RICK
MOFINA

LAST
SEEN

mira

mira

ISBN-13: 978-0-7783-1099-0

Recycling programs
for this product may
not exist in your area.

Last Seen

For questions and comments about the quality of this book, please contact us at
CustomerService@Harlequin.com.

www.Harlequin.com

Printed in U.S.A.

This book is for my hero, my father

LAST
SEEN

LAST
SEEN

Suspicion always haunts the guilty mind...
—William Shakespeare, *Henry VI*, Part III, act 5,
scene 6

The First Day

The First Day

1

River Ridge, Illinois

"**Y**ou're doomed!" the fat man on the stool said.

He was missing two lower front teeth. Peppered stubble whorled on his cheeks; vines of long hair framed his face. His eyes locked on Gage as he extended his hand, raising his voice over the chaos of the midway.

"Give me your ticket, kid."

Smiling, Gage placed his ticket in the man's red-stained palm, then raised his voice. "Hey, is that real blood?"

"You tell me, kid. Look where fate has brought you." The fat man cast his tattooed arm back to the huge arching sign bearing blood-dripping words that proclaimed the attraction.

The Chambers of Dread: America's Biggest Traveling World of Horrors!

"This is so cool!" Gage said.

"Cool? How old is your young soul?"

"What?"

"How old are you?"

"Nine!"

The man's eyes narrowed into reptilian slits as he assessed Gage, then his dad, then his mom. They stayed on Mom long enough to border on being unsavory before coming back to Gage. Then the man knocked on the wooden advisory bolted to the metal barricade next to him.

Warning! This attraction may be too intense for pregnant women and people with heart conditions. It is not recommended for children under the age of 12 unless they are accompanied by an adult.

A fat finger, tipped with a long, yellowed and chipped fingernail, pointed at Gage. "Mark my words, kid. These Chambers is cursed. No one who enters is ever the same when, *and if*, they leave. Now's the time to run home with your mama. Otherwise, move ahead. Next! You, there! You're doomed!"

"Whoa!" Gage's laugh betrayed excited nervousness as he and his parents inched forward in the crowded line that snaked between barricades to the entrance. The aroma of deep-fried food, grilled meat and cotton candy wafted from the food stands. He felt his mother's hands on his shoulders before she leaned into his ear.

"You're sure you're okay to do this, sweetie? You're not too scared?"

"Mom, I'm not scared!"

"We could skip this and get something to eat over there."

"He's fine, Faith. You're always babying him," Gage's dad said, while checking messages on his phone and texting responses.

Always working, Faith Hudson thought, irritated. It was as if his phone was part of his anatomy. Now he was dialing.

"Seriously, you're calling someone?"

Phone pressed to his ear, Cal flashed his free palm to Faith, signaling her to quiet down. She bit her bottom lip, hesitating, then said what she was thinking. "And I was going to thank you for making time for us today."

Cal never heard her, focused on his call. "Yeah, it's Hudson," he said into the receiver. "You gotta tell Stu the number's wrong in the story—it's fifty thousand, not five… Right. Good. Bye."

He turned to his wife. "I'm sorry, what'd you say?"

"Nothing."

Cal looked at her for a long moment while across from them the Polar Rocket erupted with a diesel roar, frenzied squeals and Led Zeppelin's *Immigrant Song*. After absorbing everything that Faith's silence screamed at him, Cal leaned into her ear.

"I had to make that call—it was important."

"They're always important calls."

"I had to correct an editing error. What were you trying to tell me?"

She stared at him. "I was *going* to thank you for

making time to be with us, but you're *not* with us. You're working."

"Cripes. I'm here, Faith."

"Are you?"

"Please, don't start."

"No, no, I'm not." Faith glimpsed the family behind them, the mother and father awkwardly pretending not to be watching them. Immediately Faith rubbed Cal's shoulder lovingly and smiled for all to see. "Everything's fine. Really."

Sure, everything's perfect, Calvin Hudson told himself, turning from Faith and scanning the top of the Mega-Roller Ferris wheel. She'd never truly understood his work, he thought. He was a journalist; it was in his DNA. The demands were 24/7. She never really grasped how deeply involved he was with his stories. He couldn't just switch it off, like she insisted; or like she could at the PR firm. Now there were rumors of layoffs at his paper, the *Chicago Star-News*, making him uneasy. He had to work that much harder to prove he was still valuable to his editors. Jobs in the business were scarce. But the way Faith had said, "Don't worry, we'll get by on my salary and you'll find something else," had wounded him. How could she be so dismissive, as if his position in life didn't matter, as if she *wanted* him to lose his job. She had no clue how much he'd given to it—his blood, sweat and tears along with much of his soul. She had no idea the things he'd done.

And if Cal's uncertainty about his job at the paper wasn't bad enough, the situation at home was worse. He and Faith were no longer as intimate as they used to be. She had grown colder over the past few years. Their lovemaking was infrequent. Her displays of affection—spontaneous handholding, touching or even kissing, which used to be common—were now rare.

She'd become more impatient, more demanding. And the way she babied Gage… "Is your pizza too hot for you? Want me to cut it for you? Maybe that movie's too scary for you?" The boy was nine. And he clearly hated when his mother treated him this way. It was no wonder Gage lived for any free time with his dad—with Faith, it was as if he was drowning and desperate to come up for air.

But no one knew that Cal and Faith were grappling with these problems—not their relatives, not their friends. "We don't need everyone to know our business," Faith had decreed.

In keeping with a job as a public relations manager, appearances were important to Faith.

Given her personality and her professional skills, she was good at hiding the truth when it counted. Maybe that's why buried in a corner of Cal's heart was the fear that Faith would take Gage and leave. Cal would never see it coming.

He forced himself to shift away from all these thoughts and stay positive. He found comfort in the line he had on a potential reporting job overseas. The chances that he'd get it were slim, but if he did it would mean a big change in their lives.

Still, no matter what he and Faith felt, Gage came first.

Cal looked at his son, thinking that he must sense his parents were having problems.

Like powerful telescopes scouring space for signs of life, kids like Gage could pick up infinitesimal traces of parental discord. They'd internalize it without voicing a word, while alone at night in their beds they'd hope and pray that everything between Mom and Dad would be okay.

Looking at Gage in his beloved Cubs cap and T-shirt, the one with the faded mustard stain, his khaki shorts and sneakers, Cal felt a surge of love for his son. He would do anything for him.

No matter what problems Cal and Faith had, they needed to show Gage that they were still a family intact; that's why they were here at the River Ridge Summer Carnival. Every year the big traveling midway of games and thrill rides visited their suburb on Chicago's West Side for ten days. Gage had ached to come, specifically to respond to the double dares from his friends about going through the Chambers of Dread.

"Marshall and Colton said they were going to get their parents to come to the fair today, too. I hope so because if I see them I'm gonna tell them, *'In your face, dudes!* I conquered the Chambers of Dread!'"

Cal mussed Gage's hair, smiling and thinking that maybe this fear, the kind that was manufactured and sold, would take their minds off the real things they feared in their lives. Maybe for a short time they could pretend to be a happy family.

Cal glanced back at the fat man on the stool, saw him raise a walkie-talkie and say something into it.

The Hudsons were next in line.

As they entered the Chambers of Dread through the yawning jaws of the Demon King, the carnival barker's warning of doom echoed.

Cal and Faith exchanged measured looks before they and Gage stepped into the darkness.

2

Thick waist-high fog enveloped the Hudsons in the dim light; wisps of it curled around Gage's chest as they began their journey through the Chambers of Dread.

Screams from the unseen visitors mingled with moaning in the darkness ahead of them. They moved toward ominous rumbling, coming to a passageway formed by a large, tunnellike drum, continually spinning, inviting visitors to step through the Portal to the Grim World Beyond, according to the twisted neon sign above it.

Keeping their balance while walking through the portal with a few other people, the Hudsons found a deeper darkness on the other side and began moving slowly through a maze when a large, cloaked figure emerged in front of them.

"Oh my God!" Faith gasped as the figure raised a severed human head before them, then vanished.

"It's not real, Mom!" Gage laughed.

"I know, sweetie. It just startled me. Are you okay?"

"Yeah, this is so dope!"

But the underlying nervousness in Gage's voice worried Faith, making her wonder if he'd be okay. Especially with what seemed to be up ahead.

Agonizing pleas beckoned them to the Dungeons of Dread and a darkened narrow walkway that reeked of rotten eggs and had water trickling down its jagged stone walls.

"Oh, no, let go! No!" a teenager ahead of them shrieked.

Something scratched at Faith's ankles. Then it gripped them before she kicked free. Looking to her feet she saw clawlike hands reaching out from barred windows where the condemned, confined in a subterranean prison, grabbed desperately at them, calling, "Save us! Don't leave us!"

Hurrying through the dungeons, the Hudsons came to another dark twisting connection echoing with wails, growing louder as they got closer to the next chamber.

There, the entire scene glowed in flickering orange, yellow and red as flames licked from a massive mound of wood and bramble. A large post protruded from the center. Bound to it, a woman wrapped in a white nightshirt, her head shorn, face glistening, her eyes inflamed, screeched, "So you think burning me, the witch queen, will be my end! Fools! I curse you all! I'll torment you from hell!"

The temperature soared, giving the scene a heightened degree of authenticity. Faith saw one man point out for his wife how the flames were controlled from a gas line, that the wood pile was a prop, like the gas fireplace in an expensive home.

"Did you hear me?" the witch queen screamed. "You're all cursed! *Forever!*"

Faith found kinship with the witch queen.

Her writhing against her bindings echoed how Faith felt, bound to her heartache. Cal had grown distant over the last couple years and she didn't know why. After one of his big stories he'd grow pensive. Faith didn't know what was happening with him. Whenever she tried to talk about it, he'd shut her down. He'd become absorbed in his work and was never home. She was always alone, making her feel that he preferred the long hours of working with cops, criminals and street-smart, pretty female reporters to being with her.

Had he fallen out of love with her? Once, she'd overheard him on a call joking to someone that journalists were truth seekers and PR people were professional liars. Did he feel that way about her? Most of her work was for big nonprofit groups and charities, and that was the only time she'd heard him talk that way, so she let it go.

Or tried to.

Faith needed to hold things together for Gage's sake. But it wasn't easy. She knew Gage idolized his father and lived for any free moment Cal spared for him. But it only happened when it was convenient for Cal. How many times had he canceled at the last minute on promised father-son days to see a movie, or the Cubs, or check out video games because he had to work late?

Gage was crushed every time. He was resilient, but still, it broke Faith's heart.

Cal had promised her that he would leave the crime beat and advance up the editorial ladder toward a more stable job and life. It never happened—and she knew it never would because he loved what he was doing. That's why she saw the looming layoffs at the paper as a chance for him to start something new, for them to reconnect. Because little by little she felt something was slipping away from them. They were growing apart, forcing Faith to take a hard look at taking control of matters because she and Cal couldn't go on like this.

They used to be so much in love. What was happening to them?

The cries of the witch queen soon faded as the Hudsons navigated another labyrinthian connection to the next chamber where they were met by the distinct sound of vigorous chopping. Then, emerging in the gloomy darkness, they saw a man in a blood-streaked apron swinging a cleaver, blood running down his arm while he chopped slabs of meat on a table.

"Whoa!" Gage said. "It's the insane butcher!"

Legs and arms, some twitching, were displayed on the hooks and chains near the butcher as he worked. His hair as wild as Medusa's, his face contorted and smeared with blood, as he stopped his work to offer the Hudsons delicacies from an array of bowls. One was filled with eyeballs, one brimmed with fingers and another held brains.

"Gross!" Gage laughed.

"No, thanks," Cal said.

As the Hudsons moved on with a small group, the light grew increasingly darker, making it nearly impossible to see each other, let alone Gage's face. The actors and sets were of a higher caliber than Faith had anticipated and she worried that Gage was going to have nightmares after this.

She reached for his hand but he shook her attempt away.

"I'm not a baby, Mom!"

Suddenly the air filled with a loud hellish combination of perverted circus music and a thousand fingernails scraping on chalkboards. They came to a clown, malevolent makeup covering his face. Enormous fangs jutted from his head. He sat before an organ on a stool of bones while playing a demonic tune on a keyboard of little skulls, offering entertainment at the gateway to the next chamber.

It was the darkest passage yet.

Faith felt the floor beneath them undulating as thunder cracked. They were walking on something twisting, rolling and squirming.

Something slimy and *alive*!

Sudden lightning flashes revealed they were on a stream of snakes.

"Oh God!" Faith screamed, rushing ahead, thinking they couldn't be real—they must be some sort of animatronics or CGI, though they sure felt real.

The connection, dimly lit with the lightning flashes, led them through a cavern-like passage overwhelmed with spiders and bats, forcing Faith to swat frantically at her face and hair.

They're not real, Faith assured herself, swatting around her hair.

"Gage? Cal?"

"Right behind you," Cal said.

Continuing in the next narrow connection they were nearly blind in the dark. They came upon rumbling so powerful everything vibrated. Feeling their way forward they brushed against earthen walls that were moving, closing in on them, forcing them to turn sideways to pass through. Sounds grew louder with the foreboding rumbling and heightened the sickening sense of being crushed and entombed.

"I don't like this," Faith said.

"Keep pushing forward," Cal said. "It'll be okay."

The walls were actually constructed of foam and, after the initial horror, the passage ended by opening to the next scene: a figure standing in a cemetery. Her skin was alabaster, her white gown torn and filthy as if she'd just crawled from her grave. She hovered a few feet over the burial grounds threading around headstones, stopping before the Hudsons and snarling at them. Throwing her head back, she opened her mouth to vomit a stream of blood that gushed by them.

"The executioner is coming for you and there's no escape!"

Struggling to distinguish the entrance to the next scene, Faith, Cal and Gage searched the cemetery for an exit in vain before they were motivated to look again by the sudden rattle of a revving chain saw.

"There, by the crooked tree!" Gage shouted.

The lid of an upright coffin had opened, inviting an escape just as the executioner materialized from across the graveyard. A huge man, face wrapped in a ragged, grotesque mask, held the saw high over his head, gunning the motor as he approached them.

"Let's go!"

Gage ran through the coffin door, his parents behind him with the chain-saw maniac pursuing them.

They entered the final chamber where the floor was akin to a big plate, a flat, spinning wheel, large enough to hold a car. The room went pitch-black. Faith couldn't see her hand in front of her face as the floor rotated. She couldn't see Gage or Cal as the air exploded. Earsplitting, menacing metal music thudded in time with the sudden hyperflash of strobe lights, creating confusion and terror. In the chaos, Faith now glimpsed Gage and Cal—was that them?—moving on the far side of the spinning wheel.

Or was she seeing other people?

"Gage! Cal!"

The music roared and she failed to hear a response—if there was one—as the floor turned and turned, disorienting her. Through the strobes, she spotted half a dozen curtained portals just as the chain saw's whine grew louder, alerting her to the fact the lunatic was in the room.

"Save yourself!" a recorded demonic voice boomed. "Choose your exit now, or perish!"

Faith sensed that the saw-wielding lunatic had stepped onto the wheel and had her in his sights. *That saw better not be real*, she thought before jumping to one of the curtained portals. Her heart skipped as the floor beneath her gave way and she fell onto a cushioned rubber slide that dropped in darkness for a few seconds before gently delivering her to the lighted, safe world outside.

Catching her breath, Faith stood, stepping aside as a teenage girl slid down the chute behind her. Blinking in the sunlight, regaining her composure, Faith looked around the landing zone of half a dozen chutes that webbed out to deliver visitors on a large air mattress.

"Hey!" Faith spotted and joined Cal, who'd exited at the farthest chute. "That was wild! Where's Gage?"

Cal's grin began melting as he looked at her, then around.

"He's not with you?"

"No, I thought you had him?"

"No, I saw him with you."

"Cal, where's Gage?"

Faith and Cal searched the chutes delivering a thrilled survivor every few seconds. Gage would be next. He had to be next. The seconds grew to one minute as their hearts continued to pound. Two minutes passed, then three.

Time ticked by with no sign of Gage.

3

"I can't believe this," Cal said as he and Faith walked the perimeter of the chutes, searching the slides and the clusters of people shuffling along the exit barricades for Gage.

He wasn't there. He wasn't anywhere.

"Maybe he got out ahead of us and ran to another ride?" Faith said. "Maybe he went to a food stand?"

"I doubt it, but wait here for him and I'll check."

Cal shouldered his way through the exit lines, battling frustration and unease while searching the rivers of people that were flowing into the midway crowds. *Gage wouldn't have left the chutes without us,* he thought. *He knows better. Unless he was confused and figured we'd got out first and left without him? Maybe he rushed to the next ride. No. No way. He'd wait. He's a good kid—he's sharp, like his mother. No matter how tempting the midway would be he'd wait for us.*

Come on, Gage, come on. *Where is he?*

Cal continued, turning full circle, bumping into

people, scanning faces of boys Gage's age until they began blurring. Cal scoured the Polar Express—nothing there. Then he stopped in front of the Zipper where Bob Seger's *Hollywood Nights* was throbbing amid the grind of the thrill ride's diesel and roaring crowds.

No sign of Gage.

Quickly, he circled food stands that were selling burgers and fries, pizza, ice cream, nuts, pretzels and cotton candy, scanning the people ordering, waiting or those eating at the small tables nearby.

No sign of Gage.

Cal thought it unlikely Gage would travel down this way alone in such a short amount of time, and trotted back to Faith at the Chambers of Dread.

Her hope that he'd have Gage with him died on her face as they exchanged sobering looks.

"He hasn't come out here," Faith said, turning to the chutes. "Do something, Cal!"

Near them, they saw a man in his thirties wearing a work shirt with an embroidered Ultra-Fun Amusement Corp roller-coaster logo above his left pocket, a ball cap and Ray-Ban sunglasses. Obviously a midway worker, he was helping women recover at the slides, his rolled sleeves displaying tattoo-laced biceps.

"Our son hasn't come out yet," Cal said. "Can you help us?"

The man was unshaven; his long hair curled from his cap, the toothpick in the corner of his mouth punctuated an expression that told Cal he'd been everywhere, seen everything, heard it all and was bored.

"People get hung up in there. Take it easy, pal, he'll be out."

"He's only nine!" Faith interjected. "He was right at the exit curtains with us and he's not here. It's been more than five minutes!"

Cal saw Faith's body reflected in the man's mirrored glasses as he assessed her summer top and shorts. His toothpick shifted and he nodded to the Chambers.

"Did you see him on the spinner?"

"Yes, if that's what you call the last thing before these slides, yes," she said.

"Hang on." The man unclipped a walkie-talkie from his studded belt, turned and spoke into it. "Alma, it's Sid. We got a straggler in the spinner." He turned to Faith. "What's he wearing?"

"A Cubs T-shirt, ball cap and sand-colored shorts, khakis," Faith said.

"Got a lotta kids wearing that same stuff," he said.

"A *blue* Cubs shirt and ball cap," Cal added. "And he's wearing sneakers, blue SkySlyders."

"How old did you say?"

"Nine," Faith said.

After Sid relayed Gage's description into the walkie-talkie, it crackled and a woman's bored-sounding voice said, "Roger. Stand by."

"Your people can see in the dark?" Cal asked.

"We got infrared cameras everywhere in the Chambers and Alma watches from a control desk."

Several moments passed with Sid's silent calm countering Cal and Faith's anxiety, projecting an attitude that this sort of thing happened all the time. He scratched his whiskered jaw, then raised his walkie-talkie again.

"Check the graveyard and the crusher."

"Stand by. I think…" the radio said. "Yup! Got him. He's coming your way."

"Oh, good!" Faith said, relief washing through her.

"He should be at the chutes about…now," the radio said.

A middle-aged woman with glasses whooshed down one slide, then two teenage girls shot down another, then a big-bellied man followed by a boy in shorts and a Cubs T-shirt—*a red one*. The kid looked more like twelve.

"That's not Gage! That boy's not our son!" Faith said.

"We need to do something now, Sid!" Cal said.

Sid held up a hand to stem their rising concern and he spoke into his radio.

"Alma, that's not him. Go back farther—the witch, the clown, the butcher—and double-check. Shorts and Cubs T-shirt. Nine years old."

"A *blue* T-shirt!" Faith said.

Sid shook his head. "The cameras don't pick up colors, just shades, black, white and in between."

A few more tense moments passed, then Faith said, "Sid, we're losing time and this is getting serious. Gage could've fallen. He could be hurt or unconscious in there! You've got to shut it down, turn on the lights and let us search for him now!"

"Relax, ma'am. We have procedures for these situations."

"Then use them, dammit!" Faith said.

"Hang on." Sid pulled the walkie-talkie to his mouth and took a few steps away, but even with the noise Faith and Cal could hear him.

"Still nothing, Alma?"

"Still looking."

"Call a Code 99."

"Vaughn won't like it."

"Call it." Sid turned back to the Hudsons. "What's your son's name?"

"Gage Hudson," Faith said.

Sid nodded and relayed it to Alma, setting in motion Ultra-Fun Amusement Corp's procedure for a serious incident at an attraction. Within minutes, more staff emerged amid radio dispatches and workers talking on cell phones. Some went to various points to help visitors leave the Chambers of Dread through emergency exit doors and down stairs, apologizing and handing them vouchers for a free return. Other staff converged at the chutes. One of them, a man in his early sixties with a white cowboy hat and aviator glasses, had a private huddle with Sid before he came directly to Faith and Cal. He was wearing a navy golf shirt with the Ultra-Fun logo.

"Vaughn King—I run the midway attractions." He nodded. "We'll find your son, folks." King, face tanned with neat, trimmed white stubble, presented an air of authority as he turned and spoke softly into his phone.

Cal and Faith heard a loud announcement being made within the confines of the Chambers. It was muffled but they could make out a woman's voice on the PA system calling Gage's name, telling him to report to a staff member.

"We've shut down the ride," King said. "We turned on all interior lighting. We've got staff inside who know every nook and cranny looking for your son. All the actors at the scenes are looking, too."

"Does this happen often?" Cal asked.

King's gaze was fixed on the Chambers as he stuck out his bottom lip.

"It happens. In Kansas City, we found a teenager who'd huddled in a corner of a set, her eyes shut tight. She'd refused to open them. Found the Chambers a little too scary. In Indianapolis, we had an eighty-three-year-old veteran off his medication who wandered behind the butcher's scene without the actor knowing. Found him sleeping behind the meat props. In Cincinnati, a woman fainted near one of the spinner's exits. Unfortunately, no one noticed until we searched for her. It happens."

"What about the exits?" Faith asked. "We never saw exit signs inside."

"They're dimmed but activated and illuminated in an emergency."

"Gage could've gone out one of them," Cal said.

"An alarm goes off when they're opened. Staff would've been alerted and that didn't happen."

Ten tense, solid minutes passed without results. King glanced at his watch, then spoke softly into his walkie-talkie. He looked at his watch again, bit his bottom lip and turned to Faith and Cal.

"Does your son possibly have a cell phone?"

King's question thrust the situation up to a more serious level.

For a second Cal recalled how Gage had begged them for his own phone. Most of his friends had phones. But Cal and Faith had said no—it cost too much, he was too young, he'd be tempted to use it in class to play games. They'd refused to give him his own phone for all those reasons, at first. Then they'd caved and got him one, and Gage promptly lost it. They got him a second one and he'd lost that, too. So that was it. No more phones.

Now their rationale seemed infinitely feeble because, facing what they were facing, they'd have given the world to go back in time and get him another phone.

"No." Faith blinked back tears. "He doesn't have a phone."

King's Adam's apple rose and fell. He removed his sunglasses and his blue eyes were tinged with concern.

"I'm sorry, folks, but we can't seem to find him."

4

Cal couldn't accept what Vaughn King was implying—that somehow Gage had vanished.

"That's ridiculous. He didn't just disappear," Cal said. "He's in there."

Faith cupped her hands over her face. "Where else could he be?"

King stared at Cal, then Faith.

"Our people have already searched. Are you certain he didn't exit ahead of you and wander down the midway?"

"He was with us in the spinner!" Faith said. "Let *us* search for him."

King removed his hat, drew his forearm across his brow, a gesture suggesting that allowing the public access during a Code 99 was against company policy. A second later, as if he'd convinced himself that this situation was exceptional, or maybe to diminish potential liability—*we did everything to help those parents*—King found himself nodding and clicking the speaker on the small walkie-talkie again.

"This is Vaughn. I'm bringing the parents inside to search." To Cal and Faith, he said, "All right, let's go."

His radio crackled. "But, Mr. King, the policy prohibits—"

"I know what the policy says." King cut the speaker off. "I'm bringing them in!"

The key ring on King's belt jingled as they all hurried toward the entrance. Moving around the other side of the attraction, Cal saw the Chambers of Dread for what they were: a series of interconnected truck trailers, forming an interlocking network that claimed to be America's Biggest Traveling World of Horrors! He noticed the empty stool belonging to the fat ticket taker who'd eyed Faith and wondered if he was helping search for Gage.

King led them through the jaws of the Demon King. There was no fog when they entered; bright lights lit the inside. Their footsteps echoed as they rushed through the spinning portal, which was now stationary. Gage had to be in here. The ever-present thud of the midway outside hammered a deadened rhythm as Cal and Faith looked for their son.

"Gage!" Faith called. "It's okay! Come out now. It's Mom and Dad!"

All the interior walls were painted black; so were the floors and ceilings, where Cal noticed nozzles of the sprinkler system and the surveillance cameras. Suddenly the air exploded with ear-piercing staccato beeps. A side exit door opened and closed as a young woman in an Ultra-Fun shirt holding a walkie-talkie stepped inside.

"We checked the area around this exit, Mr. King. We didn't find him."

"Thank you, Hayley."

Cal looked at the small exit light overhead and how the door was also painted black. It blended in with the walls, like camouflage, almost invisible.

"Hold on, I want to look out there," he said.

The girl let Cal step through the door. The alarm bleated as he took stock of the backside of the structure, one not seen from the midway crowd. His heart was thumping faster now as he saw tentacles of huge power cables flowing on the ground and breathed in the smell of diesel and hydraulic fluid wafting from the generators and the pumps powering the rides nearby. The area was congested with an array of truck trailers, positioned to form narrow walkways leading to RVs and campers where Ultra-Fun staff lived while on the road—a netherworld of latter-day gypsies. Cal scoured the area, then the alarm bleated and King appeared on the stairs with Faith.

"Mr. Hudson!" King shouted. "The alarm would've been activated if your son used one of these exits!"

Cal took a second sweep under the trailers for anything that would lead him to Gage. Finding nothing, he conceded King's point and returned.

Resuming their hunt in the Chambers, Faith and Cal came to the large cloaked figure they'd encountered earlier, the one toting a head. The figure had adjusted the costume. In the naked light, Cal and

Faith saw that he was an acne-faced young man of linebacker proportions.

"Hi, Mr. King. We've searched everywhere in our section. He's not here."

"Thanks, Lonnie," King said, moving on to the area smelling of rotten eggs—the Dungeons of Dread. Opening a door, he led the Hudsons down a few short steps to a cramped dugout set behind prison bars where actors with clawlike prop hands shook their heads.

"He's not with us, sir," a young woman—one of the "damned"—said.

Cal, Faith and King kept going, coming to another exit door, tripping the alarm. At this one, Faith exited and took the stairs, which landed tight to a chain-link fence. Trailers were backed against it. An empty lot stood on the other side of the fence, earthen, muddied and pot-holed with discarded tires, a stove and a filthy sofa—a menacing patch of misery.

"Gage! It's Mom, honey! Gage!"

The fear that had seeped into her voice was unmistakable, Cal thought, joining her and searching the confined area for several minutes before returning inside. Once more they'd activated the alarm, underscoring their desperation on their way to the next set.

The air smelled as if a gas stove had been switched off when they got to where the burning witch queen had cursed them. The room's temperature had dropped a little from the oven-level it had been during the act. The actress had left her stake and was still searching the edges of the prop wood pile.

"I'm sorry, ma'am." The witch shook her head. "He's not here but I'm sure you'll find him, don't worry."

Moving quickly to the next set they were greeted by the insane butcher still clad in his bloodstained apron and surrounded by props of limbs. Faith was thankful they'd stopped twitching. Still, the scene sent a shiver coiling up her spine. She dropped to her hands and knees, looking under the table and around the suspended torsos. Cal crawled on the floor from the opposite side, the chains creaking as they brushed against the props, which marked them with streaks of stage blood.

"Gage! Gage, come out, son!" Cal called as the butcher and King exchanged a look.

They'd found nothing here.

The butcher shook his hideous face, telling the Hudsons, "We looked everywhere in this section, folks. He's not with us."

Cal and Faith hurried ahead with King, stopping to inspect the areas surrounding every exit that they came to. They didn't find Gage with the fanged clown, who'd hefted the organ from a wall in order to look behind and under it. There was nothing to search at the river of snakes and the cavern of bats and spiders. Those areas had been filled with computer-generated images. Under the lights, these sets were void of anything searchable.

Gage was not among the tombstones in the

graveyard. There, the wretched zombie woman offered a sympathetic smile, shaking her head— "He's not here"—but with her makeup she came off looking like the possessed girl in *The Exorcist*.

In the spinner, the large round floor was motionless. At the six curtained exits leading to the slides, they saw the chain-saw executioner. He'd pushed his mask up to the top of his head, revealing the face of a handsome man in his thirties.

"I'm so sorry if I scared your little boy." He offered the Hudsons a small, warm smile. "He's not here but I'm sure you'll find him."

They didn't.

Cal and Faith's search of the Chambers had proven to be fruitless.

"This way." King led them to one of the exits, and the outside stairs down, returning them to the chutes to where a small group of Ultra-Fun staff had gathered.

Amid the chattering walkie-talkies, some of the staff cast looks of awkward pity at the Hudsons standing helplessly at the slides—their faces bearing small smears of stage blood. It had now been nearly half an hour since Cal and Faith had last seen Gage, yet all around them the fair kept going, people kept squealing with joy, the thrill rides kept spinning and twirling, the music kept rocking, as if nothing had changed.

But everything had changed.

Faith's breaths started coming in gasps; her hands started shaking. "Cal, this can't be happening, not to us!"

"Take it easy."

"Maybe, maybe Marshall's and Colton's families are here and this is a big joke to scare us? That's got to be it, right?"

"Faith, I don't think so."

"No. No!" Faith's knees buckled and Cal caught her. *"Gage!"*

Gage couldn't be missing, Cal thought. It couldn't be true. Maybe it was part of some pranking TV show? He struggled to grasp it all but their futile search of the Chambers with its grotesque faces and sets was a descent into Dante's circles of hell.

Cal felt something monstrous had raked a claw across their lives while the screams of the midway grew louder and he reached for his phone. His fingers were trembling when he pressed the numbers for 911.

"River Ridge Emergency Dispatch, what's your emergency?"

"My son is—" Cal started but his heart was hammering in his chest and his mind was swirling with disbelief. He glanced at Faith, her anguish piercing him. He couldn't believe this was happening. What kind of parents lose their kid? He had to stop thinking that way and stay in control.

"Sir, what's your emergency?"

Cal gripped his cell phone with such force he nearly cracked the casing. "My son is missing." He resumed reporting Gage's disappearance, but for one burning instant he felt trapped in a dream.

Wake up, go to Gage's room—you'll see he's there. Wake up!

But Cal didn't wake up because he wasn't dreaming.

5

Four minutes after Cal's call, River Ridge police officers Angie Berg and Erik Ripkowski arrived at the chutes. Already briefed by their dispatcher, they wasted no time and followed procedure.

"We need to talk to you separately, folks," said Berg, reaching for her notebook before taking Cal aside while her partner stayed with Faith.

The two officers had been close by. Today was their third shift on midway patrol, which was considered a semivacation usually involving nothing more than community relations duty. Berg had become partial to the fudge, while Ripkowski loved the Polish dogs. Up to now, their most serious call had been a woman who'd attempted to steal a fifteen-year-old girl's phone. Turned out the woman was the intoxicated mother of the boy the girl had dumped. The woman's husband, who was embarrassed, apologized and took his wife home.

But the Hudson call was different.

It went well beyond a midway nuisance, and of

all the young officers on the River Ridge force, Berg and Ripkowski were two of the brightest.

"Take a breath, sir, start at the beginning," Berg, her sandy hair pulled up in small bun, told Cal, her pen poised.

At this point Gage had been missing for almost forty-five minutes.

Nearby, Ripkowski, whose bodybuilder arms strained his uniform, was taking careful notes as Faith recounted to him what had taken place. At the same time the officers had requested that Vaughn King, who was watching from the distance, keep the Chambers of Dread closed and keep all staff on hand.

"We mean everybody." Ripkowski pointed his pen. "Nobody leaves."

After obtaining the Hudsons' initial statements, details on Gage's height, weight, hair and eye color, Berg and Ripkowski moved fast, making a number of transmissions on their shoulder microphones and calls on their phones, to their sergeant, and to the River Ridge Fairgrounds security and operations people.

"Do you have a recent photo of your son?" Ripkowski asked. "We need to get it circulated as soon as possible."

Faith rummaged through her bag, seizing her phone. "Last Saturday—no, sorry, it was Sunday—Gage went to his friend Ethan Clark's birthday party. I've got a picture." She swiped through images, stopping at Gage smiling for the camera while behind him some joker, likely Marshall, was holding up two fingers bunny-ear-style above his head. "See, he's wearing the same blue Cubs shirt. It's got the mustard stain from his hot dog at the party. I told him to put it in the wash." Faith was almost embarrassed. "I wanted to get the stain out but it's his favorite shirt."

"Okay, send it to me now." Ripkowski held up his phone displaying his email. His phone chimed receipt of the picture after Faith, fingers shaking, typed it into her email app and sent the photo. Ripkowski then forwarded it to a number of addresses and made a call, speaking urgently to a fairgrounds person while nodding to the billboard-size TV screen suspended high above their section of the midway.

The sign was flashing with ads, selfies and images of people having fun at the fair, much like the giant screens at Times Square. There were four screens overlooking the grounds, one at pretty much every compass point.

"Here we go," Ripkowski said.

Faith gasped when the screen suddenly went blank, then popped to life with Gage smiling down at her, the words *Lost/Missing* shouted above his head. Gage's name and description appeared next to his face, in missing-person poster-style with a message urging anyone who'd seen him to call 911.

"That's up now and will stay up on all the screens," Ripkowski said. "I'll send copies to you and your husband to spread the word, too."

In the minutes that followed, Cal and Faith called the parents of Gage's friends hoping that by some wild coincidence they were in fact also here, and maybe Gage had seen them and joined them.

"Hey, Pam, it's Faith. This is going to sound weird, but are you guys at the fair today?"

"No, I'm home doing a wash. Dean's with Colton at Walmart looking at fishing rods, or reels, or some man-thing. Why, what's up?"

Faith stifled her tears, cupping her hand to her face as she spun around in the chaos, seeing Cal on his phone, hearing him speaking to their friends the Thompsons.

"Jack, any chance you, Michelle and Marshall are down here at the fair right now?" he was saying.

Those calls and the others they'd made didn't yield Gage, but their friends, shocked by the gravity of Gage's disappearance, began mobilizing to come to the fairgrounds to help. Cal and Faith, both ashen-faced, watched from a few yards away as the search for Gage continued widening with great speed. There was one thing that could help.

Cal called Stu Kroll, his editor at the *Star-News*.

"It's Cal again—listen—"

"Hey, it's okay, we caught it. Changed it to fifty. It's all good."

"No, Stu, listen. Our son's missing down here at the River Ridge fair."

"What do you mean?"

"I'm going to send you his picture and information from the police—"

"The police?"

"Yeah, it's looking serious. We need to get the

word out now. Would you guys put it up on the site and tweet it out?"

"I—I'm not sure. I mean, you're an employee—"

"Please, Stu! Please! I'm sending it now. I gotta go."

Ripkowski and Berg had arranged for a River Ridge patrol car to park at the Hudsons' house just in case Gage somehow made his way home. Cal and Faith contacted their nearest neighbors— Ethan's parents, Sam and Rory Clark—who upon hearing the news immediately agreed to join the police at their house to watch for Gage.

Meanwhile, the fairgrounds chief, Herb Dulka, had trotted to the chutes, phone pressed to his ear, joining Ripkowski and Berg, who'd waved in Vaughn King, while more police officers and other security people arrived.

"We've circulated Gage's picture force-wide," Ripkowski said. "It'll be up on social media any minute now, notifying everyone across Chicago, the state, the entire country. And I'll talk to my supervisor to ensure we cover all our bases and look into possibly issuing an Amber Alert."

Dulka said, "We've given the photo to all our people on the grounds at the gates and in the parking lots and we're starting the shutdown process for the announcement."

"Good." Berg turned to King. "Our people and firefighters are going to search the attraction and we're going to take statements from all of your people working it."

"Not a problem." Vaughn nodded.

"But first—" Ripkowski nodded to the Chambers "—what about your cameras in there? You got surveillance footage? It might show us something."

"Yes, we have cameras and we're working on getting the footage but there's a problem."

"What's the problem?"

"The playback's frozen. The Chambers took a lightning strike last week when we were in Milwaukee and the system's been skittish ever since."

"We need that footage," Ripkowski said.

"We're working on it."

Near them the Polar Express emitted a hydraulic sigh as it slowed. Then the Zipper groaned to a halt as ride cycles ended and riders disembarked. People were kept off and the rides across the midway remained idle while everywhere the blaring rock music at each ride ceased.

"Almost ready." Dulka was on his phone, then nodded. "Okay, go!"

A public address system awoke, screeching feedback, then a woman's voice crackled through it with a message that came through loud and clear.

"Attention everyone. We have an emergency. We're looking for a little boy, Gage Hudson. He's nine and he got separated from his folks near the Chambers of Dread a little while ago. Gage's picture is up on the big screens. Please take a look now, then look around you. Gage, if you're seeing this, go to any ticket booth, police officer or security person, and they'll find your folks for you. Everyone, please look around your area for Gage and let's get him back to his folks. Please, do it now—it'll only take a moment. Thank you."

The chaos had been subdued and a somber air fell across the thousands of people at the River Ridge Fairgrounds. It was soon interrupted by the distant calling of people shouting, "Gage!" from various corners, as if engaged in a Marco Polo game. But it wasn't long before the murmuring gave way to demands for the party to resume as some calls devolved into "Gage, you're in deep shit!" and "Your mama's gonna whip your ass, Gage!"

During the fifteen minutes the midway was halted, no walkie-talkies crackled and no phones rang to end Cal and Faith's agony. No one had spotted Gage. With each terrible, surreal second that passed, Cal and Faith felt their horrible fear increasing and their panic rising.

It was all they could do to keep from falling off the earth.

6

Gage comes out of the portal with Faith and Cal,
they pass the cloaked figure, move to the dungeons
where hands claw at them; Gage's eyes glow; the
infrared images of the Hudsons are captured in
shades of gray, black and radiant white; the Hud-
sons move through darkness; ahead and behind
them other groups creep with trepidation: a man
and woman holding hands, two teenage girls hold-
ing each other, their eyes and teeth blazing, moving
beyond the phosphorescent flames of the burning
witch, then the insane butcher, the fanged clown;
some people are cowering, others are crouching in
the cave of bats and spiders; Gage, Faith and Cal
rush across the zombie graveyard pursued by the
chain-saw maniac to the coffin doorway when they
vanish in the sudden flash of a static snowstorm.

"Play it again," Ripkowski said.

He was with Berg and Vaughn King in the
cramped, dimly lit control room attached to the
Chambers of Dread. They watched over Alma Mc-
Cain's shoulder as she operated the attraction's

console bank of infrared security cameras. A can of diet cola, a half-eaten slice of pizza and a *Lord of the Flies* paperback were next to her. Small TV screens displayed images for each section of the Chambers, but the system had malfunctioned for the final sets. Alma pecked at her keyboard, replayed the footage, but it was futile at the spinner.

"This is where it freezes and won't work. It's given us trouble since the lightning strike in Milwaukee."

"Did you see anything unusual when you watched this live when the Hudsons went through?" Ripkowski asked Alma.

"No, but to be honest, I wasn't looking at the spinner at that time."

"Were you reading?"

"No, I was not reading. I take my book with me on breaks."

"Did an emergency door alarm activate anywhere today?"

Alma exchanged a quick glance with King before saying, "No."

"So—" Berg tapped her pen on the screen "—we've got four emergency exits and six exit chutes with no recorded video. Erik, what do you think?"

"We need IT's help to recover that footage if they can—either our people, or Chicago PD, somebody with the expertise—because this is where the boy vanishes. And we're going to need statements ASAP from everyone on duty today."

Then Berg and Ripkowski stepped outside to

update Cal and Faith amid the noise of the midway, which, with the exception of the Chambers of Dread, had resumed action at full throttle.

"Did the cameras show you what happened?" Cal asked.

"No, they've got technical trouble with their system," Berg said. "But we're going to have experts look at it."

"Dammit." Cal's eyes were brimming, for it was now close to ninety minutes since Gage had vanished. "What about the RVs and trailers behind the rides where all the midway people live? Did you check there?"

"We're on it." Berg moved the Hudsons slightly so they could see between the rides; uniformed officers were knocking on trailer doors. "Our people, and Cook County officers, are canvassing in there right now," Berg said. "Few people are home, most are working the midway. The chances someone was around to see anything are slim."

"There must be something more you can do!" Faith's voice broke, then she turned to King and Dulka, letting loose with her frustration. "Why did you start the fair again? Please shut it down so we can keep looking! Our son is missing!"

"Ma'am," Dulka said, "we're taking this very seriously. We're going to keep your son's picture up on the big screens all day. We've closed the Chambers. We have our staff on the grounds searching for him. We're doing everything we can, but we've got thousands of paying customers."

Faith's head snapped to the officers.

"You're the police! Can't you order them to shut it all down?"

"Not at this time, as no crime's been committed," Ripkowski said. "Everyone's coopera—"

"But there has to be more you can do to find Gage!" Faith shouted. "What about bringing in detectives and the FBI?"

"We're bringing in canine units and we're—" Ripkowski and Berg's radios crackled. "Erik, Angie! We've got him at the south gate!"

Cal and Faith ran to the gate with Ripkowski and Berg. Faith's heart was racing and she fought back tears as their small posse wove through streams of fairgoers.

Cal's jaw was fixed in restrained relief when they came to a wooden outbuilding standing to one side of the gate where two security staff waited; both of them were in their teens.

"Where's our son?" Faith asked.

"Inside that door, with the cops." One of the security kids pointed. "He was so smart, ma'am— kept yelling that the man with him was not his father. That got our attention."

When Ripkowski opened the door, Faith and Cal felt their hearts plunge. The boy in the chair, under the watch of two officers, was wearing a blue Cubs shirt but dark-colored shorts and—

"He's not our son," Cal said.

Faith steadied herself against the doorframe as a man behind them said, "This is huge mistake!" Two other officers had placed plastic handcuffs on his wrists. "Trevor, for God's sake, tell them the truth!"

The boy, who appeared to Cal and Faith to be eleven or twelve, screwed his face into an icy grimace, then spat, "You're not my father!"

At that moment a distraught, breathless woman arrived with a girl of about seven, who was clutching a big blue stuffed bear, as if to shield her from what was unfolding. The woman asked, "Don, Trevor, what's going on?"

Ripkowski approached the woman. "Can you show me some identification? Do you know these people, ma'am?"

"I'm Marjorie Bricker." She fished her wallet from her purse. "He's my son, Trevor, and he's Don Zaret, my fiancé. What is this—why're you arresting him?"

"Marj," Zaret started, "Trevor was trying to pass himself off as the missing kid—"

"We told you to keep quiet!" one officer said.

Zaret continued, speaking faster. "He made it look like *I'd kidnapped him*. I told these officers that it was because I wouldn't let him ride the Rocket Blaster by himself."

"I'm warning you, sir!" the officer said as Zaret got one more plea in.

"Remember, those were your instructions, Marjorie. No Rocket Blaster or Avalanche!"

The woman was showing Ripkowski photos on her phone of the family together. "See, he's my son!"

Ripkowski turned to Trevor. "Is this all true?"

Trevor looked at his mother, then at the Hudsons. He was perceptive; he'd figured out who Cal and Faith were and knew the seriousness of what had befallen them. He'd seen the sober reality up on the big screens. Now, reading the pain in Cal's and Faith's faces, he turned to Marjorie Bricker and his chin crumpled.

"Why do you have to marry him, Mom? Did you stop loving Dad?"

"Oh, sweetheart, of course not. I'll always love your father." Marjorie hugged the boy, turning to the Hudsons and police, stifling her tears. "My husband—Trevor's dad—was a soldier. He was killed in Afghanistan just over two years ago. Trevor's had a hard time accepting Don in our lives."

Zaret, still cuffed, blinked at the ceiling.

"Please." Bricker turned to the police. "This is all a misunderstanding."

The arresting officers were processing the explanations.

"Look," one of them said. "It's going to take some time for us to sort things out. We're going to need to verify everyone's ID."

Marjorie Bricker turned to the Hudsons. "I'm so sorry. Please understand."

Cal and Faith nodded but they didn't understand. How could they?

At this point nothing made sense to them.

Absorbing their heartbreak, they made their way back to the Chambers to face the mounting horror of Gage's disappearance.

7

Yellow plastic police tape had gone up around the Chambers of Dread.

America's flag of tragedy, Cal thought, his mind pulling him back to crimes he'd known as a reporter. Like when he'd watched a grieving husband look through closets and drawers for a photo of his wife, killed in a hit-and-run—"I'm sorry, she was shy about having her picture taken."

Or the time an inconsolable mother had shown him her murdered son's bedroom, his towel still damp from his shower that morning. He'd been shot in gang-war cross fire the day he'd received his acceptance letter from Loyola.

Cal never forgot interviewing a chain-smoking priest who'd given last rites to a great-grandmother stabbed and robbed on the street after buying groceries, his hand shaking with each pull.

In writing their stories, and so many others like them, Cal had accepted what he was: an invader.

Intruding on people's torment at the most horrible time of their lives was what he did for a living. Sure, he could always justify and rationalize it as his job—the champion of a free press. But he hid the creeping fear that one day there'd be a reckoning, a price to be paid for these and his other sins—including the one that haunted him to the point where he questioned his worth as a reporter. As a person.

But over time, as his professional armor had hardened, he'd grown smug, thinking he was immune to being touched by crime. It couldn't happen to him. It just couldn't. He was a middle-class family man, a decent guy, living in a good West Side neighborhood.

But here he was, grappling with a terrifying reality.

His son was missing.

A fact so chilling it numbed him.

It was now more than two hours since Cal and Faith had seen Gage.

Cal was waiting at the Chambers while Faith took a turn searching the immediate midway again. Gage had to be out there somewhere. If he'd run off to play some kind of game intent on popping up and saying, "Guess I really scared you guys!" Cal swore he would kill him. But Gage wouldn't ever play a joke like that. *He's a good kid.*

Checking his phone Cal saw that the *Chicago Star-News* had posted Gage's picture and details about him online. He called the newsroom.

"Stu, it's Cal. Anyone contact the paper with anything on Gage?"

"Sorry, Cal, nothing yet but nutbars. Wish I had better news."

Cal dragged both hands over his stubbled face as he hung up. He was a smart reporter, skilled at his craft; there had to be something more he could do. He racked his brain, then texted Stu with an idea. The moment after he sent it, his phone rang. It was Faith.

"On my way back—anything?"

"Nothing."

The police alert on Gage's disappearance had triggered several actions. One was the swift response of the River Ridge Neighborhood Patrol. A dozen volunteers, with more on the way, had arrived at the fairgrounds wearing lime green vests. They were equipped with radios, cell phones, maps, experience in searches and a "can-do" attitude.

"We have always found who we're looking for," the patrol leader, who was a retired cop, assured the Hudsons. "Little kids, Alzheimer's patients who've wandered off...sooner or later, we find 'em."

With the blessing of Herb Dulka and Vaughn King, the patrol had set up, near to the Chambers, a temporary Gage Hudson Search Center, consisting of tent canopies and several folding tables, all provided by the fairgrounds and midway. In quickly organized operations, the patrol fanned out to search the fair and neighborhoods surrounding the grounds.

Cal and Faith had taken turns scouring the midway with searchers, going up and down the avenues, looking behind rides, behind games of chance, in restrooms, picnic areas, all while Gage stared down on them from his picture on the giant screens.

Back at the search center Cal and Faith saw firefighters probing the underbelly and the roof of the Chambers. Others had gone inside to examine the interior. So far, they'd found nothing. A dog barked and the Hudsons turned to a police officer and a panting German shepherd.

"Folks, Officer Peddet. This is my partner, Champ. We're here to help. Do you have anything belonging to Gage that he would have worn?"

Faith reached into her bag. "I've got his hoodie. I'd brought it in case it got chilly, or rained."

"Good, don't take it out yet." Peddet, who wore large glasses, making him look like Clark Kent, led Champ and the Hudsons closer to the chutes of the Chambers and the exit stairs near the back. "This is the area where you last saw your son?"

"Actually, inside on the spinner," Cal said.

"Okay, we'll go inside. I'll take the hoodie with me now."

Faith withdrew the soft blue hoodie. Champ yipped as Peddet let the dog sniff the fabric.

"We'll try to pick up Gage's scent," Peddet said, "but we've got a lot of smells in the air. It'll be challenging and may take some time."

Cal and Faith watched as Peddet and Champ left to search for a trail, Champ's leash jingling as he tugged at it.

At that moment, Cal's phone rang. It was the *Star-News*.

"Cal, its Bannon. Do you have a second?"

He repositioned his grip on his phone. "Yeah."

"Stu just assigned me to call you for comment on the story we're doing, but if there are more ways we can help, you let us know."

Cal was grateful Stu had taken his suggestion earlier, that the *Star-News* do a quick story.

"Good, what do you need, Rich?"

"Just tell me what happened—what's going through your mind?"

Cal hesitated, thinking how Bannon had asked exactly what he would've asked a parent if he were doing a story. Cal exhaled, quickly related the history of events, ending with: "We're deeply concerned but hopeful we'll locate him."

"Thanks for talking to me and good luck. I'll get a story up fast as I can. You should know that Stu's sent Lori Kowski and Franco to the fair."

Cal knew that the case of a missing child would draw media attention. And it did. A TV news crew from Channel 9 was the first to arrive, followed by reporters from the *Chicago Tribune*, the *River Ridge Review*, *Chicago Sun-Times*, Channel 77, WBTN Radio News, Channel WT2 and, as expected, Lori Kowski, a reporter, and Franco Ginnetti, a photographer, from his own paper.

Security staff had helped keep Cal and Faith out of view, taking them to a trailer for privacy to prepare to speak to the press.

"This can't be real," Faith sobbed.

"Maybe he wandered off," Cal said.

"Why didn't you let me hold his hand, Cal?"

"Because he's doesn't want to be babied. You're always smothering him, Faith."

"How would you know what he wants or doesn't want? You're barely ever home!"

Cal shook his head bitterly. "You should've been watching him, Faith."

"Don't you dare put this on me! You had him."

"Me? He was with you on the spinner."

"No, he was with you! I told the police I last saw him with you."

"That's what you told them?"

"It's the truth."

Cal looked away, took a breath, then looked back.

"We have to stop this. We have to stop fighting because in about one minute we're going to step in front of the cameras and ask people to help us find our son."

Faith hugged herself while shaking her head. "I don't think I can speak to them."

"We've got to provide a united front. We've got to keep pushing the word out. Just stand by me. We'll keep it brief and I'll do the talking. Can you do that…for Gage?"

She cupped her hands to her face. "I need a moment," she said.

"For what?"

She reached into her bag. "I have to fix my hair and face."

Upward of twenty newspeople were waiting near the Chambers when Cal and Faith came out. They were joined by Dulka, King and Officer Bryan De-

Santo, a River Ridge police spokesman who led off the news conference with a short summary and update on the ongoing search before turning to them.

"Gage's parents have agreed to take a few questions," DeSanto said, triggering a deluge as cameras flashed on them.

Cal was ruggedly handsome with his soft stubble, dark eyes and dark hair. Faith, even anguished, had the fresh-scrubbed face of a natural beauty, framed by blond shoulder-length locks with a slight wave.

They were the all-American middle-class couple.

"Mr. Hudson, was your son was abducted?"

"There's no evidence of that."

"No calls for ransom, no one claiming responsibility?"

"No, nothing to suggest he was abducted."

"But you go into the ride and leave without him? Isn't it likely that someone, somehow, kidnapped him?"

"We don't know what happened."

"What do you think happened?"

"We just don't know."

"Could he have met someone online?"

"I'd say no, that's not possible."

"How can you be sure?"

"He goes on chat forums, but he only talks to people he knows. Gage is very responsible, and we've got controls on his computer games—we monitor things. He doesn't even have his own phone."

"Could he have wandered off?"

"It's not like him. He's a smart kid—he's responsible."

"Has he ever run off before?"

"No."

"Could he have been threatened, or bullied?"

"Not that we know of."

"Is there a reward?"

"We haven't reached that stage yet."

"Isn't he a little young for that attraction? Maybe he got frightened and ran off?"

"Maybe, but not likely. Gage wanted to come to the fair. He wanted to go into the Chambers of Dread as part of a harmless dare with his friends, to prove he wasn't afraid. And he wasn't. In fact, he'd refused to let his mother hold his hand."

Cal noticed Officers Berg and Ripkowski were among people at the periphery of the news pack to observe the conference. Ripkowski was on his phone feeding information to someone on the other end.

Standing with them was a black man, over six feet tall, wearing dark glasses, a jacket and matching slacks. Next to him was a white woman, in her late thirties, wearing a blazer and jeans. The woman's arms were crossed but she held an open notebook and pen, paused from writing things down. Her dark hair was pulled back in a taut ponytail. Her eyes were like black pearls locked on Cal and Faith, examining them, as the press continued with questions.

"Cal, most of us know that you're a reporter with

the *Chicago Star-News*. Mrs. Hudson, do you work outside the home?"

Faith shot a glance to Cal, who nodded.

"I'm a public relations manager," she responded.

"Who do you work for?"

"Parker Hayes and Robinson in downtown Chicago, the Sears—I mean, Willis—Tower."

"Cal, back to you—given that you're a crime reporter, could your son's disappearance have any possible link to one of your stories?"

"What? Like someone out to get me?"

"Yes."

"I think that's a huge leap."

"Thank you." DeSanto held up his palms. "One more, then we'll wrap it up." He pointed to Lori Kowski, from Cal's paper, the *Chicago Star-News*. "Go ahead, last question."

Cal saw Franco Ginnetti clench his eye behind his camera, taking aim at him and Faith. Lori and Franco knew them. He'd worked with both of them, and Faith had met them at several *Star-News* social gatherings. Gage had played with their kids at the paper's Christmas party. The moment was unreal as Cal braced for Lori's question.

"Faith," Lori started as Franco fired off a few frames. "As a mother I can't imagine what you're going through right now and my heart goes out to you. Is there anything you want to say to your son, or people who'll be following this story?"

Faith brushed back the hair that had curtained in front of her face.

"We just want to find Gage. Please, if anyone

has any information, no matter how seemingly trivial, please help us. Gage, always remember Mommy loves you. You have to be strong and re- member that no matter what happens I love you, sweetheart, and we're going to find you!"

Faith brushed back her hair again, scanning the media group and the people who'd gathered at the edges.

That's when she saw him.

He was wearing a ball cap pulled down low, but Faith would recognize him anywhere. What was he doing here? What if Cal saw him?

Subtly she made brief, intense eye contact, giv- ing him a nearly imperceptible shake of her head, as if to say, *Leave—now.*

8

Faith stared at a glass bead rosary on a silver chain.

Her friend, Pam Huppkey, had pressed it into her hand when the news conference ended. Pam was active at Saint Bartholomew's where her son, Colton, went to school with Gage and their other friends.

"I called Phyllis with the school association at Saint Bart's." Pam blinked back tears. "They're making up color fliers with Gage's picture and putting a group together to go door-to-door around the park right now." Pam hugged her with a tiny clinking sound. Pam was partial to hoop earrings and bracelets. "We're going to find him. Okay?"

Faith nodded, still staring at the rosary's Madonna and Child while running her fingertips over the crucifix. "Thank you, Pam."

Michelle Thompson, Faith's ever-poised Realtor friend and Marshall's mom, hugged her. She gestured to her husband, Jack, the other half of "the Terrific Thompson Realty Team," according to the ads on many of River Ridge's bus stop benches. He was several yards away talking with Cal and making calls on his phone.

"Jack's getting the community association and ball team parents involved in the search. We're here for you, honey. We've got your back. We're gonna find him." Michelle glanced at the newspeople lingering near the exit chutes. "Come on, let's talk over there."

Faith's friends took her away from the press to a quiet corner under the search center canopies where they continued comforting her.

"Tell us, what do you think happened?" Michelle asked.

"I don't know, I swear I just don't know. We were in the spinner part, the last section. Gage was with us. There was loud music, flashing lights. The floor spins in a circle and this guy with a chain saw is chasing you. It's chaotic and confusing. I glimpsed Gage with Cal before I got on a slide to leave. Oh God, where is he?"

"He just can't disappear like that." Michelle threw a look toward the chutes, then to Cal in the distance. Faith and Pam followed it to see Cal with Michelle's husband. Now the men were talking to police and security staff.

For her part, Pam looked long and hard at Cal, bit her bottom lip, then took quick inventory of their immediate area. She drew in close to the other women, dropped her voice.

"I thought I saw someone, but I'm—" Pam

stopped, as if catching herself thinking out loud. "I'm sorry, I'm not sure."

"What are you talking about?" Faith stared at her.

"I thought I saw someone in the crowd at the press conference."

"Who?" Faith shot at her. "Someone from where? From what?"

Pam caught her breath and swallowed hard, shaking her head.

"I'm sorry, I'm not sure."

"Who do you think you saw?"

"I'm confused."

"For God's sake, Pam!" Faith chastised her. "If you saw something important, it could be a lead! So march over there and tell the damn police who or what you think you saw right now."

Pam waved her hands in front of her. "No, no, I'm sorry! I'm confused! I didn't see anything!"

"So you didn't see anyone?"

"I didn't. I'm so sorry."

"It was either real, or it wasn't, Pam—one or the other."

"It wasn't!"

"You better be damn well certain."

"I didn't see anyone. I'm just upset for you!"

"You're *upset* for me?" Faith's condescending glare, her eyes scanning Pam head to toe in icy assessment, barely masked what she was thinking: that while Pam, a stay-at-home mom, was a loyal friend, Faith regarded her level of intelligence to be somewhat lower than hers and her other friends'.

"Christ, Pam," Michelle said. "As if Faith isn't facing enough pain now."

"I'm sorry," Pam continued. "It's just that nothing adds up, nothing makes sense. How does a little boy just disappear?"

"There could be any number of explanations," Michelle said. "We just don't know."

"Stop it," Faith said. "It's my fault. I should've been holding his hand. I'm his mother! Why wasn't I holding his hand?"

"Don't blame yourself. Cal was there, too. Anything could've—" Michelle stopped when she saw Cal approaching.

He quickly acknowledged Michelle and Pam, sensing his presence had abruptly ended a serious discussion. Then he took Faith into his arms and kissed the top of her head.

Faith made a display of rubbing his shoulders with affection, subtly glancing beyond him to the dispersed crowd to secretly confirm the man had left.

"We're going to check the lot where we parked," Cal said. "Gage might've tried to make his way to the car. You stay here, in case he returns."

"You really think Gage went to the car?" she asked. "Would he even know how to find his way back to it?"

"I don't know. Maybe. We have to check."

Cal noticed that Faith, a lapsed Catholic, had a rosary in her hand.

"What's this?"

"Pam gave it to me."

"Oh, I see." Cal glanced at Pam, then looked at the rosary briefly before closing his hands around Faith's and the rosary. He squeezed encouragement, then she cupped her hands tenderly to his face before he left with a small group for the parking lot.

They didn't find Gage at section B, space number 23, southwest of the fairgrounds where they'd parked their Ford Escape.

And as the afternoon passed, no sign of Gage had surfaced in the ongoing search of the fair and the surrounding neighborhoods, some of which had been canvassed four times by ardent volunteers. The periodic announcements appealing to fairgoers for help continued but to no avail. Alerts had gone to Amtrak and bus terminals, to O'Hare and Midway airports and to the Chicago Transit Authority, but nothing had emerged.

Gage's disappearance had become Chicago's top news story, drawing national interest. Some networks used footage recorded by fans across the country from inside the Chambers of Dread, noting that it was billed as America's Biggest Traveling World of Horrors. Every news report also included footage of Cal and Faith, who, even in their heartbreak, were a photogenic couple.

Tips began flowing to River Ridge police from the Amber Alert but they were vague, nothing concrete. "I thought I saw that kid with a Slurpee at a 7-Eleven but I'm not sure which one." Or, "I tell you I saw a boy like that running down the midway, that's all I know."

The sun sank and night fell over the River Ridge Fairgrounds. The midway continued bustling with flashing and pulsating lights while the rock music hammered. But by 11:30 p.m., the crowds had thinned, food stands began closing; the rides began shutting down and the music was silenced.

At midnight the gates were locked.

Near the Chambers of Dread, desperation was mounting.

While Faith and Cal waited at the search center with clusters of police, security staff, volunteers and media, a funereal stillness had gripped the grounds, bringing the Hudsons to the next stage of their anguish.

"Faith." Cal took her hands in his, hearing the tremor in his voice. "It's time to go home."

"Go home?" She stared at him as if he'd just uttered the vilest words imaginable.

"Go home and rest, Faith. You can look again after some sleep."

"Go home without my son?"

A surge of panic filled her eyes and she began shaking her head at the devastating weight of what had befallen them. The threads of her restraint unraveled and one by one they snapped as her facade of calm and reason exploded with volcanic might at the awful, terrible horror.

"No, no, no. I can't go home without him. No, I can't! No, I can't! No, no!" Faith began chanting, pulling at her hair as if she'd lost her mind.

"Gage!" She stood, screaming full bore in a gut-twisting pitch, as if barbed wire were scraping her vocal cords. *"Gage!"*

Cal moved to console her; she fought him off. Michelle and Pam, along with their husbands and police, rushed to help but she twisted and writhed, sobbing before crumpling to the ground in a heap.

They struggled to help her; one of the officers radioed for EMS and within two minutes a siren yelped. An ambulance, lights flashing, inched toward them. From a distance news cameras captured Faith's breakdown as paramedics checked her signs.

"She needs to rest," one of them said.

"Take her home," Cal said, giving them the address. "I'll sign whatever waiver you need. I'll ride with you. Just take her home."

She didn't fight as they transferred her to a gurney, lifted her into the ambulance and drove off. Cal was at her feet. A paramedic watched over her while she continued calling softly for Gage.

Looking upon his wife, struggling to maintain control, Cal felt he had melted into a strange dreamlike river. As they rolled through the fairgrounds he was stabbed by the thought of how they'd come here together as a family and were now retreating like troops crushed by an overwhelming enemy.

The streets of River Ridge looked alien to him.

Nothing was real anymore.

More news crews were waiting on the lawn and sidewalk of the Hudsons' house when they arrived, shouting questions at them. Cal waved them off. Samantha and Rory Clark, their neighbors who had a key, had hurried outside the Hudsons' house to help. The paramedics brought Faith inside and suggested she take an over-the-counter sleeping pill.

They put her in bed; Cal sat alone with her, not knowing what to do as his exhausted brain throbbed with thoughts of Gage.

He couldn't sleep, so after she drifted off he went back downstairs.

Officers Berg and Ripkowski were still in the house.

"We can ensure our people stay the night with you, to be prepared for anything. It's your option," the officers had told Cal.

"Yes, I'd like it if someone were here for now."

Along with Officers Berg and Ripkowski, Michelle and Pam had arrived with their husbands and offered to stay in the room with Faith. Samantha—"Sam" to her friends—had made strong coffee. Cal needed to be alert. He drank two large cups, fighting to hang on to himself while sitting in his kitchen with his friends.

For a burning instant he envied and hated them.

They knew where their kids were. They hadn't lost a child. He knew what they were likely thinking: *I wouldn't have let my kid out of my sight for one second—not like Cal and Faith, not me.*

Cal then loathed himself as his friends expressed their genuine, heartfelt concerns, urging him to eat and rest.

How can I sleep not knowing where Gage is?

Is he terrified? Is he hurt somewhere? Is he locked away? Oh God, please tell me where he is.

Cal knew what he had to do.

He hurried to the storage closet, next to the kitchen. He opened a big backpack, stuffed it with items from the kitchen and closet. He got a couple of flashlights, tapped them to test the batteries, grabbed Gage's hockey stick and headed for the door.

"Where're you going, Cal?" Officer Ripkowski asked.

Rory Clark glanced at the others, who were puzzled.

"Gage may have tried to walk home."

"You think so? It's about two miles and he's only nine, Cal," Ripkowski said.

"I know. I showed him once how to get to our place from Blossom Avenue and it leads to the fairgrounds. I'm going to track back to the car and search along the route he might've taken."

"I got a flashlight in my car." Rory nodded to the other men. "We'll come with you, unless you officers think that's a problem?"

"Go ahead," Berg said, reaching for her radio. "We'll advise our people and wait here."

In the following hours, with two news crews in tow, Cal and his group of suburban fathers walked the route Gage might've taken. They searched front yards, backyards and driveways, raking their flashlights under cars. They looked in alleys and behind strip malls. Cal used the hockey stick to probe trash cans and poke hedges and shrubs.

All the while the men called out for Gage, they stopped late-night dog walkers, joggers and people on bicycles to ask for help, showing them Gage's picture on their phones. And the group consulted with every River Ridge police car they encountered, patrolling and on alert in the hunt for Gage.

They arrived at the River Ridge Fairgrounds finding the Hudsons' SUV was the only vehicle remaining in the southwest parking lot. A patrol car had been watching it from a distance and the men checked in with the officer before moving toward it.

A cold wind kicked up, tossing papers and sending empty Old Milwaukee cans tumbling across the desolate expanse where the Ford Escape stood fast, as if keeping a lone vigil for Gage.

Cal unlocked it, opened the tailgate and lowered the rear seats.

As his friends watched, trying to understand Cal's actions, he unpacked Gage's small sleeping bag and spread it carefully on the rear. Then he set out prepackaged cheese and crackers, peanut butter and crackers, three juice boxes, apples and bananas. Gage loved those snacks. Next to them, he set down Gage's favorite handheld video game, the one he'd left on the kitchen table before they'd come to the fair.

Gage cherished the little game and Cal knew it would be the first thing he'd pick up if he returned to the car. Cal inserted fresh batteries, brushed the game tenderly with his fingertips before typing on the small keyboard. A couple of men watching over Cal's shoulder saw his brief message,

Gage, we're searching for you everywhere. You're not in trouble son, just stay here and we'll come and get you. We love you, Mom and Dad.

A few people sniffed and throats were cleared as the men turned away.

"Guys, let's search along the edge of the lot by the fences and the alleys," one of the men said, intending to give Cal privacy.

The other fathers moved away across the lot in different directions, leaving Cal alone sitting on the Ford's tailgate.

As the wind kicked up, Cal remembered that Gage didn't have a jacket or hoodie and wondered if he was cold, wherever he was right now. It may have been Cal's exhaustion, his strained emotions, but at that instant Cal was hit, like a sledgehammer to his gut, with the probability that he would never see Gage again.

He sobbed into his hands as the wind carried his pain into the night and Gage stared down on him from one of the big screens that were still lit over the fairgrounds, with the words *Lost/Missing* and *Last Seen Wearing* calling out above his description and blazing in the darkness.

I'm so sorry, Gage. I'm so sorry for everything I've done, son.

9

"*M*om, help me!"

Faith hears him first, crying out, then screaming for her.

"*Mom, help me! Please come and help me, Mom!*"

He's still in the Chambers of Dread. It's where he's been all this time.

Faith gets in her car, flies to the fairgrounds, scales the fence, rushes into the horror house, passes through the jaws of the Demon King, plunges into the darkness, following Gage's pleas.

"*Mom, please, please, help me!*"

"*I'm coming, sweetheart! I'm coming!*"

A cloaked figure points the way for her with a blood-dripping head. Faith blurs through the labyrinth, races by the flames of the burning witch queen.

"*Hurry, Mom!*"

Faith comes to the fanged clown thumping a malevolent tune on the keyboard of skulls at the organ and nodding the way for Faith over the river of snakes, through the cavern of bats and spiders. She weaves through the tombstones in the grave- yard as the zombie points. "He's in there!"

"Mommy, help me!"

Gage is lying on a cutting table and the insane butcher—surrounded by twitching limbs and bleeding torsos—raises his cleaver over Gage's neck.

Faith screams at him, "Stop!"

She rushes to Gage, but hands clawing at her lower legs, wretched hands of the damned from the Dungeons of Dread, keep her back. She struggles, reaching toward Gage, his eyes ballooning as the cleaver begins its descent. She cries out to him— oh God—straining, almost reaching him—almost!

"Why didn't you take my hand, Mommy?"

"Gage! No! I'm here! Mommy's right here!"

Faith fights to break free—to save Gage—but the hands are holding her...pressing her down... voices are calling to her...

"Faith! Faith, honey, wake up!"

She gasped and startled awake. Michelle and Pam were with her, holding her down.

"You're having a bad dream," Michelle said.

Battling through her torpor Faith discovered she was at home in her bedroom.

"A dream?"

"Yes, it's just a bad dream." Pam nodded.

"Gage is home?"

Before they could stop her, Faith bolted from her bed and hurried to Gage's room. She called for him but the deathly quiet of his empty room and his empty bed that was still made stopped her cold.

"Gage?"

She picked up his pillow, held it to her chest and pressed her face into it, smelling a trace of him.

That's all she had now, that and her guilt.

Was this the price she'd have to pay for her sins?

"Faith, honey." Michelle and Pam took her shoulders. "Let's get you back to your bed. You need to rest."

Racked with unrelenting agony, Faith slammed her back to the wall and slid to the floor. Through her sobs, as Michelle and Pam helped Faith to her bed, they heard her say, "I'm being punished! I'm being punished!"

Officer Angie Berg heard it, too, and made a note of it in her log.

The Second Day

10

Thirty minutes before dawn under a coral sky a man and woman stepped out of a blue Chevy Impala and walked to the front step of the Hudsons' house.

The woman was in her early thirties, white, five foot four, slender, hair pulled in a tight ponytail. She was jacked up on Starbucks. The man, midthirties, was black, six foot two, with a bearlike physique, calm and confident. Both had clipboard folders.

They rang the doorbell.

When Cal, who'd had about forty-five minutes of sleep since returning from the fairgrounds, opened the door, the woman spoke.

"Mr. Hudson? I'm Detective Rachel Price and this is Detective Leon Lang, River Ridge Police."

Both held up leather-cased wallets showing their badges and IDs. Cal remembered them. They'd been standing with Berg and Ripkowski at the press conference.

"May we come in?" Price asked.

A new wave of concern rolled over his face. "Did you find Gage?"

"No, sir, not yet," Price said.

"What about the car? Did he come to our car in the parking lot?"

"I'm sorry, no. But we've got more people involved and there are things we need to do as soon as possible, so may we come in?"

Cal surrendered the door and walked them inside.

"There's coffee in the kitchen," he said.

Some of the Hudsons' friends were in the living room; some were asleep and others were talking softly on phones. The TV was tuned to a breakfast news show. Sports highlights were on. The volume was low.

"I'm sorry. It must've been a rough night," Price said.

Cal rubbed his face and messy hair and nodded.

"Excuse me." Price noticed Officers Berg and Ripkowski drinking coffee in the kitchen, studying maps on the counter with two men. "I need a private word with our people before a fresh crew relieves them."

Price went to the kitchen, and Lang spoke up. "Sir, can you show me your son's room?"

Cal led him upstairs and down the hall to Gage's room, which seemed to shrink when Lang stood in the middle of it, taking stock without touching anything. He noticed Gage's posters—the Cubs, the White Sox, Bears, Bulls and Blackhawks—nodding to one that was a mosaic.

"Your son likes Pokémon?"

"Yes."

"So does my daughter. She has the same poster. Not sure what generation that one is." Lang had a soft, infectious smile that became all business when he shifted gears. "Mr. Hudson, we're doing everything we can to find Gage."

Cal nodded, then said, "Look, I'm going out to continue search—"

"Excuse me, Mr. Hudson." Cal turned to see Price had come in behind him. "We're going to need you and your wife to come to our offices so we can talk."

"Talk?"

"We want to go over everything very carefully with both of you and we should go now."

"What's going on?" Faith had emerged from their bedroom clutching a robe around her. "Who are these people?"

"They're detectives and they want us to go with them to help with the search for Gage."

"Cal, Faith." Price made sure she had their attention. "Has anyone contacted you claiming to know your son's whereabouts, or to demand ransom? Maybe they contacted you in some way we're not aware of?"

"No," Cal said. "We would have alerted your people here."

"Good, okay. Now, we'd also like to request your consent to allow us to search your home and conduct other aspects of our investigation—on your phones, computers, vehicles, bank records, credit cards, that sort of thing. We'll have the paperwork at our office." They all watched Lang close Gage's bedroom door by hooking his pen behind the knob. "Right now we'd like to seal your son's bedroom, along with the rest of the house, so our techs can process it. I've got a log here—" Price tapped her folder "—from Officer Berg. We'll also collect DNA, and fingerprints from you and everyone who's been in the house since Gage's disappearance to create an elimination set. We'll get details on where your volunteers have searched and who was involved. Mr. Hudson, being a crime reporter, I'm sure you understand these steps?"

"Wait! I don't understand. Why do this?" Faith's bloodshot eyes searched their faces for the answer. "Why search our private lives, our home? Why take our fingerprints? Gage isn't here. You had two cops sitting in our kitchen all night. Get out there and search the city. Search the freakin' fairgrounds, talk to those tattooed lowlifes working on the midway!"

"Faith." Cal grabbed her shoulders. "Honey, this is what they have to do. It's procedure."

"That's right, Mrs. Hudson," Lang said. "We're sorry if it's upsetting but we need to do this. Believe me, we've got a lot of people working to locate your son."

"I don't understand." Faith pulled at the cuffs of her robe to wipe at her tears. "I don't understand any of this."

Cal hugged her, then turned to the detectives. "Do we have time to take a shower?"

"A quick one," Price said. "I'm sorry, but time is crucial."

Half an hour later, as Cal and Faith accompanied the detectives to their sedan, Faith froze, having trouble catching her breath.

Gage's bicycle was in the front yard beside the walk.

For a burning instant she thought he'd come home from riding through the neighborhood, leaving his bike on the lawn like he always did, and her heart soared with the relief that he'd returned to her.

She reached out to touch Gage's bike but was stabbed with the cold, hard truth: he'd neglected to put it the garage before they'd gone to the carnival because he was so excited.

Cal put his arm around her, calming her, moving her along as they were caught in the glare of TV cameras and the staccato flash of newspaper photographers.

Mary Kitterly, a Chicago TV news reporter, turned to her camera, which had tracked the Hudsons' walk to the car live for its morning news broadcast. She was reporting to her anchor in what the station was calling a "Breaking Exclusive."

"That's right, Bob." Mary gripped her microphone with one hand and steadied her earpiece with the other. "Sources tell me that River Ridge detectives are taking the couple, Cal and Faith Hudson, in for what they call 'interviews.' Now, this comes less than twenty-four hours after the mysterious disappearance of their nine-year-old son, Gage Hudson, from the River Ridge midway."

"Mary, that's an interesting turn of events in what is a very troubling case. Is there anything more you can tell us regarding the parents being escorted from their home by police?"

The camera and Mary turned to see the perfect middle-class couple seated in the Chevy sedan before the doors closed and it whisked down the sleepy neighborhood street.

"Bob, experts we've talked to have assured us that this is routine in cases involving missing children and does not imply any suspicion or role in the boy's disappearance. It should be noted that it's our understanding that the parents were the last to see the boy before he vanished..."

11

The River Ridge Police Department was head-
quartered downtown, across from city hall, in the
Lewis D. Boatellick Building, a restored five-story
glass-and-stone example of Midwestern civic ar-
chitecture, named for the first officer killed on
duty.

Most cops called it "the Boat."

Price and Lang avoided the news crews huddled
out front, driving through the secured entrance
to the building's underground parking garage. It
smelled of exhaust, engine oil and cement when
the detectives led the Hudsons to the elevator.

They stepped off at the fourth floor and went
down a corridor coming to a fluorescent-lit squad
room. The walls were lined with maps, file cabi-
nets, case-status boards, shift schedules and glass-
walled offices. A large flat-screen TV suspended
from the ceiling was tuned to an all-news channel.
The middle of the room was open with an assort-
ment of large desks cojoined in pairs.

"Please have a seat." Lang rolled out two chairs

beside their desks. "First, we need you to sign the consent-to-search authorizations."

"They're ready. I'll get them," Price said, going to another office, returning with a file folder and placing a legal-looking document on the desk before Cal and Faith, who tried to read the several stapled pages.

"This allows us to immediately begin collecting material from your home—fingerprints, DNA— and search your computers and phones for anything connected to Gage." Price extended a ballpoint pen to Faith, who stared at it without accepting it.

Lang said, "Gage's disappearance could be tied to someone who was in your home, contacted you or hacked your computer or phone. Unless we investigate, we won't know."

Cal and Faith hesitated while Price kept the pen extended.

"We could get warrants," Lang said. "This is faster, lets us send an evidence team to your house right away. And our IT people can clone your phones right here right now in a very short time. That way we'll monitor all the calls here, so if someone contacts you for a ransom, or finds Gage, or he tries to call you, we're on it. No time is lost."

Cal was nodding but Faith remained hesitant as the detectives looked at them.

"But you'll also go through all of our private information?" she asked.

"With your consent," Price said.

"I don't have a problem with that," Cal said. "Whatever it takes to help find Gage, right, Faith?"

"Yes," she said, "of course."

Cal and Faith signed, then handed their phones to the detectives. "Thank you," Lang said. "We'll take these to IT."

"What about the police officers at our home?" Faith asked.

"What about them?" Price said.

"How long will they be living with us?"

Price and Lang exchanged a glance.

"Are you uncomfortable having them there?" Price asked.

"A little," Faith said.

"We've posted officers there for support and for your safety during this time," Price said. "But after we clone your phones, they can be available at your discretion. Any time you'd prefer they not be inside, you tell us. We can post them outside, okay?"

"Thank you," Faith said.

"Good. We're going to get some coffee, fuel for the job," Price said. "Can we get you coffee, juice, water?"

The Hudsons declined.

"We'll be back in a few minutes." Price offered a small smile. "And once we're done the interviews we'll take you down to processing for your prints and swab for DNA, then get you home."

Price and Lang left, leaving Cal and Faith alone.

"I didn't understand the consent we just signed." Faith blinked back her tears. "I almost feel like we need a lawyer. I can't think at all."

"This is all procedure. One way or another

they'll get what they want and we have to cooperate so they can focus on Gage."

"I'll do whatever it takes to find him but I'm so afraid, Cal, I can't think." Faith cupped her hands to her face.

Cal's impulse was to put his arm around her but he abandoned the idea. Taking stock of the squad room, he pointed his chin to one of the outlying offices. Two men in sports shirts, wearing shoulder holsters, were questioning an overweight tattooed man.

"Look, that's the ticket taker. The guy who was in front of the horror house when we went in," Cal said. "I didn't like the way he eyed you."

"You noticed that, did you?"

Cal studied her for a moment.

"Yes, I noticed," Cal said. "He gave off a bad vibe."

Faith let a few tense seconds pass before she nodded to another office where two other detectives were talking to a man. "That's the chain-saw guy. At least they're talking to the carny people. That's a good thing."

As the minutes swept by, Cal and Faith looked at the desks. Their sides were pushed against a wall under a corkboard of notes, calendars, phone lists and personal items. To one side there was a framed degree from Elmhurst College for Rachel Price and a photo of her beaming in formal blues, with two men to her left and two men to her right. *Congrats, little sis! The fifth cop in the family! Doug, Spence, Danny and Deke* was penned below it.

On the right side, there was a framed degree in Criminal Justice for Leon Wesley Lang from the University of Illinois. There was a snapshot of him with a woman and a little girl, about Gage's age, by a mountain lake. The girl bore a resemblance to Lang.

Each desk had a computer monitor and keyboard. File folders were fanned over the work area and notebooks were bound with elastic and neatly stacked. On one of the desks were splayed copies of the morning editions of the *Chicago Tribune* and the *Chicago Star-News*. The headline in the *Star-News* said Star-News Reporter's Son Vanishes in River Ridge Fair Horror House. It ran atop photos of Gage in his blue Cubs shirt and Cal and Faith at the press conference.

Faith's hand flew to her mouth. "Cal," she said, her voice quavering. "I don't like this. What're we really here for?"

"They need to know exactly what happened and we have to help."

"It's making me nervous. Will they need to know everything about us?"

Cal looked at her.

"They're going to ask us whatever they feel they need to ask us, Faith. That could be anything. Are you ready for that?"

She stared back at him. He was unable to read what was behind her eyes but her tone cooled when she finally said, "Are you, Cal?"

For a moment, neither of them breathed.

Suddenly she took his hand, squeezing it with

both of hers, as if she'd been cued by Price and Lang's return.

"All set?" Price smiled briefly, taking note of the handholding. The detectives had returned with ceramic mugs of coffee, their clipboard folders and the Hudsons' phones. "Thanks for those. Now, Cal, if you'd come with me, and Faith, if you'd go with Leon."

They led them to the far end of the floor, down a hall with several closed rooms. Price indicated Interview Room 402 on the left side for Cal, while Leon did the same for Interview Room 403 on the opposite side for Faith.

"We don't want to be interrupted," Price said, "so we'll talk in these interview rooms."

Before they entered, Faith threw her arms around Cal, surprising him with a kiss on his cheek and a tight hug, her body trembling against his.

Again, she searched Cal's face.

Then she turned and joined Lang.

12

Still feeling Faith's kiss, Cal stepped into Interview Room 402.

He took a quick look at the small room, barren of furniture but for the hard-back chairs on either side of a table with a wood veneer finish.

As a reporter, Cal had been inside enough police stations, precincts and districts to know how investigators truly regarded these rooms. All of them were like this one, bright and sparse with white cinder-block walls that seemed to be closing in on you.

Interview room? No, these were battlefields where truth waged war against deception.

"Have a seat, Cal."

The chairs scraped on the vinyl floor and Price took her place across from him, set her mug on the table, then her folder, which she opened. She tapped her pen against the pad while scanning her notes.

She was pumped for this.

Cal swallowed. Most of the saliva in his throat had dried.

Hang on to yourself and keep it together.

Price pulled a small recorder from her jacket, switched it on and set it down between them. "This little one's for me. I want to take down everything accurately." She gave him a smile, nodding to the camera pointing at him from the ceiling in the corner of the room. "We record all interviews, a precaution for you and for us. Do you have a problem with that?"

"None."

"Okay, good," she said. "We've gone over your statements but I want to begin with you telling me everything that occurred yesterday when Gage disappeared, from the time you got up, to the time you went to sleep—or tried to. Include everything you did, everyone you interacted with, whether by phone, email, in person, tell me everything."

Cal took a slow, deep breath, then for the next twenty minutes he recounted the day—how it was a day off for both him and Faith, how they'd taken Gage to the fair, to the Chambers of Dread, and the nightmare that had happened after that.

"So, Gage wanted to go into the Chambers because his friends Marshall and Colton had dared him?" Price made notes. "Is that correct?"

"Yes."

"Tell me more about Gage. Has he ever wandered off?"

"No."

"Does he have any learning disabilities?"

"No, he's a bright child, takes after his mother."

"Any attention disorders?"

"No."

"Would you say he's shy, quiet, bold, talkative, a leader or a follower?"

"He's quiet, a follower. He's social—he's got his friends."

"Is he mostly happy? Unhappy?"

"Happy. He's happy."

"Does he take risks?"

"No, he's cautious."

"Would you say he's a fearful, anxious child, pessimistic?"

"No, he's positive, easygoing."

"Any behavioral problems at all?"

"No. And he does well in school."

"Has he tried drugs that you know of?"

"He's nine."

"We both know age doesn't seem to matter these days."

"No, he hasn't touched drugs."

"How does he interact with strangers?"

"You mean when he meets new people, or creeps?"

"Any way you want to answer."

"He knows to stay away from strangers, but he's respectful when he meets new people with us, that sort of thing."

"Does he have access to the internet?"

"Yes, at school and at home."

"Has he ever met or communicated with a stranger online?"

"No, there are guards on what he can access at school and at home. These things are monitored."

"What does he do online?"

"He plays games and he chats on a site called ELZ, the earLoadzone. It's for younger kids and he only talks to people he knows, like his buddies Marshall, Colton, Ethan and their friends."

"What sort of things do they talk about?"

"Movies, video games. They talked about the Chambers of Dread—that's mostly where they dared each other to go on it."

"You sure he only talks to his friends? People can lurk on these sites."

"We monitor it closely. We can see who he talks to. So can the parents of the other kids."

"All right, but we're going to want to look into his history and who chatted with him. Does he have a cell phone?"

"No."

"Have you noticed any strange activity in your lives within the last few months? Say, strangers asking for directions, wrong numbers, strange vehicles, anything that struck you as odd or out of the ordinary?"

"No, nothing like that."

"Has Gage ever expressed or displayed any fear, unease or discomfort about anyone in particular?"

"No."

"Who would you say he is closest to?"

"Besides us?"

"Any way you want to answer."

"Well, after us, I'd say his pals Marshall, Colton and Ethan."

"Has Gage ever stayed away from home?"

"Sure, camp and sleepovers with his friends."

"Has he ever snuck out without permission?"

"No."

"Run away from home?"

"No."

Price paged back through her notes.

"Okay, let's go back. Take me through the attraction again. Everything you can remember—who was ahead of you, who was behind you. No detail is too small. And with respect to you, Faith and Gage, who was with who right up until you realized Gage was missing."

Cal related everything he could recall, noting how the fog, the darkness, the loud noises and flashing lights often made things chaotic, confusing and hard to distinguish details.

"But at no point did Gage allow either you or your wife to hold his hand?"

"That's correct."

"What was his demeanor?"

"He seemed nervous but in a fun way, like he was scared but having fun. Excited."

"Did you notice anyone talking to him, hanging around him?"

"No, well, outside he had a short conversation with the ticket taker. That heavy guy you got out there."

"What was the nature of that conversation?"

"The guy was trying to jazz him up about the ride. It was short, but he seemed to enjoy an extra-long look at Faith."

"What about inside? Did you see that guy or notice anyone hanging around Gage?"

"No to both, but again it was hard to make out details inside."

Price made notes and tapped her pen.

"Let's go back a bit to the spinner before you exited," she said. "You say you thought Faith had Gage, that you thought you saw her with him at the exit?"

"Yes."

Price blinked a few times and made a note, then Cal asked a question.

"I thought you guys were trying to retrieve footage from the video recordings inside the ride."

Price shook her head. "We've got nothing helpful so far. The techs are still working on that."

"Did you talk to other people who were in the Chambers and those chutes at the same time we were there?"

"We've been trying to locate them—it's difficult. But with the media coverage a few are beginning to step forward. We're talking to them."

"What about that canine unit?"

"Nothing so far."

"What about tips?"

"Nothing concrete has come in but we're following up all possible leads."

"The neighborhoods surrounding the fairgrounds?"

"We're still working them but nothing yet."

"Nothing?" Cal's jaw muscle twitched and he indicated the squad room. "What about the people working the attraction? The carnies…what did they tell you?"

"Like I said, we're still talking to everybody and we're still searching and canvassing. Look, being a Chicago crime reporter, Cal, I'm sure you have an understanding of the anatomy of these types of investigations."

Cal understood very well.

Price let a moment pass, then said, "There are only a few explanations for what happened. Gage wandered off, was perhaps disoriented, or he was lured or enticed, or he was abducted."

Abducted.

Here it comes.

Up to now Cal had been hanging on by his fingertips, struggling not to break, fighting to work around the keening in his head. He shut his eyes tight because what he'd feared, what he'd been denying, what he knew in his gut, had swallowed him. Gage was likely abducted and Cal knew from his own reporting experience that if an abductor intended to kill their victim, stats showed they'd do it in the first four hours. And if a kidnapper was seeking ransom, they make contact within twenty-four to forty-eight hours. The likelihood that Gage was dead, or that they'd never see him again, increased with each passing second.

"Cal?"

He opened his eyes, not having realized he'd closed them.

"Until we have a clear picture of what happened," Price said, "no one is above suspicion. You understand that, don't you, Cal?"

He swallowed and nodded.

"And you know we have to clear you and your wife so we can cross you off our list?"

Cal nodded.

"Now." Price sipped some coffee. "Are you okay to keep going?"

Cal thought of Faith across the hall, wondering how she was enduring.

"Cal?"

"Yes."

Price looked at her notes. "Are you involved in, or do you have knowledge of who may be responsible for, your son's disappearance?"

Cal shook his head. "No, I'm not involved and I don't know who took him."

"Do you or your wife use illegal drugs?"

"No."

"Has Gage ever been exposed to any form of physical, sexual or emotional abuse in your home?"

Cal shook his head.

"Do you have a gambling addiction?"

"We went to Las Vegas for fun and gambled a little, that's it."

"Do you have any debts?"

"Just the mortgage, car payments, credit cards, like most people."

"Who handles the finances in your household?"

"Faith. We each have separate accounts, but we have joint accounts, too, and Faith uses those to handle household finances."

"And these separate accounts...they're private from each other?"

"That's right. We agreed to do things that way when we got married."

"All right." Price made notes, then moved on. "You're a crime reporter with the *Chicago Star-News*."

Cal nodded.

"You don't really cover much crime here in River Ridge, or the other 'safe' suburbs. You cover the big stuff downtown and across the country?"

"Yes, I work near the *Tribune* building, and if the story's big enough, the paper sends me wherever we need to go. Although we don't travel as much these days—they've tightened budgets."

"In your line of work, you report on a lot of dangerous people, correct?"

"Yes."

"Your stories helped put a lot of people in prison?"

"I just report the facts."

"This came up at the news conference, so I want to ask—can you think of anyone in your past who may have threatened you? Anyone who might want to settle a score with you? Or anything you may have done to anger someone to the point that they'd want revenge against you?"

Cal exhaled slowly as his mind raced back over his years and the stories blurred.

"People get pissed off and have said things to me."

"What sort of things, what people?"

"Usually relatives and friends of suspects, or criminals."

"And what did they say?"

"'I'm going to kick your ass, you write bullshit.' 'Why didn't you write the truth about such and such?' But that's pretty common. I mean, not everyone's happy with what you report. But I never took any of it seriously."

"Why not?"

"Because it's just people blowing steam—people say things. No one's ever acted on anything."

"So far."

"No one so far."

Price nodded and made notes. "You ever cross the line on your job, Cal?"

"What do you mean?"

"Break the rules, get your story wrong, really piss off a subject or burn a source, that sort of thing?"

"What're you suggesting?"

"Not suggesting anything. Just want to know if you think there's anyone out to get you."

Cal steepled his fingers and touched them to his chin. "We covered this, Detective. Yes, I've pissed people off with my work."

"Who, how?"

"I already told you, some people don't like it when you write the truth about their situation. But that's part of my job. If I thought for one second that Gage's disappearance had any connection to my work, to anything I'd done, I'd be screaming that fact to you."

Price took a moment to process his response.

"Okay, let's move on. Your newspaper, the *Chicago Star-News*, has been bleeding staff in recent years and there's talk online and in the business pages that more layoffs are coming—that's got to put a lot of stress on you."

"It makes you think about what you're going to do if you lose your job. I've been with the *Star-News* a long time and reporting jobs are pretty hard to come by these days."

"So there's some stress in your home?"

"No more than anyone else in this economy."

"What about you and Faith?"

"What about us?"

"Tell me about your relationship. How did you meet?"

Cal remembered the first time he saw Faith. She was on her phone, upset and in tears. He was immediately infatuated. After approaching her, he'd learned that her boyfriend had broken up with her and he thought, *Who'd be stupid enough to break this girl's heart?* So he asked her out and they fell in love.

"We met in college."

Price smiled. "And Gage is your only child?"

"Well, after Gage, Faith miscarried once and we never had another."

"Oh, I'm sorry. When was that?"

"Two years after Gage was born." Cal blinked several times.

Price made a note. "And Faith is with a public relations firm downtown?"

"Yes."

"How would you describe Faith, Cal—is she calm or a nervous person?"

"She can be both."

"How would you describe her intelligence?"

"Her intelligence?"

"Yes, is she a genius, a linear thinker, slow to grasp things?"

"No, she's very intelligent, way smarter than me, graduated near the top of her class. She was in Mensa for a while."

"Mensa? Really?" Price made notes. "Is she generally liked by others?"

"Yes."

"Is she religious, devout?"

"She's Catholic, goes to Mass. Well, not as much as she used to, but she's still involved in the school and church."

"What about you?"

"I was raised Catholic, was an altar boy, but I stopped going to church a long time ago."

"Why? Were you abused or something?"

"Too much hypocrisy for me."

"So you lost your faith."

"No, guess you could say that I put it on the shelf."

Price made notes. "Back to Faith—is she a good mother, attentive, or career-focused?"

"She's a good mother. Gage is her world."

"Would you say she's confident or self-conscious?"

"Both, depends on the situation. She can be sensitive and sensitive to other people's feelings."

"Is she restrained and controlled or does she give in to urges and temptations?"

Cal hesitated at the word *temptations* and met Price's eyes, wondering where this line of questioning was headed.

"She's a disciplined, hardworking, devoted mother who has a weakness for banana milk shakes and tacos."

"What about her spending habits?"

"She likes to shop—she's fashionable. She buys things for Gage. But she's not out of control or anything. In fact, she earns more than I do."

"Does that bother you?"

"No."

"Really?"

"Really."

"Tell me about her hobbies, likes, dislikes?"

"She picks the mushrooms and onions off her pizza or salad. She loves to read, mostly general fiction. She belongs to a book club. She likes TV crime shows."

"Really? What kind?"

"The true-crime stuff—*Dateline, The First 48*, unsolved murder mystery stuff, forensic stuff."

"And you?"

"No, I don't watch those shows."

"Funny, I would think it would be the other way around." Price made notes. "Have you ever been unfaithful to her, Cal?"

"What?" Cal shot her a look for offending him. "No."

"Has she ever been unfaithful to you?"

Price sipped from her mug, as if she'd just asked him the time of day, watching him from over the rim. Cal swallowed and looked into her eyes. They were indifferent to any pain she may have caused as she waited for an answer. Cal suddenly imagined Faith across the hall and Lang asking her a similar question.

"No. She's a good wife and our marriage is solid."

Price nodded and made notes.

"Sure, we argue from time to time. I've ticked her off and she's ticked me off. Mostly it's me ticking her off, but that's what a marriage is."

"I wouldn't know. I'm not married."

A soft knock sounded at the door.

A man in a suit, who looked senior to Price, stuck his head in.

"Excuse me, Rachel? Something's come up. We need you now."

13

Long before the knock on the door had ended Detective Price's interview with Cal, across the hall in Interview Room 403, Detective Leon Lang slid a tissue box closer to Faith Hudson.

"Faith, I know you're devastated and exhausted but the sooner we get through this, the faster Detective Price and I can go to the next step."

"I've told you everything." She touched a tissue to her eyes. "How can I sit here talking to you when every fiber in me is screaming that my child, my baby, is missing and when—" her fingers tightened into fists, her knuckles whitened "—when I don't know where Gage is, if he's safe, if he's warm, if someone's hurting him."

"I know this is hard but we have to work together to help Gage, all right?"

Lang's soft smile was assuring, his tranquil demeanor calming. That he had a daughter close to Gage's age made his compassion genuine.

"All right." Her voice was barely a whisper.

"Good," he said, and consulted his notes. "Before we move on, I want to go back to the last moment you saw Gage. You say that you saw him in the spinner at the exits with Cal?"

"Yes, the last I saw him he was with Cal."

"You're certain about that?" Lang checked his notes. "Because in your initial statement to Officer Ripkowski you indicated you weren't sure."

"Yes, there was confusion—the floor was spinning, the strobe lights and the guy with the saw—but I'm sure I saw him with Cal." Her chin crumpled.

"But he obviously wasn't with Cal when you exited."

"No." She shook her head and brushed her tears.

"All right, I want to move on. Does Gage take any medication of any kind?"

"No."

"Does he have any chronic illness or injury or condition?"

"No."

"Has he ever needed or received counseling for any issues?"

"No."

"Any problems in school?"

"Academically?"

"Start with that, yes."

"No, his grades are good. He likes school. He completes his assignments. He's very bright. He told me he wants to be an architect, that he wants to design buildings and stadiums."

"What about peer pressure or bullying at school?"

"No, nothing that I'm aware of."

Lang made notes while Faith glanced again at the camera up in the corner that was recording everything.

"Has anyone moved in or out of your neighborhood recently?"

Faith thought. "The Robinsons at the end of the block—they're accountants. They retired and moved to Nevada about two months ago. A family—the Carrutherses, from Seattle—moved in with twin teens, a boy and a girl. They keep to themselves, pretty much. I think the dad works at O'Hare for United or Delta."

"Have you observed anyone taking special interest in Gage?"

"No."

"Anyone acting suspicious around him?"

"No."

"Tell me about Cal, his personality. Just quick descriptors—would you say he's calm or nervous?"

"Calm."

"Overly suspicious or overly trusting?"

"Well, he's a crime reporter, so I'd say suspicious."

"Self-centered or a team player?"

"I'd lean to self-centered."

"Heartless or compassionate?"

"Depends."

"How?"

"If he needs an interview with someone, he can be as compassionate as he needs to be. If he's trying to beat his competition on a story, he can be heartless, ruthless even."

"Would you say your husband is a giver or a taker?"

Faith considered the question for a moment. "A taker."

"A taker?"

"He's often at work, or with friends, or sources. Taking Gage to the fair was like a gift of his time to us."

"Would you characterize him as a workaholic?"

She nodded.

"Is that a source of tension for you and Cal?"

She took a moment to respond. "No. We've adapted."

"Would you say Cal is solitary or needs to be with others?"

She brushed a tear from the corner of her eye. "Solitary."

"Deceptive or truthful?"

"Truthful, unless he's suspected someone has deceived him."

"What do you mean?"

"If he's dealing with unsavory types for a story, that sort of thing, he'll do whatever it takes to get at the truth."

"Would you say he was arrogant, or humble?"

"Somewhere in between, I suppose."

Lang made notes.

"All right. Now, Faith, prior to Gage's disappearance, was there any significant event in his life and yours—a school problem, a relationship or family issue, something involving police, anything?"

Faith began shaking her head. "No, nothing out of the ordinary."

"Any recent stress in your family, say, with something financial, a death?"

"Cal's worried about losing his job at the paper."

"And what kind of stress has that put on you and Gage?"

"We try to keep that from Gage, but I told Cal we could survive on my salary if we tightened up on things."

"And Cal's reaction?"

"He didn't really want to talk about it."

"Faith, do you have any marital stress at all now, or in the past?"

She swallowed and blinked quickly. "A few arguments here and there, like most married couples, but no."

"Aside from the workaholic thing, is Cal a good father?"

"Yes."

"A good husband?"

She nodded.

"Faith, I have to ask these questions, but before you answer, you must understand that no matter what the truth is, all we care about is finding Gage, all right?"

"All right," she said, unsure of what was coming.

"Do you suspect anyone of being involved in Gage's disappearance?"

"No."

"Are you involved in your son's disappearance?"

"No!"

"Did someone help you to cause his disappearance?"

"No, absolutely not!"

Lang made notes, glancing at the time on his mini digital recorder.

"Has Cal ever been unfaithful to you?"

"No."

"How would you characterize his attitude toward infidelity?"

"Oh my God, Detective, what do you think?"

"You tell me. Is he indifferent to it?"

"It's wrong."

"Have you ever been unfaithful to Cal?"

Faith clenched her tissue; her breathing quickened and she turned as if counting the cinder blocks in the wall.

"Listen, Faith," Lang said. "All we care about is finding Gage and to do that we need a foundation of honesty and truthfulness."

"No, Detective Lang, my answer is no."

He held her in his gaze for a moment, then made notes.

"Good, that's good." He resumed looking at her with a hint of his warm smile. "You work as a public relations manager downtown at Parker Hayes and Robinson?"

"Yes."

"Do you have any reason to believe someone in your workplace would want to harm Gage?"

"You keep asking me the same questions. The answer is no."

Lang was flipping back through the pages of his notes when there was a knock on the door and Detective Price leaned into the room.

"Leon, something's come up. We have to go."

"Okay." Lang turned to Faith. "Excuse me," he said to her. "We're pretty much done."

In the hall beyond the detectives, Faith saw Cal and a uniformed officer.

"What's going on?" Cal said. "Will somebody tell me?"

"Hold on, Mr. Hudson." Price turned to Faith and said, "Officer Ramirez will take you and Cal downstairs so we can swab your cheeks for DNA and collect your fingerprints—all routine, I assure you. Then she'll drive you home."

"Wait!" Faith saw men in the squad room pulling on jackets, talking on phones, heading out, the heightened activity signifying some sort of development. "What's happened? Is this about Gage?"

"Please." Lang nodded to the uniform. "Carmen, would you?" Then to the Hudsons: "Please go with Officer Ramirez, she'll get you home."

"Please tell us!" Faith's eyes widened. "Did you find Gage?"

Hands went to Faith's shoulders to nudge her toward the elevator but she shook them off.

"Why won't they tell us anything? Cal, did they find Gage? Please! Somebody tell us! *Did you find our son?*"

14

14

A few miles from where the detectives had been questioning Cal and Faith, Officer Neil Peddet and his partner were searching for Gage Hudson.

"What's up, buddy? You got something?"

Champ, his purebred German shepherd, was panting and wagging his tail, signaling to Peddet that he'd picked up the scent again.

"Was he around here? Are we getting close?"

Champ yipped, as if to say, "This way." Snout to the ground, poking here and there along the lawns and sidewalks of the postwar houses on Emerson Avenue, he pulled hard on the sixteen-foot line Peddet had put on him. He brought them to a gravel patch that led to a tired-looking, one-story strip mall.

Champ was excited.

All the signs were good, Peddet thought, while keeping his optimism in check. Champ had had the same reaction yesterday while they were searching the perimeter of the fairgrounds, picking up something on the other side of the fence. It had taken them deeper into the surrounding neighborhoods. But Champ kept losing it and Peddet knew that it could've been a false lead, another dog or a scent similar to Gage's.

It could've been any number of possibilities.

But it could be Gage.

They'd worked late into the night, before knocking off at midnight and returning in the hour before dawn, resuming their work using the scent on Gage's unwashed hoodie.

Deep down Peddet was hopeful.

You've got to expect the unexpected.

He knew that the evening and early-morning hours were usually best for tracking. This morning was also ideal because there was no wind, which could disperse a scent.

Besides, Champ excelled at his job. Two months earlier he'd worked on a three-mile search to find a fifty-year-old female patient who'd wandered from the hospital. Before that, in the spring, Peddet and Champ had helped the state police search Big River State Forest near Wisconsin where a disturbed man had abducted and hidden his three-year-old cousin. Champ had tracked them to a lean-to shelter the man had built by a river.

Pretty good, considering Champ started life as an underdog, abandoned and nearly starved to death as a pup before an animal rescue shelter gave him to the River Ridge police. "I got a feeling about this one," a staff member had said. Champ was assigned to Peddet, whose previous dog had recently died of natural causes. They bonded and

Champ was trained at the Illinois State Police K-9 facility in Pawnee. Now, he was a happy, affectionate, hardworking two-year-old who lived with Peddet and his family.

Champ barked, a strong "this is it" kind of bark, practically dragging Peddet toward the rear of the strip mall, an aging building called Emerson Plaza. It had six units: a hair and nail salon, a florist, a tax office, a hardware shop and a corner store. One business was boarded up.

It was still early and no vehicles were parked in the rear lot, which was unpaved and pocked with potholes. Empty liquor bottles, beer cans, a discarded suitcase and a rusting bicycle with the front wheel and seat missing were strewn about the dilapidated rear wire fence.

Why don't the tenants or the landlord take care of this place?

The air reeked of dead cat and buzzed with flies and wasps, clouded in an ungodly looking corner of the lot where the grass and weeds were choking the fence.

"Tell me you're not interested in that cat," Peddet said.

Champ barked, tugging him instead toward the two large steel Dumpsters near the building. Both were overflowing with trash that had spilled onto the ground where two skinny dogs, spotted with mange, were rooting for food. Champ's growl sent them running, one of them with what appeared to be a pizza slice in its mouth, the other with what must have been a rag.

"Is that what's got you revved up, those strays in the garbage?"

Peddet reached for his phone to call animal protection when Champ rushed toward the Dumpsters. He ignored the first one, going to the second, rising on his hind legs, pressing his front paws to it, wagging his tail as if he wanted to climb into the container.

"Oh, it's this Dumpster?" Peddet put his phone away.

Champ gave a little cry.

"Okay, okay, hang on." Peddet unclipped his heavy gloves from his utility belt and searched the ground, finding a discarded curtain rod to use as a poker. "It's likely someone tossed out some food, or something smells like a treat to you, that's what's got you going."

Champ barked.

"Hang on."

Peddet gripped one of the top doors and hefted himself up the side, standing on the steel sleeve, and looked in. The container was nearly full, crowned with plastic garbage bags. Some had split and were leaking swept-up hair from the plaza's salon. The thing stunk with squadrons of flies strafing heaps of dead flowers and God knows what else.

"Not much here, pal." Peddet poked the rod into more garbage bags, cardboard boxes and magazines, cartons of rotting eggs, boxes of spoiled vegetables, plastic water bottles, cans, pizza boxes and rotting fruit.

Champ barked.

"I don't know, buddy."

Peddet was about to poke a corner when he froze. He'd spotted it as if it were there waiting for him.

Tucked in the far corner and easy to miss was the pristine sole of a small sneaker, almost glowing amid the garbage. Peddet's pulse skipped as he braced himself, pulled off one glove, tucked it under his arm and fished his phone from his pocket.

He'd done his homework, he knew the description, but wanted to confirm and scrolled through the full details concerning Gage Hudson.

Peddet read quickly. Gage Hudson, four feet seven inches tall, between sixty-five and seventy-five pounds, wearing a blue Cubs ball cap, blue Cubs T-shirt with a mustard stain, light-colored shorts, SkySlyder blue sneakers, size five, with neon green laces in a zipper pattern. Soles are rubber with a diamond and sawtooth traction pattern.

Before leaving that morning Peddet had obtained photos of the SkySlyder sneaker and its sole from the database. Now he checked them again on his phone, then looked at what was in the Dumpster.

From what he could see, the shoe was definitely a blue SkySlyder, without question. He could see a hint of blue and green neon lacing, but only a hint. The shoe was encased in trash. The sole had the same pattern and the number five was encircled, indicating the size.

"Good work, Champ, good job!"

Peddet knew not to disturb a crime scene, to leave everything as he'd found it. But as he thumbed his supervisor's number, a chill cut through him and he stared at the small sole.

Is it just the shoe in there or, like the tip of an iceberg, is there a corpse beneath it?

He had to know.

Peddet leaned closer and gently poked the rod into the trash again as it dawned on him.

If Gage was in there, he could be alive.

15

"You've got to relax, ma'am."

Faith struggled to keep her fingers from shaking for the fingerprint analyst. She still didn't know why the detectives had moved out so fast.

Maybe they found Gage. Was he okay? Was he hurt?

They'd already swabbed the inside of her cheek for DNA. The processing unit was having trouble with its scanners, the analyst had explained, so they had to use the ink-and-paper method.

"Okay, ma'am, we'll try again." The analyst, a heavyset woman with a crew cut, tossed the smudged card. "Just relax your arm and look away—don't try to help me."

Faith pursed her lips and nodded, letting the analyst roll her index finger on the ink pad, ensuring her fingerprint pattern was evenly covered with ink. Then she rolled the finger from side to side on the card, making sure it was even and the pressure was sufficient to get a clear impression.

"Good, we've got it." The analyst smiled. "We'll just continue with the other fingers."

Faith shut her eyes, battling the nightmare engulfing her.

She should've been holding Gage's hand. Lang's questions kept playing through her mind. *Are you involved in your son's disappearance? Did someone help you to cause his disappearance?* Now here she was in this room where they fingerprint criminals, while out there, somewhere, there may be a lead on Gage and no one would tell her.

"All done. You're free to go back with the others," the analyst said. "There's a citrus-based cleaner, a pumice stone and water at the sink to the left by the door."

Faith washed her fingers, scrubbing herself nearly raw, but the stains would not come out. Afterward, she joined Cal in the hall where he was waiting with Officer Ramirez. Faith looked at Cal, hoping for an update, but he shook his head.

"No news," he said.

Faith noticed that Cal's fingers looked like hers. The fingerprint ink was faded but obvious, as if she and Cal had been marked guilty of a horrible crime: parents who'd failed to protect their child.

During the drive, with Faith and Cal in the back seat of the car, Officer Carmen Ramirez had switched off the police radio and inserted the earpiece to her portable unit on the front seat beside her. *She's shielding us,* Cal thought. *She doesn't want to risk us overhearing any transmissions.*

Whatever's happened can't be good. If they

found Gage safe they would've told us, Cal thought. *They should've told us. We deserve to know.*

Frantic, he pulled out his phone and used his apps to search his newspaper's newsfeeds and databases for breaking stories. In seconds he'd scoured the Associated Press, Reuters, then Twitter, Facebook and Google News, bracing himself for whatever might surface.

But there were no new developments. He kept searching before finally tapping Officer Ramirez's shoulder.

"Can you tell us what happened? What's going on?"

"I'm sorry, sir. I really don't know."

Cal contended with the sickening sensation that something significant was unfolding around them. He looked at Faith staring trancelike out the window, gripping a tissue in one hand and the rosary Pam Huppkey had given her in the other.

He started making a call to the *Chicago Star-News* to find out if his paper knew what had happened, but at that moment his phone vibrated with a text from Channel 77, a Chicago TV news station.

Mr. Hudson, would you comment on the discovery?

Discovery?

Cal's stomach rose and fell. *God, what did they find?*

Faith turned and saw him reacting to his phone. "What is it?" she asked.

"A TV station—something's going on. I don't know what it is." Then to Officer Ramirez: "Something's happening! Dammit, you've got to know!"

"Sir, I'm sorry. I'm not looped in."

Cal went back to his phone and texted, We're not aware of a discovery. Can you elaborate?

The station didn't respond immediately, forcing Cal to speculate while considering the times he'd been on the other end of the phone calling an anguished family. The *Star-News* policy was clear: it was not a reporter's job to inform a family of a death. That was for the police. If a family was not aware, the reporter was to back off. But not every newsroom had the same policy. Cal knew of reporters who went fishing with a family, bluffing by asking them to comment on "the new development" when in fact there was no new development.

Was Channel 77 fishing with him? Not likely, given the way the detectives had torn out of headquarters. Cal didn't know what to think. Channel 77 hadn't got back to him by the time they'd turned down their street. The car slowed as they neared their house and he and Faith sat up, not believing what they were seeing.

Yellow crime scene tape bordered their yard. Unmarked police vehicles filled their driveway. Crime scene technicians were pulling on coveralls and entering their house carrying equipment. A group of newspeople recorded from the street.

Ramirez touched one hand to her earpiece, then grabbed her portable radio and said a subdued "Ten-four," then she turned to Cal and Faith.

"Because the techs are processing your house, it's been arranged to take you to your neighbors', the Clarks."

Sam and Rory Clark lived four doors down. Upon spotting the Hudsons, news crews that were parked outside their house, some with cameras on their shoulders, trotted over to join those already at the Clarks' house. The instant Cal and Faith stepped from the police car, questions were tossed at them.

"What's your reaction to the discovery?"

"Have police confirmed what they found on Emerson Avenue?"

"Can you give us a statement?"

Bewildered, horror blossomed on Faith's face.

"What's happened, Cal? What're they talking about?"

"Don't say anything," Cal said, pulling her to him as they rushed to the house with Ramirez. "Don't look at them and don't say anything."

"Tell me what's going on!" Faith screamed at Ramirez.

"Please, ma'am, let's get inside," the officer said.

Samantha and Rory Clark greeted them at the door, closing it to the news cameras scrutinizing them from the street. Inside they comforted Cal and Faith with hugs.

"Did they tell you what's been happening?" Sam asked.

"No." Faith shook her head. "Do you know anything?"

"No."

"Something's happening now on Emerson, though," Rory said. "There've been suggestions on the TV news. We're watching now. Come on in, we've got fresh coffee and some food in the kitchen."

Michelle and Jack Thompson rose from the sofa, joining Pam and Dean Huppkey in the kitchen, consoling the Hudsons, offering encouragement.

"We've been praying hard." Pam clasped her hands over Faith's.

"If there's anything we can do," Dean said.

Cal nodded but kept his eye on the TV, catching something.

"Turn it up," he said.

Rory found the remote and raised the volume.

"Stay with us. We'll take you live to the scene after this break..."

"What scene?" Cal looked around, his gaze stopping at the two uniformed officers who'd replaced Berg and Ripkowski at the Clarks' house. "Does anyone know what they're talking about?"

Head shaking from the two officers. "Sorry, sir."

Like everyone, Cal kept his eyes on the TV but he also reached for his phone and made a call. Commercials cut into the newscast, health insurance for senior citizens. *"After your death your family will receive..."*

"Chicago Star-News, hold please," said a young woman's hurried voice.

Cal cursed under his breath. The newsroom assistants were too quick to put people on hold when they were busy. He watched a luxury sedan cut across the desert, raising a curtain of dust. *"The drive to your new horizon."*

"Chicago Star-News, how may I direct your call?"

"Stu Kroll, please."

"Mr. Kroll's in a meeting. May I put you through to his voice—"

"Get him! It's Cal Hudson!"

A second passed, then the young woman shouted, "Stu! It's Cal!"

Three seconds later: "Cal, man, how can I help?"

"What the hell's going on at Emerson?"

A silent beat passed.

"Tell me what you know, Stu."

Cal saw the TV screen cut to a jittery live aerial shot, capturing a neighborhood from above.

"They found something," Stu said. "We don't know what it is, but it looks serious."

The TV images pulled in on activity surrounding a strip mall. Police vehicles dotted the area. It was cordoned off with tape. The focus was at the rear of the mall, on one of the Dumpsters. Technicians in coveralls were carefully working around it but the entire Dumpster was draped with huge yellow tarps.

"Cal?" Stu, who was likely watching the same images in the newsroom, said gently, "Do you want to talk to us?"

Cal didn't answer, transfixed by what he was seeing. He knew the significance of the tarps. They protected evidence from contamination.

And whenever news cameras were near, they also concealed a corpse.

16

Cal and Faith watched the TV news chopper's vibrating aerial view of the forensic technicians in white coveralls working behind the strip mall.

In the short time that had passed since the Hudsons had arrived at the Clarks' home, police had erected a canopy over the tarps and the Dumpster. Every few minutes a technician would emerge from the canopy and transfer bagged evidence to one of the police trucks parked nearby.

"Please, why can't you tell us what they've found?" Faith pleaded with the officers in the house.

"Ma'am, we're not part of the work at that site," Ramirez said. "We don't know."

"But they found something!" Faith was sitting between her friends on the sofa. "What does this mean, Cal?"

Almost whispering, he said, "I don't know."

But Cal knew.

He and Faith were distressed but they were not stupid people. Deep down both knew that those bags could be holding something that could be identified as a piece of evidence, or a weapon.

Anything.

"We should be there, Cal." Faith stood. "We should go now."

Ramirez and the other officers traded quick glances before Ramirez stepped forward. "Excuse me, but it would be best if you stayed here."

"Why?" Cal asked. "We're not under arrest."

"That's correct. You're free to go wherever you wish... But, sir, you have to let the crime scene people do their work. I'm sure Detectives Price and Lang will advise you at the appropriate time."

"Advise us of what?" Faith said. "What do you know, Officer Ramirez?"

A phone rang. Jack Thompson answered his, turning from the group to take his call. The two other officers watched him.

Ramirez shook her head at Faith's questions. "Ma'am, I don't know anything concerning the matter on Emerson Avenue."

"I think you do." Faith's face creased with anger. "I think all three of you know. And I think you should tell us the truth. I want you to tell us if you've found our son—" she pointed at the TV "—in that Dumpster!"

"Ma'am—"

"Why are you even here, to help us or to spy on us?"

"Ma'am." Ramirez's face was sincere. "I know you're upset but I'm not part of the investigation. I don't know what they've found."

Faith looked at Ramirez for a long tense moment before relenting. She believed her. "Somebody knows what happened to my little boy." Her voice broke. "Somebody knows." Michelle and Pam supported Faith as she crumpled back to the sofa.

"Cal?" Jack Thompson extended his phone. "Call for you. Some woman. I told her this wasn't a good time but she insisted, said it was important she talk to you now."

"Who is it?" Officer Ramirez stepped between them, holding her hand out for the phone, checking it for caller ID, noting there was none and logging the call in her notebook.

"She said her name was Beth Gibson," Thompson said. "Said I showed her a house once and she met Cal and Faith at a community meeting. Just wants to offer her support."

Ramirez hesitated. "I don't think it's anything to worry about," Thompson said. "I'm in real estate. I might not remember this Gibson lady but I meet a lot of people and my number is posted everywhere."

Ramirez took the phone and spoke briefly with the caller to verify her identity until she was satisfied. Then she handed the phone to Cal and made more notes.

"Hi, Ms. Gibson?" Cal said. "We appreciate the call but this really is a bad time."

"This isn't Beth Gibson, Cal."

Cal caught his breath and his mind raced before

crashing full bore into memory, recognizing the voice on the line.

"Don't say my name, just say, 'Yes, thank you,' and go to a spot where you can talk privately."

"Yes, thank you." Cal gave the officer a thumbs-up and walked down the hall, leaning against a windowsill where he was able to see if anyone approached.

"Are you alone now, Cal?"

"Yes."

"Anyone recording this?"

"No, not this phone."

"Now, do you know who I am?"

"Yes. How did you know how to reach me?"

"I figured your friend Jack Thompson the Realtor might be with you. I saw him near you on the TV news the other day and figured they hadn't executed warrants or cloned his phone, correct?"

"Yes."

"It's been a long time, Cal."

"Why call me now?"

"I'm broken up over what's happened to your son."

"Are you?"

"Cal, after all we went through, why would you question my true feelings about people who harm children?"

"I can't talk now. Is that why you called, to share your feelings?"

"I'm watching your situation and I know that at some point they're going to lean on you and lean hard, believe me."

Cal swallowed.

"Under no circumstances are you to reveal or even hint at what we did. Do you understand?"

Cal said nothing.

"Do not breathe a word, Cal. It has absolutely no impact on Gage's case. All you need to remember is that we did the right thing and we sure as hell don't want to open a Pandora's box. Not now. It wouldn't be good for anyone if this slipped out. Do you understand?"

Cal said nothing.

"Tell me you understand, Cal."

"I can't believe you would call me with this crap at a time like this."

"I need to make sure you're thinking straight. Before I go, I want to tell you one last thing. Your situation has reignited my rage toward the vile things that slither through this world. So I want you to know that I'll help you behind the scenes in any way I can. You got that?"

Cal saw Officer Ramirez approaching.

"Yes, we appreciate your prayers. I really have to go. Thank you for calling, Ms. Gibson." Cal hung up.

"Everything okay?" Ramirez asked.

Cal responded with a slight nod.

"The detectives just alerted me to bring you and Mrs. Hudson back to headquarters straightaway. They need to talk to you both."

Do you understand?"

17

Twenty minutes later, Cal was back at River Ridge
police headquarters in Interview Room 402.

Again, he was separated from Faith, and again,
Detective Rachel Price was sitting across the table
from him, her face as sober as a funeral usher's.

The tiny red light on her microrecorder blinked
as she spoke.

"We've made a discovery at Emerson Plaza, approximately two miles from the fairgrounds."

Cal's heart began beating faster and his attention went to the legal-size pale blue file folder upon
which Price rested her hands, palms down.

"We're confident it's connected to Gage but we
need you and Faith to confirm it for us."

Price opened the folder and at that moment Cal
heard a pained cry coming from the room across
the hall.

In Interview Room 403, Detective Leon Lang
had withdrawn six crisp color photos from a folder
and set them on the table before Faith.

Her searing cry had pierced the walls and she

clamped her hands to her mouth, her tears rolling over them as she stared in horror.

"Can you identify this as belonging to Gage?"

The first photo showed the immaculate sole of a small SkySlyder sneaker, amid rotting fruit, spoiled vegetables, plastic water bottles, cans and pizza boxes. The second and third were from different angles in the trash, showing that the shoe was size five, with a diamond and sawtooth traction pattern. The next three presented the shoe on a clean surface against a ruler for recording evidence. The shoe was blue.

Faith began nodding, for she'd recognized the green neon laces, recalling how happy Gage had been after she'd helped him thread them in that zipper pattern.

Thanks, Mom, now they look so cool!

Cal ran his hands through his hair as he stared at the same images.

"Yes." His eyes glistened. "I can confirm that this is my son's shoe."

Price nodded, wrote briefly in her notebook, then looked at Cal. "Thank you. I understand how hard this must be."

"Did you—" Cal cleared his throat. "Did you find him, or anything else?"

Price let his question go unanswered for a beat.

"No." She looked at him. "But we have more questions."

Fingers trembling, Faith pulled tissues from the box, pressing them to her face.

"Oh God, is he still alive?"

Lang stared at her straight-on.

"We've found nothing to confirm that he's been hurt. And unless something emerges, we work on the belief that Gage is alive."

Faith nodded, taking deep breaths and pointing at the photos.

"What does this mean…? Where is he? Where're you looking?"

"It could mean anything. There are a few possibilities, but the key fact is we're getting closer. We're searching and canvassing the area."

Lang leaned forward so that he had Faith's full attention, and when he did, he clicked his pen and positioned his notebook.

"Now, I need your help with some new questions."

"Cal," Price started, "would Gage have any reason to be at Emerson Plaza, or have any connection to it?"

"No, it's not even near our place."

"That's right. As I said, it's two miles from the fairgrounds and just shy of three miles from your home."

"So how did his shoe get there?"

"That's what we're trying to determine."

"What about security cameras?"

"The plaza was vandalized last week and the cameras were destroyed."

"Are you thinking that it could be linked to Gage?"

"We're not ruling anything out."

"What about all those carnival workers?"

"We're still interviewing everyone who was working the attraction and those in the trailers behind it. Some people who were at the fair at the time are stepping forward and we continue to follow leads."

"I think that it had to be someone inside who took Gage."

"As I said, we're looking at everything. Now, coming back to the plaza and my questions, do you and Faith have any connection to it?"

"What do you mean?"

"Ever stopped there? Ever interacted with any of the businesses?"

"No. Wait, maybe. No. I can't remember. I'm sorry."

Price let Cal's answer stand for a moment before making notes.

Detective Lang slid a new photograph across the table to Faith.

It was taken from the small parking lot framing the store and office fronts of Emerson Plaza. There was the florist, the hardware shop, the corner store, the hair and nail salon, the tax office and the unit that was boarded up.

"We need to be clear," Lang said. "Have you or Cal ever had any dealings, even the slightest contact, with any of the people or the businesses at this plaza?"

Faith thought the strip mall looked sketchy. The fact Gage's shoe was there and in a Dumpster twisted her insides.

"Faith?" Lang said.

"No," she said.

"No?"

"No, I've never had anything to do with that place."

"I need you to think carefully because a few minutes ago Detective Price and I talked to the people who work there and a couple of them told us a different story."

Faith's face whitened.

"Faith, remember earlier today, I said how we need to work together on a foundation of honesty and truthfulness?"

She said nothing.

"I need you to be truthful with me."

She remained silent.

"Faith, do you recall being there?"

Lang clicked his pen and looked at his notes.

"Because this is what we know," he said. "A woman who works at the hair salon had stepped out to buy a soda at the corner store and said you were sitting alone in your car in the passenger seat. Sound familiar? This was about a month ago."

Faith looked away.

"The woman said you were crying. She was concerned and said she went to you and asked if you were okay. You waved her off, saying you were fine. She said she remembered this because she'd recognized you from the TV coverage of Gage's disappearance."

Lang looked at Faith.

"Is any of this ringing a bell, Faith?"

She stared at her hands on the table before her. "Is there something important you and Cal are not telling us?"

"I'll ask you again, Cal." Price reached for the folder. "Have you ever had any dealings with anyone at the plaza or any of the businesses?"

"I'm not sure."

Price slid a photo of a man in his early seventies who looked like the kind of guy who'd chat weather and sports with you on your front porch.

"Recognize this man?"

Cal shook his head.

"He runs the hardware store, and he said that four weeks ago, thirty days to be exact, you were in his shop."

"I really don't remember."

"Well, he said you spent most of your time talking on your phone, that you were quite serious so your call must've been important. However, I'm curious about what you bought."

"I'm sorry, I guess I was preoccupied. I don't remember."

"Well, after seeing you on TV and with all that's happened, Hap Varnow, the man who runs the hardware store, certainly remembered, even had a credit card receipt with the date."

Price consulted her notes.

"Mr. Varnow confirms you bought a heavy steel lock and some six feet of steel chain." Price looked hard at Cal. "Now what would you need that for? And why was your wife sitting in the car crying while you were making your purchase? And why would we find your missing son's shoe in the Dumpster in the back of that very plaza?"

Cal said nothing.

"Now, Cal, you can see how this looks. How it leads us to think that maybe you're not telling us everything we need to know."

18

Detective Lang leaned forward, turning his head so that his face was in Faith's sight line.

"Why were you crying that day? Why did you stop at that strip mall, the same mall where today we found Gage's shoe? Who was with you that day? Who was driving? Was it Cal?"

Faith began squeezing the tissue in her hands. Blinking through her tears, she lifted her head to the ceiling, as if the answer were there.

"I don't remember."

Lang leaned back. "You don't remember."

As his memory of the past dawned on him, Cal lifted his eyes to Price.

"Gage had a ball game that day," Cal said.

"A ball game? Okay." She took notes.

"He got a ride to the game with the Thompsons because Faith and I had to work and were late, so we caught up at the game at River Ridge South Park."

"Where did you and Faith meet to go to the game?"

"At home, that's when one of the coaches, or

dads, called and asked me to bring a lock and chain to the park. I didn't have one, so when we were driving to the park I saw the hardware store in that plaza and pulled in."

"Do you remember exactly who called you?"

"I'm not sure. Somebody called from the game."

"Why did they ask you to get a lock and chain?"

"Someone had tried to break into the team's equipment storage bin at the park and they wanted to secure it."

Price nodded and took notes.

"All right. But why was Faith crying in the car?"

"Faith." Lang softened his voice. "If something had upset you enough to draw a stranger's attention, I think you would remember."

"Cal and I likely had a stupid argument that day. I don't remember where we were exactly on a specific day a month ago."

"But you were with Cal?"

"Yes, probably."

"Do you remember stopping at the plaza?"

"Maybe we stopped at that plaza. I don't remember."

"You don't remember?"

"We might've been going to Gage's baseball game."

"Was Gage with you at the time?"

"No. Is this a trick, Detective? Because you told me that, according to the stranger, I was alone in the car."

"No trick, just a question. Do you remember

what you and Cal were discussing that resulted in you being upset?"

Faith looked at him, feeling her fear and fury churning. "I don't see what this has to do with the fact our son is missing and his shoe found in the garbage! My God."

Price worked over the gum in her mouth. "Can you tell me why Faith was crying in the car?"

"We argued."

"About?"

"The looming layoffs at my newspaper and how we were going to make ends meet if I lost my job."

"Anything else?"

"No. That was, and is, an ongoing matter for us."

"A source of tension?"

"I guess so."

"Is it straining your marriage?"

Cal didn't answer. He'd already said their marriage was solid.

"Cal, is it straining your marriage?"

"No, the situation was making us anxious, causing us worry, but our marriage is okay."

Price nodded, made a few notes, glanced at the time. "I think that's it for now."

"Faith," Lang said. "I understand how upsetting this is for you. Believe me, we're doing everything we can to find Gage. Finding his shoe is a break for us but we've got a lot of work to do, a lot of ground to cover, and your cooperation is critical."

Faith nodded while opening and closing the

crumpled tissue in her hands, her fingers still bearing the ink from fingerprinting.

Lang checked the time.

"Okay," he said. "I think we're done for now."

After the Hudsons had left with Officer Ramirez to return home, Price and Lang got to work comparing notes and assessing the couple's latest statements.

They'd been working for about five minutes when their supervisor, Lieutenant Tony Sosa, summoned them to his office.

"You might want to sit for this." Sosa's tie was loosened and his sleeves rolled to the elbows. Standing and studying a clipboard, he said, "We're still searching all the businesses at Emerson, as well as the boarded-up storefront."

"Anything?"

"Nothing so far. We're also canvassing the neighborhood."

"What about the midway people?"

"Still going through interviews, still got a lot of work." Sosa dropped the clipboard. "This is a helluva case. We got broken security cameras and we got several potential crime scenes. We got every person the department can spare on this case but our resources are limited, even with Cook County helping us. We're a small department and we don't have the budget for this."

"What're you trying to tell us, Tony?" Lang asked.

"As of this moment, the FBI is taking the lead."

"The FBI?" Price said. "Just when we're digging into the parents, new investigators are going to come in so the feds can bigfoot the case?"

"Rachel, they have the resources, they have the expertise. It's out of our hands."

"This is BS," Lang said.

"You know we've been looping them in since the onset, sharing everything—notes, reports, statements. The FBI's case agent will be Tibor Malko."

"Tibor Malko," Lang said. "I heard that name somewhere."

"I worked with him once when I was in Houston," Sosa said. "He's a legendary asshole and a legendary expert in child abductions and kidnappings. It's all he's done for the last ten years."

Disappointed, Lang and Price shook their heads.

"Your orders are to get any new material to the FBI, ASAP," Sosa said. "There's a case-status meeting first thing in the morning. We're setting up a formal command post, with a joint-agency team here in the second-floor meeting room. So, get to it."

"Wait," Price said. "What else can you tell us about this Malko?"

"He's got one of the sharpest minds in the FBI and he's brutal with suspects—and other investigators."

19

Bursts of sparks swirled into the night from the
fire that blazed in a steel drum among the RVs and
campers where the carnies were lodged.

It was after midnight and the hiss and crackle of
the wood had replaced the earsplitting music, diesel roars and screams of the midway. The smells of
hydraulic fluid, deep fryers and cotton candy gave
way to wood smoke and marijuana in the tranquility
that was punctuated with beer cans being opened
and the quiet conversations of another fair day's end.

Some of the women and men who operated the
rides and games of chance had gathered, as they
always did, in lawn chairs around the fire.

"It's a shame about that little boy gone missing from the Chambers. Do they have any ideas
on what happened?" Gail, a seventy-year-old pro
who ran the water-gun-balloon races, asked before taking a pull from her Marlboro, then a swig
from her Bud.

"Got to be some pervert grabbed him in the dark
is how I see it," said Lloyd, who'd been running

the Machine Gun Star game for twenty-five—or was it twenty-six?—years now.

"There's some who think maybe the parents had somethin' to do with it," said Chuck, who oversaw the Polar Rocket. "It was on the news that police were talkin' to 'em."

"That's all standard stuff," said Ted Burch, who was in charge of the Ferris wheel and had been with Ultra-Fun since 1976, longer than anyone. "What I can't figure out is how you lose a kid in the Chambers? It's just a series of connected boxes flowing traffic to the end, where everyone has to go through the spinner and down the chutes. Ain't that right, Alma and Sid?"

"That's right," said Sid Griner, who helped people at the Chambers' chutes. He had his ball cap pulled low and was slouched in his chair, staring into the flames and quietly sipping his Coors.

"What's more," Ted continued, "you got them cameras in there everywhere and trip alarms on the exit doors, right, Alma?"

Alma McCain was beside Sid, her husband on the road. She also had a man back home in Arkansas, but that was another matter. She ran the board on the Chambers and had been troubled by Gage Hudson's disappearance. She'd wrapped a blanket around herself as if she were freezing, gazed into the fire and dragged on her joint.

"I said—" Ted raised his voice "—ain't that right, Alma?"

"Yes, Ted." She exhaled smoke. "But everyone knows we had trouble with the cameras and the electric network after that lightning strike in Milwaukee. Police have sealed the ride and they're working with our mechanics and state inspectors, practically taking it apart. They've shut it down. Now Vaughn says we gotta find work on the midway. It sucks."

"Sid can help me on the Rocket," Chuck said.

"And I hear Mavis wants someone to take shifts on the basket toss," Gail said. "They're going to put all the Chambers actors in costumes over in Big Small Kiddieland while we're here."

"I tell ya—" Lloyd snorted "—I hear that the cops are going to intensify their searches. What're you hearing, Chuck?"

"I'm hearing the same thing and they're going to keep questioning everybody with the FBI taking over. I was already taken downtown and 'interviewed,' is what they call it. What about the rest of you? Alma, Sid?"

"Not yet. I mean, we talked to River Ridge police a few times already," Sid said. "We're supposed to go downtown before we pull out for Indianapolis."

"Be on your toes," Chuck said. "The FBI takes this to a whole new level. They go deep into your history, so if you got any trouble, they'll know."

Alma blinked at the flames, then shot Sid a subtle sideways glance as Chuck continued.

"And word is that they're going to make some people take lie-detector tests."

"That's serious shit," Gail said.

"You can say that again," said Johnny Lee Snow,

the actor who was the chain-saw-wielding lunatic in the Chambers. "They drilled me already. I was down there twice with Abel, our ticket taker."

"Is that all that fat ass does now, take tickets for the Chambers?" Lloyd shook his head.

"Forget that—how'd it go with the cops, Johnny?" Chuck asked.

"Unpleasant. They grilled me on what I saw, what I did. Asked me if I liked little boys, if I took the kid or knew or helped someone take him. They grilled me on my background, my possession charges, for which, for the record, I was never convicted."

"Speaking of Abel Wixom," Lloyd said, "where is that fat bastard, Johnny? He owes me a hundred bucks."

"Right after the interview downtown he said he had family trouble. He took off to California, said he'd talked to Vaughn about catching up with us on the road."

"Family trouble?" Lloyd scratched his chin. "I didn't know Abel even had a family. Are you sure the cops didn't find something out about him? I bet that old weirdo has a checkered past."

"I don't know," Johnny said. "He never told me nothin'."

"Tell me, Alma." Ted had gone mentally deep into his theories on what could've happened to Gage Hudson and came out of them with more questions. "You're sure you didn't see something on your board, on your cameras, when that family was in the Chambers?"

"Nothing." Alma's hand shook as she dragged on her pot. "Our system was malfunctioning, like I already told you, Ted and the damn police. Jesus."

"Take it easy. It just gnaws at me how strange it all is," Ted said. "What about you, Sid? Didn't the kid come by you on the chutes?"

"Never saw him, but there's a steady stream of people coming through there and they all look alike to me. You know how that is, Ted."

"Yep, sure do."

"You know what I heard?" Lloyd said. "That Vaughn is freaked right out about this. It's making his blood pressure rise."

"We all know that," Gail said. "How he's ordering us to cooperate with the cops, let them search, let them question us. Said he'd get us lawyers if we needed them. He's stressed about insurance, the liability, getting sued."

"He's stressed about losing money," Chuck added. "The Chambers is a big cash stream and now it's shut down. We don't have many more days here before we move on to Indy, but there're rumors from Ultra-Fun corporate that there could be warrants to freeze the entire show indefinitely while they investigate. If that happens, we're going to find ourselves out of work."

"Shit," Johnny said.

"I second that," Chuck said.

"Well, that's a helluva thing." Ted burped, crushed his beer can and tossed it into the fire. "And there ain't a helluva lot I can do about it tonight. It's one damned big mystery to me. I'm turning in."

"Me, too," Chuck said.

One by one, members of the group folded their chairs and retreated into their respective campers and RVs.

Only two people stayed behind.

20

Sid and Alma stayed back to watch the fire wane
until Sid downed the last of his beer. Then they
collected their chairs and Alma's blanket, and
made their way amid the cables, hoses and electrical cords to their home on the road, a white 2011
Ford Excel TS camper van parked behind the big
thrill rides.

Sid had bought the van from a dealer in Arizona. It was in good shape, had low mileage and
was comfortable for two people. It came with a
generator, a shower, a toilet and a sofa that could
be configured into a king-size bed, or two twin
beds. The galley had a microwave, sink and a small
oven; there was a flat-screen TV and DVD player,
big leather seats, an awning and a big storage unit
on the back.

Once they were inside, Alma collapsed into her
seat and cupped her hands to her face.

"Oh cripes, Sid, oh cripes. I'm so scared, so
damned scared!"

He knelt before her and gently took her hands
into his.

"We did nothing they can put on us, okay?"

"But they're looking at everything and that Ted Burch with his damn questions. Who does he think he is, Sherlock Holmes?"

"Don't worry about him."

"What if he tells the cops all his theories?"

"You've got to relax, babe. There is no way anyone can tie anything to us, okay? Trust me."

Sid held her hands firmly as she searched his eyes until she found some degree of assurance. Then he kissed her cheek and smiled.

"I'll be right back."

He reached into his pocket, pulled out his Swiss Army knife, unfolded the largest blade and went to the back of the van. Alma didn't know what he was going to do and she didn't watch. Instead, she gazed out the window at the night, trying not to think as she listened to Sid's movements.

A full minute passed before he returned with a small brick-shaped object wrapped in blue plastic. He slowly opened it, revealing a bundle of tens, twenties and fifties, bound with rubber bands.

"This is a reminder of what it's all for." He grinned, the bills snapping as he fanned them. "This is our dream come true, babe. With this we can go to California, buy into my uncle's operation of kiddie rides at the malls and make more money than we ever can here."

Alma stared at the cash but said nothing.

"This is why we agreed to do this. It's our shot, babe."

Sid stared at Alma for a reaction but only saw apprehension.

"Think back on all the pain you've been through. Take a look at how we live. Don't you deserve a better life?"

Alma blinked several times, absorbing Sid's words.

"Babe," he said, "we just have to hang on and remember that we did nothing they can link to us. We took care of everything. The system wasn't working properly, right?"

Alma said nothing.

"Right, Alma?"

"I don't know."

"Alma, the lightning strike on the system is a documented fact."

"Yes, but what if they put me on the lie detector, Sid?"

"Just keep changing your answers, make sure they're all over the map because you're scared and worried about that boy—it's natural—and everything's going to be all right."

"But, Sid, I'm so scared. What if something bad happens to that little boy?"

He looked hard at her. "Alma, we got nothing to do with that!"

"But, Sid!"

"Just keep your mouth shut and we'll get through this."

"But—"

"Alma! All we did was help somebody. Just gave

them a little help for a little cash, is all. Anything after that's got nothing to do with us!"

"But—"

"Nothing! Do you hear me?"

Tears rolled down her face.

"Alma? Do you understand?"

She nodded, but in her heart she was terrified for Gage Hudson.

The Third Day

The Third Day

21

At 5:45 a.m. the next morning FBI Special Agent Tibor Josef Malko removed his glasses and pinched the bridge of his nose while listening to Detectives Price and Lang update him on the investigation into Gage Hudson's disappearance.

Malko had been up late the previous night and earlier this morning examining every report, every interview, every video clip, every transcript, immersing himself in the case. It was obvious to him that, from the get-go, River Ridge had made mistakes.

There were elements here that didn't fit, a few coincidences and investigative gaps, Malko thought, frowning as he made neat notes. He twisted his neck in his collar, then replaced his glasses.

Some forty investigators from a spectrum of agencies had joined the case-status meeting, filling the room at tables set up classroom-style. FBI agents from the Chicago office, and five agents with the FBI's Child Abduction Rapid Deployment Team, were also participating in the case.

Gage Hudson stared at the group from a white-board at the front of the room displaying enlarged photos of him, his shoe, the interior and exterior of the Chambers of Dread, maps, notes, timelines, a checklist of canvasses and people interviewed. A large screen played partial videos collected from the Chambers, and TV news clips of Cal and Faith Hudson.

For the last thirty minutes Malko had listened to the detectives summarize the work of River Ridge PD on the investigation.

"That's where we're at," Price concluded. "We're now passing the lead to the FBI. Over to you, Agent Malko."

Nodding his thanks, Malko stood, took a moment and stroked the stubble of his bald head.

"The odds of finding Gage Hudson alive are overwhelming. Past cases tell us that immediate response in the early hours is critical. Ideally, the FBI should be involved from the beginning. In seventy-five percent of child abductions, the child is dead within three hours. After seven days that figure is ninety-seven percent. So already the odds are we're too late."

A few investigators blinked, others exhaled, shaking their heads.

"But we're not defeated because it's our sworn duty to battle those odds, to fight for the hope that remains."

Malko waited to ensure he had everyone's attention.

"Many of you are case-experienced investigators and know what I'm going to tell you. Some of you may need reminding of these tenets of investigation, especially child abductions. You will find that families are not perfect, but that does not make them suspects. You'll also find families who will appear perfect, but that doesn't make them incapable of heinous acts.

"We've seen abductions that were fabrications to cover up deeper family problems or an accidental death. We've seen people who appear innocent orchestrate abductions with accomplices. We've seen someone with a connection or vendetta against a family as the perpetrator. And we've seen clear, stranger abductions by disturbed individuals. All possibilities must be pursued and they must be pursued simultaneously.

"Never fall victim to tunnel vision. It's a dangerous thing. Keep an open mind on all theories. It's crucial that all of them, no matter how unlikely, are considered and exhaustively pursued. As investigators, we know that everyone lies, especially when they are under stress or concealing other truths. Nothing should be assumed and no one should 'seem credible.' You must *prove* that they are, or are not, credible. For example—" Malko turned to Price "—who is Beth Gibson?"

Price's back stiffened.

"A woman from the community who called to wish the Hudsons well."

"And how do we know that?"

Price searched her notes for an answer.

"You won't find confirmation there," Malko

said. "There's no report in the file documenting that anyone listened to Gibson's conversation with Cal Hudson. Nor is there follow-up on why Gibson needed to call through Jack Thompson's phone."

"Hold on." Price found a page in her notes. "Our Officer Ramirez spoke briefly with the caller and determined there was nothing unusual. Beth Gibson had called to convey her support to Cal."

"Did she?" Malko said. "Did you know that Gibson's number belongs to an untraceable prepaid disposable phone? What legitimate well-wisher uses one of those? Yet I see no follow-up. We have no idea about Gibson or her conversation with Cal Hudson. This is an investigative gap."

Price's face reddened; she pursed her lips and made notes.

"And the chain and lock Cal Hudson bought... did we confirm where it is right now, and how it's being used? Or do we assume it's where Cal Hudson told us?"

"We haven't got that far yet," Price said.

"Detective Lang, have you lit up the neighborhood for known sex offenders and predators?"

"Not yet."

"Have you scrutinized Ultra-Fun Amusement Corp's permits?"

"Not yet."

"I've taken steps to arrange a thorough physical and mechanical examination of the attraction with local and state inspectors, and a specialist with the FBI."

Price nodded as Malko continued.

"Have you run the employee list of the Ultra-Fun Amusement Corp through NCIC and sex offender registries?"

"Not yet," Lang said. "It's on our list. Our people are still interviewing and just getting into background."

"Did you check on Ultra-Fun's complaint history while touring? Has anything similar or relevant happened with this company in the past in other cities?"

"Not yet," Lang said. "Look, we don't have a lot of people."

"You do now. We'll work together to quickly assess and determine what we have here so we can concentrate our investigation in the correct direction. Can we conclude that Gage Hudson was kidnapped? There's been no ransom demand. Or did he wander off? Was he lured away by an adult? Or possibly other children near his age? Was he taken by a stranger, or is there parental involvement? For example, I looked at one random tip called in from a person who claimed to have been with her daughter behind the Hudsons in the line waiting to enter the attraction. This person says she's a psychologist, and reports that by their body language and facial expressions and the tone of the few words she'd overheard, she believes the Hudsons could've been arguing about something before entering. This could be vital or it could be nothing. But it's just one more thing we need to follow.

Investigators continued taking notes as M began running down what still had to be don

"We need to delve deeper into the Hudson family history, including Gage's background. We need to talk to relatives, friends and neighbors. And, as noted in the case file, Cal Hudson is a crime reporter with the *Chicago Star-News*. We'll examine his stories for anyone who may hold a grudge against him and we'll look at Faith and her professional background.

"We're going to question all fair and midway employees. We're going to examine the partial video we have of the Hudson family in the Chambers and track down fairgoers who were near them at the time of Gage's disappearance. We can make a public appeal through the media.

"We're going to canvass and recanvass targeted areas, the strip mall where the shoe was found and the area surrounding the fairgrounds. I see reports that no one was home at some of the houses being canvassed. This is unacceptable. We keep going back to every address."

"Give me a break—if no one's home, no one's ," one detective half snorted. "What if people simply out of town? Jeez."

ko's eyes narrowed at the man who'd inter- "Then you will find out where they went, y went and why they went. That's called vork, sir."

honished detective cursed under his red his head to make a note. Staring said, "Let me be clear. I'm not here s and coddle egos. I'm here to save ock is ticking against us." Malko looked at the others, then resumed. "We need to search other Dumpsters for more potential evidence and contact trash companies about collection schedules and landfill sites."

Pages snapped as investigators continued taking notes.

"I understand obtaining video surveillance recordings has been problematic," Malko said. "We need to identify all businesses near the strip mall and fairgrounds and key areas in between that use security cameras. We'll review them for leads. Note that some businesses record over previous recordings each day or every forty-eight hours, while others don't.

"The FBI's Evidence Response Team will help collect potential evidence at all relevant locations. This includes the Chambers of Dread attraction, the fairgrounds, the Hudsons' residence, cars, offices of employment, cell phones, computers, Gage Hudson's school and any locations or items that may arise.

"We'll set up a webpage for the case to solicit tips with a 1-800 number. I see that Faith Hudson's employer, the advertising firm Parker Hayes and Robinson, is offering a twenty-five-thousand-dollar reward for information on the case. That should help. And depending on the circumstances, we'll see about another press conference with Cal and Faith. If this is a stranger abduction, this will be the Hudsons' chance to talk to the abductor directly because in nearly all cases abductors watch coverage."

Malko removed his glasses and began cleaning them with a small cloth.

"We've got people here from Chicago PD, the state, Cook, other counties and departments. We're authorized to draw on other agencies. The FBI will pursue and expedite all necessary warrants. We'll start tasking assignments and get moving immediately. Agents Peller and Wills—" Malko nodded to them "—will assign, coordinate and log. Thank you."

After several minutes the room emptied, leaving Malko alone studying the case file. As he worked, he overheard the others grumbling about him in the hallway.

"What's with that guy?"

"Does he think we're backwater idiots?"

"We shouldn't have to take his shit. What makes him such a prick?"

As Malko repeated the last question in his mind, his jaw muscles began throbbing and he wanted to shout the answer to them.

What makes me such a prick? How about witnessing autopsies of abducted children?

Instead, he picked up his phone and swiped the screen to a photo of a pretty little girl with a big smile, the light in her eyes as bright as the sun.

Eight-year-old Sally-Anne Marie Sanderson.

She hadn't shown up at school one day. When she vanished, she became one of Malko's first missing-child cases and he'd believed every word her mother and father had told him, believed that she'd been abducted by a stranger. Eventually he'd uncovered the truth, that Sally-Anne Marie was being abused by her parents, that she'd been hurt so badly they feared she wouldn't recover. So they hid her. The whole time Malko had led the search for the abductor, Sally-Anne Marie had been locked in a box, half-buried in the soil of a crawl space under her home.

By the time they found her, she was dead.

The medical examiner concluded that Sally-Anne Marie had been alive for days and would've survived if investigators had learned the truth earlier.

Malko had failed her.

That was nearly ten years ago. Sally-Anne Marie Sanderson's death had changed him, and he'd vowed at her grave site to attack every investigation with all he had and to never again believe what suspects said when it came to the life of a child.

Malko then swiped to photos of Faith and Cal Hudson.

Their missing son's shoe is found at the strip mall where dad bought a chain and lock while Mom bawled her eyes out for reasons neither can seem to recall.

He doubted the credibility of what Faith and Cal had told investigators.

Every instinct told him that the Hudsons were concealing the truth, and no matter what it took, he would rip it out of them.

Ever since Sally-Anne Marie Sanderson, he always did.

22

Half an hour later, Malko was standing on the Clarks' doorstep.

"Federal Bureau of Investigation." He held up his ID for Rory Clark, who, looking beyond him, saw Detectives Price, Lang and two other grim-faced men. "We need to speak with Mr. and Mrs. Hudson. Alone, without anyone else present in the house." Malko closed his ID.

Clark showed the investigators in, conveyed their request to everyone inside, whereupon the group prepared to leave, deciding to meet at Michelle and Jack Thompson's home in Breezy Hill several blocks away.

As they gave Cal and Faith parting hugs and encouragement, some shot awkward, uneasy glances at Malko, who forced a half smile. Once the house was cleared, Malko turned to Faith and Cal and indicated they talk in the living room.

"You know Detectives Price and Lang," Malko said, introducing himself and the other agents. "Let's sit down."

"Did you find Gage, or…or other things?" Faith remained standing, cupping her face with her hands.

"No, nothing like that," Malko said. "First, I want to advise you that the FBI is now leading the investigation. We've put considerably more resources on the case and will keep adding people as needed. Please, sit down."

She swallowed and sat beside Cal.

Malko leaned forward, resting his elbows on his knees, pressing his fingertips together, and looked at the Hudsons.

"I'll come to the point. We need you to help us clarify matters pertaining to certain aspects of the case."

"Clarify what matters?" Cal asked.

"Some details as to timing, as to consistency of statements you've given and threads we need to tie up."

Malko let a few seconds pass, then got to it.

"We'd like you both to submit to a polygraph examination as soon as possible." Malko studied the Hudsons' reactions.

"A lie detector?" Faith said. "You want us to take a lie-detector test?"

Cal said nothing as Faith's anger rose.

"I don't believe this!" She fought her tears. "We've been interrogated, asked horrible questions—"

Sensing an eruption, Cal reached for her arm. "Faith."

"We've been fingerprinted." Her voice grew

louder. "Our home's been seized. We've been forced out of it so forensic people can go through our things!"

"Faith," Cal said again.

"You're listening in on our phones, and now you want us to prove that we're telling you the truth about our son's disappearance? We're his parents. We're not criminals! How in God's name does this help Gage?"

Unfazed, Malko looked at her and Cal as if studying specimens.

"I understand how upsetting this is for you," Malko said.

"How could you?" Faith spat. "Is your child missing?"

Malko blinked slowly, his mind racing with memories of small bodies on morgue tables, thinking how this world had failed them; how a piece of him had died with every case until there was little left for sympathy, especially for those he suspected of lying during an investigation.

"A polygraph," Malko said, "is a tool we use to ensure we're concentrating on the correct areas, so that our investigation is thorough. I assure you, we're examining every possibility in our effort to find Gage."

"What about the people at the plaza where you found his shoe?" Cal asked. "And the people living around there?"

"We're pursuing that fully, as well."

"Are you questioning the midway people, the carnies?" Cal asked.

"We are and we're executing warrants at the fairgrounds," Malko said. "Cal, as you're likely aware from your work, agreeing to submit to a polygraph examination is strictly voluntary. You can refuse. That's your right. As you know, the results cannot be used in court."

"But any statements we make during the process can. In fact, you might even Mirandize us. Isn't that correct?"

Malko gave a polite nod. "It is. But the bottom line here is that your cooperation would be helpful to the investigation. It could lead to Gage's safe return. Wouldn't you do anything to help us find your son?"

"Of course we would," Faith said.

"Will you agree, then?" Malko asked. "We can do it later this afternoon."

Faith and Cal exchanged looks for a moment, then Cal responded.

"We'll talk to a lawyer first, then get back to you."

"Certainly. As you wish. We'll stand by," Malko said, feeling the promise a fisherman feels at the first little tug of his line.

23

The men standing outside the Chambers of Dread sipping morning coffee from take-out cups were with Ultra-Fun, the county and the Illinois Department of Labor.

Their conversation halted when a woman in her late forties, wearing coveralls with a duffel bag hoisted over her shoulder, ducked under the crime scene tape and joined them.

"And you are?" Rex Dunne, Ultra-Fun's lead engineer, appraised her.

"Quinn Hardy, FBI structural engineer," she said, allowing an awkward moment to pass before the men recovered with introductions and handshakes.

As a woman in a male-dominated field, Hardy was used to this sort of reaction. But as an MIT grad, with some twenty years' worth of investigating aviation disasters and terrorist attacks around the world, she had more experience than her colleagues combined.

"Thanks for sending me the floor plans and

other documents last night to study," she said to Dunne.

"Sorry, with the name Quinn I thought you were a guy," Dunne said.

"Happens all the time. My dad, God bless him, wanted a son." Hardy smiled while surveying the Chambers, empty and silent before them, as were the fairgrounds, which hadn't opened yet. "Let's get started with a walk-through. First with the lighting the same as it was when Gage Hudson entered."

Hardy caught the valid permit decal on the lower exterior wall near the entrance. She knew that in order to get the permit, state law required amusement rides and attractions operating in Illinois be inspected before operation and once a year after that.

Bud Porter, the white-haired man walking near her, had been inspecting Ultra-Fun's rides for the state for the last seven years and carried a binder thick with documents and plans.

In keeping with permit requirements, Ultra-Fun had also provided proof to the state that they'd conducted criminal history and sex offender registry checks for all employees. That information had been passed to the other investigators but Hardy knew that often it was not accurate.

That was for Malko and his people to sort out.

The Chambers of Dread was sixteen years old and had been reconfigured and renamed every few years. The attraction was erected in a maze-style. Its construction consisted of several interconnected tractor trailers, some of them double-wide, making it one of the largest traveling scare houses in the country.

It was conceived around a system that moved guests along a twisting walkway from "scare set" to "scare set," arranged such that exits weren't clear due to the theatrical distractions and low illumination.

After her first slow walk through the Chambers in the darkness, Hardy requested a second walk with all lighting activated. Passing through she took note of all exits, fire extinguishers, the security exit alarms and the close-circuit camera system.

On her third, fourth, fifth and subsequent tours through the Chambers, Hardy took pains to examine the walls, touching, pressing, knocking and tapping them, checking for anomalies, inconsistencies, things hidden or concealed.

In the set of the insane butcher, Hardy detected an unusual creak-squeak and give-and-take underfoot. Dropping to her hands and knees she noticed a small latch, recessed, almost hidden in the flooring. Pulling a screwdriver from her pocket, she hooked the latch and heaved open a small wooden door, just under two feet by two feet.

Concealed beneath it was a compartment the same size and about six inches deep. It resembled a cupboard or drawer space under the floor. A square metal bracket was screwed to the center of the space.

"What's this, Bud?" Hardy asked. "It's too small to hide much and it doesn't lead anywhere."

"I don't know." His binder crackled as he flipped through older records, floor plans and manuals. "Here." He tapped a laminated page. "I think that goes back a few years to when they called the attraction Terror Town. Looks like this was a spring-loaded pop-up scare, no longer in use."

"Hmm." Hardy sat on the floor examining how well it was constructed and concealed.

"What're you thinking?" Brian Lodge, with the county, asked.

Hardy tapped her screwdriver to the hidden compartment.

"Over the years this attraction has evolved with the complexity of an illusionist's trunk or cabinet. And given that we intend to go over every inch of its walls, floors, ceiling, underbelly and roof, I'm thinking this is going to take a couple of days."

"A couple of days?" Dunne repeated.

"Yup. And I've got a hunch we're going to find a few surprises."

24

Michelle and Jack Thompson's home was a two-story stone colonial, with a yard sheltered by two-hundred-year-old oak trees, in keeping with what people might expect real estate professionals to own.

Michelle, Samantha and Pam went to the kitchen while their husbands went to the living room, turned on the TV and checked their phones for any news.

The air was taut with apprehension in the wake of the FBI taking Cal and Faith away.

"Any word?" Michelle asked, setting down a tray of fresh coffee while Samantha and Pam brought sugar, milk and cookies.

"Nothing," Dean Huppkey said. "Why do you suppose the FBI showed up like that?"

"Maybe they got a new lead in the case?" Rory Clark said.

"If they did, it can't be good," Jack said. "Could be they found something."

"Besides the shoe, what do you mean?" Sam asked.

"What I mean," Jack said, "is that if they already found Gage's shoe in that Dumpster, think what else they could find. I hope I'm wrong, but it just doesn't look good."

"We can't give up hope," Michelle said. "I just can't imagine how much they're suffering right now. If anything like that ever happened to Marshall I'd be shattered. I'd go to pieces."

Pam Huppkey twisted her bracelet while listening to her friends.

"Right from the start—" Rory pointed his finger at the air "—I said it has to be someone inside who took Gage, a customer, a worker. He couldn't just disappear like that. What else could it be?"

"Maybe he ran away?" Dean said. "Colton told us that Gage told him he thought his parents were arguing more than usual."

"Probably worried discussions over Cal's situation at the paper," Jack said. "You know, with the rumored layoffs and all it's understandable. It's not like their marriage is in trouble or anything like that."

As the group debated scenarios and guessed at the FBI's presence, Pam withdrew into her thoughts, tormented by what she'd seen—or thought she'd seen—at the press conference at the fairgrounds.

It was that man, standing at the back watching Cal and Faith talk to the reporters. She'd recognized him under that ball cap. She'd seen him before. Or had she? She was unsure if it was really him.

Pam had taken art classes, even produced a number of portraits. She knew she had a good eye for faces.

In her heart she knew it was him. Yes, she was sure. And when she glimpsed Faith, she saw by her demeanor, the flash of recognition, she knew the man, too.

Knew him well.

What should Pam do?

She began twisting the tiny cross on the chain around her neck, her thoughts pulling her back several months to when her friend Marcia, who lived nearly ten miles away in Oak Brook, had called her to go shopping and have lunch at the big new mall there.

They were in the food court when Pam spotted Faith at a table nearby. What a lovely coincidence. Pam had thought maybe Faith could join her and Marcia.

She was about to go to her table and surprise her when Pam's phone rang and she sat right back down. Dean was calling, something about his car and running late. But as Pam had talked with Dean she'd noticed that Faith was not alone. She was sitting with a man, a good-looking man wearing a sport coat.

Maybe he's a client of hers, Pam thought. *But wasn't it odd that they would be meeting way out in Oak Brook, so far from her office downtown?* Pam noticed that they seemed to be having an intense conversation. She abandoned her plan to approach Faith, grateful the latticework of the small partition surrounding her section had made it nearly impossible for Faith to see her.

Pam had no idea who the man was, or what she'd witnessed.

Whatever was going on was none of her business. Besides, she'd always felt a little intimidated by Faith. Her friend was so smart and pretty and she had that power public relations job in a downtown skyscraper. Pam was happy to be her friend but Faith subjected her to subtle moments of almost cruel condescension.

Like that time Pam was invited to help Faith, Michelle and Samantha host the school fundraiser at the River Ridge Golf and Country Club. Faith's eyes trailed over Pam's top and skirt with a glint of disapproval before she smiled and said, "Oh, don't you look nice."

Then at the book club when Faith had suggested they read something by Joyce, Pam had said, "Oh, I've never read her, is she a new author?" Faith touched her shoulder and smiled a bit coldly. "James Joyce, sweetie, the Irish writer, and *he* has been dead for some time."

Yes, Faith always made her feel a little self-conscious, for being a stay-at-home mom who never finished college. That's why Pam thought that maybe she'd misread the incident at the mall and had told no one about it.

That's what she thought at the time.

But now, Pam was convinced she'd seen the same man at the press conference on the fairgrounds, shortly after Gage had vanished.

Was his presence related to the boy's disappearance?

What should she do?

Paralyzed with fear and confusion Pam couldn't decide.

The detectives had not yet talked to her, or Dean and the others, but Jack said they should all expect to be questioned at any moment.

Faith was Pam's friend and she wasn't sure what she'd seen or what was going on. But Gage was missing, and if they found his shoe, did that mean… Oh, what should she do? It was none of her business. Or was it?

"Pam? What do you think?" Sam asked.

"I'm sorry?"

"Are you okay?" Michelle asked.

"Yes, why?"

"Pam, you're crying. This is hard on everyone. All we can do is keep hoping and praying, right?"

Nodding and smiling weakly, Pam twisted the cross around her neck.

25

Pounding on the side of their van woke Alma Mc-Cain and Sid Griner.

"What the—" Sid wrapped a sheet around his naked body, went to the door to find Chuck dragging hard on a cigarette.

The fair and midway hadn't opened yet and they'd slept late.

"Get your asses in gear." Chuck pointed his cigarette hand to the distance. "FBI's here and they want everyone out so they can search our places."

The yip of dogs pulled Sid's attention to the end of the RVs and campers where he saw agents in FBI raid jackets, along with River Ridge and Cook County people, huddled with Ultra-Fun and fairgrounds bosses.

"This is way more serious than before," Chuck said. "I'm just giving you a heads-up, partner."

Sid shook the bed as he rushed to get dressed. "Get up, babe. FBI's getting ready to search everything. You gotta help me take care of things right now!"

Alma groaned a sleepy protest.

Sid looked out the window in time to see Vaughn King, Herb Dulka, the fairgrounds chief, and some well-dressed people pass by. Word spread fast that all Ultra-Fun and fairgrounds staff were to meet immediately in front of the Polar Rocket.

"Get up!" Sid kicked the bed. "This could be trouble."

Then someone shouted at their van, thumping it as they passed by. "Get out now, leave everything untouched!"

Alma said nothing, quickly pulling on a hoodie, panties, pants, socks and shoes, then working with Sid to take care of what they needed to.

Seconds ticked by, then more thudding shook their van as a dog barked and its leash jingled. It was close, very close.

"Alma! Sid! Meeting in front of the Rocket, now. Let's go!"

"We're getting dressed!" Sid shouted as he and Alma worked.

"Leave the van and touch nothing. Let's go!" the voice shouted.

A moment later, Sid and Alma emerged from the van, taking stock of the activity. Sid was wearing a baggy T-shirt under an oversize flannel plaid lumberjack shirt. Ensuring that no one saw them, they took a detour around several rides, stopping unseen for a moment in a narrow alley of trucks, portable toilets and generators before going to the front of the Polar Rocket, arriving just as the meeting began.

Vaughn King and Herb Dulka had introduced two men in expensive-looking suit jackets from some law firm who spouted off some legal mumbo-jumbo before King took over.

"So, bottom line, people," King said, "the FBI is executing search warrants as part of the investigation for the missing boy. They'll search everything."

Soft mutterings and grumbling rippled through the group.

"This is fairgrounds property," Herb Dulka added. "And as you heard, all of you are either employed by Ultra-Fun Amusement Corp, the fairgrounds, the town or the county. You have a legal obligation to cooperate or face obstruction charges."

"Be assured," King said, "we will cooperate and we will open on time today. So, go to the canteen, have some breakfast, then wait by your home and the agents will tell you when it is released for you to reenter."

Little more than an hour after breakfast, after much speculation with other carnies in the canteen, Sid and Alma waited outside their Ford camper while an FBI team searched it.

Sid dragged shakily on a cigarette, listening to the dog panting and yipping as agents sifted through their belongings. He exchanged a few nervous looks with Alma.

Inside, FBI Agent John Fitzwell noticed his K-9

partner, Samson, was interested in the closet in the rear. Fitzwell opened the door.

Samson barked and panted encouragement.

The agent's eyes focused on the panels inside the closet and how the seams of certain wall panels seemed ever-so-slightly ajar. He ran a gloved hand along them, then took his knife from his utility belt, using the blade to pry at them, noticing just how loose they were.

He removed one of the panels.

The dog continued to bark.

"Whoa!" Fitzwell said. "What do we have here?"

26

Chicago, Illinois

"This is as serious as it gets."

Gina Preston-Gold set her pen upon her yellow legal pad after the Hudsons had detailed their situation.

"The FBI's polygraph request puts you in a difficult spot."

Cal knew Gina from trials he'd covered for the *Star-News*. She was a Yale grad who'd started with the Cook County state's attorney at the Criminal Prosecutions Bureau in the Felony Division. Then she worked for the US Attorney's Office before going into private practice and becoming one of Chicago's top criminal defense attorneys.

When Cal called her for help after the FBI requested polygraphs, she'd agreed to drop everything for a free emergency session at her office, high up in the John Hancock Center. If they needed her beyond today, it would get costly. She had been following Gage's case; most people had. It was high profile across greater Chicago. "I'm praying he'll be returned safely to you," she'd told them, her eyes glistening with sincerity.

Now, she bit her bottom lip.

"Before I go into options and strategies, let me state a few things. I understand your reluctance to submit to a polygraph. But the common view would be that if you're innocent with nothing to hide, you'd jump at the chance to take a test."

"We understand that," Cal said.

"And it looks bad if you try to avoid it, even though it's your right to do so."

"Yes, we get that," Faith said. "But the idea of the test makes me so nervous."

"Sure," Gina said. "A lot of people fear that something will go wrong and make their innocence somehow come across as guilt."

"Exactly, that's a factor." Faith reached out and took Cal's hand in hers. "We're a close-knit family, a deeply loving family, with nothing to hide."

Gina paused to process Faith's somewhat odd assertion, then resumed. "Your reaction and concerns are normal. Look, at this stage it's not my job to judge your reasons or decision. My job for now is to outline a few things so we can proceed."

"Okay," Cal said.

"First off, you could hire a private examiner and we'd administer the polygraph right here. It's pricey but sometimes police accept the results."

"What's the advantage?" Faith asked.

"It's less stressful for you, it reduces chances

of unfair or leading questions and it can be kept confidential."

Faith turned to Cal. "That sounds good, what do you think?"

"Let's try that. How do we start?"

"Simple." Gina reached for the business card Cal had provided. "I'll reach out to this Agent Malko and confirm if he'll accept private polygraphs. Why don't you wait in our boardroom—this shouldn't be a long call."

Alone in the boardroom, Cal and Faith stood at the floor-to-ceiling windows taking in the breathtaking view of Chicago's skyline and Lake Michigan.

"It's surreal." Faith touched a tissue to her eyes. "Don't you think?"

"What do you mean?"

"Standing here, not knowing where Gage is, police pushing us to take a lie-detector test." She turned to him. "I'm so scared, Cal. What will they ask us? What if things go wrong?"

Cal searched her eyes, unsure of what they held. "We just have to tell the truth to keep them focused on searching for Gage and whoever took him."

Tears rolled down her face.

"Why didn't you let me hold his hand?"

"Faith. Please."

"Why was it so important that I not hold his hand?"

"What the hell are you implying?"

"If I was holding his hand, he'd be with us right now."

"Are you trying to blame me for this?"

She turned away.

Cal shook his head. "Jesus, I don't believe you."

A knock sounded at the door and a moment later Cal and Faith were back in Gina's office.

"The FBI said no to a private polygraph," she said. "They won't accept the results. They want you back in River Ridge to undergo testing with their polygraph guy as soon as possible."

"So what do we do now?" Faith asked.

"I'll lay it out for you," Gina said. "While the FBI may say the polygraph is routine, a tool to clear you, you must assume that for whatever reason, to them, you could remain suspects. Okay? The stakes are very high."

She looked hard at Faith, then Cal, before continuing.

"Now, submitting to the test is voluntary. It's your right to refuse. But there are pros and cons," Gina said. "Agreeing to the FBI polygraph clearly shows that you're working with them, that you're willing to do whatever is needed to find Gage— you're cooperating with the investigation."

Cal and Faith nodded.

"However, as you know, the results are not admissible in court, but any statements you make while under testing can be used against you. Anything that arises from the test could drive their investigation in a new direction. Do you understand?"

"Yes," Cal said.

"The results, no matter if you pass or fail, will not guarantee that they will cease considering you a suspect, unless new evidence surfaces."

"Yes, we get that," Cal said.

"If you exercise your right to refuse a polygraph, there's a good chance your refusal could be leaked to the press and the public would know. This will stigmatize you in the court of public opinion. It creates the impression you have something to hide, while any innocent concerned parent would take a polygraph in a heartbeat to find their child."

After Gina allowed the Hudsons a moment to absorb what she'd presented, Faith spoke up. "I think we should do it."

Gina looked at her, then at Cal.

"Do you agree?" Gina asked him.

He nodded. "Let's do it and get it over with."

"All right, then. I'll call Agent Malko."

27

River Ridge, Illinois

"All set?"

FBI Agent Larson Ward double-checked the contacts of the sensors connecting his polygraph system to Cal Hudson.

"Remember, I expect you to be nervous, that's okay. Breathe normally and consider this a conversation where you only answer yes or no."

Cal nodded and took in the small meeting room at River Ridge police headquarters from his comfortable chair facing a painting of a beach lined with palm trees Ward had put up to help him relax.

Earlier, Ward, a soft-spoken, bookish man with frameless glasses, had taken Cal privately through the phases of the exam: the pretest interview, when he'd asked about Cal's physical and mental state, then the discussion of Gage's disappearance. Afterward, he'd explained how the polygraph worked.

Ward said that the sensors he'd connected to Cal's heart and fingertips would measure his respiratory activity, galvanic skin reflex, blood, pulse rate, breathing and perspiration; that his responses to his questions would be recorded on a moving chart on Ward's large laptop.

The FBI polygraphist would later analyze the results and give the investigators one of three possible answers: Cal Hudson was truthful, Cal Hudson was untruthful or the results for Cal Hudson were inconclusive.

Cal was familiar with lie detectors. He'd taken a polygraph exam previously for a crime feature he'd written about the process.

Now, set to begin, he thought of Faith, isolated in another room waiting her turn as he struggled to harness his emotions and remain calm. Still, he couldn't keep from thinking of all aspects of the process, how even confirmed liars are willing to take the test, how the only people who try to beat it are those who are untruthful. Cal knew the research showed that the technology was accurate about ninety percent of the time; that people tested tell the truth about sixty percent of the time and lie thirty percent of the time; and that test results were usually inconclusive ten percent of the time.

Yes, Cal knew more about the process than most people. But none of it mattered now.

No, not when I'm sitting here wired to a lie detector and the FBI's read me my Miranda rights, and two detectives, two FBI agents and my lawyer are sitting behind me. Days ago we were a family at the fair. Now Gage is missing. The clock's ticking on his life. And they suspect me.

"Here we go, Cal," Ward said. "Are you relaxed?"

Cal took in a long, slow breath and nodded.

"Do you intend to answer my questions truthfully?"

"Yes."

"Is your name Calvin Hudson?"

"Yes."

"Are married to Faith Hudson?"

"Yes."

"Do you have a son, Gage?"

"Yes."

"Is Gage missing?"

"Yes."

"Do you know where Gage is now?"

Cal swallowed hard and hesitated.

Ward's eyes were fixed on his laptop's screen and the graphs.

"Cal, do you know where Gage is now?"

"No."

"Do you know what happened to Gage?"

"No."

"Do you know how Gage came to be missing?"

"No."

"Did you conspire with anyone to cause Gage to disappear?"

"No."

"Do you suspect anyone directly of taking Gage?"

"I think it was a midway worker, or maybe—"

"Cal, please answer yes or no."

Cal nodded.

"Do you suspect a person or persons directly of taking Gage?"

"Yes."

"Have you ever abused Gage?"

"No."

"Are you aware of any abuse of Gage in your home?"

"No."

"Has Gage ever expressed or indicated he'd been abused by anyone?"

"No."

"Are you employed at the *Chicago Star-News* newspaper?"

"Yes."

"Are you employed as a reporter?"

"Yes."

"Do you report on crime for the newspaper?"

"Yes."

"Have you reported on child abductions?"

"Yes."

"Do you possess above-average knowledge of police investigative procedures and tactics?"

"Yes."

"Are you involved in Gage's disappearance?"

Cal swallowed. "No."

"Do you know how your son's shoe came to be in a Dumpster at Emerson Plaza?"

"No."

"Have you had any dealings with the people or businesses at Emerson Plaza?"

"Yes."

"Did you mislead police earlier when you denied having dealings with businesses at Emerson Plaza?"

"No, I didn't remember, that's all."

"Yes or no, Cal."

"No."

"Did you purchase a chain and lock at Emerson Plaza several weeks before your son's disappearance?"

"Yes."

"Other than for locking up your son's team's baseball equipment at the ball park, was there any other intended use for the chain and lock?"

"No."

"Did you know that investigation has determined that the chain and lock are not in use at the ball park?"

"No."

"Do you know the location of the chain and lock now?"

"No."

"Was Faith with you when you purchased the chain and lock?"

"Yes."

"Was she in the store?"

"No."

"Was she in the car?"

"Yes."

"Was she aware of the intended purpose of the chain and lock?"

"Yes."

"Do you know why she was crying in the car at the time you purchased the chain and lock?"

Cal hesitated. "Yes."

"Was it because you were arguing?"

"Yes."

"Were you arguing about the chain and lock?"

"No."

"Were you arguing about Gage?"

"No."

"Were you arguing about your relationship?"

"Yes."

"Are you happy in your marriage?"

Cal took a moment. "It's complicated."

"Yes or no. Are you happy in your marriage?"

He sighed. "Yes."

"Have you ever lied to Faith?"

Cal blinked quickly and looked to the ceiling. "Yes."

"Have you ever been unfaithful to Faith?"

"No."

"Have you had sexual relations with another person who is not your wife while married to your wife?"

"No."

"Do you trust Faith?"

"Yes."

"Do you think Faith has ever abused Gage?"

"No."

"Do you think your wife has the potential to harm your son?"

"No."

"Has your wife ever been unfaithful to you?"

"No."

"Do you think your wife is honest?"

"Yes."

"Do you think your wife is deceitful?"

Cal swallowed hard. "No."

"Do you think your wife is involved in Gage's disappearance?"

"No."

"Do you know of anyone who may have reason or cause to take Gage?"

"No."

"Is the name Beth Gibson familiar to you?"

"Yes."

"Did she call you recently?"

"Yes."

"Had she ever called you before?"

"No."

"Did you meet her at a River Ridge community meeting?"

"Maybe, I don't remember, I—"

"Yes or no."

"Yes."

"Do you know why she used an untraceable phone and called Jack Thompson to reach you?"

"No."

"Did you know our investigation shows that no one named Beth Gibson is listed on tax records, voter registration or Illinois state driving records is residing in River Ridge, or any of the surrounding communities?"

"No."

"Did Beth Gibson call to wish you well in the search for Gage?"

"Yes."

"Did she ask to speak with Faith?"

"No."

"Did Beth Gibson raise any other subjects in your conversation?"

Cal hesitated. "No."

"Is Beth Gibson involved in Gage's disappearance?"

"No."

"Do you have reason to *suspect* Beth Gibson is involved in Gage's disappearance?"

"No."

"Have you provided investigators all the information they should have in order to pursue Gage's whereabouts?"

Cal inhaled and licked his lips. "Yes."

"Are you withholding any information from investigators about your life or activities, past or present, that may have a bearing on Gage's disappearance?"

"No."

"Are you being truthful, Cal?"

Cal froze.

Are you telling me the truth, son?

Time stood still and Cal was a kid again, a teenager going out on night calls with his dad, who operated his own towing business. It was his dad's dream that he take over and Cal told him it was his dream, too. But over time, Cal realized he didn't want that life, recalling his dad's big callused hands, the dirt under his fingernails, his perpetual back problems and chasing after people to pay him. When they went to car wrecks, Cal would be fascinated with the reporters who sometimes arrived on scene. One night, on a long drive home from an accident, Cal's father started talking about Cal's future and the business. That's when Cal told his father that he wanted to be a journalist.

"So all this time you lied to me, letting me think you were going to take over."

"Dad, I'm sorry."

"Are you sure you don't want the business? Is that how you feel? Are you telling me the truth, son?"

"Yes, Dad."

His old man gazed out the window for a long time without speaking. The next day he told Cal he understood, but Cal knew he'd broken his heart. He could see the hurt in his eyes. Six months after Cal started at the *Chicago Star-News*, his father died of a heart attack and Cal could never get past feeling that he'd died a disappointed man because his son never carried on the business he'd built. And as his coffin was lowered into the ground Cal thought, *Can any of us be truly happy in this world?*

Cal looked hard at the beach and palm trees in the painting and was pulled back to when he, Faith and Gage went to Florida. He could hear the ocean rolling up on the sand; he could see Gage silhouetted against the sun and diamond waves as he collected shells in a moment of perfect family bliss that was gone, gone, gone.

Now, as Ward hammered at him with question after question, tears rolled down his face because he realized all of his failures had brought him to this aching point and that he may never see his son again.

"Cal? Are you being truthful?"

"Yes."

Ward leaned into the screen and scrutinized the readings on the graphs.

28

"Are you responsible for Gage's disappearance?"

"No." Faith's voice quavered.

"Do you know who is responsible for Gage's disappearance?"

"No."

"Are you concealing the identity of the person who is responsible for Gage's disappearance?"

"No."

Faith blinked repeatedly, a sign of stress, as FBI Agent Larson Ward's relentless questioning continued well into her polygraph exam. In her troubled, strained state of mind, for an instant scenes from her life shot through her thoughts.

Faith was fifteen when her father, an insurance broker, died of a heart attack. He was a workaholic. Watching his casket being lowered into the ground, she almost hated him for abandoning her and her mother, who was a high school math teacher. Faith's mother, a quiet, private woman, never grieved in public, even with relatives near. But at night, Faith would hear her crying in her room.

During the years that followed, Faith sought comfort in books. She was a voracious reader. She was smart, always scoring at the top of her class, and even though her dad's insurance policy covered her college tuition, she worked at several jobs. She yearned to get away, to be out on her own.

She met Cal at college. Her boyfriend at the time had just broken her heart and Cal was there when she needed someone. They fell in love, got good jobs, got married and built a good life. When she had Gage she was the happiest woman on earth. That changed two years later when she lost her second baby; coming home and sitting in the room that was to be the nursery, staring at the rolls of new wallpaper she had planned to put up, the change table, the dresser and the empty crib—it had felled her.

Faith and Cal tried for over a year to have another baby but she never got pregnant and Cal was not interested in seeing fertility doctors or other options. It was as if he'd given up hope for a second child.

Faith had always blamed herself for losing the baby. Cal coped by disappearing into work at the paper, closing himself off to her. It hurt her knowing he was working long hours on intense stories, often with pretty reporters who looked up to him.

A part of Faith felt abandoned and utterly alone. And then a few years later, Cal had retreated even further, with no explanation.

Prior to her polygraph test, as Agent Ward took Faith through the process as he'd done with Cal, her stomach twisted. Her world was falling apart, she was losing another child and they were submitting her to a lie detector as if she were responsible.

Ward had seated her in the same chair before the same beachfront painting. FBI agents, River Ridge detectives and her lawyer were seated behind her. Now, the readings on Ward's laptop showed that Faith's heart rate was elevated.

"Faith?"

"Sorry?"

"Was it your idea to go to the fair?"

Fighting her tears, she remembered Gage's pleas.

"Can we go to the fair, Mom, please? They've got this haunted house called the Chambers of Dread and it's so scary! Colton and Marshall said it's got this guy, the insane butcher, and he's chopping a guy on his table. There're bloody arms and legs hanging everywhere. And there's this witch burning up. And they got this guy who chases you with a chain saw!"

"It sounds too scary, honey."

"Mom, I'm not a baby! Colton and Marshall dared me to go inside. Can we go, please, Mom? Please. I'm begging you, please!"

"Faith, was it your idea to go to the fair?"

"It was Gage's idea and I suggested to Cal that we go."

"Please, just yes or no."

"Sorry."

"Was it your idea to go to the fair?"

"No."

"When you arrived at the fair did you have any altercations or disagreements with others?"

"No."

"Did Cal have any altercations or disagreements with others?"

"No."

"Did Gage have any altercations or disagreements with others?"

"No."

"When you arrived at the fair, did you notice anyone acting suspiciously toward Gage?"

"No."

"Once inside the Chambers of Dread, did you notice anyone acting in a suspicious manner toward your family or Gage?"

"No."

"Were you concerned for his well-being inside the attraction?"

Faith shut her eyes, remembering how she feared that he'd have nightmares, how Cal had admonished her. *"Don't baby him."* Remembering... reaching for Gage's hand, Gage shaking it away telling her, *"I'm okay, Mom! I'm not a baby!"*

"Faith, were you concerned for his well-being?"

"Of course, yes. It was scary. Sorry. Yes."

"Did you keep within close proximity to him?"

"Yes."

"Were you present when Gage disappeared?"

"Yes."

The deafening, menacing music, the flashing lights, the floor spinning; the confusion, chaos and terror; seeing Gage with Cal, or was it someone else? It was Cal, it had to be Cal.

"Were you close to him when he disappeared?"

"Yes."

"Did you see who Gage was with before he disappeared?"

"Yes."

"Was it a stranger?"

"No."

"Was it a friend?"

"No."

"Was it his father, Cal?"

"Yes."

"Do you think Gage's disappearance is the result of Cal's action?"

The readings on Larson's screen fluctuated as seconds ticked by and tears rolled down her cheeks.

"Faith, do you think Gage's disappearance is the result of Cal's action?"

"I don't know."

"Yes or no, please."

"I don't know."

"Do you suspect Cal of being responsible for Gage's disappearance?"

"I'm not sure—no." She shook her head. "No."

Ward made quick keystrokes, then penned notes and resumed.

"Not counting your mortgage, credit cards, car loans, do you have other debts?"

"No."

"Do you gamble?"

"No."

"Have you taken drugs or medication today?"

"No."

"Do you abuse any prescription drugs?"

"No."

"Do you consume illegal drugs?"

"No."

"Do you owe money to any private individual?"

"No."

"Is your family living beyond its means?"

"No."

Ward made more notes.

"Have you ever abused Gage?"

"No!"

"Has Cal ever abused Gage?"

"No."

"Are you aware of Gage being abused by someone outside of your home?"

"No."

"Has Gage ever indicated to you that someone acted inappropriately toward him?"

"No."

"When you and Cal stopped at Emerson Plaza a month ago, did you know Cal was going to purchase a lock and steel chain?"

"I—I don't remember."

"Just yes or no."

"No."

"Did you know why Cal purchased these items?"

"Now I do but at the time, no. So, no."

"Do you know the location of the chain and lock now?"

"I'm not sure—I think—no. No."

"Were you crying at the time the chain and lock were purchased?"

"Yes."

"Were you crying because of something related to Gage?"

"No."

"Do you know why Gage's shoe was found in the Dumpster behind Emerson Plaza?"

Faith was crying now. "No."

"Do you know who Beth Gibson is?"

"No."

"Do you ever recall meeting Beth Gibson?"

"No."

"Have you ever spoken to Beth Gibson?"

"No."

"Did you know Beth Gibson called your husband after Gage's disappearance?"

"Maybe, no, I don't remember. No."

"Would you agree your marriage is strong?"

Faith hesitated. "Yes."

"Would you agree your marriage is troubled?"

"Uh—no. No."

"Are you happy in your marriage?"

Faith didn't answer.

"Are you happy in your marriage, Faith?"

"Yes."

"Are you being truthful with your answers?"

"Yes."

"Do you trust Cal?"

Faith took a moment to answer. "Yes."

"Has Cal ever lied to you?"

"I don't know."

"Yes or no?"

"I don't know."

"Have you ever caught Cal being knowingly deceptive or lying to you?"

Faith was silent as seconds passed.

"Faith?"

She remained silent.

"Okay, moving on. Faith, have you ever deceived Cal?"

The readings on Ward's screen lurched wildly.

"Faith, have you ever deceived Cal?"

She stared at the painting, at the beach and palm trees, until they blurred.

"Faith," Ward said, "please answer: Have you ever deceived Cal?"

She swallowed hard. "Yes." Then she choked back a sob. "I mean, no. No!"

"Faith, try to relax. Have you ever deceived your husband, Cal?"

"No." Her face creased with pain; the readings of the polygraph continued swaying as if scratching in desperation.

"I can't..." Faith said.

"Take a slow breath," Ward said.

"I'm sorry. I'm guilty."

"Faith," Gina Preston-Gold sat upright. "Don't say anything more."

"I'm guilty!"

"Faith, what are you guilty of?" Ward asked.

"Don't answer!" Her lawyer stood. "Let's stop this now."

"I'm guilty of being a horrible mother because I didn't watch my son!"

Faith buried her face in her hands.

Malko, Price and Lang exchanged glances.

29

Still reeling from their polygraph exams, the Hudsons arrived home that afternoon to an unsettling scene.

The evidence team had finished processing their house, but Cal and Faith were jolted by the aftermath.

Blackish, graphite fingerprint powder was smudged and streaked on the walls, the windows, the TV, the counters, the tables, the chairs, the doors, doorframes, doorknobs, light switches and mirrors. Every cupboard, closet, sofa and drawer had been rummaged as if a maniac had rampaged through each room.

At every turn the intrusion screamed *suspicion*.

The forensic team had left a list of cleaning companies the Hudsons could hire. Nice touch.

Since investigators had already cloned their phones and processed their residence, Cal and Faith had requested the police presence be removed from their home. They wanted to absorb the latest developments privately. The FBI compromised by putting a marked River Ridge patrol car in front of the house, while another kept vigil in the rear lane. A handful of newspeople were huddled on the street. But thankfully no police officers were inside, giving Cal and Faith a measure of solace in the fact that they were alone.

Cal sat in front of the TV and muted the sound. Then he called Stu Kroll at the *Star-News*.

"Are you hearing anything?"

"We'd heard you and Faith were being questioned again, this time by the FBI. Do you want to talk to us about that? Go on the record?"

"No, and I don't want to be quoted. This is just a conversation, okay?"

Kroll considered the request, then said, "All right."

"Are you hearing anything about the search for Gage, Stu?"

"Not much, but we're digging hard. How're you and Faith holding up?"

"I feel useless. I should be out on the street hunting for him, investigating this like a story, but I'm numb. I can barely think straight. It's a nightmare."

"You got to hang in there."

"Stu, I was thinking, could you get an Ultra-Fun employee list and run the names through sex offender registries, and also look at those residing in River Ridge—make calls, do some door-knocking? You never know what you could find."

"Already got Lori and Jacobs on it."

"That's good."

"As long as we have the bodies in this newsroom

we're doing all we can. You gotta stay strong, Cal. They're going to find him."

"Thanks, Stu. I gotta go."

After hanging up, Cal knew that he should be making more calls for updates on searches, canvasses, police tips, any breaks, anything he and Faith needed to do. But he was depleted from the polygraph, from lack of sleep, from everything.

He stared blankly at commercials on the smudged TV screen.

Faith was in the kitchen making tea. As the kettle boiled, the very air in the house seemed to pulse with questions.

Their home was hollow without Gage, as if its soul had been ripped away. Faith couldn't hold back her tears as the kettle whistled and they grappled with the evisceration of their lives. Cal's thoughts shifted to the polygraph and he cast an apprehensive glance at his wife.

"What'd they ask you?" Cal said.

"Horrible questions."

"Tell me."

She cupped her face in her hands and took a breath.

"Who is Beth Gibson, Cal?"

"They asked you about her?"

"Yes. Who the hell is she?"

"We don't even know her. She's from the neighborhood, one of Jack's real estate clients who called to wish us well."

Faith stared at him for a long uncertain moment.

"What else did they ask you?" he said.

"If you or I ever abused Gage. It's vile that they'd even ask that."

"They have to ask, you know that."

"They asked me if I was happy in our marriage."

"What did you tell them?"

"I said yes."

"I see."

A taut moment passed between them.

"Did they ask you that question, too, Cal?"

"Yes."

"And?"

"I said yes, I was happy."

"You did?"

"I did."

"They also asked me if I thought you'd ever lied to me."

"What did you say?"

"I told them the truth."

"Which is?"

Cal stared hard at her and repeated himself. "Which is?"

"I said that I didn't know if you've ever lied to me."

Slightly wounded, he nodded.

"Didn't they ask you the same thing about me?"

"Yes," he said. "I told them you'd never lied or deceived me."

Faith blinked several times, thinking. "They asked me if I thought you were involved in Gage's disappearance."

"What did you say?"

"I said no."

"They asked me the same question and I gave them the same answer."

She nodded and slowly lowered her head to gaze into her tea.

"What else did they ask you, Faith?"

She didn't respond.

"Did they ask you about the plaza and the lock and chain?"

She looked at him without speaking.

"What else did you tell them?"

She raked her fingers through her hair, while shaking her head.

"I'm tired, Cal. No more questions. I'm going to our room."

Alone in the living room Cal wrestled with whether he could trust Faith's answers while at the same time he struggled to understand the FBI's fixation on the chain and lock, racking his brains, sifting through his memory of that day.

He was not clear on all the events, only that now—oh God, now—they'd found Gage's shoe.

And the FBI thinks there's a connection to me, the lock, the chain and Gage's shoe in the Dumpster. That's just not right. So where's that lock and chain?

Cal reached for his phone and called Jack's number. He didn't care if police were listening.

"Hey, Cal, how're you doing?" Jack said. "Faith texted Michelle, said you were polygraphed. How'd it go?"

"It was rough but we survived it."

"That's good. Cal, I'm glad you called—things

have been happening. More people are helping with searches, going door-to-door with flyers and blasting things out online. Everybody's working to get Gage home."

"I've got to ask you something."

"Sure, anything."

Cal explained what he remembered from a month earlier concerning Gage's ball game and the request to get a lock and chain.

"I remember that someone busted into the team's equipment locker," Jack said, "and Dean was real pissed about it, but I never called you."

"I thought it was you."

"No. Maybe it was Dean."

"Okay, I'll call him."

"Cal, wait—"

But Cal had already hung up and was punching in the number for Dean Huppkey, relieved to reach him. After giving Dean a summary, Cal asked him about the lock and chain.

"Yeah, that's right," Dean said. "Some idiot busted into the equipment locker by the bleachers at the ballpark. We knew you were on your way, so I asked you to bring a lock and length of chain."

"So what happened to it?"

"We didn't need it. Remember? We found the groundskeeper and he took care of securing the locker. I told you to keep the stuff you bought, or take it back. Why're you asking me this now?"

"It's just—I got it at the plaza where they found..." Cal could barely get the words out. "Where they found Gage's shoe."

"You're right, Cal, that is a strange coincidence. Is there some sort of connection, maybe to someone at the plaza?"

"I don't know. Nothing's making sense." A tone sounded in his ear. "I gotta go, Dean, I'm getting another call."

Cal answered his incoming call.

"Hey, it's Jack again."

"What's up?"

"I needed to tell you, that woman Beth Gibson called me again, looking for you."

Cal froze with disbelief.

"Cal? You there?"

He adjusted his grip on the phone and lowered his voice. "When did she call, Jack?"

"This morning. Asked if you were with me so she could speak to you."

"What'd she want?"

"Wanted to know how you and Faith were doing. She said she was concerned, especially after I told her that the FBI came to the house to speak with you and Faith privately. What's with this Gibson woman with her calls and questions? You sure there's nothing going on with her? Maybe the FBI should be looking at her?"

Cal didn't answer. He couldn't understand why she was taking such a huge risk. She had to stop calling. It was too dangerous.

"Cal? I said, should the FBI look into her?"

He tried to sound casual. "Nah, I don't think so. In my line of work you meet a lot of eccentrics—she seemed harmless."

* * *

After the call, Cal hurried to the garage, grateful they'd parked their cars there, out of sight of the press. The forensic teams had been through their vehicles. The interiors were laced with fingerprint powder. Cal knew they would've inventoried the chain and lock if they'd found them.

It didn't matter. He had to find them.

He searched their Ford Escape, under the seats, in the storage areas. Then he searched Faith's car—the front, the back, the trunk. He even lifted the trunk carpet to search the reservoir for the spare and the jack.

It was futile—no trace of the lock and chain.

He searched the garage but it was in vain, as well.

What did he do with them?

He searched the plastic recycle tub holding discarded newspapers that sat next to the workbench. Leafing through the old papers he discovered something that stopped him cold.

A small ad in an old community flyer had been circled in pen.

What was this? He hadn't circled it—it had to have been Faith. How did the forensic people miss this?

Cal dragged his hands over his face. His mind was swirling.

He tore the page from the flyer and returned into the house.

30

Faith stood at the door to Gage's bedroom drowning in guilt.

Guilt for all the sins she'd committed in her life that had brought her to this nightmare. She opened the door, stepped in and was staggered by the violation. Fingerprint powder smeared the walls, windows, doors, everything.

Gage's things were practically ransacked.

Yes, she'd expected it, but nothing had prepared her for the cold, dark reality hitting her like a blow to the stomach, for this room was sacred to her. This is the room where she had read to him when he was little. *Green Eggs and Ham* and *Paddle-to-the-Sea* were his favorites. This is the room where she'd taken care of him when he was sick, where he still liked to snuggle with her and where he'd once said that he wanted to marry her because his mom was the best mom in the whole wide world. Gage was a sweet boy, a trusting boy who believed that everyone was good and believed everything she and Cal told him.

This was the room where Gage dreamed.

Faith could almost see him now lying on his side, his hair mussed, sleeping sound and safe below his poster of the Chicago Cubs. Looking around she saw the things he treasured, the things he touched, thinking how they were now somehow desecrated with fingerprint powder.

There was the Lego stadium and skyscraper he'd built, his remote control helicopter, his ball glove, his book of world records. He'd page through it for hours, asking her, "Hey, Mom, do you know how tall the world's tallest man is?"

Faith nearly smiled at the memories.

How he loved playing games on her iPad, and how he'd play forever if she let him. How he loved watching the *Simpsons* or *iCarly* and eating pizza or nachos.

Faith picked up one of his T-shirts, a Chicago Bears shirt he got at a game he'd gone to with Cal.

Cal.

Why had she agreed to the polygraph?

It had left her devastated and confused. The piercing insinuations and accusations...about abuse, drugs, money, the lock and chain, about Cal and their marriage.

Their private lives were none of the investigators' business.

Yet their questions had spawned others in her mind.

Who was Beth Gibson? Why were the police concentrating on Gibson and Cal?

The questions whirled around Faith as she stared at Gage's shirt.

She held it to her face and was consumed by guilt.

I should've been holding your hand.

She breathed in her son's scent.

Will I see you again?

She knew the odds, knew the statistics; she knew the probabilities in cases of missing children.

All of them told her that her son was dead.

I won't believe you're dead. Everyone's preparing me, telling me that I should brace for the worst. But I won't accept it, I can't. I know I'm going to see you again. I carried you inside me, next to my heart—every fiber of my being tells me I'm going to see you.

But her pain came in waves and her guilt was overwhelming.

Hugging Gage's T-shirt, Faith raised her head to the window.

She shifted her thoughts to the street, zooming in on the vehicle parked near the end of the block.

She knew that car. She recognized the man sitting behind the wheel.

Her breath caught in her throat.

First he shows up at the press conference, and now he's watching my house.

Silently, she cursed, willing him to leave. *I don't need this—not now.* She prayed he'd leave before Cal caught a glimpse of him—and before the police did.

31

Cal found Faith in Gage's bedroom holding one of his T-shirts.

She seemed startled when he entered the room.

"Where did you go?" she asked, her voice quavering.

"The garage, to search for that lock and chain."

Faith stared at him. "They asked me about it."

"And?"

"I told them I don't remember."

"You don't remember?"

"I don't remember, Cal."

"You were there, Faith. In the car when I bought it."

"Why are they so focused on them?"

"Because I bought them at the plaza where they found Gage's shoe. It looks bad. They likely think it could be related and I'm somehow behind his disappearance."

"Are you?"

Cal froze, taken aback by her question. "What?"

"Why don't you tell me why you bought that lock and chain?"

His eyes narrowed. "I can't believe you'd ask me this."

"Why not? It's what the police have been asking both of us for days. They must know something we don't."

Dismayed, Cal shook his head.

"I bought that stuff," he said slowly, "because someone had tried to break into Gage's team's equipment storage bin at the park. Dean called me on our way to the game and asked me to. You know this—you were there with me."

"I was upset. I don't remember everything."

"Well, that's the truth."

"You still didn't answer my question. Are you involved?"

"No, Faith. Are *you* involved?"

"Just stop it! Oh God, what's happening to us?" Faith stared at him, then her eyes went around the room before she thrust her face into Gage's T-shirt, keeping it there until she'd regained some composure.

"Did you find the stupid lock and chain?"

"No." He watched her reaction. "Do you know where it is?"

"I have no idea."

They stood there, together but alone, trapped in the horror of Gage's disappearance. His room was like a flag of hope, or the portent of a shrine with the specter of his death looming, underscoring how helpless they were, desperation slowly coiling around them.

"Cal." Faith's voice was soft as she kneaded

Gage's tearstained shirt. "Are you telling me everything?"

"What do you mean?"

Faith ran her fingers over the material, thinking.

"I'm going to ask you a question and I want the truth," she said.

"What is it?"

"Are you seeing someone else?"

"What?" Incredulous, he stared at her for a tense moment. "Why are you asking me this now?"

"At the *Star-News* summer picnic I saw you with Chelsey Blake."

"So?"

"She's pretty and I saw what she was doing."

"What was she doing?"

"I saw her slide her arm around you, and she ran her hand up and down your back. It was so familiar, so intimate. And you're never home."

"Don't do this."

"You're always working."

"Faith."

"What's going on? Are you going to leave me for her? I want the truth."

Cal shut his eyes, took in a deep breath while shaking his head.

"For God's sake. Chelsey's affectionate with everyone. We'd been working together on a story when her boyfriend broke up with her at the same time her mother died. She needed a shoulder but I'm telling you nothing happened, or *is happening* with her. She left the paper months ago. She's not even in the country anymore."

"Okay, then who is Beth Gibson? And why did you take her call in private the other day?"

Cal could feel his face flush and he covered it with both hands. "I told you—she's just another caller from the neighborhood who wanted to wish us well and give her support. We've had dozens of people call us, most of them strangers. I don't know her."

"That's it?"

"Yes, that's it. I don't get this. What's going on with you?"

She didn't answer as she studied Gage's T-shirt.

"Faith, what the hell are you getting at?"

"I'm scared. I don't know what to believe."

"You don't know what to believe?" He shook his head. "What about you? What're you keeping from me? Huh? I'm working at holding this family together. You know I'm looking for a new job, something to provide for us and give us all a new start. What're *you* keeping from *me*?"

"I don't know what you're talking about."

"Do you think I'm stupid, Faith?"

"What're you talking about?"

Cal reached into his back pocket for the page he'd torn from the flyer, tapping the ad circled with blue ink, and thrust it at her.

"This!" he said. "I found it in the recycle bin."

Faith's face reddened as she stared at the ad for a divorce lawyer.

"This goes beyond 'thinking about a separation,' which is what you told me in the car that day on our way to Gage's ball game. You sure went a step further with this. So what else have you done? Have you been planning something, Faith?"

"Cal, no, you don't understand."

A ringing sounded in Cal's shirt pocket, halting their argument. He looked at the number—the *Chicago Star-News*.

"Is this Cal?" the caller asked.

"Yes."

"I'm so, so sorry to bother you. It's Joannie, at the paper."

The young newsroom assistant was breathless.

"It's okay, Joannie. What is it?"

"I got this woman on the line who's asking for you. She refused to leave a message. She just said that it was critical that she speak to you, that it was a matter of life and death about Gage!"

"Transfer her to my phone now."

Faith asked, "What's going on?"

Cal held up a hand for her to wait while the line clicked.

"Hello, is this Cal Hudson?" The caller was a woman, sounded like she was in her midthirties or forties.

"Yes."

"Cal Hudson whose son is missing?"

"Yes. Who's calling?"

Silence.

The caller ID display on his phone showed the newsroom switchboard number because the call had been transferred from there to his phone. He found the recording button on his phone and pushed it.

"Who's calling?" he repeated.

Nothing.

"We have your son, Mr. Hudson."

"Oh God!" Cal squeezed his temple with his free hand. "Where is he? Let me speak to him—please!"

Cal's pleas were answered with silence.

"Is he safe? Where is he? Please! I'm begging you! Let me talk to him!"

"We can't allow that." The voice was calm, monotone.

"Cal?" Faith, realizing what was unfolding, rushed to him, placing her hand on his arm. "What is it? Did they find him?"

At that instant her phone rang. She looked at it and nearly dropped it as she fumbled to answer.

"Faith, this is Agent Malko. Are you near Cal?"

"Yes, standing next to him."

"We're getting a location for the caller. Cal's got to ask for proof of life. He must keep the caller talking. We're moving on the address."

She whispered Malko's instructions to Cal, who nodded.

"I want to speak to my son!" he told the caller. "How do I know this isn't a hoax?"

No response.

"Tell me!" he shouted. "How do I know?"

"Because I have his other shoe."

His heart pounded, tears stinging his eyes.

Faith tapped Cal's shoulder, repeating what Malko was telling her in a whisper so the caller couldn't hear. "The press has reported the shoe, but only we know that they found the left one. Ask the caller if they have the right or left shoe."

"Which shoe?" Cal said. "Do you have the right or left shoe?"

Silence crackled over the phone.

"I have the right shoe."

Cal ran his hand over his face, turning to Faith. His expression said it all. Faith's face crumpled as she reported back to Malko. Cal pleaded with the caller. "Please, what do you want? Is it money? We'll pay! Please, let me speak to Gage, please!"

"You won't be speaking to him ever again because today is his last day on earth."

The line went dead.

32

Chicago, Illinois

Within seconds the FBI had traced the location of the call to the southwest side of Chicago.

It originated from an address at the fringes of Archer Heights, a community with a large Polish population near Midway airport.

The FBI alerted the Chicago police.

The information came up on an emergency dispatcher's screen. She immediately circulated the call to the Eighth District, advising no lights and no sirens to the responding Chicago police units in the Archer Heights area. Within four minutes they'd locked on to the location, a low-income strip of the city's Bungalow Belt.

While marked units held back, a lone unmarked car rolled by the address, which was near a vacant lot where several old men were leaning against an eviscerated F-150 pickup truck, passing around a bottle wrapped in a paper bag.

The residence was a long-neglected bungalow-

style house with cracks webbing the foundation.
The brick walls were crumbling, the front porch
sagged, paint blistered on the doors and windows.
The yard was a riot of wild grass, entwining weeds,
shrubs, trash and patches of a dying hedge. It had
a small ramshackle garage with swing-out doors
shut tight.

They were secured by a lock and chain.

A Chicago PD SWAT team was rolling on the
address with an ETA of twenty-two minutes. More
CPD units converged on the area establishing an
outer perimeter to seal all traffic moving in and
out. People whose homes were in the line of fire
were quickly and quietly evacuated.

Out of sight, a block west, the SWAT team
had set up a command post in the parking lot of
a church. The commander was informed that the
house had no complaint history and the primary
resident was Kazik Pulaski, aged seventy-two. His
name was run through several police databases.
Pulaski, a retired Chicago bus driver, now disabled
and using a wheelchair, did not come up in anyone's system.

The commander had directed his team to estab-
lish an inner strike zone around the house by first
sending in scouts to determine lines of fire and
safety points. Once they were good to go, squad
members wearing helmets, armor, headset radios,
and equipped with rifles and handguns, began taking positions. Sharpshooters moved to key points
while the utility man, the breacher and other team
members lined up on the house. The squad pressed

against the brick walls as they got in place around the front and rear doors. Sharpshooters found positions in neighboring yards.

At the same time, a small, heavily armed team, equipped with bolt cutters, had lined up on the garage.

While team members settled into their positions awaiting instructions, the commander used the hood of an unmarked Ford Police Interceptor to study maps while outlining the hot zone, consulting with the FBI and determining an entry and rescue strategy.

Despite Pulaski's clean background, it was decided that surprise was critical given that a hostage could be used as a shield in a protracted standoff. Circumstances warranted a no-knock forced rapid entry. The commander requested eyeball reports from the team members in position.

The house's windows filled the sharpshooters' scopes.

"We've got a white female in her forties, lying on a bed in a bedroom in the southwest corner. No weapons seen," one sharpshooter reported.

"Elderly male in a wheelchair watching TV in the living room," a second team member reported.

"No sign of occupants or movement in the garage," a third reported.

The commander made final checks with the team leaders.

All was green.

The commander said, "Go!"

Flash-bang grenades smashed through windows. Amid the deafening noise, smoke and chaos, SWAT members charged through the front and back doors to the living room, shouting orders to the man. "Police! Hands over your head now!"

Members rushing into the bedroom yelled at the woman. "Get on the floor, on your stomach, now! Hands behind you! Now!"

"What the hell's this?" the old man in the wheelchair protested as his hands were cuffed in front of him.

Outside, SWAT members cut the chain and began pulling open the doors to the garage.

In the house, all bedrooms were checked. The bathroom was checked, closets were checked, the basement and attic were checked. Special equipment was used to scan the walls, floors and ceiling for body mass. The house was inspected three times for any trace of Gage Hudson.

Nothing was found.

The woman's bedroom reeked of body odor.

After handcuffing her, SWAT members helped her to a sitting position on her bed. She had long, unkempt hair. She was wearing stained sweatpants and a black T-shirt with a death's-head image. She revealed that she was missing most of her teeth when she smiled at the SWAT members and said, "Hello."

After the smoke cleared, the chaos gave way to calm. Several agents in FBI windbreakers entered the house and began searching it while others went to the living room and bedroom to question the two occupants.

In the living room, the old man nodded, acknowledging he was Kazik Pulaski.

"It's my daughter" was all he told them of the woman.

That was it. He sat in silence, tears rolling down his face, as agents continued questioning him in vain.

In the bedroom, an agent searched the woman's bag on her dresser, finding ID indicating she was Ula Pulaski, aged forty-one.

"You're Ula Pulaski?"

"I am."

"Where's Gage Hudson?"

"I want a lawyer. I know my rights."

"Where's Gage Hudson?"

"I'm not sayin' nothin'. I want a lawyer. I know my rights."

"What is your relationship to Kazik Pulaski?"

"He's my father. I want a lawyer. I know my rights."

The agents surveyed Ula's room, while another called in a request for Ula Pulaski's name to be run through NCIC and several other criminal databases. There was a laptop computer on a desk, next to a landline phone. The desk was cluttered with news clippings concerning Gage Hudson's disappearance.

One agent marveled at a wall papered with posters from horror movies. One of the posters featured a year-old promotion for The Chambers of Dread!

America's Biggest Traveling World of Horrors! Lining another wall, floor-to-ceiling, was a bookcase filled with horror books, classics to contemporaries, Edgar Allan Poe to Stephen King.

Another agent found a scrapbook bulging with clippings of Chicago crime stories, some of them stories with Cal Hudson's byline.

Several empty medication containers were scattered on the desk and night table. An agent read the name of the doctor listed on Ula Pulaski's prescription to a police dispatcher.

Police had reached the doctor and the call was connected to the requesting agent at the scene. It took a few moments as the agent absorbed the doctor's explanation.

Ula Pulaski was her outpatient from Great Lakes Memorial Psychiatric Institute.

"She'd suffered a head injury when she and her father were walking near their home and were both struck by a dump truck that had blown a tire. The tragedy also resulted in her father's incapacitation," the doctor told the agent who was standing in Ula Pulaski's bedroom.

"Ula used to write paperback crime and horror novels and had always followed real cases closely. From time to time, mostly when Ula's off her medication, she calls people she learns about from the news, gets confused and says inappropriate things. I assure you, she's no threat to anyone."

At that point, another FBI agent held his phone out to the agent on the call with the doctor. The screen showed that Chicago PD databases revealed that Ula Pulaski had a history of making disturbing calls to real victims of high-profile crimes, all during her time as an inpatient at the institute.

The agent nodded, then thanked the doctor, telling her that there would be a follow-up for the investigation.

Then he called Tibor Malko.

33

River Ridge, Illinois

In a corner of the second-floor command post at River Ridge police headquarters, FBI Agent Malko ended the call, set his phone down and stared at his laptop screen.

The hope that they'd find Gage in Archer Heights was gone.

There was nothing connecting him to the Pulaskis' house and nothing in the garage but a 1999 Chevy Cavalier on blocks, tires, spare parts and dusty crates of junk. The chain and lock were different from those purchased by Cal Hudson at Emerson Plaza, according to the receipt from the plaza hardware store. Moreover, Pulaski's doctor confirmed that Ula Pulaski had been at the institute for an appointment at the time the Hudsons had reported Gage missing. On the shoe, Ula Pulaski had had a fifty-fifty chance of guessing correctly, and she had.

The Archer Heights call was a dead end.

After he'd informed Cal and Faith, Malko's stomach tensed.

With each passing second, the chances of finding the boy alive melted. Malko stared at Gage Hudson's face on his screen. How did he vanish? Did he wander off unseen and was then abducted? Maybe he was lured by other kids, kids slightly older. Or did something happen inside the attraction, amid the chaotic darkness?

Malko could not stop considering the two people who were with Gage just before he'd disappeared.

Cal and Faith Hudson.

Everything about them seemed wrong. There was no way he could rule out parental involvement. Not yet. But if they were involved they would've had to have had help.

He really didn't have any solid evidence.

Not yet.

There was the lock and chain, which they couldn't find. There was the connection to the strip mall, Gage's shoe and the Dumpster—the mother sobbing in the car, an indication of marital stress. Taken together they were troubling factors but at this point only circumstantial. They could have absolutely no link to the parents. But they were so disturbing and so coincidental Malko would be a fool not to pursue these aspects, no matter where they led, because something about the Hudsons didn't feel right.

Malko removed his glasses and rubbed his tired eyes, remembering his words about the dangers of tunnel vision. He needed to keep an open mind on all theories. All possibilities had to be weighed and pursued.

And that's what the joint forces operation was doing.

Glancing at the status boards at the far end of the room, Malko saw that they still had a long way to go. He looked at the tips—one hundred and thirteen so far, some so vague they were useless, others with potential for a break.

He scrolled through them. There was the woman who'd claimed her neighbor had kidnapped Gage. She said she saw the man, "a certifiable creep, digging a grave in his backyard." Turned out he was gardening and the neighbors were feuding over property lines. Then there was a man who'd reported that he'd overheard a fat man with tattoos in a bar bragging that he "knew exactly what happened to that Hudson boy." But the caller was too drunk to remember anything about the man, or the name or location of the bar. Then he said that maybe he'd dreamed about the incident.

Then there was a grandmother who'd reported seeing a distraught boy matching Gage's description crying in the back seat of a car driven by a "very stressed-looking" man and woman at a Calumet City gas station. Investigators used security camera footage and credit card records to track the vehicle to Hammond. They confirmed that the boy in the car was not Gage. He was half his age and had been suffering from an ear infection. His parents were both nurses who'd been working double shifts. The call was another false alarm.

And there was no ransom demand. No one claiming responsibility.

Malko glanced at the time, thinking how the outstanding work on other aspects of the case was mounting and everything was a priority.

FBI agents and River Ridge detectives were continuing their questioning of the employees on duty at the Chambers of Dread, other workers with Ultra-Fun Amusement Corp and employees of the River Ridge Fairgrounds. Most of the people they'd interviewed had alibis, but some were flagged for additional questioning and polygraphs.

Like Sid Griner and Alma McCain, who were working at the Chambers of Dread. They were due to arrive for another interview.

Malko clicked to more files and reread the notes made by Price and Lang when the detectives had interviewed the couple. McCain was on duty in the control room where she operated the attraction's bank of infrared security cameras and monitored the emergency exits. An alarm would sound if an exit was used. Then there was Griner, the man she lived with. Griner worked the chutes, helping people as they slid out the main exit. He was also listed as a technician who helped assemble and tear down the Chambers, so he had expertise with the attraction.

Malko considered the notes he'd made in the margins.

Something about McCain and Griner ate at him. He couldn't put his finger on it but he didn't trust the responses they'd given Price and Lang. It could've been related to the fact that McCain and Griner each had troubling histories.

Then there was the disturbing element of what we found in their van.

Malko's phone buzzed with a message telling him that McCain and Griner had arrived. Right on time.

He gathered his files and started for the interview rooms.

McCain and Griner were in key positions when Gage Hudson disappeared from the Chambers.

They have to know more than they've told us.

34

The tapping of Malko's pen on the table as he read Griner's file was the only sound in the interview room, interrupted only by the swish of Griner drinking from the bottled water Agent Sue Marsh, who'd been working on the carnival workers' interviews, had given to him.

A solid minute had passed since Malko and Marsh had entered the room and identified themselves and Malko had taken up Griner's file.

Now, without looking up from the file, Malko said, "Sidney Clydell Griner, age thirty-five, born in Lufkin, Texas. When you were five years old your drug addict mother was murdered by an outlaw biker. You bounced around foster homes, were in and out of school. Then you were in and out of the military and in and out of jail until you found your calling with Ultra-Fun Amusement Corp."

Malko closed the folder, took stock of Griner—his muscular tatted arms, the lines and pocks in his unshaven face, his long hair pulled into a ponytail, his ball cap on the table—then looked him in the eye.

"Been a hard life for you, hasn't it, Sidney?"

"You play the hand you're dealt." He shrugged. "Sir, I prefer to be called Sid."

"Ultra-Fun lists you as a technician. You help the mechanics assemble and tear down the Chambers, maintain it and fix problems. You must know the attraction like the prison art on your skin, huh, Sid?"

"It's my job to know it, sir."

"Given your expertise with the Chambers, do you have any thoughts or theories as to what happened to Gage Hudson? How he disappeared?"

"Maybe he wandered off," Griner said. "It's been known to happen."

"Maybe he wandered off?" Malko nodded. "That means he wandered right by you while you were helping guests at the chutes."

"There are six chutes. I can't watch them all. Makes the odds that people get by me pretty good and I'm not responsible for someone's kid."

"Ultra-Fun operations policy says you're responsible for the safety of all patrons. Do you think Gage Hudson, who patronized your attraction, is safe now, Sid?"

Griner gave it a moment's thought. "That didn't come out right. I'm sorry, sir."

"Fine. Now tell me, how could he disappear? Was he taken out one of the emergency doors?"

"Maybe, but it would've tripped the alarm."

"Some of the other people on duty at the Chambers, and the few customers we've talked to, insist that no emergency door alarm sounded in the time frame of Gage Hudson's disappearance. The alarms were never tripped, according to..." Malko paused, turned to Marsh, who was taking notes on her tablet, which rested on several more folders. She slid Malko one of them. "Alma McCain, who worked the control console for the Chambers."

Griner shrugged.

"And the cameras were malfunctioning at that time," Malko said.

"The electrical system was acting up since Milwaukee," Griner said.

Malko nodded. "We checked weather records and Wisconsin and Cook County permit records and maintenance logs. There was an electrical storm and a lightning strike. But that was almost two weeks ago. You can understand how we're concerned about this?"

"Yes, sir."

"The fact that the alarms and cameras malfunctioned at the time Gage Hudson disappeared is troubling. Doesn't that seem troubling to you?"

"I suppose it does."

"You suppose, do you? Well, it sure as hell should because you better believe it raises a flag for us."

Griner said nothing.

"According to records, the structure of the actual attraction is over ten years old. It just gets reconfigured and renamed for marketing reasons from time to time to make it sound like a whole new attraction."

"That's my understanding."

"Tell me, Sid, is there any conceivable way Gage Hudson could've exited the Chambers without going through the chutes? Maybe a trapdoor, a hidden escape?"

"I don't know."

"You don't know? But you're an expert at assembling and tearing the thing apart. You just told us that it's your job to know."

"Look, I told you, the kid must've got by me and wandered off."

"All right." Malko tapped his pen and went to his notes. "Do you know what we found in your van, Sid?"

"No, no one told me."

Marsh slid her tablet to show Griner photos of the hidden storage compartment behind the wall of the closet.

"What we found in there, according to the inventory list, is five hundred dollars in cash and eight grams of marijuana. Under this state's new pot law, that's a civil offense punishable with a fine of up to two hundred dollars and maybe jail time. Now, you're no longer on parole, so the violation is not automatic, but it could pose a problem."

Malko looked at Griner.

"Quite frankly," he continued. "I don't care too much about the pot right now. Here's what I think. I think it's almost like you and your girlfriend, Alma, wanted us to find your stash. And that whatever else was in there is gone, and that concerns me greatly. Want to know why?"

Griner said nothing.

"I'll tell you why," Malko said. "We measured that secret compartment and the dimensions are big enough to conceal a child of Gage Hudson's size."

Griner just stared at him.

"The dogs might not have detected anything but now we're going to have the FBI's evidence team comb through that space."

Griner blinked several times and reached for his water—a sign, Malko knew, that Griner's throat was dry, a symptom of nervous tension.

"They're going to be looking for any DNA or trace of anything connected to Gage Hudson. They're good."

A tense moment passed as Malko glared hard at Griner.

"Are you involved in Gage Hudson's disappearance, Sid?"

"No, sir."

"Do you have knowledge of who may be responsible for Gage Hudson's disappearance?"

"No, sir, I do not."

"Prior to his disappearance, have you ever communicated with Gage Hudson?"

"No, sir."

"With any member of his family?"

"No, sir."

"Anyone with a connection to his family?"

"No, sir."

"Do you know an individual by the name of Beth Gibson?"

"No, sir."

"Do you know of any individuals who might

wish to harm the Hudson family? Exact retribution or revenge?"

"No, sir."

"Have you had any reason to be near or at Emerson Plaza on Emerson Avenue?"

"No, sir."

Malko shuffled the pages of Griner's file.

"You've got quite a list of accomplishments over the years, Sid—assault, burglary, domestic violence, threats. In Kentucky, you were convicted of assaulting a woman you were living with, struck her with a toaster. In New York, you pleaded guilty to malicious destruction of property after you broke into a woman's home, stole cash, her computer, her TV, then destroyed her car. But before that you threatened to kill the woman and *steal* her six-year-old daughter."

Malko looked Griner in the eye.

"Pretty nasty work, not something to be proud of, is it?"

"I was messed up and I took treatment inside."

"All right." Malko leaned forward. "Now, I want you to think hard before you answer, Sid. Are you aware in your circles, say your old inmate circles, or anything on the fair circuit, of any talk or rumors as to who may be behind Gage Hudson's disappearance?"

"No, sir."

"Again, do you have any connection to the Hudson family?"

"No, sir."

"Did someone approach you to assist them in

any way with what resulted in Gage Hudson's disappearance?"

"No, sir."

"I think you've been bullshitting us, Sid. If you're involved in any way in Gage Hudson's disappearance, or have any information about it, you better tell me now, because if the FBI finds out later that you've misled us, we'll bring the hammer of justice down on you without mercy."

"I'm not involved and I have no information, sir."

"You know, Sid, you're likely the last person to have seen Gage Hudson before he vanished."

Griner said nothing.

"All right, you say you're not involved."

"Yes, sir."

"You've got nothing to hide?"

"Yes, sir."

"Would you agree to submit to a polygraph examination?"

Griner swallowed.

"Yes, sir, I'll do anything to help find that little boy."

35

"Is there something you're not telling us, Alma?"

Alma McCain could no longer make eye contact with the two FBI agents questioning her.

She didn't like police stations. Her life had only been made worse whenever she had entered one.

Now, sitting in Interview Room 403 and looking at the white stone walls, Alma was unsure if she was shivering from the air conditioner—or fear.

Hold it together, she told herself. *Like Sid said, we got nothing to do with it. Really? Nothing at all?* She glanced up at the ceiling corner and the camera they said was recording the interview. *It's like an all-knowing eye, watching me. How much do they know about me, about my life?* She blinked back tears. *But what happened to that little boy? His poor mom and dad. Stop. Hold it together. We're so close to our dream. So close. Don't we deserve a better life? It's been more than an hour now and these two agents are pushing me so hard with their questions.*

Marsh, the woman, was a sharp dresser and had

nice nails. She was stern-faced but seemed to show Alma a degree of warmth, unlike the man, Malko. He gave her a bad feeling. His black eyes boring into her just like the big python in the reptile tent.

"Can you answer the question, Alma?" Malko repeated.

She needed to think. She knew that they'd already talked to Sid, but because they'd kept them apart she had no idea what they'd asked him.

Or what he'd told them.

"Alma?" he repeated.

She sat a little straighter and looked at him.

"Yes. I mean, no, I've told you everything."

Malko held her in his gaze long enough to convey his doubt.

"Let's go over it all one more time so I'm clear." He shuffled papers. "Your job is to monitor all the cameras. Tell me again—what're you looking out for?"

"The guests. We don't want anyone freaking out, or having a heart attack, or harming other guests. We don't want people falling or getting hurt, that sort of thing."

"That it?"

"No, we also want to be sure guests don't hurt the staff, or the actors, or damage the sets. Sometimes when people are scared they react by punching or kicking the actors. We watch for that, too."

"So, did you see Gage Hudson leave the Chambers of Dread?"

"No."

"One more time, walk us through events surrounding his disappearance."

"Sid called me on the radio saying we had a straggler in the spinner and described him to me—a nine-year-old boy with a Cubs T-shirt, ball cap and shorts. I searched all the cameras in the Chambers but never saw him. Then Sid called a Code 99 and Mr. King took over and we shut it down and everyone searched. Mr. King even took the parents through the Chambers to help search."

"What about the emergency exits? Could Gage have gone out one of the emergency exits?"

"An alarm sounds if the doors are opened and no alarm sounded."

"Is it possible that the alarms may have malfunctioned?"

"Maybe, but they're on a separate system. If someone went through the door, we would've known."

"Okay, but the cameras didn't record everything, right?" Malko asked.

"No, they're on a different system and were spotty after Milwaukee."

"Let's go back to the alarms for the doors. Can they be disarmed? Switched off?"

"Yes, at the door with a key."

"What about at the control panel where you work? Can they be switched off manually there?"

"Yes. That usually happens when we break down a ride after a fair, or for maintenance."

Malko leaned forward and steepled his fingers before his chin.

"Did you at any point surrounding the time frame Gage Hudson disappeared switch off the alarm system, even accidentally for a brief moment?"

Seconds ticked by before Alma answered. "No, I did not."

Malko read her face for deception. "Alma, would you agree to come back and submit to a polygraph examination, to help us?"

All the saliva dried in her throat as she swallowed, her mind reaching back for Sid's advice on the lie detector. *Just keep changing your answers, make sure they're all over the map because you're scared and worried about that boy.*

"Alma?" Malko said. "Would you agree to a polygraph?"

"Yes. I want to help."

"Good. Thank you. We're almost done here. Let's switch gears." He opened a folder and slid a photo toward her. It showed a laptop with a photo of Gage Hudson displayed on the screen.

"Why do you have this on your laptop, Alma?"

Was this a trick? She shrugged as if it were obvious. "That's what police sent out when it all happened and I've been praying for him."

"Praying for him?"

"Yes, like everyone, hoping that you find him and return him to his mom and dad."

"Prior to his disappearance, did you have any contact with Gage Hudson?"

"No."

"Online?"

"No."

"With his family?"

"No."

"Do you have any information about anyone who may have ill will toward the Hudson family?"

"No, I don't. I don't know the family."

Malko then slid a physical color photo, five inches by seven inches in size, to her. It was a head-and-shoulder image of another boy about the same age as Gage Hudson.

"We found this among your belongings in your RV."

Alma leaned over and looked at it, her face softening.

"Is this your son, Kyle?"

Her face creased as she nodded.

"Tell us what happened to him."

"You know. You have my file there. Please don't make me."

"We'd like you to tell us in your words."

Fighting her tears she stared at the ceiling.

"Kyle was seven. His father was out of the picture. I was raising him alone, struggling to make ends meet. It was hard. One day Kyle was watching a kids' show and got rope from our storage and learned how to make a lasso. He was twirling it, playing cowboy in the living room. I told him to stop. He didn't. The rope hooked our TV and brought it down, smashing it to pieces on the floor. I'd just bought it and I lost my temper. I yelled at him, grabbed his arm and twisted it hard. Something cracked, he screamed and I took him to the hospital."

She looked down at the photo.

"I can't. Please don't make me go through this."

"You'd broken his arm," Malko said. "Hospital staff said you'd been drinking. Social services were called and they took Kyle away. They determined you weren't fit to be Kyle's mother and placed him in a foster home, isn't that correct?"

Alma nodded. "They were wrong," she said. "It was an accident, a flash of anger."

"Then what happened?"

"There was a fire in the foster parents' home. Smoking in bed, they said, and the parents and Kyle they were…they were…"

"No one in the house survived the fire."

Alma's tears fell on the photo.

"But something happened before the fire," Malko said, passing tissues to Alma as he continued. "You'd gone to the foster home and tried to kidnap Kyle, to steal him back, but the foster father stopped you, didn't he?"

"I needed Kyle back with me. He was my son! I needed to tell him how sorry I was."

"Do you feel somehow responsible for his death?"

Alma stared at Malko, knowing it was in the reports.

"If I hadn't hurt him——" Alma's voice grew small "——he wouldn't have been in that house and he wouldn't have been in the fire. He'd be alive."

Malko looked at her as she struggled to compose herself.

"You'd give anything to have him back, wouldn't you?"

Alma nodded.

"You ache to have your child in your life, don't you?"

She nodded again.

"You know you weren't an unfit mother, that people make mistakes. And each day you see happy families, like the Hudson family, go by in your cameras and you die a little more and you want to take back what the system took from you."

Alma blinked as if awakening. "What? No, nothing like that."

Malko stood.

"And your pain's been building over the years, hasn't it?"

"No, stop!"

"Maybe you're thinking you deserve a 'do-over' with another boy?"

"No."

"You've admitted you control the alarm system. You can switch it off."

"Yes, but I didn't."

"And your boyfriend, Sid Griner, knows all there is to know about the Chambers. Did you two do it together?"

"Stop this, it's crazy."

"Are you involved in Gage Hudson's disappearance?"

"No."

"You're not telling us everything, Alma!"

"I am!"

Malko slapped his palm on the table.

"You did something, Alma! What did you do?"

"Why're you so cruel?" she cried. "I don't want to talk to you anymore. I want a lawyer."

She thrust her face into her hands and sobbed.

36

In River Ridge police headquarters, Malko splashed water on his face.

It had already been a long day and it was not over.

Reaching for paper towels, he couldn't help his gut feeling that Griner and McCain were hiding something.

Malko knew they were lying and was confident the polygraphs, which were being arranged through Ultra-Fun's attorneys, would show that.

They needed to look hard at all the carnies and guard against falling victim to one approach. There were a lot of elements in play.

Back at his desk, Malko resumed work and saw a message that pleased him. A warrant was obtained to ensure the Chambers of Dread attraction remained at the fairgrounds and intact so investigators, with help from experts, could continue working on the entire structure, including its faulty security camera system, for potential evidence.

On other fronts, the Illinois state police were

helping review the statewide sex offender database to identify persons convicted of certain crimes against children. They'd started with those residing near the fairgrounds, then went out by a ten-mile radius, knowing that an individual could come from anywhere. Many disturbing people had surfaced but so far in the ongoing search, all those questioned were alibied.

Investigators were still poring through the canvass reports, and they were beginning to examine security footage collected from businesses and residences between the fairgrounds and Emerson Plaza.

The forensic team was processing physical material collected from the Hudsons' home and vehicles. Agents were looking at bank and credit card records. They were studying information contained on their phones and computers.

Malko knew they were looking closely at Gage's chat history on the earLoadzone and they'd interviewed his friends Ethan Clark, Colton Huppkey and Marshall Thompson.

"What we mostly talked about on ELZ lately was the Chambers of Dread," Marshall had told agents. "That it was supposed to be the scariest thing ever."

Ethan Clark had said, "People on ELZ were talking about the insane butcher, the burning witch queen and the guy who chased you with a chain saw."

"We talked about it at school, too," Colton had told the FBI. "We knew it was coming to town and we were daring each other on who would be brave enough to go in and who would be first." Colton then blinked quickly at the agents. "You're going to find him, right? Gage is going to be okay?"

The agents promised Colton they'd do all they could to find his friend.

Some of the cyber experts had suggested adults posing as children could've accessed the site. But it was challenging to nail down. Some visitors had the skill to erase their trail on ELZ, perhaps the work of protective tech-savvy parents.

Other investigators were beginning interviews with Cal and Faith's friends, coworkers, neighbors, as well as Gage's teachers, coaches, his friends and classmates. And people who'd claimed to be in the Chambers of Dread, or at the fair, when Gage vanished were coming forward.

The list of people to speak to was growing. Malko glanced at the time again. Pamela Huppkey, a close friend of Faith Hudson's, was coming in for an interview shortly.

He opened another file. A small team of agents was studying all the major crime stories Cal had produced for the *Chicago Star-News*. Starting with the most recent and going back, they were looking at cold-blooded criminals, their families and associates, who may have taken Gage as an act of vengeance. The agents made notes, intending to consult Cal.

Malko's shoulders and neck had knotted with tension.

What were they missing? Was there something

he wasn't covering? How does a little boy disappear from an enclosed area? Did he wander off? Was he taken? He hadn't yet eliminated the parents as suspects, so which way should he point the investigation?

A shadow fell over Malko and he raised his head to FBI agent Larson Ward, the polygraphist who'd administered Faith and Cal Hudson's exams, standing before him with his computer.

"I've concluded examining the Hudsons' results. Is now a good time?"

"Yes."

Ward set up his laptop and began rolling through and pointing at the peaks and valleys of the graphs.

"We still have a lot of people to process, Tibor."

"I know."

"We've made the parents a priority as you requested."

"Yes, thanks. Can we get on with it, Larson?"

"First, it's important to note that we have to take in a spectrum of emotions and reactions, from the innocent parent suffering from guilt for what's happened, to the offender who knows who is responsible for the crime."

"Ward, I'm familiar with the cautions."

"Given the high profile and the emotional atmosphere of this type of case there are a lot of potential factors to bear in mind when evaluating the responses and readings. Individuals could be responding as part of a diversionary tactic to protect someone, or deflect suspicion. It could be a matter of misperception, such as an honest error, or there could be mental health issues, or other stressors at play."

"Ward, yes, I've been through this many times. What do you have?"

"Based on my readings of the results, I conclude that both Cal and Faith Hudson were untruthful in their responses. They're concealing something."

37

Pam Huppkey twisted the straps of her bag while taking stock of the small, barren room where she waited.

With its four cinder-block walls, plain veneer table, hard chairs and stained ceiling tiles, it seemed clinical, cold and smelled of floor cleaner.

Pam had never been in a police station in her life but when the FBI requested an interview regarding Gage Hudson's disappearance she drove to River Ridge police headquarters as soon as she could.

She wanted to help, but deep down she was nervous and jumped a little when the door opened.

"Thank you for coming, Mrs. Huppkey," said the man who'd entered the room with a woman. His tie was loosened and his shirtsleeves were rolled up to his elbows. The woman was wearing a conservative business suit. She had short hair cut in a layered bob.

They were unsmiling as the man closed the door behind them. They set file folders on the table and took the two chairs opposite Pam.

"I'm Tibor Malko with the FBI. This is Agent Sue Marsh. Can we get you anything—coffee, tea, water?"

"No, thank you."

Malko and Marsh opened their folders.

"As you know," he began, "this is a large investigation and part of our job is to talk to everyone in Gage Hudson's circles to help us with any information that could lead to us finding him. We don't want to miss anything."

Pam saw that they were looking at pages that resembled the questionnaire form that she and Dean had completed. She saw penned asterisks in the margins. Her nervousness bordered on fear, for she was uncertain what she should say, given the secret that had been gnawing at her.

"You, your husband and son are good friends with the family," Marsh said.

"Yes, our son, Colton, and Gage go to Saint Bartholomew's together. I work part-time as a volunteer in the admin office there."

"And you're quite involved with various activities?"

"Yes, I volunteer with school and church groups. Our boys play on the ball team. Dean helps coach."

Malko and Marsh continued with seemingly routine questions about the length of the Huppkeys' friendship with the Hudsons, the frequency of interaction, before moving to specifics about Gage's disappearance.

They pressed Pam to identify anyone in Gage's circle who may have been recently exhibiting unusual behavior. They asked her to detail anything out of the ordinary concerning the Hudsons in the forty-eight hours before Gage vanished. Then they wanted her to characterize Cal and Faith's reaction to Gage's disappearance, their demeanor, what they said, what they did.

"Every iota of information is relevant," Malko said.

As they continued, Pam grew increasingly anxious, twisting the tiny cross on the chain around her neck—a reaction that was not lost on Malko and he saved it in his mind the way a skilled card player keeps an ace in reserve. He held on to it until their interview with Pam neared its conclusion.

"I think we're done, Mrs. Huppkey," he said. "But before we wrap up, let me ask you—is there anything else you think we should know? It could be crucial, no matter how trivial, or embarrassing, or unrelated it may appear."

Malko casually stroked the stubble of his bald head while his eyes, like black ball bearings, drilled into Pam's as if he knew a truth was hidden there.

"Anything at all that might be weighing on you, Pam?" Malko asked, using her first name for the first time.

She twisted her cross, grappling with whether she should reveal her most disturbing and secret observations about Faith Hudson. Pam's desire to be a good friend, to mind her own business, became entangled with the acrimony she'd buried for years about her friendship with Faith.

Faith had always had a prickly side to her and could be a bit of a bitch. Pam could not help but feel that at times the pretty and high-octane businesswoman, working in a downtown skyscraper, looked down at her, the plain-looking, religious, suburban school mom.

Above all, what had happened to Gage had chilled Pam to her core and in her heart she knew that if it had happened to Colton she'd want everyone to do all they could to find him—*no matter what it was.*

"There's one thing," Pam said.

Malko's expression was stone-cold. He said nothing.

"A few months ago—" Pam cleared her throat "—I saw Faith do something that troubled me and I've never told anyone about it."

"What did you see?" Malko said.

Pam related the shopping lunch with her friend Marcia at a mall about ten miles away in Oak Brook, and how she'd spotted Faith in the food court with a man.

"He was a rather handsome man. I have no idea who he was," Pam said, recounting how Faith had never seen her, and how she thought the man was a client, possibly. But that their conversation seemed so intense.

"That's the only word to describe it," Pam told the agents.

"Were they arguing?" Malko asked.

"I'm not sure. But at one point it looked like the man touched Faith's hand. Then, when he shifted in his seat, his jacket opened a bit and I saw the handle of a gun in a shoulder holster."

"You're absolutely certain that it was a gun?"

"Yes."

Malko glanced at Marsh, who made a note.

"Go on," Malko said.

"Later—" Pam cupped her hands to her face "—this keeps getting stranger, but later, when we were leaving, I saw Faith with the man in the parking lot next to her car. I mean, what are the chances that we'd be in that lot at the same time? It's almost as if I was meant to see this."

"Did Faith see you?"

"Oh, no, I'm sure of it. There was some distance between us."

"Were they driving together?"

"No, but I saw Faith touch his arm before they parted."

"Was your friend Marcia with you at the time? Did she witness this, as well?" Malko's face betrayed no emotion.

"Yes."

"Anything else?"

"Yes. I believe I saw that same man again the day Gage disappeared."

"Where?" Malko asked.

"He was at the fairgrounds, standing at the edge of the crowd during the press conference."

The only sound audible for next moment was the scratching of Marsh's pen as she completed notes.

"Please don't tell Faith I told you this. Please."

"I assure you," Malko said, "all information is

confidential and we request that you not share any aspect of this conversation with anyone, either. It could be integral to the investigation."

Malko absorbed Pam Huppkey's revelations. She had given them a new lead.

Pieces were beginning to fit.

38

Oak Brook, Illinois

After Pam Huppkey left the room Malko had stared at his notes while tapping his pen on the table.

"What do you think?" Marsh asked.

"We need to find this guy. We may have something here."

Malko and Marsh moved fast in the minutes and hours following Pam's account of Faith's meeting with an armed man who she'd later spotted at the fairgrounds.

Pam had consented to let the FBI scrutinize her credit card records. From her purchase of a salad lunch, it didn't take long for them to pinpoint the date and time she was at the food court at the Oak Brook Victory Mall.

Malko reached out to the mall's security office and was connected to chief of operations, Norm Garfield.

"Absolutely, we archive all of our surveillance footage. Our system's state-of-the-art," Garfield said over the phone as Malko and Marsh headed westbound on I-88 in an unmarked Bureau car.

Less than half an hour later, Garfield greeted them at the administration office, extending his meaty hand over the reception counter.

"Terrible thing about the Hudson boy. Happy to help. Follow me."

Garfield walked with a limp, then told them the reason. "Twenty-six years on the job with Chicago PD and in my last week before retirement we come up on a bank heist in progress and I take a round in the leg. But I did better than the perps. They died on the street."

Garfield opened the door to the mall's dimly lit security control room with its vast console of monitors and control panels.

"We've got nearly a hundred cameras throughout the mall," he said. "We monitor all entrance/exits, all storefronts on all levels. All common areas—elevators, hallways, the parking lots, the loading zones. We even have them set up to watch the roof."

"You're covered well," Malko said.

"We've got the capacity to archive footage for years. We monitor for everything from terror threats, to missing kids, to car thefts, parking lot accidents, slip-and-fall liability claims—the whole shebang."

Garfield introduced Malko and Marsh to Len Lockerby, the duty officer in the swivel chair operating the console.

Lockerby shook hands with the agents.

"I think I've got what you want here, based on the date and times you provided," he said. "Watch monitor twenty-one."

In the crisp, clear, slow-motion images of shoppers eating in the food court, Malko recognized Pam Huppkey. Not far from her table, on the opposite side of a latticed wall, he found Faith Hudson with a man.

"That's our subject." Malko produced a pen and nearly touched the screen. "Can you follow this man's movements?"

Lockerby manipulated the controls. Camera perspectives shifted several times as they tracked the man leaving the food court and walking with Faith through the mall to an exit/entrance, then the parking lot.

The cameras covering section fourteen captured Faith placing her right hand on the man's arm before they parted.

"Follow him," Malko said, wishing they'd had surveillance of this caliber at the fairgrounds and near the strip mall Dumpster where they'd found Gage's shoe.

Lockerby operated the controls so that the images shifted to the man getting into a pickup truck.

"Looks like a Ram 1500, 2016," Marsh said.

"Can you pull in tight enough to get his plate?" Malko asked.

"Not a problem."

Lockerby activated the zoom function and easily captured the Illinois plate, prompting Malko and Marsh to jot it down in their notebooks.

"Okay, just freeze everything for a moment." Malko and Marsh reached for their phones and launched a series of urgent calls, making demands for the tag to be run immediately through a spectrum of databases, ranging from the Illinois Department of Motor Vehicles, state and county records, sex offender registries, to regional and national law enforcement and terror list databases, as well as the FBI–run National Crime Information Center and Violent Criminal Apprehension Program. Then for the next several minutes, the two agents took notes as information streamed back to them.

The man who Faith had met was Roy Simon Tate, a Deputy US Marshal.

"We've got more." Marsh, phone pressed to her head, nodded, then signaled for Malko and whispered in his ear. "Tate's assigned to Witness Security Program."

Malko and Marsh exchanged a silent look.

"We need to confirm if the Marshals Service is running anything involving the family," Malko told her. "And that's not going to be easy. It's going to take calls by people far above our pay grade."

Malko's phone rang with a callback with additional information.

"You're not going to believe this," the FBI agent on the line said to Malko. "From the years 2013 to 2016, Roy Tate moonlighted as a security consultant for the River Ridge Fairgrounds."

"That's confirmed?"

"It is. Apparently he came close to a conflict

of interest disciplinary issue with the Marshals Service and ceased his relationship with the fairgrounds administration."

After the call ended, Malko stared at the frozen screen while mentally taking stock of the new information they'd uncovered concerning Faith Hudson and Roy Tate.

This took everything to another level. Malko didn't know what they were dealing with here, but they had to be getting closer to the truth behind Gage Hudson's disappearance—what that truth was, he didn't know.

Not yet.

39

River Ridge, Illinois

On the screen, two toddlers laughed and splashed joyfully in a wading pool.

"That's Gage and Ethan in our backyard."

Rory Clark had turned his tablet and the home video to Leon Lang and Rachel Price, who were interviewing him in his office in the old municipal building. The River Ridge detectives were working through their list by coordinating appointments visiting people where they worked or lived.

Things went faster that way.

"My wife put all the family videos in one big folder. This one of the boys is my favorite," Clark said. "Don't know what prompted me to look at it last night. Maybe it was your call." The squeals of delight ended when Clark closed the video, tears standing in his eyes. "Any leads on Gage? Ethan asks us every hour if you've found him."

"We're following up on several possibilities and we're hopeful," Price said.

Sadness washed over Clark as he nodded.

"Sam and I have probably known the family longer than anyone else. We met them twelve years ago when they moved into the neighborhood, just four doors down. Before Gage and our son, Ethan, were born. The boys grew up together."

At the outset, the soft-spoken civil engineer with the county, who managed drainage, utility and transportation projects, was reluctant to talk to them at all. He couldn't, "in all good conscience," betray what he felt was the Hudsons' confidence—their "private matters."

"We assure you, all information we collect is confidential," Price said.

Clark stuck out his bottom lip. "You just want me to answer questions and give you my observations?"

"That's right, sir," Lang said.

"And this is all confidential?"

"That's right."

Clark picked up an old slide rule and moved the cursor thoughtfully, then moved the slide as if calculating how to respond.

"Sir, all information is critical," Lang encouraged him. "You may have the piece that could help us locate Gage."

Clark nodded, put the slide rule down carefully.

"Okay, go ahead."

For the next half hour Price and Lang went through their questions before gradually inviting Clark to offer his thoughts.

"I don't think Cal's been happy in their marriage," Clark said.

"And what makes you think that?" Price asked.

"He never stated it outright, but it was what he'd said in our private conversations."

"What do you mean?" Price asked.

"Whenever Cal had the time, he'd walk over to my house and we'd watch a game and talk over a few beers."

"What would you talk about?" Lang asked.

"Work, who pissed us off, politics—but mostly about the Cubs, the Bulls, the White Sox and the Blackhawks. But over the last ten months Cal started asking me if Sam and I were happy, if we'd ever had problems, if I ever felt like she was going to leave me, or if I felt like leaving her."

"Did he indicate that he and Faith were having problems?" Lang asked.

"No, he said he was just curious. Then one night out of the blue, we're watching a Cubs game and Cal had downed quite a few beers, more than usual, and he kind of loosened up, you know. He's staring at the screen and he says that there were times that he'd wished that he could just start over with his life, that there were things he'd done that he regretted, that he wished that he could just disappear."

"Did he say what these *regrettable* things were?" Price asked.

"No, and I asked him. But he refused to tell me. He said they were secrets he'd carry to his grave."

Price and Lang exchanged looks.

"Did Cal give any reason for making such a statement?"

"No, he was cryptic and at first I chalked it up to stress at his newspaper, the looming layoffs, all the beer he'd had and the fact the Cubs were losing. Then as it got later he tells me that if he ever wanted to, he could disappear and no one would ever find him—he'd go 'off the grid.' He said that he had a lot of police and criminal sources. He said there were things he could do to create a new identity, things he knew about credit cards, about counterfeit cash. He said he'd learned a lot from his years on the crime beat."

"Did he ever elaborate on why he'd disappear, or where he'd go?"

Clark shook his head. "He just kind of let that go and he never said anything about it again."

"And what did you make of all this?" Price asked. "Was it just beer talk or something more?"

"I always believed that Cal was exceptionally street smart because of his job. Now, when I think about it, yeah, it's troubling, with Gage gone and Cal's marriage talk. I don't know what to think. You'll keep this confidential, though, right? Because this could mean absolutely nothing."

"Confidential. We assure you," Lang said.

"Tell us." Price moved on to a new subject. "Is the name Beth Gibson familiar to you?"

"No, I don't think so. Wait. Isn't that the person who called Cal on Jack Thompson's phone when everybody was at our house right after Gage's disappearance?"

"Yes. Do you know this person, or anything about her?"

Clark shook his head.

"Ever meet her?" Lang asked.

"No."

"Let's shift gears again," Price said. "Are you involved with Gage and Ethan's baseball team?"

"I go to the games and help manage the team when I can."

"Do you recall about a month ago if the team's equipment storage locker at the park near Emerson Boulevard was vandalized or damaged?"

"Not really, no."

"Do you recall anyone contacting Cal to buy a new lock and chain for the locker?"

Clark shook his head. "Maybe Dean Huppkey or Jack Thompson might remember something like that. I don't. Is it important to the case?"

"Just something we're following up on," Price said.

Clark looked at her for a moment, then at Lang before asking them, "What do you think happened to Gage?"

"We don't know. That's what we're trying to determine," Lang said. "What do you think transpired, Mr. Clark?"

"Me?"

"Yes, what do you think happened to Gage?"

"I don't know. I honestly don't know." Clark stared beyond the detectives at the wall behind them, searching for an answer. "How does a nine-year-old boy disappear from what is essentially an enclosed space while with his parents? I've gone over it a thousand times in my head and I swear it just doesn't make any sense."

40

Cal Hudson's heart sank.

In the moments after Agent Malko had told them that the FBI's lead on the woman who'd claimed to have Gage was a dead end, Cal was at a loss.

The woman was unstable. The call was a fabrication. She had no connection to Gage.

"Maybe you missed something! I'm going to drive to Archer Heights and search the property myself!" Cal had told Malko, grasping for hope as it evaporated.

"You won't be permitted to do that," Malko had said. "Cal, listen to me. You and Faith have to be prepared for this emotional roller coaster. We're going to see more of this sort of thing—false, exaggerated or distorted confessions, useless information from attention-seeking citizens and disturbed individuals. I'm sorry, but it's all part of the case."

Beneath Malko's halfhearted attempt at consolation Cal knew that the FBI had not cleared him or Faith.

The Archer Heights setback had hurt. It became

enmeshed with Cal's other fears—the FBI's suspicions toward them and his belief that, with the separation talk and now the divorce ad, Faith was keeping something crucial from him. The increasing mistrust fed the tension mounting between them and they withdrew into themselves to confront the real and growing horror.

Gage could be dead.

It was almost too great to bear, so much so that now, as Cal struggled with it, he welcomed the interruption of a phone call and answered.

"Mr. Hudson, this is Agent Dee Lewin with the FBI. We need you to come to River Ridge police headquarters as soon as possible."

When Cal arrived, Agent Lewin and Agent Grant Hern told him they had been conducting an exhaustive review of the major news stories he had written over the past five years for the *Chicago Star-News*.

"We're looking for plausible, potential acts of retribution by the subjects in your stories," Lewin said.

The agents were set up at a desk on the same floor as the rooms where Cal and Faith had been interviewed and polygraphed. Seeing no sign of Malko, or Detectives Price and Lang, he inquired after them.

"They're out conducting interviews and following leads," Lewin said, offering him a chair. The desk reflected the agents' work, with a computer terminal, two laptops, a tablet and several notebooks. The plastic trash can next to it overflowed with takeout wrappers.

Lewin got down to business. "We've done an analysis of all the stories you've written for the paper."

"That's a lot of stories."

"Yes, and in the case of major stories we've also reviewed related reports by other news outlets, TV news and social media. We've conducted a threat assessment in the same vein as we do for law enforcement personnel who are threatened or deemed to be at risk."

"Cal, we'd like your input on our results." Hern began clicking on pages cued up on the large monitor. "It's evident you've dealt with a spectrum of dangerous people, murderers, rapists, pedophiles, organized crime figures, and while most of your stories are about Chicago-set crimes, you've traveled across the country and internationally to sketchy areas and have gone into prisons to interview death-row inmates and a range of convicted criminals."

"That's true," Cal said. "But in most cases I was never threatened."

"Most, but not all," Lewin said. "Of all the hundreds of stories we reviewed, these are the ones that concern us most, so far. They're in no order, but let's start with this one. A murderer, a Chicago native, killed a retired couple in Berkeley, California. But after the California Supreme Court overturned his conviction he walked off death row."

"Lance Leonard Oakley."

"You covered his case extensively, interviewed him in prison before his release. One day Oakley called your newsroom, claimed you'd promised him a job and friendship," Lewin said.

"I never offered him those things and he knew it."

"Yet he told a Chicago TV station that you'd lied to him and he'd never forget it," Hern said. "Do you think he could've taken Gage?"

"No. Oakley was always boastful. He's just not that bright. Look, it should be in the story somewhere, or in your files, that Oakley was assessed and has the intelligence level of a child. So you can't give him much weight."

"Still, he shouldn't be underestimated. We're attempting to locate him."

"Last I heard he was homeless in Toronto and kind of out of his mind from drugs and alcohol."

"Fine, then there's Faustino Carlos Avila," Hern said, "a serial killer and a cartel executioner who murdered ten people from the Chicago area in the Arizona desert before fleeing. You covered his case in depth. Some say that your reporting helped police capture him in Buenos Aires, Argentina. You flew there but he was angry and refused to grant a jailhouse interview. Upon his extradition to the US for trial he told the *Chicago Tribune* that he would spend every day in prison figuring out a way to hurt you."

"That was just talk," Cal said. "Those who mean to hurt you don't broadcast it."

"Cartels do, Cal. You know that," Lewin said. "That's why Avila shouldn't be dismissed as a possible suspect."

"Faustino was also a drug addict given to braggadocio and making all kinds of fantastic statements—he thrived on that sort of thing."

"Fair enough, but then we come to the case of Ezekiel Lyman Ezili," Hern said, "a pedophile convicted of the horrific murder of a six-year-old boy. His case was complex and garnered some profile in Chicago. You broke a number of exclusive stories on it that led to his arrest and conviction. Ezili found Jesus in his prison cell, and in a letter written from prison to the *Sun-Times*, he claimed he was innocent, that he was set up, that you were the architect of his conviction. He alleged your reports about him in the *Star-News* were police-fed fiction and called on his supporters for a day of reckoning against his enemies."

Cal stared at the monitor showing his stories on Ezili.

"Cal?" Hern said. "Do you see something in the Ezili case that stands out, given it involved a boy whose age is close to your son's?"

Cal scratched his stubble and blinked thoughtfully as if remembering, then shook his head. "No. Ezili was cryptic and nothing came of those things he said."

"But there were calls for an internal affairs investigation of the Chicago homicide detectives on the case."

"Yeah, that went nowhere. You must've learned that," Cal said.

"Still, Ezili called for action against you," Lewin said.

"Yes, Ezili was a creep but the key thing with

him was that he was murdered in prison—so, that ends that."

"Well, we don't think his threat should be dismissed."

Cal grew thoughtful, said nothing, and Lewin let a few moments pass.

"Okay, there's Henry Zutz," Lewin said, "an ex-cop who became an insurance salesman. He deceived clients, usually older, wealthy businessmen in poor health, into changing their beneficiaries, ultimately to him. He'd do this by having a business lunch with them to update their policies and he'd secretly lace their meals with poison. Several clients died—but the last one survived and his wife, who'd never trusted Zutz, alerted police to investigate."

"Yes, Zutz was smart, calculating and cold-blooded," Cal said.

"Upon his arrest and conviction he proclaimed his innocence and vowed revenge, saying that he'd start by suing you and the *Star-News.*"

"Our legal people said his case was groundless and there's no way he can follow through on any of his threats from prison. I think he spends most of his time in solitary."

"True, but he made threats," Lewin said. "Finally, there's Dillford Lee Sikes, a white supremacist who murdered a nine-year-old boy in Rockland, Illinois. He was convicted but escaped from prison during a hospital transfer. He fled to Canada where he murdered a ten-year-old boy in Winnipeg, was arrested and escaped again.

"You went full tilt on his case, obtaining his US and Canadian prison records, and began calling his network of family and friends. It led to his arrest in Reno, Nevada, where he'd taken on a new identity, married a widow and started a new life. He vowed that his white supremacist friends would help him get back at you because, according to what he told *USA TODAY*, 'I'd be a free man if it wasn't for Cal Hudson of the *Chicago Star-News*. Someday he'll pay for destroying everything I worked for.'"

"More jail cell boasting from a two-time child killer," Cal said. "The guy's locked up."

"You can't dismiss these cases as completely harmless, given that some of them involved boys similar in age to your son," Hern said. "Especially now, in light of what's happened."

"I don't dismiss them. Believe me, I don't. You should know that I thought about all of these cases, racked my brains about the possibility that any one of them might somehow be connected to Gage's disappearance," Cal said. "They're all violent, dangerous, sick, twisted people. But I've dealt with them all and I don't believe they're involved. I think it would be a waste of resources to pursue them."

"What makes you think that?"

"These people are vermin but they're all behind bars, or in Ezili's case dead, or in Oakley's case lost on the street. I just don't think that they have the resources, or the desire, or the ability, or power, to get anyone willing to risk being arrested by stalking my family to the Chambers of Dread and taking Gage to get back at me. That's a Hollywood scenario. I know they have no love for me, but their reality is a day-by-day struggle for survival in prison. Getting back at me is tough-guy talk to scare me, but it truly wouldn't be a priority for them. I really think we're getting distracted here."

"We understand but can't rule them out, Cal," Lewin said. "We can't leave any stone unturned. We've already made arrangements for agents to track each subject down and go into prisons and question each of these people. We're going to investigate their contacts for the past six months—for any connection."

Hern looked hard at him. "Why do we get the feeling that maybe you don't want us looking into these people? Is there something going on that you're not telling us?"

"No! If you have enough people, go ahead and look, absolutely. But I don't think—" Suddenly tears filled his eyes. "In my gut, I think that it was some member of the public who was in the attraction with us, or someone associated with the carnival or fairgrounds, carnies or fair people. I—I..." Cal's hands were shaking as he covered his face. "I'm sorry, I haven't slept or eaten and I can't stop thinking that I'll never see Gage again." He sobbed. "I can't stop thinking that he's dead and it's our fault for not watching over him. I'm sorry."

Lewin put her hand on Cal's shoulder and kept it there as a few minutes passed and he regained his composure.

"We know this is hard," Lewin said. "Everyone on this case is working flat-out to find Gage. We're pursuing over a dozen possible angles of investigation. Just about every agent, cop, trooper and deputy is a parent. They take something like this to heart. We've got people coming in on their own time to help."

"Thank you." Cal nodded his appreciation just as a burst of activity in the hall drew his attention and that of the agents.

Malko and several other people were hustling a man toward the interview rooms. At one point, as the man passed by, he looked directly at Cal, who felt a sudden stab of unease.

He'd seen him before. Where? Then it clicked. He was among the people watching them during the news conference at the fairgrounds... Who was he?

Cal heard the faint clink of metal against metal. That's when he saw that the man's wrists were in handcuffs.

41

Later that day Roy Simon Tate eyed FBI Agent Sue Marsh while massaging his wrists after she'd removed his handcuffs.

"Can we get you anything, Roy, a soft drink or coffee?" Malko asked.

Tate shook his head slowly.

Dressed in faded jeans that complemented his slim waist and a T-shirt that revealed his tattooed, muscular arms, he projected an air of power and quiet control. A few longer strands of his thick, combed-back hair fell against his temples. Dark, intelligent eyes that seemed as if they missed nothing shone from his weathered, craggy face. It bore a few days of stubble and a peppered goatee, accentuating his rugged features.

Malko took his time reviewing the file folder with Tate's background. Age: forty-two; divorced father of a teenage daughter living with her mother in California; at age twenty he donated a kidney to save his brother's life. Tate was a Deputy US Marshal with a stellar record of tracking down fugitives. He was currently assigned to the Witness Security Program. He'd served with the US military and saw action in Iraq and Afghanistan, where he was taken prisoner and tortured by rebel forces. He'd escaped by killing two guards with his bare hands.

As dangerous as a coiled cobra, Malko thought. Tate never resisted arrest when they'd boxed in his truck near his townhome, except to say, "What the fuck is this?"

Closing the folder, Malko indicated the camera in the upper corner of the room. "I expect you know how these things go, Roy?"

Tate said nothing.

"You've got to be asking yourself, why would the FBI arrest you, a decorated veteran, and an outstanding cop? Why would the FBI pat you down, search you, Mirandize you, put you in cuffs and haul you in here? What do they know, or *what do they think they know*?"

Tate remained silent.

"Now, you've waived your right to an attorney, which indicates you're confident about your innocence."

"I've done nothing unlawful."

"That's good, Roy. But from this point on, I hope you'll see the wisdom in cooperating with us. You'll want to weigh your answers carefully. The truth is a wise strategy."

Tate stared at Malko.

"You're familiar with the case of Gage Hudson?"

"It's all over the news."

"We've confirmed that the family is not in the witness program."

Tate shrugged. "I can't discuss any knowledge of people in the program."

"We understand. We took care of that. We need to know about your relationship with the Hudsons."

"I don't have a relationship with the family."

"You're telling us you don't know them at all?"

"I didn't say that and you didn't ask me that."

"Do you know the Hudsons?"

"I met them once at a party, a Christmas party for law enforcement and Chicago press people. That's it."

"Once?"

"That's what I said."

"You were divorced at this time?"

"Yes."

"Subsequent to that party, did you maintain contact with them?"

"No. I don't know the family."

Malko absorbed the answer, then flipped through pages of Tate's file.

"Your divorce records indicate that your wife complained of psychological abuse. What's that about?"

Tate's gazed drifted to his hands and he took a long moment before responding.

"After I returned from service, I had trouble coping. PTSD, they call it. I had nightmares, suicidal thoughts, bouts of rage." Tate hesitated and looked at nothing. "I never hit her but she did take the brunt of my problem. I don't blame her for leaving. I'd lost myself and it cost me my family."

"Did you seek therapy?"

"I did. I was one of the lucky ones. I had good help and I worked at it and I recovered, accepting that I had been changed. I started over and focused on getting a life. Friends helped me get a position with the Marshals Service. But that was a long time ago. I put that all behind me."

Malko nodded.

"We see that for a few years you moonlighted as a security consultant for the River Ridge Fairgrounds."

"To cover child support payments and pay my divorce lawyer. Those things tend to be expensive."

"Certainly," Malko said. "But during that time you became familiar with all matters of security for the fairgrounds, especially during the River Ridge Summer Carnival."

"That was the job."

"You also became familiar with Ultra-Fun Amusement Corp's policies, practices and the safety and security of their attractions when they were in town."

"Also part of the job."

"That would make you something of an expert on its vulnerabilities, wouldn't you agree?"

"Yes, it was my job to know."

"Are you familiar with Sidney Griner and Alma McCain?"

"No."

"They're Ultra-Fun employees who operated the Chambers."

Tate shook his head. "Names don't ring any bells."

"So you've had no association with them for your security role?"

Tate shook his head, saying nothing, and Malko let a long moment of silence pass before shifting the subject and resuming the interview.

"Is the name Beth Gibson familiar to you?" Malko asked.

"First time I've heard it."

Malko nodded patiently, accepting Tate's response while flipping through the file.

"Ever buy or use a disposable phone?"

"Maybe, I don't know."

"That's your answer?"

Tate said nothing.

"You know, Roy, this case has drawn a lot of attention and a lot of tips. Some have been implausible, while others give us concern. Nevertheless, we store all of them in databases. Now, you've established with us that you have no relationship with the family, yet a neighbor of the Hudsons, who is with the Neighborhood Watch program, took note of your license plate. She'd spotted your pickup truck in front of the Hudson home two weeks ago at two in the morning, then again down the street soon after Gage Hudson vanished."

Malko consulted the notes in the folder.

"When asked about that, you told our people that you were part of an operation. We subsequently

checked and have since been told that there was
no operation on the date and time your vehicle was
spotted. What do you make of that, Roy?"

Malko watched Tate carefully, the muscles in
his jaw pulsing as he waited for an answer that
never came.

"Why in the world would your vehicle be there,
if you have no relationship with the family and
they're not in the program?"

Tate still said nothing.

"You've got a nice little townhome in Rogers Park—that's a heck of a long way from River
Ridge, don't you think?"

Tate remained silent.

"Have you ever been to Oak Brook?"

"Maybe."

"Ever been to the new mall they got there, the
Oak Brook Victory Mall?"

"Maybe."

"It's such a long way from Rogers Park. Why
drive all the way there?"

Tate shrugged.

"Was there something there you wanted to buy?"

Tate shook his head. "I don't remember."

"Could this be the reason?" Malko removed another folder, opened it and carefully placed several
photos on the table—clear still frames captured
from the mall's security camera showing Tate with
Faith Hudson. "From the video we've seen, you had
quite a conversation with Gage Hudson's mother,
one that carried right out into the parking lot."

Tate stared hard at the photos, his jaw throbbing.

"What's this about? Why were you meeting Faith Hudson?"

Tate sat in silence.

"Roy, I'm disappointed that you would mislead us, a man of your position and caliber."

Still, only silence across the table.

"One more thing," Malko said. "We have a witness who places you at the news conference the Hudsons gave shortly after Gage vanished. You can see how we'd be concerned that, when considered with everything else, you just happen to be at the fairgrounds within hours of Gage's disappearance. Yet you state you have no relationship with the family."

Tate's eyes went around the room as if the white cinder blocks were moving in closer and closer.

Suddenly a chair scraped as Malko stood, leaned on the table and thrust his face into Tate's.

"You better give your head a shake and get your shit together, Roy, because while we have you here, we're disemboweling your life and scouring the entrails for your link to Gage Hudson."

42

Rogers Park, Illinois

More than fifteen miles north of where Roy Tate was being questioned, the FBI was backing a white panel van into the driveway of his townhome.

Bob Turley, manager of the Prairie Valley Breezes complex, slid on his bifocals while standing near the address rereading the papers FBI agent Jim Gerard had given him.

"You have the key?" Gerard asked.

"Yes, but I don't understand. This is all so sudden and—" Turley was incredulous, staring at the words on the pages from the United States District Court for the federal warrant to search Tate's residence. "And you know that Roy's a law enforcement officer. There's got to be a mistake."

"No mistake, sir." Gerard waved ahead to other agents arriving wearing raid jackets and windbreakers with FBI emblazoned on them. "We don't want to force the door but we have authority and you wouldn't want to be deemed as obstructing us."

"Of course not." Turley lowered the pages. "He uses our cleaning services. I have a key right here."

Turley was shocked by the FBI activity because this part of Rogers Park had always been a tranquil enclave of urban professionals. Turley then nodded respectfully to the agent who held a small camera and was recording the search.

The agents entered Tate's residence with guns drawn, sweeping through every room. The town-home was modest, a 1,097-square-foot multilevel atop a two-car garage. It had two bedrooms, two bathrooms and a kitchen that opened to the living room. The master bedroom had a whirlpool tub and separate shower. There was a study, a laundry room and a number of large closets.

Agents found no sign of Gage Hudson, or anyone else present, after clearing every corner of the townhome.

Then with quick, cool efficiency, the search team snapped on latex gloves and commenced execution of the warrant setting out to search everything within its scope. Every one of the agents was experienced with the procedure and familiar with the evidence listed.

The warrant encompassed potential trace evidence belonging to Gage Hudson—blood, hair, fibers, items of clothing or other personal items—any record of communication between Tate and members of the Hudson family, any weapons, any pornographic material, any items associated with the River Ridge Fairgrounds, the Chambers of Dread.

The list went on.

Aware that Tate could've disposed of or hidden evidence, the search team probed and examined every storage area with expert efficiency. While Tate had had the opportunity to conceal evidence, it had been diminished by the very speed and surprise with which Malko had arrested Tate away from his home.

Bearing in mind that time was ticking down on Gage Hudson, Gerard and the team moved as fast and as thoroughly as possible, searching for documents, photos, videos, records, wherever they could be stored—in computers, phones registered or disposable, containers, books or artwork. They'd noticed he had a large collection of books on the subject of Roman military history, campaigns, commands and ranks.

They seized Tate's personal computer, which contained security manuals for the fairgrounds and Ultra-Fun Amusement Corp; they vacuumed floors, seized the lint trap in his dryer and collected the traps in his drains, to examine the matter collected for trace evidence.

Time was slipping by and nothing had yet emerged.

Looks like we're going to strike out here, Gerard thought. The creeping sense of failure stung because Malko had drilled into them that this was their best chance to secure evidence, if it existed.

"We can't hold Tate for long," Malko had said. "If we miss anything with this search and release him, any evidence that does exist will be gone."

Tate, being a seasoned law enforcement officer,

would be smart about these things, Gerard admitted as he moved to consult with other team members.

Agents were going through Tate's Ram pickup in the driveway in front of a small audience of local boys on bicycles who'd gathered to watch from across the street. One agent working the truck shook his head at Gerard, indicating the truck held nothing so far.

Then the first newspeople arrived from two TV stations. Crews hoisted cameras onto shoulders, aiming them at Tate's townhome as Gerard, the back of his FBI jacket turned to them for a strong visual, moved into the garage and closed the door.

The garage was spacious and neat, with walls painted battleship gray and a polished concrete floor. Storage shelves stood along the right wall. They were jammed with cardboard boxes and plastic tubs. The opposite wall held shovels, brooms, a ladder and a coiled hose.

A workbench stood at one end with a big red metal toolbox on the counter; the wall above it held power tools, boxes of supplies.

"Anything?" Gerard said to the agents searching.

"Nothing yet. Wait, hold on!"

At that point an agent at the workbench who had been searching worn, torn cardboard boxes kept under the bench stopped and stared into one.

"Hey, Gerard, over here, look at this!"

Gerard joined the agent and when he saw what they'd found in the box under the bench his pulse kicked up.

He reached for his phone to call Malko.

43

River Ridge, Illinois

As the door to the interview room opened, Roy Tate downed the last of his tepid coffee, crushed the foam cup and dropped it in the trash can next to the table.

Malko had returned. He dragged a chair to Tate's side of the table and sat in it, invading his space.

"You need to start telling the truth," Malko said.

Tate eyeballed him with icy calm.

Malko never lost sight of the fact that this man had been tortured by enemy forces, had witnessed decapitations and was not easily intimidated.

He was prepared for the challenge. A second agent sat at the table with a file folder, a new one.

"We've executed search warrants on your home, your truck," Malko said. "Things have taken a turn."

Tate stuck out his bottom lip, nodding as if amused.

"Consequently we've got a number of critical points of concern, Roy."

"Do you."

"You told us that you'd only met the Hudsons once and that you've had no relationship or contact with them since. We've seen footage that shows you lied to us, especially about your relationship with Faith."

Tate shrugged as Malko continued.

"A witness places you at the Hudson residence, either visiting or lurking."

Tate said nothing and Malko let a moment pass. "You have expertise in security at the fairgrounds and with Ultra-Fun Amusement Corp."

Tate scratched his nose.

"You can't adequately explain why you were at the fairgrounds around the time Gage Hudson vanished, giving you a window of opportunity to commit the crime."

Tate stared at his hands.

Malko stood and moved behind him, leaning into Tate's ear.

"Roy, we're starting to connect the dots and we're seeing a line that points straight to you."

The accusation hung in the air for a long, tense moment.

"Before you respond, you'd better think carefully, because as I've told you, things have taken a turn. Your situation is now a whole lot worse than it was when we started."

Tate stroked his chin. "I met Faith Hudson at the mall by chance," he said. "We just bumped into each other and she asked me how things were going. She said she'd lost friends in Iraq and was supportive."

"Really, a woman you'd only met once, and just happened to bump into at the mall, is going this deep into conversation with a man who's practically a stranger? You want me to swallow that one?"

"That's what happened."

"Then you show up at the fairgrounds when her son is missing?"

"I saw the alert on social media and since I used to work there I hurried down to offer help. Things seemed to be well in hand so I hung back."

"Never approached Cal or Faith to offer sympathy or support?"

"I stayed out of the way."

"All this for a family you told us that you didn't know and had no relationship with? You know what that's called, Roy?"

Tate said nothing.

"That's called changing your story." Malko slammed his palm hard on the table next to Tate. "Stop the bullshit and tell us where Gage Hudson is!"

Malko nodded to the agent sitting across the table to slide the folder to Tate so he could see the contents.

"These," Malko said, "are pictures of a chain and lock we found in your garage. The serial numbers match the chain and lock purchased by Cal Hudson at Emerson Plaza, where we found Gage Hudson's shoe in the Dumpster out back."

Tate stared at the photos.

"Now, how did these items end up in your possession?"

Tate said nothing.

"You know we're going to have these items analyzed for trace, for DNA, for blood, hair. We're not done yet. We're still going through your house and truck for trace, too. You know the drill, Roy."

Tate's Adam's apple rose and fell as he swallowed.

"Are you ready to stop the lies and tell us about your involvement in the disappearance of Gage Hudson?"

Tate shuffled through the photos, thinking, not speaking.

"Who else is involved, Roy? Who are you protecting?"

Tate didn't respond.

"Is it Faith? Cal? Both of them? Is it Beth Gibson?"

Tate didn't answer.

"What did you do with Gage Hudson?"

Tate kept staring at the photos.

"The facts are piling up against you. Now is your chance to unburden yourself, to come clean, Roy."

Tate slid the photos back into the folder.

"I want to exercise my right to an attorney."

44

At the time Roy Tate requested an attorney, Faith Hudson was home alone slipping into a dark, bottomless chasm.

She stared blankly at the TV news, doing all she could to hang on to herself after the call by the disturbed woman who'd claimed to have Gage. Any hope the call had given Faith had melted away and nothing new had emerged in the search for him.

Now, she feared he may never be found, that he was hurt.

Or worse.

Her mind burned with scenarios of Gage suffering, crying out for her, overwhelming her with helplessness as she struggled to keep hope alive.

Her battle was made harder since Cal had gone to help the FBI scour his stories for leads hours ago, leaving their home dripping with mistrust in the wake of their argument following their polygraphs. Faith pushed herself to get past the pain of the accusations rising between her and Cal over Gage's disappearance.

But she couldn't escape feeling that something was going on.

Again, she tried calling and texting Cal but he didn't respond.

Why won't he answer me? What's taking so long? What could he be telling the FBI? Did they discover something about Gage? About Cal? Or me?

What's happening to us? Why do we suspect each other?

Faith suddenly remembered how she and Cal had been watching a movie about a fugitive. He had criticized the movie's hero's decisions, and boasted that he could do a much better job—that if he needed to, he could disappear, create a new identity and never be found.

Sure, he was only joking then, but Faith believed that if Cal wanted to vanish "off the grid" as he'd teased, he *could* do it. And now it didn't seem so much of a joke.

What if he'd planned to leave me and take Gage?

No, she had to stop thinking like that.

Faith looked around the room, worry enveloping her.

She reached into her pocket for the rosary Pam Huppkey had given her and traced her fingers over the beads, the crucifix, the Madonna and Child. As she closed her eyes and whispered a prayer the doorbell sounded, pulling her from her anguish.

It was Samantha Clark, her neighbor.

"I dropped by to see how you're doing and if there's anything I can do?"

Wary of the patrol cars around her home and

possible news cameras, Faith hurried Sam inside, closed the door, then broke down in her arms.

"I'm losing my mind!"

"Oh, sweetie, it's okay," Sam said, hugging Faith, helping her to the sofa. "Are you all alone? Where's Cal?"

"He's with the FBI, going over his old news stories."

"Why?"

"For any threats, any potential retribution that could lead to Gage."

"Are there any breaks at all?" Sam passed Faith a tissue box.

"A few hours ago, this woman called the *Star-News*, they patched her to Cal. She said she had Gage."

"Oh, dear God!" Sam's hand flew to her mouth. "What happened?"

"She was a disturbed person. The call was nothing. It was a false alarm." Faith sobbed. "I don't know about anything anymore."

Sam rubbed Faith's arms. "You've got to stay strong, honey." She looked around. "How did you come to be left alone here?"

"I guess everyone's at the community hall, or searching, or getting on with their own lives."

"No, that's not right. One of us should be here with you at all times. You're not going through this alone, okay?"

Faith nodded, dabbing her eyes with the tissue. "Sam, you know the FBI made Cal and me take polygraph exams, and the questions they asked were horrible. They practically accused us of abducting Gage and now I don't know what to believe or trust. I'm losing my mind."

"No, you're not. You're going through hell. Have you eaten anything? Have you slept?"

"No, how can I? How can I do anything when my little boy's out there and I don't know if he's hurt, if he's alive, or…"

"Shh, shh, you've got to eat something and you need to rest."

Sam got Faith to take some tea and chicken noodle soup with crackers but she was unable to sleep. After eating she just sat at the table, kneading the rosary.

"I'm being punished for being a terrible mother," Faith said, tears brimming. "I should've been watching over him."

"Faith, you've got to stop talking like this and stop blaming yourself."

"I'm a horrible person. I've done terrible things. I've failed at being a good person… I just—"

"Faith, you're in shock, you're facing the worst anyone could face. Feeling guilty is normal. Please, stop beating yourself up."

Faith thrust her face into her hands and fought to compose herself.

"I don't want to stay here, Sam." She grabbed her phone. "Let's go to the community hall."

They took Samantha's car.

River Ridge police made no secret of having a patrol car follow her.

The hall was a mile away. It was a restored World War Two–era stucco building with more than two dozen vehicles parked in the lot. Inside, the walls were covered with enlarged photos of Gage, huge maps of River Ridge with colored search zones and log-in sheets. In the center, folding tables had been arranged in a horseshoe pattern where some forty people were at work, poring over maps, studying data on computers, talking on phones.

Volunteers were making and distributing flyers; search teams were being dispatched while others returned. Everyone took a moment to embrace Faith and offer words of support. Her employer had put up the reward money and had arranged for a website and app aimed at finding Gage; other volunteers were helping to widen the search into other areas of metro Chicago.

Faith left Sam and moved through the hall, drawing comfort from the effort, thanking each person who talked to her, noticing that Pam Huppkey, working alone at a separate table, had glanced at her, then quickly looked away.

What was that about?

One white-haired woman in a turquoise tracksuit approached Faith. Her glasses hung from a chain and she slid her phone into her pocket before taking Faith's hands in hers, which were vein-webbed and wrinkled, yet strong and warm.

"I'm with the Golden Grannies Gang," she said. "We're helping search everywhere for Gage. Don't you worry, dear, because I know in my heart that we're going to find your son."

"I can't thank you enough." Faith smiled before her attention went back to Pam.

She was wearing a hoodie and jeans and her trademark hoop earrings and bracelets. Their eyes met but only briefly. Faith nodded to Pam but Pam had failed to acknowledge her, instead going back to her work reviewing and crossing off names on what looked like address lists.

Faith went to her.

"Oh, Faith," Pam said, feigning casualness. "Is there any news?"

"No, nothing." Faith touched Pam's arm. "Thank you, for all you've done, for all you're doing. I appreciate this from the bottom of my heart."

"You don't have to thank me." Pam concentrated on her address lists. "We're all praying for Gage to come home."

"Thank you for giving me this rosary."

Pam nodded weakly without making direct eye contact.

"Is there something wrong?" Faith asked.

Pam lifted her head but didn't answer. She was looking over Faith's shoulder at what was happening behind her. Faith's face creased with puzzlement and she followed Pam's gaze, turning to see that two uniformed officers had entered the hall and were talking to volunteers who were nodding and pointing to Faith.

The officers approached Faith and Pam quickly, their portable radios crackling with dispatches.

"Excuse us, Mrs. Hudson?"

"Yes?"

"We need you to come with us, now."

Faith's stomach clenched. "Why? Did you find Gage? What is it?"

The radios continued with their static-filled exchanges as one of the officers lowered his volume. Volunteers had stopped working, conversations halted and heads turned to Faith.

"We don't have any further information. We need to take you to headquarters, though. Please come with us."

"But wait! What's this about?"

"Ma'am, please. We need to go."

One officer reached for Faith's arm, his radio was still squawking; but before he could turn it down it released a clear transmission. "FBI says no handcuffs. Copy?"

"Fourteen-thirty, copy," the officer said into his shoulder microphone. Then to Faith, he said, "Ma'am, let's go. Now."

As they led her away, Faith looked back at Pam, who'd cupped her hands to her face.

"Will someone tell me what's happening?" Faith said.

The reference to handcuffs had rippled through the hall with people staring at Faith in disbelief, including a student intern from the *Chicago Sun-Times*, there to do a feature on volunteers searching for Gage.

The intern held up her phone, recording Faith

being escorted by the officers, then immediately sent it to her editors with a message.

A *Sun-Times* exclusive—looks like River Ridge police just arrested Faith Hudson.

45

Is it all over?

Is this how they're going to tell us about Gage?

Faith saw nothing beyond the squad car windows.

It was getting late and the neighborhoods were a teary blur during the drive to headquarters. The officers had refused to answer her questions, so she stopped asking them, squeezing the rosary as if it were her lifeline. The blood rush drumming in her ears had muted the sounds around her.

She was numb in the elevator as it ascended to the same fourth floor where detectives and FBI agents paused to look at her as she was taken through it.

Where was Cal? He'd never answered her calls or messages from the car. Did they find something with one of his stories?

Something was wrong; she felt it.

The officers escorted her down the hall toward the interview rooms. As they neared Interview

Room 402, she saw that the door was open and gasped.

Cal was in a chair at the table.

She couldn't see the detectives—it looked like they'd taken a break from questioning him.

His gaze met hers in the instant she passed by.

"Faith! Did they find Gage? What's going on?"

"I don't know," she called back as the officers kept her moving.

Across the hall, the door was also open to Interview Room 403, where she had been questioned previously. As she passed it she looked inside and her eyes widened.

Roy Tate stared at her from a chair at the table.

He looked at her in silence as she walked by.

Her mind was reeling as the officers led her into Interview Room 404, where Malko waited at the table with a woman in a business suit. Her hair was cut in a short, neat bob.

"Hello, Faith." Malko and the woman stood while the officers patted Faith down and searched her before leaving, closing the door behind them. "This is Agent Sue Marsh. Please, sit down."

"Why bring me here like this? Did you find Gage?"

Malko stared at her for a long, cold moment. "No, unfortunately, but our investigation is ongoing."

"You keep telling me that. Why did you bring me here when you have nothing new to tell me?"

Malko continued staring at Faith, his eyes devoid of emotion.

"I can tell you this—you have the right to remain silent."

Faith was stunned as Malko continued.

"Anything you say can and will be used against you in a court of law. You have the right to an attorney. If you cannot afford an attorney, one will be provided for you. Do you understand these rights?"

Faith was frozen in place.

"Do you understand these rights, Faith?"

She nodded.

"And with these rights in mind, do you wish to speak to me?"

Faith's mind swirled with confusion and fear. Cal and Roy Tate were down the hall in interview rooms. She had no idea what they'd told investigators, no idea what was happening.

Had they wanted her to see them? Was it some kind of tactic?

"I don't understand." Her voice quavered. "Am I being charged with something?"

"No," Malko said. "We have questions based on new information and we need your help with the answers so we can determine what happened to your son. You want to help us find Gage, don't you, Faith?"

Her chin crumpled, her eyes stung.

"With all my heart."

"Good. So, do we proceed? Or do you want a lawyer, which means we stop everything?"

"Tell me what's happened. What have you learned?"

"Faith." Malko stared at her. "Are you waiving your right to an attorney?"

She swallowed and thought carefully, then began nodding. "Yes, I am. I want you to tell me what you know, right now."

"First, sign the rights waiver." Malko nodded to Marsh, who slid the sheet and a pen to Faith. She signed it with urgency.

"Is my son dead?" Her voice broke. "You tell me right now if Gage is dead!"

"We have no evidence to suggest that, Faith, and until such time we're proceeding under the presumption that he's alive but missing."

Faith exhaled slowly.

"I'm sure you've deduced that we've been talking to your husband and Roy Tate," Malko said.

"You wanted me to see them, didn't you?"

"Why do you think you're here?"

"You said you have new information."

Malko tapped one of several files on the desk. "We have the results of your polygraph and our polygraphist, who's been proven to be correct in just about every one of his cases, has concluded that you've been untruthful. That you've lied to us, Faith."

She blinked several times.

"There are things you're not telling us." Malko unbuttoned his collar and loosened his tie. "What's your relationship with Roy Tate?"

Faith didn't answer.

Agent Marsh began placing the Oak Brook mall

security photos on the table showing Faith with Tate.

"We reviewed all of your credit card and bank card records," Malko said. "We've studied all of the mall's security cameras. Seems the only thing you bought was lunch and time with Roy Tate."

Faith stared at her hands as if reading the lines raked across her palms. She began twisting her wedding and engagement rings. Malko stood and leaned over the table, drawing his face to hers.

"We need the truth," he said. "Time is running out."

Faith's stomach writhed and the walls came to life, moving toward her, offering no escape. The room began spinning, spitting up images of Gage, the insane butcher, the burning witch, the lunatic with the chain saw. Faith saw bloodied, twitching limbs. Lights pulsated, music hammered at her brain, then she saw herself in her wedding gown at the altar with Cal.

"You can't hold on to the lies any longer." Malko raised his voice.

His words cut into her with surgical precision and the wound ran deep. The truth clawed at her, forcing her to steel herself. She raised her head to meet Malko's gaze as she admitted the truth for the first time.

"I was having an affair with Roy Tate."

Malko stared at her for a long victorious moment, assessing her in a new light as he slowly pulled back.

Faith covered her face with her hand and sobbed. Agent Marsh slid the tissue box toward her.

"Why didn't you tell us this at the outset?" Malko asked.

"Because it was my life and had nothing to do with Gage."

Malko's fist came down hard on the table. "Wrong, Faith. It has everything to do with Gage."

46

Faith's eyes were iridescent with tears as her last moments with Gage pierced her memory.

How she reached for his hand, how he shook hers away.

"I'm okay, Mom! I'm not a baby!"

She should've held on to him…she should've…

She was a horrible mother for not watching over him and now she was revealed to be a failure as a wife. Faith's skin tingled with shame as Malko and Marsh stared at her for what she was: a lying, cheating adulteress.

Yes, she'd had her reasons for being unfaithful, and her suspicions about Cal, but that had been before the mounting horrors she was facing; now, her fractured life—what was left of it—had been torn to pieces.

"Does Cal know about you and Tate?" Malko asked.

Her face bunched up and she groaned for air. "God, no, I never told him. Did you tell him?"

Malko didn't answer.

"Did you tell Cal?" Faith repeated. "Are you using this against me somehow?"

Malko didn't answer, letting the uncertainty torment her before moving on with new questions.

"Tell us how your affair with Tate happened."

Faith twisted a tissue in her hands.

"I met him when Cal and I went to a big press and police party, maybe six months ago. He seemed nice."

"How did you meet afterward?"

"Not long after the party he called me at my office. He said he was in my building on business and invited me to coffee. At first I thought it odd, kind of forward, but I was flattered. I agreed to meet him."

"You were attracted to him?"

"Yes. He was charming, handsome and a good listener. We talked. He casually suggested that we should meet again. I was going through a bad period with Cal, my life was whirling... I agreed."

"Then what?"

"We met in a park, we talked, we connected and we kept meeting and talking, agreeing that we'd keep our situation secret."

"And things progressed and you became intimate?"

Faith gave him a tearful nod.

"What about Cal? Do you think he suspected anything?"

"No, he was barely home to notice. Cal was married to his job. That was part of the problem. He completely checked out. I think it was one of his stories, something happened with him. He changed."

"Which story?"

"I'm not sure which one." Faith shook her head.

"Do you think he got something wrong?"

"I don't know. I'm not sure. He never talked to me, no matter how much I tried."

"What happened to him?"

"He withdrew, like he was carrying something dark inside. It got worse when the layoffs started and the rumors flew of even more looming job cuts at the *Star-News*."

"So your marriage was not strong and you were not happy, like you told us earlier. In truth, it was strained, it was in trouble?"

Faith blinked several times as she nodded.

"He was never home. I was doing everything and I felt completely alone. I told you, Cal was married to his job. He worked closely with other women at the paper—vibrant, exciting, attractive women."

"Did you suspect he was unfaithful?"

"I had fears, suspicions. I'd seen how some of the reporters touched him—it was intimate. He made me feel alone and I hated him for it."

"So you looked outside your marriage?"

"I felt invisible until Roy came along. He was alone. I was alone." She stopped, tears rolling down her face, and stared at the cinder-block walls. "We found each other and things just fit for both of us. It felt good and it helped for a while. Roy was like medicine I needed."

Malko let a few beats pass while he stared at her. "You can see how this looks, Faith."

"What're you getting at?"

"Let's look at some facts. You lied to us about being happy in your marriage. You chose to have an affair with a man who is an expert at secrets and helping people disappear."

"I don't know what you're driving at. I broke it off with Roy." She indicated the photos from the mall. "That's what the Oak Brook meeting was about. I ended it with him there."

"How did he take it?"

"He was angry. He thought the relationship would lead to something more. He thought it would help him with his own issues."

"What issues?"

"The war. He was dealing with much more stress from what he'd experienced than anyone knew. And there was his divorce. His daughter wouldn't connect with him. In many ways he was lost."

"But you were on the brink of asking Cal for a separation. Our review of your calls and emails shows that you'd consulted a divorce lawyer. You just admitted you hated your husband."

"I know but—"

"Our review of your personal bank accounts shows that months before your son vanished, you withdrew nearly six thousand dollars in cash. It was from your account so Cal wouldn't have known about it. That amount is well under ten thousand, the threshold for which the bank would have to file a CTR, a currency transaction report on suspicious activity. Still, six thousand in cash comes in handy if you're planning something that needs seed money, doesn't it?"

"My God, that was for a bathroom renovation. The contractor wanted cash before he canceled on us. I got a refund."

"We've got no record of the money going back into the account," Malko said. "Let's look at some other factors. What's your relationship with Alma McCain and Sidney Griner?"

"I've never heard those names."

"They were working at the Chambers when you reported Gage missing. Griner was on the chutes, McCain was inside on the control board. You talked to them."

Faith thought for a moment. "Then that's all I know of them."

"They may have known Tate. I'm sure you're aware that he was a former security consultant for the River Ridge Fairgrounds."

Faith stared at Malko, then Marsh and back. "What are you driving at?"

"Given what we now know," Malko said, "the possibility that a stranger took Gage at random is growing more and more unlikely."

"What are you insinuating?"

"We think you needed Roy Tate for more than attention and affection."

"What?"

"We think you were somehow involved in Gage's disappearance."

"That's crazy!"

"Is it?" Malko nodded to Marsh, who set down more photographs. "Then why did we find the lock and chain that Cal bought at Roy Tate's residence with your fingerprints, Tate's fingerprints and Gage's DNA all over them?"

Faith gasped. "Oh God—is Gage dead? What happened?"

"You tell us." Malko stood. "You were there when Cal bought the chain. You were sobbing in the car. We know why he bought it but it wasn't needed. What happened to it after that is a mystery, other than that we found it in Tate's possession with your prints all over it. We don't know the details, Faith, you do."

"I don't know how it got there, but none of this makes any sense. I'm telling you I broke it off with Roy! I couldn't go on. It's true that I was contemplating separation, but for Gage's sake and for my sake I needed to work things out with Cal. We would start talking about our problems but he wasn't there, mentally—it was like he'd checked out of our relationship. He spent more time at work. As painful as that was, I was willing to do whatever it took because I believed we needed to save our marriage, to keep our family together. But as much as I tried with Cal, even after ending it with Roy, it was looking more and more futile. I was so torn on what to do."

"Stop lying to us, Faith. You had an affair with a man who is expert at tracking people and helping them disappear. A man who was also expert at security for the fairgrounds and the midway attractions. A man who by your own admission was desperate to start a new life with you!

"And then we find Gage's shoe in the Dumpster where Cal bought the lock and chain that we later find at Tate's, with your and your son's trace evidence on it! When are you going to start telling us what you did and who helped you to do it?"

Faith felt the room spinning, thrust her face into her hands and sobbed.

Malko and Marsh remained silent as her gasps bounced off the cold walls and her shoulders shook.

A long moment passed, broken by a soft knock at the door.

An FBI agent stuck his head in, ready to face Malko's wrath for the interruption.

"Something's come up," the agent said.

47

In the hall outside the interview room Malko and Marsh looked at the images the agent was showing them on his phone.

"These just came in, from the warrants."

Malko's lower jaw tightened as he studied the photos. This was a break, another big piece. The agent handed him a folder with hard-copy prints of the images and notes.

"And they're expediting processing for trace and DNA analysis."

Malko tapped the folder in his hand, thinking and looking at the doors of the interview rooms. All the players were here—Cal, Faith and Tate.

Marsh studied a new message on her phone and nodded to the door. "Tate's got his lawyer in there with him now, Tibor."

"All right," Malko said. "Let's do this. We'll start with Tate."

They entered the room. A man in a dark suit with glasses and a neatly trimmed beard halted his muted conversation with Tate. Their attention went to the agents, prompting the man in the suit to stand.

"Mitchell Slotter, attorney for Mr. Tate. And you are?"

"Agents Tibor Malko and Sue Marsh."

They sat. Slotter moved his briefcase to the floor beside the table and consulted his tablet.

"I acknowledge Mr. Tate is still under the Miranda caution and take this time to inform the FBI that my client states that he has no involvement in the disappearance of Gage Hudson."

Malko said nothing as the lawyer continued.

"Mr. Tate is prepared to cooperate with the investigation by answering your questions with me present to advise. He will also agree to submit to a polygraph examination in my presence."

Marsh's eyebrows rose slightly.

"Thank you," Malko said, then looked directly at Tate. "So, Roy, you were banging Faith Hudson?"

Slotter's jaw dropped.

"This is an outrageous question," he said, "and I fail to see what bearing it has on the case."

Tate had no reaction and said, "We had an intimate relationship."

"And what did you hope that relationship would bring you?"

"Don't answer," Slotter said. "I don't see this as being relevant."

Malko ignored him. "Care to cooperate and answer, Roy?"

"Ever since the boy disappeared, it's been eating

at me," Tate said. "I want my attorney here, but I got nothing to hide."

"That's wonderful."

"I'll answer any question you've got with the truth."

"Terrific, so what did you hope to get out of a relationship with Faith?"

"I thought we had a future together. She was my chance to start a new life. I was living in a dark place. I was messed up from the war, from my divorce."

"You were counting on Faith Hudson to help you climb out of your personal hell?"

"You could say that," Tate said. "I had strong feelings for her."

"Did you ever meet her son, Gage Hudson?"

"No."

"Did you and Faith ever discuss her leaving Cal and getting custody of Gage? Was that a factor in your hope for the relationship, a part of the plan, Roy?"

"It was discussed. I said I'd do whatever she wanted me to do to help her get on with her life."

"So you felt you were on track to have a new life with Faith and Gage, a new life that you desperately needed?"

"Yes."

"Things were looking up for you—you had hope, isn't that true?"

"Yes, that's true."

"Until Faith had a change of heart, realizing that she wanted to stay in her marriage and work things out. So she broke it off with you. She took away that hope, leaving you alone to deal with your issues, didn't she?"

Tate swallowed hard and said nothing.

"It hurt when she ended it, didn't it, Roy?"

Tate glared at Malko, his eyes burning at him for ripping open his wounds. "It hurt."

"I'm sure," Malko continued. "Of all the horrors and pain you've endured, this was another knife in your heart, wasn't it?"

"It hurt, that's the truth. What do you want me to say?"

"You were angry at Faith for hurting you, for giving you hope, then taking it away?"

"I was angry."

"Who could blame you, Roy? All your adult life you gave it your all and still people wanted to hurt you. You gave everything to your country and you were captured and tortured. You came home and your wife couldn't understand and divorced you. You find Faith, a woman alone, like you, and she helps pull you out of your abyss, then—" Malko suddenly smacked his hands together with a loud crack "—that bitch lets go of the rope and you fall back into hell."

Tate's eyes brimmed with tears.

"Did you want to hurt her, Roy? Did you entertain getting back at her?"

"I advise you not to answer," Slotter said.

"I was hurting," Tate said.

"Yes, you were hurting badly and then two

months after Faith Hudson destroys your world, her son disappears."

Malko let that statement hang in the air before resuming.

"And we find that you're an expert in keeping secrets and helping people disappear, a person with knowledge and expertise in security at the fairgrounds and with the midway attractions. We find that you were at the location where Gage Hudson disappeared within the time frame he disappeared. We find a lock and chain that Cal bought in your residence with Gage's DNA and your fingerprints on it. All the dots are connecting."

Marsh set out the photos again.

"You've seen these, Roy. We'll make copies for Mitchell."

Slotter studied them, then said, "This is weak evidence wrapped in a lot of circumstance, Agent Malko."

"I was not involved," Tate said.

"How did the lock and chain get to your garage?"

Tate took in a long breath and let it out slowly.

"After Faith ended it, I went to her home when I knew she'd be alone to ask her to reconsider. I told her that she was just nervous about starting a new chapter and that I would help her get custody, help her move, help her get on with her life, whatever she needed.

"I told her that I needed her, that she filled a painful void and with her I felt whole again. I needed her to hang on to my sanity so I could start over. But she was afraid and very uneasy that I'd shown up at her home, fearful Cal, Gage or a neighbor might come upon me being there."

"What was the outcome and how does it relate to the lock and chain?"

"Faith rejected me again, only this time she was colder about it. It was as if her being at home had somehow made her a different person than when we were alone together. I felt like she was pushing me over the edge of the earth. I was angry. When I left I called her a selfish, whoring bitch."

"And the lock and chain?"

"I went out through the garage. I wanted to put my fist through something, and I know this will sound stupid, but that day I needed to buy a chain—I was going to help a friend tow a car— so when I saw the lock and chain in the garage I stole it on my way out. I thought about using it to trash Faith's car, but instead I just left. It was hanging from a bicycle, likely Gage's, which is why it might've had his DNA. Maybe he scraped a knuckle and bled on it, how would I know?"

"Let me get this straight. You're reeling with anger, you want to hit something…so you stole the chain from the garage?"

"Yes."

"Your accounting for the chain seems weak."

"It's true. I just grabbed the damned thing. I was going to buy one, so hell, I thought, I'll just take this. It was a stupid spur-of-the-moment impulse."

"Sounds like a far-fetched story you're feeding us on how the chain got to your place."

"It's the truth. And the reason I went to the fairgrounds is because I saw the alert and went down to see what I could do to help, behind the scenes, given that I'd worked there and I knew Faith."

"Quite a tale, Roy," Malko said. "Do you know what Gage was wearing when he disappeared?"

Tate scratched his stubble thoughtfully.

"From the description issued, I think a Cubs T-shirt, shorts, sneakers."

"And a Cubs ball cap."

"Right, a ball cap."

"Like this one." Malko removed new photos from the folder, setting them before Tate. "We found this in a box marked Goodwill, wrapped in a jacket, as if someone had intended to hide it." Malko tapped the photos. "This is exactly like the blue, youth-size adjustable cap that Gage was wearing when he disappeared. How did you obtain this hat, Roy?"

Surprise and what seemed like dismay dawned on Tate's face but he said nothing.

"You're not going to tell us how the cap got there?" Malko asked.

"Are you telling me that's Gage's cap?" Tate said.

"We're testing it for DNA, Roy."

"You won't find any."

Malko stood and leaned over the desk and closer to Tate.

"You were prepared to help Faith disappear with Gage, but when she rejected you, you exacted vengeance, didn't you?"

Malko met Tate's stare but said nothing.

"Or is the breakup just a story you and Faith worked out to cover for the plan to abduct her son and disappear together?"

Tate continued staring at Malko.

"Ultra-Fun's records show that Sidney Griner and Alma McCain were employees during the period you were a security consultant."

"So?"

"They were working in key areas of the Chambers when the Hudsons reported Gage missing. It's possible that you could've arranged for them to help you, or someone entered and left the Chambers with Gage unseen and unrecorded."

Tate shook his head. "I'm not involved."

Malko's gaze telegraphed strong doubts as he continued.

"Is Beth Gibson involved?"

Tate said nothing as Malko pulled in even closer and whispered. "Now's the time to tell us—where's Gage Hudson, Roy?"

48

Cal waited alone in Interview Room 402, his mind boiling with confusion and fear.

Why did Malko and Marsh pull him away from the other agents to wait here for more questions?

Something big was unfolding around him, but no one would tell him a damned thing. They'd left him to stare at the cinder-block walls, his thoughts jumping from having seen a man who was vaguely familiar taken by in handcuffs, to seeing Faith being escorted past his room.

Why did they bring them in? Why were they keeping Cal here and not letting him talk to Faith? There must be a break in the case.

Cal's attempt to deduce what that break might be was futile and as minutes swept by his focus veered to the FBI's scrutiny of some of his darkest stories. He analyzed the reason for his reaction to the ones they'd cited.

Maybe he'd appeared too quick to dismiss them but he couldn't let them dig into those stories—one of them in particular. And if they found out who

Beth Gibson was, and how she was connected, he would be finished. Why was she haunting him and raising the specter of what they did? It had nothing to do with Gage.

Cal paused, thinking over that last assertion. His breathing quickened with a chilling fear.

That story can't possibly be tied to Gage. No, there's no chance. How could it be? Cal's anxiety careened around the stark, cold room, taking him back to the man in handcuffs. Who was that guy? What did he have to do with the case?

The door opened with Malko and Marsh entering the room.

"Why's Faith here? Can I talk to her?" Cal said.

He tried reading their sober faces as they positioned chairs and sat.

"There've been developments," Malko said.

"Is it Gage? Did you find him?"

"No."

"Where's Faith? I want to talk to her."

"We'll get to her," Malko said. "First, you need to start telling us the truth."

"What do you mean?"

"You and Faith failed your polygraphs."

Cal's face reddened. "Come on. We know how reliable those things are," he said.

"Our guy's track record is nearly perfect, so no more bullshit, Cal." Malko's eyes flicked to Marsh, who was working on her phone. "We want you to look at something."

Marsh cued up a video clip, which she turned

to Cal. It showed the man Cal had seen earlier in cuffs. He was sitting alone in an interview room.

"Do you know who this is, Cal?"

"He looks familiar. I think I met him…it was at the Christmas party last year, that's it. I think he's a cop and his name is Tucker or Taylor."

"Tate. Roy Tate."

"Yes, that's it," Cal said. "So what's he got to do with anything?"

"What can you tell us about him?"

"Not much. I only vaguely remember meeting him at a police and press party. I never worked with him. Wait. Roy Tate. Yeah, now that I remember, he's with the US Marshals Service. I don't really know the guy. Why're you asking me?"

"Are you sure that's all you can tell us?"

"Yes, why?"

A long moment passed, then Malko leaned forward and looked Cal in the eye.

"Your wife's been having an affair with him."

Cal's attention shot from Malko to Marsh and back as if this were a sick joke.

"Is this some sort of strategy?" he said.

"No."

"Faith and I have had serious problems but this is a lie."

"It's the truth. She's admitted it to us."

"I don't believe you. It's some kind of mind game you're playing, part of a cruel plan."

Marsh worked her phone, calling up another video clip for Cal. In this one Faith was in tears confessing to the cinder-block walls.

"I was having an affair with Roy Tate... I felt invisible until Roy came along. He was alone. I was alone...we found each other and things just fit for both of us. It felt good and it helped for a while. Roy was like medicine I needed..."

Cal felt the room spin. Faith's admission was like a sledgehammer to his gut.

It couldn't be true.

The agents allowed him time as he sat there staring at nothing, his heart breaking under the crushing devastation.

How could he be so stupid? Of course it was true. Faith wanted a separation; she'd circled an ad for a divorce lawyer...she was ready to give up on them.

Absorbing the blow, Cal's mind retreated over time to when he'd first met Faith, to their first date, falling in love, their wedding day, their honeymoon and Gage's birth, Gage's childhood, to his disappearance, to this moment—this torment.

How could she betray him? Betray Gage? How could she do this?

With his life in flames Cal battled to process the revelation. Faith's words echoed in his soul, spearing him again and again with the truth: he was not entirely blameless. He'd sown the seeds for this. He was never there for Faith because he'd become consumed with work, with setting things right to relieve the guilt he felt over things he'd done...

"Cal?" Malko pulled him from his thoughts. "Do you accept that Faith's affair with Tate is a fact?"

Cal took in a long breath, wiped at his tears and nodded.

"Brace yourself, there's more."

"More?"

"It gets worse. We have reason to suspect Faith and Tate are involved in Gage's disappearance."

His heart skipped a beat. "I can't believe this—"

"We found the missing chain and lock, with Gage's DNA and Faith's and Tate's prints on it, in Tate's residence in Rogers Park."

Cal stared at Malko in disbelief.

"We also found a ball cap identical to Gage's hidden there, as well, that we are currently processing for DNA."

Cal started shaking his head.

"Tate worked with the US Marshals Witness Security Program. He's an expert at ensuring people disappear. He also worked with the River Ridge Fairgrounds as a security consultant. They may have had others assist them."

Cal said nothing.

"Is there anything you know that might help us?"

"I—I don't know anything…this is too much…" He stopped. "What about the carnies?"

"We're looking hard at them. Is it possible this Beth Gibson is involved?"

Cal swallowed hard, shook his head.

"I doubt it. I told you—she's a stranger who called to wish us well."

"The circumstances under which she called are very suspect, Cal. We're not ruling out any other possibilities but at this point we think Faith and Tate are behind your son's disappearance."

Dragging both shaking hands over his face Cal withdrew into his thoughts and fears, struggling against a current of shock and disbelief.

It made no sense. Why would Faith do such a thing? She could easily get custody in a divorce. But she's smart, so smart. No, he couldn't believe it—but he'd hurt her, abandoned her, forced her to turn to another man.

But if Faith *did* do this, then there's a good chance Gage was still alive—*he has to be alive.*

Cal shook his head, unable to find a thread of thought.

What if Malko and the FBI have got it all wrong? What if it was someone else? In which case, time was ticking down on Gage's life.

49

Two hours after Malko and Marsh had talked to Cal they'd gathered with other investigators for a call on the case against Faith Hudson and Roy Tate and the potential for charging them with kidnapping.

River Ridge detectives Rachel Price, Leon Lang and Lieutenant Tony Sosa, their supervisor, were with them in the closed-door office for the call.

On the line was Melissa Miller, assistant special agent-in-charge of the FBI's Chicago office, Bennett Boyle with the Cook County State's Attorney, and Earl Luckett with US Attorney for the Northern District of Illinois. Both jurisdictions were involved because no one yet knew where the case would land.

Everyone had read through the report Malko had distributed earlier.

Malko started the call. "I think we're building a solid foundation for a strong case."

"I wouldn't say strong." Boyle could be heard flipping through pages. He was one of the state's most experienced prosecutors. "What's your take, Earl?"

Earl Luckett, a veteran of trials involving violent street gangs, corruption, terrorism and kidnappings, was legendary in Chicago.

"I don't think this is solid enough, Tibor. Where're you headed here?"

"We're looking at the emerging picture. Everything points to Faith Hudson and Roy Tate, her unhappiness in the marriage, her affair, his expertise and the physical evidence."

"You're talking about the lock, the chain and the ball cap?" Boyle asked.

"Yes. It's all very damning."

"How? How you can link the purchase of the lock and chain—and the subsequent discovery—to Faith, Tate or anyone's involvement in Gage's kidnapping?"

"Look at the context. It's where they were bought and where they were found. We've found Tate's prints and Gage's DNA on them. They could've been used to restrain Gage."

"Not really," Luckett said. "They were in the family's possession and Tate admits to stealing them. The prints and DNA are all plausible, defensible."

"Why are you fixated on that lock and chain?" Boyle asked. "What proof is there connecting it to Gage Hudson's disappearance?"

"Again, it's in the context of its purchase, that it was bought at the same strip mall with a Dumpster where we found Gage's shoe."

"But how can you tie the shoe to all of this? You didn't find the chain affixed to the shoe," Boyle said. "The lock and chain are not strong pieces of evidence in my book."

"There's Faith and Tate's affair," Malko said.

"Both admitted to it," Boyle said. "That's not an offense."

"But Faith lied to us about it earlier," Malko said.

"Yes," Boyle said. "That alone is a small piece. You need much more."

"You report finding a ball cap similar to Gage Hudson's in Tate's possession. Where does that stand?" Luckett asked.

"We're still awaiting the DNA analysis."

"So you haven't confirmed the cap is Gage's?" Luckett asked.

"Correct."

"I don't know about what you have so far," Luckett said.

"I'm telling you everything points to Faith Hudson and Tate. He was helping her make a preemptive strike against Cal."

"But they both claim they broke it off," Boyle said. "If so, you then look at Tate making an act of retribution against her. Your theories bounce around."

"The breakup could be a cover story," Malko said.

"Look," Luckett said. "Tate's cooperated, even with his lawyer, and he's agreed to a polygraph. Do you have his results?"

"Not yet, we're in the process of setting it up."

"Your case is not strong enough to sustain charges," Boyle said.

"I agree with Ben," Luckett said. "We sure as hell couldn't go to a grand jury with this. You've got some building blocks but you have not yet removed all reasonable doubt."

"You report that both Faith and Cal Hudson failed polygraphs. Have you ruled out other suspects? Someone from the midway? A stranger? Have you ruled out Cal?" Boyle asked.

"Almost."

"Almost?"

"Everything's pointing to Faith and Tate."

"So he could still be considered a suspect, or anyone else for that matter?" Luckett said.

"If I may," Detective Rachel Price said. "I understand the FBI is still analyzing Cal Hudson's news stories for possible acts of retribution."

"Yes, that's in progress," Malko said.

"As are interviews with fairgrounds and midway workers, along with chasing down a number of tips."

"That's correct. All of those aspects of the investigation are ongoing."

"Well, given the situation I think we should adhere to the advice you gave us all at the outset, Tibor," Price said. "We shouldn't fall victim to tunnel vision. We have to keep an open mind on all theories and, no matter how unlikely, they must all be considered and exhaustively pursued."

"Agreed," Luckett said. "If you're holding anybody I suggest you release them. You don't have a case yet, Tibor. You've got a lot of loose ends but at this stage they really don't add up to much. You need to bring us something solid. This thing is still wide open."

50

Setting flour, eggs and sugar on the counter
alongside the other ingredients, April Kohl kept
an anxious eye on the time and her thirteen-year-
old daughter, Breeana.

When she wasn't on her phone texting, she was
staring out the window of their big kitchen on Wil-
low Breeze Lane in River Ridge.

"What's bothering you, honey? I thought you
wanted to help me with these cupcakes for my
book club. It's getting late and I've got to get going
on them."

"I'm fine, Mom. Sure, I'll help."

"Really? Because for the last few days you've
been pretty quiet. Do you not like going to summer theater class?"

"I'm fine," she said to her phone.

"Because you begged us to enroll you and you
know how much it cost. We can still get a partial
refund if you don't want to go. But your class is
going to perform *Cats* onstage at the end of the
summer and your dad and I—"

"Mom, stop! I like theater class! I don't want to drop out! Okay?"

"Okay."

April wiped her hands on her towel and un-muted the TV above the counter, anticipating the end of the commercials.

"Do you want to break the eggs into the bowl, Bree?"

Face in her phone, Breeana approached the counter like a robot devoid of emotion or inter-est. *Something's going on with her*, April thought.

"Is there anything you want to talk about?"

Breeana offered a weak shrug, which April took as an opening to take things slow, just as the news resumed with a story on Gage Hudson, the boy who'd vanished at the River Ridge Summer Car-nival.

"Oh." April increased the volume.

"Do we have to watch that, Mom?"

"Honey, I've been following this story. I'm just praying they find that little boy safe. He looks like a little sweetheart. My God, it's so sad—his poor parents."

The report showed footage of Gage's picture, then the fair, which was still going on, then the Dumpster where his shoe was found.

"Two eggs, Bree, break two into the bowl."

April sensed her daughter hadn't responded and turned to find her riveted to the news report, then texting and glancing at the TV, as if she was con-veying information about the report as it continued.

"Two eggs, honey. I'll get the milk."

Breeana put her phone down and picked up the first egg as the report showed Cal and Faith Hudson talking to reporters. Then there was footage of police asking for people with information to help.

Breeana's hands shook while tapping the egg on the edge of the glass mixing bowl as the reporter, who was standing in front of the Hudson home, was saying, *"And sources close to the investigation tell us that earlier today the FBI conducted polygraph exams on Cal and Faith Hudson, fueling speculation that they've not been ruled out as suspects in the mysterious disappearance of their son from the attraction known as the Chambers of Dread. We'll show that number for the tip line again on your screen."*

"Bree! Careful, you're missing the bowl."

April paused the TV report, then tore paper towels from the roll, deftly catching the yolk and white before it slimed over the counter along the drawers to the floor.

"Goodness," she said. "Pay attention! Seriously, what's up with you?"

Breeana froze and was on the verge of tears when she reached for her phone but a second later it was seized from her hand. April slapped it to the counter.

"Talk to me, Bree, your mother. Not your friends. I'm right here."

Looking as if she were about to shatter, Breeana backed away from April until she was stopped by a wall. Defeated, she slid down, her top bunching up behind her. She pulled her knees to her chest, tightening into an emotion-charged ball. Sobbing, she choked out the words, "I'm sorry, so sorry!"

"Honey." April lowered herself to the floor. "Sweetheart, what is it?"

"It's something bad, Mom! So bad and it's my fault and I don't know what to do. I want to die, Mom."

"Honey, what is it?"

"Something horrible happened to me and it has to do with that little boy on TV."

51

"Bree, listen to me. Take a deep breath."

April stroked her daughter's hair. Breeana kept her face down, nodding while sobbing.

"Now, honey, take your time and explain everything to me."

April's mind raced with worry at what could be troubling her daughter. And how in God's name could it be related to the missing boy? Breeana could be as dramatic as any teen, but April had never seen her like this. There was a sudden dark, underlying current that frightened her.

Several seconds passed before Breeana raised her head, allowing her mother to dry her tears with the dish towel.

Breeana swallowed hard, her voice quavering as she began.

"On the day that boy went missing…"

"Yes?"

"I didn't go to theater class."

April absorbed the seriousness of the offence—tuition for the class had stretched their budget—but she said nothing.

"Hannah and I skipped it."

"This is Hannah Dawkins, the girl whose parents take drugs?"

"Mom, please! That's just a stupid rumor because her dad used to be in a rock band."

"Okay, sorry. So you and Hannah cut class. What happened?"

"They were painting sets and we didn't want to, so Hannah got them to believe that there was a family emergency, that we had to go but would be right back, and one of the teachers, who I think is only eighteen, believed us. She didn't make us sign out or make any calls or anything."

April bit back on her anger at the school and Hannah. She never liked Hannah, never trusted that girl. She was always looking for trouble.

"Our plan was to go to the fair. It was only a few blocks away."

"The fair?"

"Yes. Hannah had money from her birthday, so we went. We played games, we went on rides. Got food. It was fun. Then we saw the Chambers of Dread and Hannah was, like, 'Oh, I bet it's not *that* scary. Are you too scared to go inside, Bree?' I was a little scared. I'd heard things about it. But I lied and told her I wasn't scared, so we decided to go."

"And Hannah was paying for everything?"

"Yes, so we got in line and, well, you know how Hannah has boobs now, and she likes to show them."

"Yes."

"She was wearing this little top and, well, there's this fat guy on a stool who takes your ticket before you go in. He's got these bushy sideburns, and missing front teeth and ugly tattoos—he's real creepy—and we're waiting in line and he looks at me and says, 'You look scared there, sunshine.' 'Not really,' I told him. Then he looks at Hannah, right at her shirt and her cleavage, and says, 'What about you, sexy? This is the scariest attraction in America, gives people heart attacks! Are you scared?' Hannah tells him, 'Do I look like a baby to you, asshole?' Then he starts laughing, this kind of creepy laugh. 'No,' he says, looking right at her shirt. 'My, my but I can tell *you two* are scared. Don't worry, I'll escort you.' Hannah and I didn't know what he was talking about. We told him we didn't need an escort but he goes, 'It's our policy,' and calls on a radio for another worker guy to take his place and then goes in with us into the haunted house."

April could feel her stomach begin to churn as Breeana continued.

"Well, we just ignored him. Hannah kept telling him to go away but he laughed, said this was part of his job, and he hung around us all the way through. The place was so dark and full of noise, flashing lights and people screaming, we sort of forgot about him. The actors were really good but there were lots of surprises and we got scared a few times. Even though it looked real, we knew it was all fake. It was all fine, nothing really happened with the creepy guy. Until near the end."

"What happened?"

Breeana hugged herself and stared at her knee-caps.

"What happened near the end, Bree?"

"There's a guy with a chain saw who chases you from the graveyard into this big room with a spinning floor that has these curtains that are the exits, which let you out onto these kind of slides. The music is superloud and there's flashing lights and the chain saw guy and it's really confusing and Hannah and I ran the wrong way, right into the creepy guy, then he—"

Breeana drove her palms into her face to wipe her tears.

"Then he what? What did he do, Bree?"

"He ran his hands all over me, Mom! He rubbed and squeezed at my chest and grabbed my privates. I screamed but it was so loud in there—everyone was screaming. I knew it was him because in the flashing lights I saw his side-burns and tattoos and he's laughing and saying, 'You're going the wrong way.'"

April felt her flesh crawl and anger erupt.

"He did the same thing with Hannah, grabbing and rubbing. She screamed and told him to F-off and we ran from him, jumped through the curtains and got away."

April's hands were shaking as she patted Bree-ana's face with the towel.

"We were so scared and so disgusted and ashamed."

"No! Don't be ashamed! This was not your fault."

"We didn't know what to do and we saw this couple asking people about their boy. They couldn't find their son. Then Hannah said to me she thinks she saw the creepy guy go toward them in the spinning room but she's not sure. But we were so scared we left and ran back to class."

"Did you or Hannah tell anybody about this?"

"No. Mom, I was so scared and ashamed and confused because we skipped class and I kinda thought it was my fault and then it's all over the news that boy is missing and Hannah thinks that creepy guy went for him after us and now...now... they found the boy's shoe in a Dumpster and if we told maybe that creepy guy would come for Hannah and me next! Mom, I'm so scared!"

"Shh—take it easy, Bree. It'll be okay, it's going to be okay. I promise."

As April held her distraught daughter in her arms she glanced at the TV. The screen was frozen with the tip line number for anyone with information on Gage Hudson to call.

As April soothed Breeana she eyed her phone.

52

Faith is resplendent in her wedding gown, her smile gloriously brilliant.

And here she is honeymooning in a bikini on the beach at Paradise Island, Bahamas. A few years later she's holding Gage in her arms minutes after his birth, her face radiating joy.

As night fell, Cal bit back on his emotions sitting in the dark, watching home videos on their big flat-screen in the living room. His memories bouncing from their blissful times to Faith's words in a police video.

"I was having an affair with Roy Tate... I felt invisible until Roy came along. He was alone. I was alone...we found each other and things just fit for both of us. It felt good and it helped for a while. Roy was like medicine I needed..."

Her words, her admission, compounded by the FBI's suspicions that she was *actually behind Gage's disappearance with her lover*, had stabbed Cal in the heart, leaving him unsure of anything in his life.

"Cal?" Faith was behind him in the darkness, at the kitchen counter, the light of the TV flickering on her tearstained face. "Cal, I am so sorry."

He didn't respond or even look at her.

"I know it's pathetic to say, but—" her voice broke "—God, I am so sorry."

He never moved.

"Cal, we have to talk."

He was frozen with pain while his mind swirled with a million cliché questions: *Why? How could you? You vowed to be faithful, remember? Do you love him?* But his questions orbited the greater, monolithic wound.

"The FBI says that you and Tate took my son. Is that true, Faith?"

"No."

"Because if it is, I swear, somehow, some way, I'll make sure you both burn in hell."

"Cal, it's not true!"

"Why should I believe you? You're a lying cheating, deceitful whore. You're not fit to be the mother of my son."

"*Our* son, Cal. He'll always be *our* son!"

"*Always be?* What the hell're you talking about? Is he dead?"

"Cal! Stop it!"

Cal continued staring at the TV, shaking his head.

"I don't know you, Faith. You're a stranger to me. I'll sleep in the spare room from now on until we, or I, get Gage back, then we'll deal with all this."

He heard her break down with great gasping sobs but did not move or say anything. Minutes passed before she spoke again.

"I didn't take Gage! You have to believe me. I admit what I did and I know I hurt you. I know the pain I caused but I refuse to take all the blame for what happened to us."

Cal leaned forward and with his elbows on his knees cupped his face with his hands, bracing to accept his role in the fracturing of his marriage.

"You're not so innocent in all of this," she said. "You were never around. Yes, there are pressures at the newspaper. Your industry's under siege with budget tightening and layoffs. I get that, but something happened to you."

"What're you talking about?"

"Something fundamental happened a couple of years ago or so, and you changed. I would ask you if anything was going on but you would never talk to me. You'd stay out till all hours. I think it had to do with a story you were working on."

"What story?"

"One of the big murder stories. I can't remember which one—the Teddie Turco case, the Oakley case, Faustino Avila, Ezili—there were so many. But something happened with one of them and somewhere along the line you withdrew from me, from Gage, from us."

"I was working to save my job."

"It's more than that. You grew distant and you were never home. I was doing everything. I felt alone, discarded. You made me feel like I no longer mattered to you!"

Cal turned to face her.

"And—" Faith was searching for something on her phone "—there's your thing with Chelsey Blake."

"What thing? We talked about this—there is no *thing*."

Faith marched to him and thrust her phone in his face. "Don't you lie to me. I took this at the staff and police party. Remember, I said I wasn't sure I could make it. But I did make it. I was late and I wanted to surprise you. But when I arrived I saw you and Chelsey. I took this video."

The video showed Cal and Chelsey talking in a circle of friends. Their backs were to the camera. Chelsey's hand went slowly, gently, up and down Cal's back and shoulders.

"Faith, there's nothing going on. I can explain that," Cal said.

"Oh, sure you can," Faith snapped. "But you tell me what I'm supposed to think. I see you two at the picnic, then at this party. God, it's so obvious, Cal!"

"Nothing's going on. People were drinking. Someone made a joke that we were like a football team in a huddle. She could've just as easily given me a high five. Faith, Chelsey is, well, she's affectionate. She'd gone through some hard times and we'd worked closely together. Besides, I told you, she left for a job with a news service in Kuwait months ago."

"I know. And Kuwait is only a plane ride away, Cal."

"What's that supposed to mean?"

"Remember how you told me how you could disappear and no one would ever find you? Maybe you and your girlfriend planned this all along, being two investigative reporters."

"What? For chrissakes, I was joking about disappearing—we were watching a movie."

"Maybe you took Gage and were planning to disappear with your girlfriend, Chelsey? And if it's not her, maybe it's this Beth Gibson. You tell me, Cal—did *you* take Gage?"

He got up and left the room, the TV frozen on an image of Cal and Faith dancing at their wedding reception.

They were so happy then.

A portrait of another couple in another time.

The Fourth Day

53

At 6:59 a.m. the next day *Practical Homicide Investigation* was splayed open on the passenger seat of Officer Clayton Burke's patrol car.

He'd been studying the textbook whenever he had a free moment and hoped to cover the section on suspects during his shift today.

Burke had been a River Ridge patrol cop for five years. It was time to put his criminology degree to use. He wanted to take his shot at making detective, then ultimately land a job with the FBI, DEA or ATF.

But that dream was pushed farther away when Burke's request for a special assignment with the multiagency investigation of Gage Hudson's disappearance was never granted.

"Don't fret, you've got plenty of other duties," his supervisor had said.

Still, Burke remained keen and lived for the FBI's briefings on Hudson, devouring every aspect the lead investigators were able to share.

"Be alert," Malko, the lead FBI agent, had

drilled into them. "That seemingly trivial, mundane, inconsequential bit of information you come across could be the key to everything. We're all on this case."

That's why Burke was on guard for anything.

But now, rolling through his zone at the top of his early-morning shift, he needed coffee and wheeled into one of his favorite places, Hart's QuikStop Print and Postal. Mel Hart operated the little family business with the help of his daughter Rhonda, who was easy on the eyes and, as Burke recalled, wasn't dating anyone these days.

The smell of freshly brewed coffee filled the shop and a few early-bird customers were at the copiers or mailboxes when Burke entered.

"Good morning, Clay," Mel called from the counter.

"Hey, Mel, how're things?" Burke poured himself a coffee.

"So-so, you know."

Burke noticed a woman slide her key into the lock of her mailbox, then pull out her letters and flyers.

"You're by your lonesome again," Burke said to Mel. "Where's Rhonda?"

"In Green Bay."

"What's she doing there?"

"Visiting her big sister. No law against that, right?" Mel laughed.

"Well, it ought to be a felony just going to Packer country. Tell her I said hi." Burke sipped his coffee, set two dollars on the table and started for the door when something the woman at the mailboxes said stopped him.

"Darn, Mel. This one's not mine. It's for someone named Cal Hudson and, silly me, I wasn't looking and I opened it."

Burke turned to the woman who was holding a large brown envelope.

"Let me see that, Alice." Mel moved his glasses from his forehead to study it. "Yup, his box is 1212. Darnell missed the slot again."

"Excuse me." Burke approached them. "Mel, is that for Cal Hudson, the father of the missing boy?"

"Oh, yes," Mel said. "It's terrible. Yes, Cal Hudson, the reporter. He rents a box here."

Burke's instincts kicked in.

"Please set the envelope on the counter and don't let anyone else touch it," he said, thinking it could be a possible ransom note or nothing at all. Not wanting to take any chances, he took precautions. "Ma'am, I'm going to need you to stay here awhile."

"Why? I didn't look inside. Am I in trouble?"

"Nothing like that, bear with me, please."

Burke leaned closer. The envelope was addressed to Cal Hudson. Burke's eyebrows climbed slightly. It had some Arabic lettering. Return address was the Global Gulf News Agency in Kuwait City, Kuwait.

"Mel, you're absolutely certain Cal Hudson, the father of the missing boy, rents a box here? Because he lives on the other side of town."

"Yes, Clay. I rented it to him a long time ago."

"How long we talking?"

"A couple of years."

"Has Cal been in to check his mail here since his son went missing?"

"Gosh, no."

"What about his wife?"

"No. She's never been in here. The box is rented to Cal. I remember he said how reporters need a secret postal address."

"Really?"

Studying the envelope, which the woman had opened, Burke was tempted to look at the contents. As he considered what to do he was guided by the FBI agent's words—that a seemingly small bit of information could be the key to everything.

"Mel, have the FBI or any of my people been in here to look at this box, execute a warrant or talk to you about it?"

"No." Mel stuck out his bottom lip and shook his head. "What're you thinking, Clay?"

Burke held up one finger, turned, got on his phone and called headquarters. In seconds he was connected to a River Ridge lead detective on the Hudson case.

"Detective Price, this is Clay Burke. I patrol in Bradfield, Zone Three. This may be nothing, but did you know Cal Hudson has a private PO box across town and he's got an eight-by-eleven letter waiting for him here from a news agency in Kuwait?"

"No, we didn't know that. How'd you find out?"

"It's complicated, but I'm looking at the opened envelope right now."

"What's in it? Is it a ransom?"

"I don't know. I haven't looked inside. We don't have a warrant."

"How did it get open?"

"A woman opened it by accident. It was misplaced in her mail slot."

"Put your gloves on and take a look in case it's a ransom note."

"But we don't have a warrant."

"These are exigent circumstances, the hot pursuit principle."

"Give me a second."

Burke wedged his phone between his shoulder and ear, reached for his utility belt, tugged on his gloves and pulled out the contents, which were pages of government forms and a note.

"Is it a ransom note?"

"No, it looks like a visa and work permit for a job in Kuwait City."

Silence filled the phone.

"Hello, Detective?" Burke asked.

"Wait. What's your twenty?"

"Hart's QuikStop Print and Postal at 2322 Lexington."

"Okay, hold the line."

Burke heard sounds at the other end like Price was getting someone to make other calls. Muffled voices and several long seconds passed before Price came back on the line.

"Clay, secure everything and wait right there. We're sending people."

54

"Why did you conceal from us the fact you have a secret mailbox?"

Cal swallowed hard, dragged his hands over his stubbled face, while sitting across from Malko and Sue Marsh at headquarters.

He was now facing the fourth day of Gage's disappearance and the anguish that Faith was not only unfaithful—he could no longer stomach being in the same bed with her and had moved to their spare bedroom—but was suspected of taking their son. Now he'd been hauled back into headquarters for more questioning without being told why. His inability—to sleep, to think—was exacting a toll.

"I'm sorry but I don't understand."

"Cal, early in the investigation we'd asked you to provide all the addresses you used where you could potentially receive a ransom note. You gave us your home and work addresses but concealed the fact that you rent box number 1212 at Hart's QuikStop Print and Postal, located on 2322 Lexington Boulevard."

"I'm sorry, with everything going on, I forgot."

"You didn't forget. You lied to us and I think this could be a reason."

Malko slapped copies of documents on the table; a number of pages fanned out. Among them Cal saw a Kuwaiti visa application form, passport photos for him and Gage, an employment contract from the English-language Global Gulf News Agency, a health certificate and a work permit.

"You were planning to leave the country with your son but never said a word about it to us. Why?"

Cal stared from the records back up to Malko and Price. "This is not what it looks like."

"Don't try to lie your way out of the facts," Malko said. "Look at the handwritten note on Global Gulf News letterhead. It's from Chelsey Blake. People at your newspaper told us you were very close to her and that she had a thing for you before she took a buyout and a job overseas. Faith told us that she feared that you were unfaithful with another reporter at the paper."

"I know how this looks but you're wrong."

Ignoring Cal, Malko continued. "Look at what Chelsey's saying in her note to you. 'The applications you copied to me look good…the job is yours if you want it…don't worry about the language, most of the people you'll deal with speak English, and the agency provides interpreters…and the school American diplomats use will hold a space for Gage…this will be an exciting new start, Cal.'

This has every indication of an international parental abduction."

"I'm telling you this isn't what it looks like."

Malko stood up, walked around the table and leaned into him.

"No? We also discovered that you recently withdrew seven thousand dollars in cash from an account you don't share with Faith."

"I needed it because I was thinking of going to Kuwait to look into the job."

"You're on thin ice with that one, Cal. Come on, who needs that kind of cash in today's world?"

"No, you're twisting things. This is crazy."

"Is it? Shortly after you report Gage missing, you get a call from Beth Gibson that we can't trace. Was that Chelsey? We know it's possible to route an international call through a prepaid disposable phone."

Cal shook his head.

"Maybe you had help from Sid Griner and Alma McCain, two people who worked in key positions on the Chambers of Dread? Maybe you paid them to help make Gage vanish in the chaos of the dark. It's a perfect venue. Maybe you enlisted someone, one of your trusted criminal sources, to disappear with Gage, throw his shoe in the Dumpster to create a false trail."

"This is idiotic." Cal pointed his finger at Malko. "First, you tell me Faith's cheating and that you suspect her and her boyfriend took Gage. It all points to them, you said. But now...now because I looked for a job in Kuwait, you think I took Gage.

Do you know how absolutely stupid this sounds? What's worse, it tells me that you guys don't have a damn clue what you're doing!"

"That's good, Cal. Try to turn the tables. You're smart. We may not have all the pieces but you know all the angles. Maybe you had your people take Gage up to Canada to fly to Kuwait from there. We know there are entry points where you can just walk across the border."

"This is beyond stupid." Cal stared at the ceiling.

"Remember how you bragged about how you could disappear? Remember how you said you wanted to vanish and start your life over?"

"Who told you that?" Cal shook his head. "Why in hell would I attempt such a thing? Draw all this attention, traumatize Gage? You're insane."

Malko leaned closer to Cal. "Because somehow you knew Faith was cheating on you and you were going to ensure she paid for what she did to you."

"Not true."

Malko fished through the papers and plucked a document. "Here's your work permit, issued by the General Department of Immigration Affairs in Kuwait. It states that if your spouse or family members are accompanying you, you must confirm that on the form for it to be valid. You've got Gage listed but nothing for Faith."

Cal closed his eyes and drew a slow breath.

"Now, we've contacted our FBI legal attaché at our embassy in Kuwait City. He's working with

Kuwait police to question Chelsey Blake. We're going to get to the truth, Cal."

His face reflected an empty stare.

"One more thing." Malko held up his phone. "Here's a news feature you wrote about all the countries that have no extradition treaties with the United States. Kuwait is among them. You knew that, once you got there with Gage, there would be little we could do to bring you or Gage back to America. This is all part of the plan, isn't it, Cal?"

"I'm telling you, you're wrong." Tears rolled down Cal's face. "Yes, I was considering a job in Kuwait where the pay was more than double. But that was out of fear of losing my job here. Chelsey was helping me because she's a contact in my professional network. Look, at the time, I didn't know where my marriage was headed. Faith and I had problems and I wasn't sure if she would leave Chicago, or join me later. I didn't know—I wasn't thinking clearly. You have to believe me."

"Why?"

"Because it's the truth!"

Malko leaned into his personal space.

"But you've lied to us so many times before, Cal."

55

"It's okay, Bree, you're not in trouble. Just a few more questions."

Breeana Kohl liked Detective Carol Lopez's smile and her pretty earrings. She was nice. So was the other lady detective, Rachel Price, who got her her favorite chocolate milk to drink.

Still, Breeana was so scared.

After her mom had called police the previous night about what had happened to her inside the Chambers of Dread, they told her to bring Breeana to the police station first thing in the morning.

Breeana knew it was important because they wanted to talk to her without her mom beside her in a separate, ugly room and wouldn't let her use her phone. They made her turn it off.

"Sweetheart, you can hold it, if it makes you feel comfortable, but no talking to anyone at all," Carol had told her at the beginning.

The detective had a nice calm voice and she wanted Breeana to call her by her first name. She told her how in her job she'd talked to lots of kids who'd had similar things happen to them and that it was important for Breeana to take her time and just tell them what happened.

It was so hard but Breeana did it.

She didn't know how long it had taken for her to tell them everything but now Carol was going back over the story.

"So you're sure that after this guy rubbed his hands all over you and Hannah he moved toward Gage Hudson in the spinner area?"

Breeana nodded.

"Even in the dark with the music and noise, you're sure?" Rachel asked.

"Yes, because that family was close to us in the line. I remember the boy had the ball cap and T-shirt. Hannah and I both saw him when those lights flashed like lightning, but we never saw him outside at the slides and then his parents were there and looking around for him…"

"Just so we're clear," Carol said, "you're certain the man who did this was sitting on a stool in front of the Chambers."

"Yes, he was the one taking your ticket and talking on his radio letting people in a few at a time, like he was controlling how many went in."

"Okay, we're going to show you some pictures and we want you to see if he is in any of them." Carol nodded to Rachel, who began swiping through a tablet, then turned it to Breeana.

She looked carefully at all the faces of the men, held her finger over one image, then lifted her eyes to Carol.

"Him," Breeana said.

"Any doubts?"

She shook her head and suddenly began crying. "He's the one who did it. It was so awful. I feel so…so…dirty!"

Carol rushed around the table to comfort her.

After a long moment and helping Breeana brush away her tears, Carol said, "You did great, Bree. We're done. There're just a few more things I have to tell you, okay?" She made eye contact and smiled.

Breeana nodded.

"We'll take you to your mom and we need you to wait for some paperwork. But if you ever want to talk to a real expert who helps kids when this kind of stuff happens we have a nice lady, Celeste Spring—she's a doctor—who will be happy to talk to you. And she really is great."

Breeana nodded.

"Now, sweetie, it's very important we keep our conversation here confidential. We're going to talk to Hannah, too, later today. But you cannot talk to Hannah about it. It also means you cannot tell anyone besides your mom and dad. We'll talk to them, and Hannah's folks, too. It's important, so we can find this man and make sure he doesn't hurt anyone else. Okay?"

"What if when you find him he thinks it's me who told you and he gets mad and wants to find me?"

"He's not going to be able to do that," Rachel said, "because he'll be going to jail, okay?"

"Okay."

"So you promise to keep this confidential?" Carol asked.

"Yes."

"Good. Let's go find your mom."

56

Abel Renard Wixom.

In the moments after interviewing Breeana Kohl, Rachel Price alerted her partner, Leon Lang, to join her. Minutes later their supervisor, Lieutenant Tony Sosa, and FBI Agent Malko were huddled around her desk looking at Wixom's photograph and the investigation's notes on him.

"He was the ticket taker when Gage Hudson disappeared," Lang said.

"Yes, he was," Price said as all investigators studied her tablet and the file notes on Wixom.

"And we've already interviewed him?" Malko said.

"Yes. At the outset of our investigation," Price said.

"Well, we'd better damned well find him and bring him in," Malko said.

"We've already alerted our patrol people at the fairgrounds." Sosa was on his phone texting.

"Look at this." Malko pointed at Price's screen. "Wixom is forty-two years old. Based in California, he's listed as being an employee with Ultra-

Fun for ten years in the position of technician. He's familiar with all the workings of all the rides and attractions."

"Right," Lang said, "and in his interview with River Ridge he said he never left his position as ticket taker during the time frame of Gage Hudson's disappearance."

Sosa's phone rang and he took a few steps away to take the call.

"And look who backed up that alibi for him," Malko said as Price scrolled through the notes. "Sidney Griner. Oh, this smells. Now we have a traumatized witness placing Wixom inside the Chambers at the time Hudson vanished. This gives him a window of opportunity."

The muscles in Malko's jawline began throbbing. "What is Wixom's history?"

Price scrolled through the notes. "Nothing showing. His record looks clean."

Malko shook his head in disgust. "No way that's right. My gut tells me something was missed here. We'll run him through every database we have access to again. Who interviewed him for River Ridge?"

Price scrolled through.

"Detective Steb Kwhaley," Price read from the screen, her eyes flicking to Lang, catching his subtle wince indicating another problem.

"Bad news." Sosa had finished his call. "Our patrol at the fairgrounds checked the site with Vaughn King. Turns out Wixom left the show immediately after his interview."

"He's gone?" Malko said.

"Wixom reported a family emergency and left in his RV."

"Is this before we had a chance to search it?" Malko said.

Price examined the file. "Looks like Wixom's RV wasn't searched."

"Did he tell them where this emergency was? Or leave contact info?"

"No."

Malko cursed, removed his glasses and unbuttoned his collar. "We're going to put out an alert identifying Wixom as a person of interest. Meanwhile, let's get Kwhaley in here."

The instant River Ridge detective Steb Kwhaley joined the group, Malko assailed him with questions.

"We want you to take a look at this file on Abel Wixom. Did you interview this midway employee?"

Kwhaley was given to wearing ill-fitting shirts and jackets, making him look like a skeleton in his clothes. On some mornings colleagues, who detected traces of alcohol on his breath, doubted his ability to function. One detective, frustrated at working with Kwhaley, had called him a "waste of skin."

Now, concern widened Kwhaley's eyes slightly as he slid on black-framed glasses and leaned in to read the information on the screen.

"Yes, I interviewed the subject."

"And did you run a background check?" Malko asked.

"I ran him through NCIC, but the system was temporarily down. I had a sense there was nothing. Wixom was very forthcoming."

"You had a sense, but no confirmation?"

"The system was down."

"Did you submit a follow-up query?"

"I may have."

"You *may have*?" Malko shook his head. "Your record shows his address is in California. Did you run him through state records?"

"I put the request in, yes."

"And?"

"They were slow to get back to me."

"That's not an answer. Did you confirm his record or lack of one?"

"Nothing came back, but I confirmed with a coworker that Wixom was not in the Chambers of Dread during the time Gage Hudson went missing, thereby eliminating him as a potential suspect."

"Who was that coworker?"

"It's in the file."

"Sidney Griner?"

"Sounds correct, yes."

"Did you know that Griner is a potential suspect?"

"No, I was not aware."

"Here's another thing you're not aware of, Detective. We just had a thirteen-year-old girl identify the subject you cleared, with no valid confirmation, as being inside the Chambers and molesting her and her friend during the time Gage Hudson was inside, and that he was moving in the direction of where the boy was last seen."

Kwhaley blinked several times. "Jeez. We need to bring him in, then."

"He's gone, Detective. Shortly after telling you lies he drove off in his RV before we even had a chance to search it. Gage Hudson could be in that RV, and now no one knows where Wixom is."

Kwhaley's eyes widened at the realization.

Malko got in his face. "I'm going to request that you be removed from this case and reprimanded. If it was up to me, you'd be fired."

57

Another day of life, Adria Zoliski sighed to herself as she headed out the rear door of her home to tend to her backyard garden.

At eighty-six, Adria embraced each day as a gift and her garden was her joy. Working on it and making food for community functions kept her happy, healthy and independent.

Surveying her immaculate yard, the sun bathed her in its warmth until she spotted something and frowned.

Oh, that lazy old man!

Adria shook her head. John, her eighty-seven-year-old husband, a retired contractor, had failed to repair the broken slats in the wooden privacy fence surrounding their yard after promising her he would do it.

Yeah, sure, he says. *I'll fix it honey. I'll take care of it.* But he was down at the coffee shop flapping his jaw with his pals. And when he wasn't doing that, he was watching sports or napping.

How many times had Adria told him the animals

were coming into the yard through the hole in the fence? The neighborhood cats, even rabbits from the ravine, and the other day she saw two sickly-looking stray dogs eating her vegetables and peeing on her flowers.

Adria had a good mind to get John's tools and fix it herself. She'd probably do a better job and it would be done quicker.

Heaven, give me patience.

But Adria chided herself. She knew there were more important things in this world. It may have been years since she'd retired from her job as an administrative assistant at the Cook County Sheriff's Office of Professional Review—what some called internal affairs—but her mind was sharp and she stayed on top of all the news, especially crime stories, like the one about the little local boy who'd disappeared at the fair.

Gage Hudson.

It's been all over the news and it hit close to home for Adria.

She cast a look to the surrounding yards and rear alley that connected the backs of the houses in this section of River Ridge. That boy's family lived less than half a block away. Adria could see their house in the distance through the trees. She didn't know the Hudsons but she thought of them and their little boy.

She couldn't imagine their agony.

She adjusted her sun hat and turned to her garden, which filled more than half of her backyard. Adria's family were farmers in the old country and the importance of growing your own food had been part of her upbringing, even in the middle of one of the largest metro areas in the country.

Her vegetable garden thrived. She grew potatoes, beets, cabbage, beans, cucumbers, radishes, carrots, onions, lettuce, peas, tomatoes, turnips, garlic, leeks, eggplant, parsley and spinach.

She also grew flowers. Breathing in their fragrance made her smile. Adria took pride in her gardening. She knew every inch of her backyard, which spot was doing well, which spot needed more tending.

She sighed again and was about to bend down to pull out some withered cabbage leaves when she stopped.

She'd caught a flash of color in the far corner.

What was that?

Something the animals dragged in or someone tossed in the yard.

Adria stepped closer for a better look.

Less than a minute later, after closer inspection and with her heart pounding, Adria called the police.

58

Clarksburg, West Virginia

You Can Run but You Can't Hide from Everything NC—I See!

Sakura Sato smiled, as she did every day, at the colorful little banner that was her daughter's art, pinned on the wall of her FBI workstation.

Sato was an FBI specialist with NCIC, the National Crime Information Center, which was one of the world's largest electronic storage houses of crime data, aiding every cop in the United States.

She loved how the omnipotent technology encompassed everything from missing persons to stolen boats. A traffic cop who has stopped a car can search NCIC to determine if the driver is wanted, or if the car is stolen. On more complex priority cases, law enforcement agencies can request NCIC staff to help.

That's where Sato played a key role.

She had security clearance to access an array of federal data banks and excelled at mining the vast web of information, or working with her colleagues to scour local, regional, national or international networks.

When the system works, justice prevails.

Sato glanced out her window at the rolling hills of West Virginia. Her section was part of the FBI's Criminal Justice Information Services and was housed in a sprawling three-story modular complex, some two hundred and fifty miles west of Washington, DC.

Sipping coffee she resumed offline searches of purged records related to a money-laundering investigation in the southeast, when Ryan Lander, her supervisor, approached, typing a message on his phone.

"Heads up, buddy. Need you to drop everything for a hot one—that missing child case out of Chicago. Something's fallen through the cracks. I'm sending notes from the requestor now."

Sato opened Lander's encrypted message and Abel Renard Wixom's face blossomed on her computer monitor.

"Got it. What d'you need?"

"Full background check, records, fingerprints, any wants, warrants, associates. A full-court press, everything. And I mean everything."

"Not a problem." Sato studied the notes. "It looks like a query on our guy was submitted earlier by an officer with River Ridge PD."

"Yup, our log shows a system maintenance glitch. The guy never followed up. In fact, he can-

celed it. Since then there's been a break and the
case agent, Tibor Malko—we've dealt with him before, not the most pleasant human on the planet—
has blown a gasket. He's resurrected the query and
we're making it a priority."

"I'm on it."

"Keep me posted."

Lander turned, taking a call on his phone, as
Sato began running Wixom through the twenty-
one files of NCIC's massive database containing
records from across the country.

She went through wanted persons, then foreign
fugitives, then identity theft records, then files of
people on probation, parole or supervised release,
or those released on their own recognizance.

She moved on to records on criminal illegal
aliens whom immigration had deported and those
with warrants removal. From there she checked
records of violent gang members, then suspected
terrorists, then on to records of people in the sex
offender registry.

She looked at property files, then records on se-
rially numbered, stolen, embezzled cash used for
ransom or counterfeit securities. She checked files
for stolen vehicles, vehicles involved in crimes and
records on stolen license plates.

Sato was getting hits, capturing and collecting
pieces of information on Abel Renard Wixom.

But she didn't stop there.

She went into the FBI Integrated Automated
Fingerprint Identification System, the mother of

all databases. The system stored fingerprint impressions and criminal histories on nearly sixty million people. Then she worked in the data bank for the Violent Criminal Apprehension Program, which was a repository for details on unsolved homicides and serial crimes.

Following those sessions Sato continued her search.

Abel Renard Wixom's last known address was in California.

After zipping off a message, she picked up her phone and followed up by calling a friend in Sacramento.

"Robbie, it's Sakura at NCIC. Did you get my message?"

"Sure did, baby. Let me see what I can do—but it's going to cost you some of that West Virginia blackberry jam."

"You got it."

Robbie Strickland, a senior analyst with California's Department of Justice, moved on Sato's request, submitting what they knew of Wixom into a number of state data banks. One of them was the California Law Enforcement Telecommunication System—CLETS—a network run by the justice department's Dawkins Data Center.

Strickland also accessed the various systems of California's department of corrections, including the Parole Law Enforcement Automated Data System—LEADS—and the Automated Criminal History System. The submission could verify parolee history, offender identification, arrest records, convictions, holds and commitments for other law enforcement agencies, even create all-points bulletins and warrants.

That's when Abel Wixom's history began lighting up all over the place.

Strickland found that Wixom was convicted of felony child molestation in Reno, Nevada, in 1990. He also had a misdemeanor child molestation conviction in Hanford, California, in 1999. Two years later he faced new child molestation charges in Santa Ana. In that case he was alleged to have fondled a ten-year-old boy behind a small midway set up in a mall parking lot. Wixom's lawyer managed to cast doubt on the allegations but not enough and Wixom had served time.

Strickland let out a small whistle.

A few years back he was released as a PC 290 sex offender.

Strickland's keyboard clicked from rapid typing. He let a few minutes pass, then called Sato back.

"I've just sent you everything."

"I'm reading it now, thanks, Robbie."

"There's more on him that you can't see. It's a file note in our system."

"What's it say?"

"Wixom's file's been flagged by an LAPD detective, Norm Howell. He's to be alerted and contacted regarding any inquiries concerning Abel Wixom."

"Does it say why?"

"No, but Howell must have more disturbing background on Wixom."

"Okay, we'll alert our people in Chicago. Thanks for this, Robbie."

"And, Sakura?"

"Yes?"

"Don't forget to send that jam."

59

River Ridge, Illinois

Back at home Cal was still feeling shaken by how Malko had grilled him on Kuwait, when loud thudding rattled the rear windows of the house.

Cal and Faith hurried outside to their backyard.

A police helicopter thudded overhead, hammering the sky.

"What's going on?" Faith asked him.

They'd hardly spoken in the last few hours while struggling with the wounds they'd inflicted on each other—the accusations, the acrimony and the fallout of the FBI suspecting each of them in Gage's disappearance. Now the sudden alarming activity around them had diverted their attention.

"Something serious," he said, taking in the activity.

About half a block from their home, a patrol car had sealed the rear alley. Its emergency lights bathed the neighboring houses, trees and fences in pulsating red and blue. Plastic yellow crime scene tape stretched around one yard.

Investigators appeared to be canvassing door-to-door. K-9 units were scouring yards and shrubs along the alley while a drone skimmed the area at treetop level. Cal saw officers posted in the lane behind their backyard keeping curious neighbors in place. Then he spotted River Ridge officer Erik Ripkowski, one of the first to help them at the fair-grounds.

"Erik!" Cal waved him to their yard. "What's going on?"

Ripkowski gave a tense glance to one of the other officers nearby. "I don't know, Mr. Hudson."

"Did they find something related to Gage?"

"Sir, all I know is that we're asking people to stay on their property at this time."

"What? Why? Is Malko or Price around? I'm going down there."

Ripkowski held up his palms. "Sir, please, we're asking you to remain on your property." Ripkowski's radio crackled. "I'm sorry, I've got to go."

Faith turned to Cal. "Oh God, this is bad. They've found something down there."

Cal's face tensed and he punched a number into his phone.

"Who're you calling?"

He didn't answer. As the number rang he focused on the Clarks' house. They lived four doors down, closer to the action.

"Hello?"

"Rory, Cal. What's going on? It's like a military operation out there and they won't tell us anything."

"They won't tell us much, either. A detective was just here asking us questions."

"What questions?"

"Did we see anything suspicious recently, like anyone in the Zoliskis' yard."

"Who?"

"The old couple who live near us. Police asked us if we saw anyone put anything in their yard."

"Did they say what?"

"No."

"Did they tell you if they found something?"

"No, but I think they did, Cal. I saw guys in the Zoliskis' backyard with shirts that said FBI Evidence Response Team."

Cal's stomach twisted as his mind raced. They've definitely found something, and by Ripkowski's demeanor toward them, it had to be related to Gage and it had to be bad.

"Cal?" Rory asked. "You still there?"

"Thanks, Rory."

Cal hung up and headed into the rear alley.

Faith joined him. "Where're you going? We're supposed to stay here."

He started trotting, forcing her to keep up.

"What did Rory say they found?" she asked. "Is it Gage? Did they find Gage?"

The Hudsons rushed toward the patrol car and sealed yard, passing K-9 units. Officers called for them to halt. Upon recognizing them, TV news crews redirected their cameras just as officers began waving at the couple.

"People, please return to your property!" uniformed officers ordered.

Cal pointed at the press. "If they can be here, I can be here!"

As if cued, two reporters approached him. "Mr. Hudson, what's your reaction to this search so close to your house?" one of them asked.

"I have nothing to say. I don't know anything."

Cal then moved to where the tape met the fence bordering the Zoliskis' backyard. Peering over it he saw Malko.

"Agent Malko," Cal called to him. "Please talk to me. Tell me what you've found."

Malko, taking in the press, shot him an icy stare, waved off the officers and headed to the tape to meet Cal and Faith, his suspicions and hostility toward them still simmering.

"Agent Malko, please tell us what's happening," Faith pleaded.

Through the space between the Zoliskis' house and their neighbors, Cal glimpsed the FBI's ERT truck. He then strained to see if there was a vehicle present from the Cook County Medical Examiner.

"What did you find?" Cal repeated.

Malko scratched the stubble of his bald head and then looked at the Hudsons for a long, cold moment.

"I'm sorry, I can't discuss anything," he said. "Please return to your property. If we need to advise you, we'll do so at the appropriate time."

"What?" Cal's jaw dropped.

Malko then turned, leaving the couple stunned. It took about two seconds for Faith to explode.

"You come back here this instant! You come back here, Agent Malko, and you tell me if my son is dead!"

60

Malko returned to Adria and John Zoliski's backyard with the Hudsons' pleas echoing behind him as officers escorted them back to their house.

He rejoined Sue Marsh and Bill Caffrey, the supervisory agent for the FBI's Evidence Response Team. They resumed studying the crisp, clear photos on Caffrey's tablet of what Adria Zoliski had discovered in her garden.

Adria told them how she'd gone out to work in her garden and noticed something in her tomato plants. At first she'd thought it was something animals had dragged in, or someone had tossed in the yard. She got her rake and plucked out what appeared to be a rag. When she dropped it on the grass to examine it, she saw that it was an article of clothing.

A T-shirt.

But small, like for a child.

Aware of the news reports on the missing neighborhood boy and details of his clothing, she called the police.

Rick Mofina

Now, in the photos, Malko and the others saw that it was a blue Cubs T-shirt, wet and soiled, but with what was clearly a mustard stain on the front.

"Are you confident that the T-shirt is Gage Hudson's?" Marsh asked.

"Well—" Caffrey swiped through the photos "—it matches his in style, color, size. And there's that mustard stain." Caffrey then juxtaposed the shirt with the photo Faith Hudson had given police of Gage wearing his blue Cubs T-shirt. "See how the stains align?"

None of the agents spoke as the helicopter circled above the neighborhood. After it passed, Malko said, "And you detected small bloodstains on the shirt?"

"Right, initial tests indicate the blood is type A. Gage Hudson has type A, so yes, I'm very confident the shirt is the one he was wearing when he went missing."

"I have no doubt that this is Gage Hudson's shirt," Malko said.

"What about the blood?" Marsh said.

"Yeah, it's troubling for sure, could mean a lot of things. We need to do more analysis," Caffrey said. "If there's nothing more, I should catch up with my people. We've got a lot of work to do."

"That's it for now," Malko said. "Thanks, Bill."

Malko and Marsh stayed at the scene a few minutes longer discussing the case while awaiting callbacks and updates. The helicopter, which was conducting aerial photography of the area, in

addition to searching, circled again as they both
looked in the direction of the Hudsons' home.

"How do you think the shirt got here?" Marsh
asked.

Malko shook his head.

"This is so close to them, Tibor, half a block
away. And with those bloodstains, it's not looking good."

"Nope," he said. "Above all else, no one outside the investigation will be told about the T-shirt.
We'll hold that back. It's key fact evidence—we
can't let any details leak out."

Malko and Marsh had already interviewed and
run background checks on the Zoliskis, who'd also
volunteered to let the FBI search their home and
property. They were both ruled out as possible suspects.

"What I don't get," Marsh said, "is how the shirt
was missed in the initial search and canvass of this
neighborhood."

"I don't think it was missed. I think it ended up
here very recently."

"Really? So how do you think it got here?"

"Stray dogs could've dragged it the couple of
miles from the Dumpster where we found Gage's
shoe. We'll see if our canine units turn up anything more here. But animals are one possibility."

"Right. Adria Zoliski spotted strays in her yard."

"But she also told us emphatically that she
works in this garden every day," Malko said. "So
timing and proximity are factors."

"Assuming it was not animals, who would put it here?"

"We can't rule out anything or anyone," Malko said. "For me, this keeps the focus on the parents and Tate."

"What about the molestation incident involving Abel Wixom?"

"He remains a suspect. It pisses me off that River Ridge messed up with him." Malko checked his phone for updates. "Still nothing new on him from NCIC. We need that data."

"What about Sid Griner and Alma McCain?" Marsh consulted her phone. "Their polygraph results came in this morning and they show that they were both untruthful."

"We're not ruling them out, either. Whoever is behind Gage Hudson's disappearance did not act alone."

"But you like the parents as the lead actors?"

"The Hudsons have marital stress and motivation to take their son as an act against the other. I know it sounds extreme but it happens. Either one of them could be associated with Wixom, Griner and McCain. Tate can't be ruled out. We have to look at the potential physical evidence that has emerged—the shoe in the Dumpster, the lock and chain, the ball cap and now the bloodstained T-shirt."

"But why would Cal, Faith or anyone place Gage's T-shirt in this yard? It makes little sense."

"It could be someone is trying to misdirect us."

Malko shook his head. "I don't know, Sue. I admit there are a lot of loose ends."

Each of the agents' phones pinged with messages they then read.

Tate's ex-wife and daughter had been located on vacation in Paris and had cooperated with French police and the FBI's legal attaché at the embassy. They all worked with the FBI lab in the US and French forensic experts to confirm that hair found in the ball cap was consistent with Tate's daughter's hair.

"Look at the daughter's statement," Marsh said. "Tate bought her the ball cap when she was visiting last year. She said her relationship with him is not a good one, that she resents him. She didn't want the ball cap and stuffed it in a box marked Goodwill without his knowledge. So the ball cap doesn't belong to Hudson."

Malko's poker face conveyed no reaction.

"Why the hell didn't Tate tell us that he bought a cap for his daughter?" Marsh said.

"He probably never knew that she'd rejected the gift. She says he bought it for her over a year ago."

There was a supplemental message on Tate he was reading. It was from Larson Ward, the polygraphist. Tate's polygraph results: truthful.

"Cripes, Tibor, so do we rule out Tate?"

Malko dragged a hand across his face as he stared at the home of Cal and Faith Hudson in the distance.

"I don't think so. He was not forthcoming at the outset and he's skilled law enforcement. Everybody's been lying to us, Sue. We're facing a huge web of deceit, and if there's any time left on that boy's life, it's getting shorter by the minute."

They stood there for a long moment waiting for the helicopter to circle again. When it did, Malko's phone rang and he answered. "Malko."

"Agent Malko, Norm Howell, detective with the LAPD."

"Yes."

"NCIC has informed me that you've been making inquiries on Abel Renard Wixom."

"That's correct."

"This guy's central to a major investigation we're running. We need to talk."

Malko glanced around.

"Okay. Let us get back to a desk. We'll call you back in thirty minutes."

61

Stinging from Malko's disdain, Cal stood in his backyard battling his anger, his thoughts swirling as investigators continued searching the neighborhood, working their way toward his property.

Watching it all, he felt his life was being torn apart.

Was his son alive? What did that couple, the Zoliskis, find? Was someone trying to set them up—set Cal up?

He glanced at Faith, sitting on the steps of their rear deck, wiping her eyes with a tissue.

Was she involved?

At this point he felt nothing but contempt for her. He didn't know what was real anymore. He looked toward the Zoliski yard at Malko on his phone. *Look at him—he thinks Faith took Gage, he thinks I took Gage. Where's he rushing off to now?*

Cal dragged both hands over his face.

How could he find out what they discovered in that yard?

Cal called his newsroom—maybe they'd picked up something on the emergency scanners. At this point he no longer cared if the FBI was listening in. He wanted to know what they'd found and that's the first thing he asked Stu Kroll when he reached him.

"We know by the radio chatter there's a lot of activity there," Kroll told him. "But whatever they found, they're being extremely careful not to discuss it on the air. Do you have any idea? Do you want to talk to us?"

"No, I've got to go. Thanks, Stu."

As he hung up, he heard Faith speak from behind him. "Cal, what did they find?"

He turned to her. "You should know. Aren't you and Tate behind it?"

"Please, don't. Just don't. You're as cruel as Malko. For all we know they could've found Gage dead a few—" she pointed toward the Zoliskis' home "—just a few doors…oh God…a few doors from his home." She began sobbing.

Cal didn't move to comfort her; instead, he turned away to resume watching the police work.

"It can't be Gage's body," he offered. "I saw nothing there from the medical examiner's office." Then, to be callous, he added, "If it was a corpse, or a body part, they'd be there."

Faith sobbed harder but he ignored her pain to contend with his own. He'd been so consumed with the investigation that he'd barely thought of what was happening to his son right now.

Forgive me, son. Please forgive me.

Exhaustion and anguish suddenly swept over Cal, bringing a torrent of images.

Was someone hurting Gage, abusing and torturing him? Where was he? Why did they find only one shoe? And in that Dumpster, like it was just so much garbage. What did they find down the street? And those people in the Chambers, people who trafficked in fear. Did they work with Tate? What did they know? What did they do?

Maybe I should shake the truth out of Faith; go beat the truth out of Tate. No, I need to focus. What about the FBI probing my news stories looking for a connection? Yes, I've crossed the line once or twice—but no one needs to know because there's no way Gage's disappearance could be connected. I mean, how could it be?

As if waking from a nightmare Cal found himself in the house, in Gage's room with his heart racing. Seeing some missed traces of fingerprint powder on the door, the walls, then confronting the deathly stillness, catapulted him back to what he did for a living. To the times when he'd intruded on the grief of the families who'd lost loved ones to shootings, fires, drownings, car wrecks, suicides, every sort of tragedy.

He recalled how he'd ask them to tell him about their loss and they would. How they'd search through computers, phones, wallets, purses, albums, shoeboxes, for a "nice" photo, pulling them off fridge doors, corkboards and walls. Then they'd show him the rooms of the departed and their belongings: a cherished stuffed toy, or a piece of jewelry, a sweater or a trivial-looking cherished souvenir.

The last things they touched.

And now, standing in Gage's room, touching his fingers to his posters of the Cubs, the Bears, Bulls and Blackhawks, seeing the blackish traces of graphite on his ball glove, his book of world records, his Lego stadium and skyscraper...*the last things he touched.*

Cal felt the karmic wheel had turned.

Heartbroken, all he wanted now was to lie down in Gage's bed and wrap himself in his sheets, but the front doorbell rang and someone pounded on the door.

He answered it to find Rory Clark on his doorstep. Beyond him, a few newspeople and a River Ridge police car were on the street in front of the house, watching. He opened the door to let Rory in, closing it behind him.

Inside, Rory held up his phone. "There's a woman calling for you on my phone."

Cal's stomach clenched—not again. "Who is it?"

"She wouldn't give her name. Just insisted that I find you and put you on the line. She says she used the internet to track down your neighbors because it's safer to talk to you on a phone police aren't monitoring."

"How would she know what phones police are monitoring?"

"I don't know. It's definitely odd." Rory passed the phone to him.

"This is Cal Hudson. Who's calling?" he asked, more for Rory's benefit than his own, since he already had a sense of who was on the line.

"It's me again."

Cal was dismayed to recognize the voice—*Beth Gibson*. Or, at least, that's what she'd called herself last time.

"Don't say my name, Cal. We need to talk without anyone hearing us."

"One minute." He covered the speaker with his hand. "Rory, I have to take this privately. I'll return it soon as I'm done."

"Hold on. What's going on? Why is this stranger calling my phone and asking for a private call? Don't you think we should at least notify the police?"

"No, I'll just talk to her and take care of it. She's an old police source."

"Cal—" Rory put his hand on his shoulder "—you know we support you one hundred percent...but the news reports make it look like investigators suspect you and Faith are hiding something."

"Rory, you have to trust me. This is okay and you did the right thing coming to me like this."

Rory was silent. Cal could see he was wrestling with his unease.

"Please," Cal said. "Just trust me."

A moment passed before Rory relented. "All right."

"Thanks. Help yourself to coffee in the kitchen," Cal said, then went to the laundry room and shut the door.

"You still there?" he said.

"I'm here. Are you alone now?"

"Yes."

"Is anyone recording?"

"No." Cal squeezed the phone, struggling with rage seething beneath the surface. "Is my son dead?"

His question was answered with silence.

"Tell me!"

"I don't know."

"You must know! They're looking near our home. It's on the news!"

"That's why I called. I saw it on the news."

"Do you know what they found?"

More silence.

"Stop the bullshit," Cal said. "You of all people should know what's going on out there."

"I believe they found an article of your son's clothing."

He steadied himself on the dryer, then struggled with his composure.

"Are you involved?"

"Cal, I swear to you, I've got nothing to do with this."

Unsure what to believe, he didn't respond.

"I called because they're clearly deeper into the investigation now, and it's critical that you never reveal what we did."

"But what if there's a connection to Gage?"

"Nothing has surfaced to point that way."

"Not yet."

"There is no connection."

"You better hope there's not because if there is—"

"Cal, my heart goes out to you. I know this is horrible."

"More than you can imagine," he said. "The FBI's leaning hard on both of us. They haven't ruled me out, or ruled Faith out. I don't know what's true anymore. I haven't slept or eaten. Our lives are in pieces. And they've pressed me on some of my stories."

"What stories?"

"Stories where I was threatened. They're looking for leads on Gage. One of them was *that* story."

"What did they know, what did you tell them?"

"They didn't know anything. They were sniffing at it but I steered them away."

"That's good."

"What if you're wrong, what if I'm wrong? My son's life is at risk. I'm thinking of telling them everything—of telling them to look at everyone connected to that story, just in case it is tied to Gage."

"No! If you even hint at it, it opens the door."

"We're talking about my son's life!"

"I know, Cal, but think. You know why we did what we did."

Cal said nothing.

"We had to do it, Cal. Right?"

"I know we did."

"And if you say one word, everything comes crashing down on everyone involved—you and me. And it would hurt everyone we love. Everyone. We'd be charged. We'd face prison time. And then what happens when you find out it has nothing to do with Gage, has no bearing on his disappearance? Then all you've done is reveal what we did and go to prison for it. What good are you to your son then? Think!"

Feeling like he was coming apart Cal took a long, hard breath.

"Cal, deep down, you know it's not connected, right?"

"That's what I thought at the outset but now I don't know what to think."

"Cal, listen to me. The person involved is out of the picture, gone—there could be no connection between him and your son. It's all in the past and we have to keep it there."

"I don't know how much longer I can do this." He choked back a sob. "It's my son."

"Listen to me, Cal. Our case is a dead end because the guy is dead. If you go there, it will not only destroy everything, but it will distract the FBI from searching for Gage. You and I will become the focus of the investigation. Do you understand what's at stake here? If you want to help Gage, you keep this thing buried where it belongs. Keep the FBI locked onto Gage. Do you get that, Cal?"

He said nothing.

"Cal, you have to hang in there."

Drained, Cal ended the call, closing his eyes against the breeze that flowed through the laundry room window to the backyard.

He leaned back against the wall, absorbing his situation, unaware that Faith was still outside and had heard his end of the call.

62

Abel Renard Wixom's face stared from the monitor on the wall at the far end of the second-floor meeting room of River Ridge police headquarters.

The lights had been dimmed and the monitor, which also held Wixom's record collected by NCIC and California law enforcement, glowed on Malko, Marsh, Detectives Price and Lang, their supervisors and other investigators who'd gathered for the call from Norm Howell with the LAPD.

"Can you confirm we're talking on a secure line and this is confidential?" Howell said.

"Yes," Price said.

"All right." Howell's voice sounded tinny through the teleconference speakers. "As you can see, using stolen identities, false birth certificates and driving licenses, Wixom is also known as Arthur Lee Wilemonte, Melvin Claude Marxe, Wardell Preston Bowles and Felix Steed Vassellef. We know him as Felix Vassellef and we've been looking for him."

"You said he's central to your investigation?" Malko asked.

"He's a key player in Illicitum Passio."

"What's that?" Price asked.

"The name is Latin. Loosely translated it means forbidden passion or suffering. It's an ultrasecret worldwide network of pedophiles that uses the dark web to distribute child porn."

"Understood," Price said. "I think we're all aware of people distributing porn online."

"This group is different. It operates on a level that surpasses any other. It goes beyond the sharing of pictures and videos. Members of Illicitum Passio have been suspected of infiltrating adoption agencies, social service departments and other offices around the globe to arrange to steal and sell children to other members. This group specializes in fetishes, sexualized torture and even ritualistic murder."

"Damn, that's the devil at work," Lang said.

"Members are also pathologically loyal to each other. Illicitum Passio is extremely sophisticated. On the dark web they use a very complex structure of guides and forums. They communicate through a dizzying array of layer upon layer of state-of-the-art encryption, characteristic of an onion router, with servers hidden around the globe."

"Where does Wixom, or whoever he is, fit into this?" Malko asked.

"Some time ago we got a tip from an internet provider after they'd accidentally uncovered hidden child porn when Vassellef—sorry, Wixom—was having a computer issue. For a moment he'd been sloppy. Shortly after we began investigating him, he vanished.

"Long story short, for more than a year we've worked with the Royal Canadian Mounted Police, also police in Europe, Asia and South America, and we were successful in infiltrating the group to a certain degree with an officer posing online as a member. We also had limited success tracking Wixom because he kept changing identities. His fingerprint records had a glitch and we missed out that he'd done time for the crimes that your investigation uncovered. Additionally, it got by us that he was a carny with Ultra-Fun.

"As you are all aware, in reality things do not go as smoothly as they do on TV, the movies or in books. Our efforts to track him were hampered. We'd get breaks only when Vassellef surfaced on the dark web in Illicitum Passio. Our investigation took a turn when we recently learned that Wixom slash Vassellef is connected to an orphanage in Thailand."

"In what way?"

"Supplying them with children."

A chill rippled around the room as Howell continued.

"And if he has the Hudson boy and he hasn't killed him, he could be planning to change his identity, take him to Thailand and sell him. Either way, if we don't find Wixom, Gage Hudson is most likely gone forever."

Malko, Price and the others darted momentary glances to each other.

"I have to tell you," Howell said, "when we

were alerted to your query we had hoped you had Wixom in custody."

"River Ridge had him for questioning," Malko said, "but before proper background on him was completed, he left the area."

"How long ago did he leave?"

"Approximately seventy-two hours ago," Malko said. "We discovered it less than twenty-four hours ago and put out an alert. We're going to intensify things because now, given additional information from you, and allegations he molested at least one child here, the situation's changed."

"Keep us looped in," Howell said.

Even before the call had ended, Malko studied the files, revisiting River Ridge information. Early in the investigation one sharp-minded officer had noted the plates and photographed every vehicle, RV, camper, van and car belonging to Ultra-Fun's staff.

We've got Wixom's RV. That's a start, Malko thought, looking at the photo of it.

"We'll get out an Amber Alert as far and wide as possible," Malko said.

"Agreed," said Sosa, the River Ridge lieutenant. "We've already alerted the Royal Canadian Mounted Police in case he entered Canada, and instructed Mexican officials, US Customs and US Border Patrol to watch for Wixom at every terminal and border checkpoint."

"I'll call the US Attorney and State's Attorney," Malko's supervisor, Agent Paul Bishop, said. "We'll push them to issue those felony charges against Wixom for what he did to Breeana Kohl and Hannah Dawkins, then we'll go public with him on our Most Wanted."

"Tibor." Agent Dee Lewin was scrolling through her tablet. "We know Cal Hudson covered pedophile cases. We need to go back over all his stories for any possible connections."

"All right. Good." Malko continued paging through his notes. "And we'll reinterview the Ultra-Fun staff, especially Griner and McCain. We'll lean on them about Wixom."

"We have to hustle," Price said. "Because the midway is only in town a few more days and I'm not sure we can get warrants compelling the entire operation to stay put."

Malko stared at Wixom's face on the monitor, then he glanced through files on Cal and Faith Hudson, Roy Tate, Sid Griner and Alma McCain.

His jaw clenched like a man preparing for war and he warned himself as he always did at critical points of an investigation.

Don't get tunnel vision. You haven't ruled everyone out yet.

63

"How many times does she need to go through this?"

Rex Dunne, Ultra-Fun's chief engineer, was losing patience with Quinn Hardy, the FBI's engineer. Hardy had shown no sign of wrapping up her meticulous search with investigators for an alternative way Gage Hudson could have exited the Chambers of Dread.

Dunne, out of Hardy's earshot, dragged his sleeve across his brow. "We've been at this, what, over thirty-six hours now."

"I hear ya." Brian Lodge with the county nodded.

"We've combed through every inch of the floor, the walls, the ceiling and outside. We examined the undercarriage and the roof. We found nothing. It's clear that the boy likely wandered off." Dunne pointed his chin to Hardy, who was at the spinner. "What's she looking at again? Is she ever going to stop?"

All the bolts in the critical areas of the spinner were satisfactory and all the nondestructive test reports, the NDTs, were in compliance, Quinn Hardy thought as she reviewed the rotation mechanism one more time.

Flipping through the binders, she checked off the occupant load records again. Then she reviewed the section's floor plans, but when she came back to the alarms she waved Bud Porter, the state inspector, over.

"The records show the electrical system took a lightning strike in Milwaukee," she said, "which made the alarms and security cameras perform erratically."

"Yes, we've covered this," Porter said. "The systems were working when I signed off."

"They could still be switched off manually."

"That's against procedure."

"But it's possible."

"It would have to be logged and there's no confirmation."

"Sometimes people forget and sometimes people lie."

"That's true." Porter sighed and turned to the others in the distance. "Look, Quinn, we've been over this thing exhaustively. We're in agreement that the attraction was performing and in compliance and we've found no alternative exits."

"I still don't know."

Hardy shifted her attention once again to the walls that surrounded the spinner to where Gage Hudson was last seen. Like the rest of the interior they were all painted black to enhance the dark. Again, she tried to imagine Gage amid the chaos of a rotating floor under his feet, flashing lights, loud music, screams and an actor chasing patrons with a chain saw.

"I can't shake this feeling that we're missing something," she said, tapping on the curving black wall and listening. The surface of the wooden wall was foam, molded to resemble ancient bricks like a dungeon wall.

"It's a divider wall." Porter flipped through his manual. "We've looked at it. The records show it was used in another incarnation when the attraction was called Horror-Rama-Tour-of-Hell."

Tapping and thinking as she walked around the other side, Hardy returned with an idea.

"Bud, humor me. Take your tactical flashlight, go to the opposite side and run the beam close to the wall, moving it slowly up and down."

Porter shrugged and unholstered his light from his belt.

"Guys," Hardy called to the others. "Kill all the lights, please."

After a ripple of muttering and switches snapping, the attraction was thrown into total darkness. The floors creaked from Porter working on the other side of the wall as Hardy stepped closer, seeing nothing, not even her hand in front of her face.

"Are you running your light, Bud?" she called.

"I am."

Still nothing—then a bright sliver of light flashed.

"Hold it," Hardy called. "There! Where you are now—move it up and down slowly." Another sliver flashed and Hardy shifted her position until a hair-line seam of light leaked through on her side.

"Okay, guys, can we have the lights back, please?"

Hardy stood still with her gloved finger on the light leak and within seconds she discerned an almost invisible section. She ran her fingers along it, up and down, noticing a very small mesh peephole about eye level. She also noticed that the wall had some give. Carefully and gently she pressed the wall until she heard a click.

Hardy froze.

The wall sprung slightly inward a few inches and she saw a track above and below, similar to the sliding doors of a closet. Hardy rolled the section of wall and it revealed a hidden passage no more than a foot and a half in width, all painted black and winding in the direction of the nearest exit door.

"Well, look at that," Porter said. "A false wall."

"Don't move or touch anything, Bud. Come with me."

Hardy rushed to the exit, went outside to the landing that faced the chain-link fence and vacant lot. She began pressing on sections of the exterior wall until she heard another click and opened a narrow door, so camouflaged by the murals painted on the exterior that it was invisible.

"Okay, come on!"

Hardy rushed back to the spinner and the entrance. She got Porter to run his powerful tactical light along the floor. Upon detecting foot impressions in the dust and other matter, Hardy reached for her phone and punched a number.

"A person with knowledge of this wall could've used it to swallow Gage Hudson in the chaos and darkness," she told Porter while it rang. "They could've taken him in a heartbeat. We're going to need the Evidence Response Team down here now— Hello, Agent Malko?"

64

Alma McCain chewed on her fingernails watching the FBI's Evidence Response Team roll its white cube van up the midway to the Chambers of Dread.

"Sid, they're gonna find out what we did. I can feel it." She stood behind him outside of their RV as more police arrived. "What're we gonna do?"

"Why don't you shut up, get back in the van and let me think." Sid Griner never turned from eyeing the increased activity at the Chambers.

Alma stomped into their Ford camper, slamming the door behind her.

This is getting so freaking serious. They've been working on the Chambers for days. Suddenly there's more FBI everywhere. She continued biting her nails while pacing. *They must know I lied on the polygraph. I tried to do what Sid told me—I kept changing my answers. I said I was upset. But it's like the FBI knows everything and so much is happening. I'm scared to death for that little boy.*

She glanced at Sid's laptop. The screen showed

the FBI's website where Abel Wixom was now one of the most wanted men in the country.

If they catch him what will he tell the FBI?

Alma ran her hands through her hair.

I bet Abel would try to make a deal. Put it all on us.

She looked through the window at Sid.

So would he. He'd make a deal and put it all on me. He'd say I was crazy because I lost my son in a fire. If things turned bad, Sid would try to save himself. He would. She bit down on her bottom lip. *I can't wait for that to happen. I've got to do something.*

Alma's breathing quickened and her eyes swept the interior for her wallet. She found it on the galley counter and slid out the business card for Grace Kelsey, the lawyer Ultra-Fun had arranged for her polygraph. Alma turned the card over and over, thinking for a moment before putting her wallet in her purse, slipping it over her shoulder and stepping from the van.

"Where're you going?" Sid asked.

"The drugstore—I need things."

"What things? I'll go with you."

"Female stuff. I'm going alone, Sid."

Almost trotting the first few blocks from the fairgrounds to the drugstore, Alma thought, *I should just get on a bus and disappear.*

By the time she'd reached the parking lot she'd abandoned the idea and gone straight to the public phone that stood in front of the drugstore.

Forty-five minutes after using it she was at River Ridge police headquarters in an interview room with lawyer Grace Kelsey at her side.

"My client has remembered more information," Kelsey told Malko and Marsh, who sat across the table from them. "And in exchange for providing you this information, we're seeking immunity from any prosecution."

The two agents flicked a stone-cold stare to Alma.

"Do you know where Gage Hudson is?" Malko said.

"No," Alma said.

"We won't make any deals. That's for the US Attorney and the County State's Attorney to determine. We have no time here. What's your information and remember you're still under the Miranda warning."

Alma swallowed and looked to Kelsey, who nodded.

"Sid and I were paid five thousand dollars to temporarily shut off the alarm system and the cameras."

"Who paid you?"

"Abel Wixom."

"Why?"

"He never told us."

"Where did he get the money?"

"I don't know."

"Was Gage Hudson the target?"

"I don't know. Abel just approached us to do it and said he would radio us when the time came and that we were to leave it off for half an hour."

"So he was watching for Gage? This was planned?"

"All I know now is that he radioed me to switch it off at the time the boy and his family entered and that's what I did. Before it all happened, all Abel said was that if we were ever questioned about it, we could use the lightning in Milwaukee as a cover for the system going down."

"Where's Abel now?"

"I don't know."

"You don't know?" Malko's chair scraped and crashed to the floor as he stood, looming over Alma. "You think hard. What else do you know?"

She shut her eyes and cried.

"Did you ever see Gage Hudson after he was reported missing?" Malko asked.

"No."

"Who abducted him—was it Griner?"

"No, Sid was outside at the chutes."

"Was it Wixom?"

"Maybe, I don't know. He was in and out of the Chambers at that time."

"Who else is involved?"

"I don't know."

"Think!"

"Abel said he was helping somebody, that they paid him, too, and that that was all we needed to know."

"Was it Roy Tate, Faith Hudson or Cal Hudson?"

"I don't know."

"Who!" Malko shouted.

"I don't know anything more."

"You've just admitted that you're an accomplice to a crime, a serious criminal act. That means you'll face charges. If Gage Hudson is dead that makes you an accessory to murder."

Alma buried her face in her arms on the table and sobbed.

"I swear, I didn't know this was going to happen! God forgive me. I'm so sorry for that poor little boy!"

"We're going to place you under arrest, Alma. And we're going to arrest Griner, too. You're both going to prison for a long time. The only thing that might help you is if we find Gage Hudson alive."

She lifted her head, her hair curtained over her tearstained face.

"I pray to God that you do. I'm so, so sorry."

65

Lone Pine County, Montana

Deputy Emmett Peak with the Lone Pine County Sheriff's Office was driving west on Highway 200, a ribbon of pavement cutting across the vast, windswept plain of eastern Montana.

Peak never tired of how the sky and earth became one in this part of the world; how you could go for miles without seeing another soul. He loved the land with its rolling hills laced with creeks, the pine-dotted coulees, the bluffs and badlands. Some two thousand people lived within the county's 2,500 square miles, giving everyone lots of breathing room. With the exception of drunk drivers and a few domestics, there wasn't a lot of crime here.

Lone Pine was peaceful.

Almost too peaceful. Maybe he should consider the Montana Highway Patrol again. Word was they were accepting trooper applications.

Peak was just beyond the exit for Cottonwood, midway through his shift, thinking about getting a turkey sandwich with fries at Buck's Diner, when a glint of chrome caught his eye.

It flashed from the windbreak near the shoulder on the north side of the highway.

What's this?

He pulled his patrol car over and got out to investigate. Tracks in the dried mud from last night's rain led into a big stand of bull pine and blue spruce thick with creeping juniper and other shrubs.

Tugging on gloves he followed the tire impressions into the thicket, using his baton to slap aside branches, soon determining that the chrome was part of a vehicle wedged at a forty-five-degree angle up against the trees, entwined in the brush. The sides were scraped and dented, the windshield shattered.

Looks like someone lost control, or ditched a stolen vehicle, which is a good indicator of a link to another crime.

Peak got the passenger door open and drew his weapon. No one was in the front.

"Hello!" he called.

He climbed inside. The interior was a mess of pots, pans, canned food, cereal and other items that had spilled from the kitchen. Empty take-out containers, wrappers and pizza boxes were starting to give off a bad smell. Clothes were strewn about.

Nobody was inside.

Peak climbed back outside and took notes. It was a camper van, a Phoenix Cruiser 2350, white on green with an Iowa license plate.

Reaching for the shoulder microphone of his

portable radio, he called in his position and the incident.

"Shelley, will you run the tag and VIN through NCIC for me?"

"Ten-four."

He read out the numbers and she repeated them.

"Got it," the dispatcher said.

Waiting on his query, Peak probed the immediate area for any sign of an injured passenger or foot impressions. The terrain was too rugged. Maybe he'd request a K-9 team come up from Miles City.

"Emmett, the plate comes back as stolen out of Sioux City, Iowa."

"Copy that. I figured. And the VIN?"

"Stand by."

The radio crackled with static.

"Oh, boy," the dispatcher said. "Emmett, we have to alert the FBI."

"Want to tell me what you have there?"

"There's an Amber Alert on this. The vehicle and a white male subject—he's got a whole list of aliases—are wanted in connection with the suspected abduction of Gage Hudson, age nine, from River Ridge, Illinois—that's metro Chicago. That case has been on the news. There's a lot more supplemental information."

"Read it to me."

The dispatcher read an overview of Abel Renard Wixom—alias Arthur Lee Wilemonte, Melvin Claude Marxe, Wardell Preston Bowles and Felix Steed Vassellef—who was a person of interest in connection to the abduction of Gage Hudson, last seen at the River Ridge Summer Carnival in the Chambers of Dread. Hudson was four feet seven inches tall, between sixty-five and seventy-five pounds, wearing a blue Cubs T-shirt with a mustard stain, light-colored camo shorts, SkySlyder blue sneakers, size five, with green neon laces in a zipper pattern.

When she'd finished, Peak blinked several times, his heart beating faster before he headed back into the camper as if remembering a detail.

"Emmett? You copy?"

"Ten-four. Alert the sheriff, tell him what we got. Let him alert the FBI." He resumed scanning the interior. "I'm going to stay with this vehicle. This could be a crime scene. Shelley, contact Miles City—we're going to need a K-9 unit."

"Ten-four. Also, Emmett, I got another call for you. Just came in. Want me to raise Randy and send him, or can you take it?"

"What is it?"

"Stand by."

While waiting, Peak kept searching the disarray. He thought that when he first looked inside he'd glimpsed something.

"Griff Johnson at the Sunset Dreams Motel—that's only four miles from you. He says he's got a bad feeling about a guest that showed up."

"What sort of bad feeling?"

"Said a man showed up without a vehicle and his clothes were bloodied and his face was scraped pretty good."

Peak froze. "Did Griff say if the guest was traveling with a child?"

"I don't have that information."

"Did Griff say if the man was still there?"

"Affirmative. And that call is only a few minutes old."

"Okay, Shelley, tell the sheriff we need assistance. We need Miles City SWAT ASAP to set up on the motel. Tell him we may have one of the most wanted men in the country in that motel, possibly with a kidnapped boy from Chicago."

66

Travis Prell, a sniper with the Miles City Police SWAT Team, lay flat on his stomach concealed by the wheatgrass in the field across the highway.

The door and window of Unit 22 of the Sunset Dreams Motel filled his scope.

Next to the motel, out of sight in the parking lot of the Rawhide gas station, Miles City SWAT Team leader, Doug Mott, had set up a command post. Using the hood of a Lone Pine patrol car he studied the motel property and floor plan, hastily sketched on the back of a diner placemat by the manager, Griff Johnson.

Mott had guided the team, supported by deputies from Lone Pine, Garfield and Prairie counties, along with Montana Highway Patrol troopers, to set up inner and outer perimeters while he developed an entry and arrest strategy for Unit 22.

Two plainclothes female officers, pushing cleaning carts, knocked on the doors of all occupied units. Other officers quickly and quietly escorted guests to a safe zone beyond the perimeter.

While passing by Unit 22, one of the officers, quickly and surreptitiously, made a check at the door and window. She heard the TV and shower, confirming activity in the room.

At the command post, Griff Johnson looked hard at the images Lieutenant Mott was showing him on his phone. The FBI had distributed photos of the subject known as Abel Renard Wixom.

"You're certain this is the man, sir?" Mott asked again.

"That's definitely him." Johnson scratched his sideburns. "His clothes were bloody. His face was scratched. He had a backpack and a duffel bag with him, but I can't say for sure if a child, like that boy, or anyone else, is in the room with him."

Mott nodded, then made a round of whispered radio checks.

SWAT members wearing helmets, armor, headset radios, and equipped with rifles and handguns, were ready. Sharpshooters had taken up key points while other team members lined up on the unit. The squad pressed against the motel's walls as they inched toward the room from either side.

"All right, if we're good to go, let's call into the room so we can end this peacefully." Mott nodded to the negotiator, Louise Reddick.

Reddick dialed the room number but the phone rang unanswered. She waited, then tried again. After four efforts, she moved closer and, using an unmarked police vehicle as a shield, spoke through a bullhorn.

"Mr. Abel Wixom." Reddick's voice crackled

across the motel courtyard. "Mr. Abel Wixom in Unit 22, this is the Miles City police, supported by Lone Pine County. We want to talk to you. For your own safety, would you exit now with your hands raised and your palms forward."

Several long, silent moments passed.

Reddick tried calling in again, then repeated the police order through the bullhorn.

No response.

Several more moments passed. Reddick turned to Mott. It was now his call.

They couldn't wait a second longer, he thought. There was always a chance Wixom could have spotted them setting up. It was a safe bet he was monitoring news; he had to know he was on the FBI's Most Wanted list, so there's no telling what he might do if he had the boy with him.

Mott made a decision and spoke into his headset. "Go! Go! Go!"

Five seconds later the battering ram smashed the door, accompanied by the deafening crack-crack and blinding flashes of stun grenades fired through the window. The team stormed the small room, flashlight beams piercing the fog as the heavily armed officers swept it in choreographed tactical movements to detect and neutralize any threat.

They tossed the mattress, checked under the bed, checked the sofa bed and checked the closet. No sign of anyone. The room was empty.

The TV was on, tuned to an all-news network. The bathroom door was closed. The shower could be heard.

"Police! Exit the room with your hands raised now!" the squad leader shouted.

Nothing happened.

The order was repeated, and still nothing happened.

The team popped the door and entered, filling the room.

"What the hell?"

A man's body hung from the center of the ceiling, a belt around his neck affixed to the overhead sprinkler nozzle.

The first SWAT member immediately hugged the man's legs and raised his weight while the second slashed the belt with a knife.

Upon lowering the man to the floor one of the members touched his fingers to the man's neck.

67

Somewhere over Nebraska

Seventy-five minutes from Denver, a flight attendant summoned Malko from his aisle seat to the front of the plane. The first officer had stepped from the cockpit to relay an urgent message.

While Malko was gone Marsh checked her phone again.

The airline provided in-flight Wi-Fi service but the connection was down. The FBI had arranged to send them encrypted secure updates via the crew. Marsh resumed studying files for several minutes before Malko returned and slid back into his seat.

"Abel Wixom is alive." Malko kept his voice low. "Tried to hang himself but they cut him down in time."

"And the boy—did they find Gage Hudson?"

He shook his head.

"This is what we just got from our people on the ground." He paged through his notes. "They've launched a major search operation."

"What about Wixom's vehicle and motel room?"

"Our ERT people from Great Falls are on-site along with a team flown in from Salt Lake. They're processing the camper and motel room."

"Did Wixom say anything useful?"

"No. They airlifted him to Billings unconscious and critical. It's uncertain he'll survive." Malko glanced at his watch. "We'll land in Denver soon, get our connection to Billings. We should be at the hospital in a couple of hours to question him."

"If he regains consciousness," Marsh said.

Malko nodded.

"Has this find gone out to the press yet?" Marsh asked.

"Not yet. We've got a head start but it'll break wide open soon enough."

As their jetliner encountered a pocket of rough air, Marsh considered the circumstances of the case so far and turned to Malko.

"This should tie everything to Wixom."

Malko removed his glasses, tapped them to his chin and said, "Not entirely. He didn't act alone."

"Agreed. We have Alma McCain's admission of her and Griner receiving five thousand dollars to help him, but it's shaping up to be all Wixom."

"No, beyond that, there's still Cal and Faith."

"What about them?"

"Remember, they each had separate bank accounts and moved enough cash to cover the amount Wixom paid McCain and Griner. We can run the serial numbers of any of the remaining paid-out cash against banks the Hudsons used."

"You're still hanging on to the idea one of them conspired with Wixom?"

"We've got a lot of unanswered questions."

"True, but with everything now pointing to Wixom, why bring the parents back into this?"

"There are factors we can't ignore," Malko said. "They lied to us. Their marriage is fractured. There's the Tate connection. There's Cal's plan to take Gage to Kuwait. The shoe in the Dumpster behind the strip mall where they'd stopped and Faith was crying in the car. There's the T-shirt so close to the Hudson home and the timing."

"Timing?"

"Given that Adria Zoliski checks her garden each day, the timing of the discovery of Gage's T-shirt makes it impossible for Wixom to have placed it there when he was driving across the country."

Marsh weighed Malko's theories.

"I know you're trying to avoid tunnel vision," she said, "but isn't it possible you're overthinking this?"

"This isn't over, so nothing can be ruled out."

He glanced up to see the first officer coming down the aisle toward them. When he arrived at their seats, he leaned in, keeping his voice low.

"Agent Malko, the captain has confirmed our connection's been restored. You can use your phones in-flight to receive and transmit messages now."

The agents' phones began pinging with a stream of messages. Malko went to the most recent. It was

from Keith Coogan, with the Evidence Response
Team processing Wixom's camper.

Agents Malko and Marsh, we're alerting you to this
item recovered in the subject's vehicle.

Malko read the description and looked at the
attached color photo of a blue SkySlyder sneaker,
size five, with green neon laces in a zipper pattern. The sole had a diamond and sawtooth traction design.

"Tibor," Marsh said. "It's the right shoe. It has
to be Gage's missing shoe."

"I know." Malko glanced down at the patch-
work-quilted landscape flowing under them before going back to his phone and the photo of Gage
Hudson smiling back at him.

Are we on the right track?

Time was running out and the odds were mounting against them.

Malko pleaded with fate to give him a break.

He pleaded for the plane to go faster and for
Wixom to recover so he could question him.

Above all, he prayed for Gage Hudson to be
alive because in the pit of his gut Malko knew that
he couldn't bear to stare at another little corpse.

68

Billings, Montana

"Duration of suspension is a critical element for near-hanging victims."

Dr. Violet Knight explained Wixom's condition to Malko and Marsh as they stood in a waiting area of the hospital's intensive care unit. The large windows presented a sweeping view of Billings.

"While early resuscitation was administered, we can't pinpoint the duration of suspension. Permanent cerebral damage is inevitable if oxygen to the brain is cut off for more than five, even three, minutes."

"What are the odds he'll recover?" Malko asked.

Knight slid her hands deep into the pockets of her white coat, then answered. "He's been intubated and he's on a ventilator. Given he's suffered head trauma, consistent with an auto accident, and given his vital signs, I would rate chances at full recovery with no neurological problems at ten percent and regaining consciousness at fifteen percent. The next few hours will be crucial."

"Thank you, Doctor. We'll stand by right here."

In the moment the doctor left, new footsteps echoed in the corridor as Scott Nesbitt, the FBI's agent in Billings, approached.

"Did he wake up? Did you talk to him?"

"No, it doesn't look good," Marsh said. "We're going to wait it out here."

"Okay," Nesbitt said. "Let's find a room to discuss status before I get back to the command post in Lone Pine."

Nesbitt found an empty office near a nursing station and closed the door. It was cramped. Shift schedules were pinned to the corkboard beside personnel lists over a table cluttered with textbooks and notes, as if someone were studying. They pulled chairs to the table and consulted the incoming messages on their phones from various investigators.

"We've got nothing on the search for the boy so far," Nesbitt said. "Nothing from the dogs or the air. There's not much out there but a whole lot of open spaces."

"Other than the shoe," Marsh said, "we don't have anything irrefutable that puts Gage in that van. Preliminary testing on Wixom's clothing indicates the blood is Wixom's."

"Hang on." Malko concentrated on his phone. "Coogan with ERT just said they've confirmed collecting partials on a window in the camper that are consistent with Gage's."

"That puts Gage in the camper," Nesbitt said.

"Yes, but at what point was he removed from

it and where?" Malko's eyes stayed on his phone. "There's more here from Coogan—they found Wixom's laptop in the motel."

"Maybe he left a suicide note in it," Marsh said. "Can they hack into it?"

"No. Coogan says it's locked with a password that's protected with sophisticated security software." Malko cursed under his breath. "A cyber expert team is flying in from Denver to work on it."

"The press find out yet?"

"The county says we just got our first call from a radio station in Miles City. You can bet it's going to snowball," Nesbitt said. "Now, on Wixom's vehicle, Montana Highway Patrol says the tires show dangerous tread wear and the left front blew. That's how he ended in up in the—"

Malko's phone rang and he left the room to take the call in the corridor.

"Agent Malko, Norm Howell, LAPD. They told me what's happened and that you're in Montana. Have you talked to Wixom?"

"No, he's still unconscious and we haven't located the boy."

"I expect you got your hands full but we've got something I thought you should have concerning Wixom's recent activities."

"What's that?"

"One of our Interpol operatives who'd infiltrated Illicitum Passio picked up recent posts by a handle that we know is used by Felix Steed Vassellef, one of Wixom's aliases. In the posts he'd boasted of picking up a fresh date for the market a few days ago while working with a partner."

"A partner?"

"Yes. And Wixom also claimed he'd been keeping a journal on a successful project while enjoying the heat. My instincts tell me he's talking about Gage Hudson."

Malko's eyes widened slightly as he searched the Billings skyline.

"Norm, you have any indication who this partner is?"

"No, but we're digging. Did you find a phone or computer with Wixom? His posts have to be in there?"

"No phone—maybe he tossed it—but we have a laptop. It's locked and we've got people working on it."

"Short of talking to Wixom, or finding his partner, your best shot at finding the boy is unlocking that computer and—"

Voices down the hall coupled with medical staff rushing into Wixom's ICU room seized Malko's attention. His pulse kicked up when he saw Dr. Knight hurry into it.

"I have to call you back, Norm."

Malko returned to the small office to inform Marsh and Nesbitt of the developments. Some twenty-five minutes later, Knight emerged from Wixom's room to find the investigators waiting in the hall.

"I'm sorry," she said. "Mr. Wixom went into

cardiac arrest. Our efforts to revive him were unsuccessful. He's gone."

Malko stared at the doctor for a moment, then he lowered his head and thought.

"Doctor, I request that we keep Wixom's death confidential. Not a word is to be released at this time. Leave it with the FBI as it's extremely critical to our investigation and efforts to find Gage Hudson."

69

River Ridge, Illinois

"For viewers who're just joining us, there's breaking news in the multistate Amber Alert case of Gage Hudson, the nine-year-old boy allegedly abducted from a suburban Chicago midway attraction a few days ago."

Cal Hudson reached for the remote and increased the volume as Faith sat transfixed before their television. No one had alerted them to the break in the case and their anxiety mounted.

River Ridge police had put extra officers around their property and it felt like the world was closing in on them.

The news anchor's voice carried over a split screen—half with aerial pictures of forensic experts in white jumpsuits working on a van embedded in brush and half showing investigators at the Sunset Dreams Motel.

"The FBI and local police have set up roadblocks and launched a massive ground search after

finding the camper van of Abel Renard Wixom in a remote section of eastern Montana. The FBI had put Wixom, a midway worker with a history of aliases and offenses against children, on its Most Wanted list, alleging that he'd played a role in the Hudson boy's disappearance from an attraction known as the Chambers of Dread."

Cal and Faith's phones were ringing. *NBC News* for Cal: "Mr. Hudson, we're seeking your reaction to developments in Montana..." The *Washington Post* for Faith: "Mrs. Hudson, can you share your thoughts on the latest events. What're police telling you?" More press calls followed—CNN, *USA TODAY*, Reuters, then his own newspaper. They declined all requests for comment. News crews arrived in front of their home as they continued watching the live coverage.

"Sources tell our network that Wixom had attempted suicide and was revived and flown near-death to a hospital in Billings where police are keeping a vigil in hopes of questioning him about the location of Gage Hudson, who has so far not been found."

"Oh God!" Faith said. "Why aren't Malko or Price telling us about this?"

Cal called Malko to demand information but he couldn't get through as images of roadblocks, helicopters and K-9 units appeared on the TV screen.

"Today's major developments are the latest in a heart-wrenching case that remains steeped in mystery..."

Footage of Cal and Faith at their first news conference at the midway was shown with an inset image of Gage in his Cubs T-shirt.

"According to sources close to the investigation, Gage's parents—Cal and Faith Hudson—failed their polygraph examinations. And, very recently, undisclosed evidence in the case has been found near their River Ridge home. Sources say the Hudsons have not been ruled out as potential suspects in their son's disappearance and how, or if, they're connected to events unfolding now in Montana."

Faith covered her face with her hands.

After more futile efforts to reach Malko, Cal rushed to their bedroom. In between calls and checking his phone, he began packing a suitcase.

"Where're you going?" Faith watched him from the doorway.

"What does it matter to you?"

"Cal, please, for God's sake."

"Montana. If they find him, I want to be there."

"I'm going with you."

"Shouldn't you stay here with Tate and get your stories straight?"

"I'm not involved! You have to believe me."

"I don't, Faith. I don't know what to believe."

"What about you?"

"What about me? I never cheated on you."

"I heard you on the phone. You're hiding something, Cal."

"What're you talking about?"

"You were in the laundry room, and the window was open. I was outside. You were talking to someone like they knew what was going on, something about one of your stories and a connection to Gage."

Cal said nothing.

"Who were you talking to?"

"I was begging an old police source for help to find Gage."

Unsure if his answer reconciled with what she'd overheard, Faith stared long and hard at Cal until the doorbell rang.

River Ridge detectives Price and Lang arrived and the Hudsons assailed them with angry questions about Gage.

"No, Gage has not yet been located," Lang said.

"I can't reach Malko," Cal said. "Why won't anyone tell us anything?"

"That's why we're here," Price said. "We have few facts—everything's still unfolding."

The detectives looked at Cal's suitcase near the door.

"Is someone going somewhere?" Lang asked.

"I'm going to Montana. If Gage is there, I want to be there," Cal said.

Price looked at Lang, then back at the Hudsons. "Cal, Faith, it might be best if you come with us to headquarters."

"Am I under arrest?" Cal said.

"No."

"Is there a court order restricting my movements?"

"No."

"Then I'm going to Montana to find my son. Excuse me." Cal went to the window. "There's my cab." He left the house, working his way through the cluster of reporters and cameras out front without commenting.

Watching from the window Lang got on his phone and called for units to follow Cal's taxi, alert airport security to confirm the airline and alert the FBI on Cal's travel.

"He'll be easy to spot." Lang saw news cars following him, as well.

At the window, watching her husband leave to what may be the death site of their child, Faith's eyes burned with fear.

"I've got to go to Montana, too," she said, turning to start for her bedroom as Price confronted her.

"Faith, wait."

"I need to be with my son."

"We can't stop you from going but you must understand there's little you can do there at this time. Come with us to headquarters. We have more questions and we can keep you updated."

Faith was torn. Hugging herself, she collapsed on a chair, rocked back and forth while tears streamed from her eyes. "I don't know what I should do. Things are happening so fast."

"What things?" Price asked.

She was silent, her eyes going around her home. "Faith? What things?"

"I don't understand it but I think Cal's involved." Price and Lang traded glances.

"I think you should arrest my husband."

70

On the way to O'Hare, in the back seat of his cab, Cal had trouble fastening his seat belt because his hands were shaking.

After repeated attempts, he succeeded.

For several miles he forced himself to pray for Gage to be alive, to be found safe and for this nightmare to end. But by the time they got to the expressway he found himself picking through the entrails of his conversation in the laundry room earlier, and the other untold horror story in his life.

With Wixom's history of aliases and offenses against children, is it possible that he's tied to what we did? It can't be. It just can't! If I reveal what we did I'll go to prison. But if I hang on, and we find that it's not tied to Gage, then the whole thing remains buried and no one will ever know.

But if I'm wrong and remain silent I'm gambling with my son's life.

A tongue of red flared in the cab's rearview mirror just as the siren sounded behind them and a River Ridge patrol car pulled them over.

"What the hell?" the driver said. "I wasn't speedin'."

Cal turned around. Behind the patrol unit was an unmarked car, grill lights wigwagging as Detectives Price and Lang got out and walked toward the cab, coming up on either side.

"Drop both rear windows," Cal told the driver.

Price leaned toward the right rear where Cal sat. Lang was on the left.

"Cal." Price raised her voice over the streaming traffic. "We strongly advise you not to go to Montana."

"Why? Everything points to Gage being there."

"We have no confirmation. For now, we think it's best you come with us. We need your help."

"My help?"

"With questions that might come out of Montana."

Cal's seat belt clicked as he unbuckled and got out of the car to face Price. "Is there something you're not telling me? Something Faith fed you?"

"Cal, if you come with us, you'll be the first to know should any news arise. We just got word. Malko and Marsh are already on their way back."

"Why're they coming back so soon?"

"The FBI didn't elaborate. Work is still ongoing there and here."

Cal saw news cameras trained on him from the distance. Traffic rushed by like his fears as he fought to hang on. Seeing an airliner climbing in the distance, he thought of how in a few hours he could be in Montana.

What if Gage is out there? What if he's dead? What if it's my fault?

He turned to Price.

"Are you charging me? Is that why Malko's coming back?"

"No."

"Are you arresting me?"

"No."

"Did something happen out there you're not telling me?"

"Cal, please just come with us."

"I'm not involved. I've got nothing to do with it, no matter what Faith or anyone else tells you. I'm not involved."

Price nodded.

"None of this is over, Cal. We don't have all the answers."

He stared hard at her as gusts from a passing tractor trailer tumbled over them.

"Rachel, you have to tell me—is my son dead? Tell me what you know."

She brushed away hair that had curtained in front of her face. "I don't know, Cal. In my heart I pray for his safety."

He searched her eyes for a trace of deception.

"Swear to me."

"I swear to you," she said. "Come with us. We need your help."

Tears stood in his eyes and he sniffed.

Exhausted and nearly broken, he watched another jet climb away like it was taking with it his last hope. Then he reached into his pocket, gave the driver some crumpled bills and asked him to pop open the trunk. He hefted his bag from it and went with the detectives.

Rew Morina

71

"Thanks again for coming into River Ridge."

FBI Agent Dee Lewin set a ceramic mug of coffee before Elka Thorne.

"Anything to help."

Thorne, in her early forties, wearing a smart blazer and her hair pulled back in a tight ponytail, was borderline attractive with an angular face. Her job as a Chicago homicide detective had hardened her smile, which was evident when she offered it to Lewin and her partner, Agent Grant Hern, before sipping from the mug.

"As I told you on the phone—" Lewin opened her file folder "—we've been reviewing Cal Hudson's stories for possible ties to Gage's disappearance and one of them concerns one of your cases, Detective."

"The Ezili case."

"Yes, Ezekiel Lyman Ezili, convicted of murdering six-year-old Teddie Turco."

"It was a horrible case."

"New information on Gage Hudson's case has

come to light," Lewin said. "We've been referencing and cross-checking it with news stories Cal has written, including his reporting on the Ezili case."

"What about it?"

"Does the term, or the name, Illicitum Passio mean anything to you in relation to the Ezili case?"

"No, I'm not familiar with it. Should I be?"

"It's Latin, the name used by a secret global network of pedophiles."

"Yeah, well, we knew Ezili was connected to several networks, as is often the case with pedophiles. I don't recall all the names. So no, I'm not surprised. This new information you've got, did it come out of Montana and the matter with Abel Wixom, your suspect? I saw on the news that he tried to off himself. Is he still alive?"

"I can't go into details because we're still processing things."

"I understand you have to protect your case, but you called me."

"Yes, and here's what I can tell you," Lewin said. "We believe it's likely Wixom did not act alone in Gage's disappearance, that he was working with others and that those others may be connected to Illicitum Passio."

For the next several minutes Lewin related what the FBI knew about the organization. How its members had been known to infiltrate government agencies related to child welfare around the world.

"Gage's abduction may not have been random," Lewin said, "but an act against the Hudson family whereby Gage was targeted. Do you have any thoughts on this avenue of investigation?"

"It's one theory. I'm not privy to all of your evidence, but what would be the motive for such an act against the Hudsons?"

"You'll recall that Ezili always maintained his innocence, charging that the press had published police fiction about him and that he called on his supporters for a day of reckoning against his enemies. After some political pressure, an internal investigation was launched."

Thorne rolled her eyes slightly, shook her head with the hint of a smile. "Yeah, you'd expect that from an evil, deranged, child-raping murderer." Her eyes narrowed. "You ever look at the crime scene photos of what he did to Teddie Turco? The internal investigation found nothing. Listen, Ezili was in possession of that boy's DNA. Our case against him was as solid as the walls of this room."

"You know he was stabbed to death by a fellow inmate at Dixon Correctional Center ten months ago?"

"Yeah, can't say I shed a tear."

"So you don't believe members of Illicitum Passio could be behind Gage Hudson's abduction, as some way to honor Ezili?"

Thorne eyed him carefully. "I think you're reaching with that one."

"Are you aware that members of the group have been known to be pathologically loyal to one another, with a cultlike devotion to vendettas?"

"That could be, but if so, why go after the Hudsons?"

"Possibly because of Cal's reporting and profile with the *Chicago Star-News*?"

She thought for a moment, a subtle wave of unease flickering across her face. "Maybe, but why not me, the lead homicide detective? Wouldn't I be the lead enemy? Why not threaten me, or my teenage daughter?"

"Have you received any threats in relation to Ezili's case?"

"No, nothing. That's why I think this is a weak theory, based on what you're sharing with me."

Lewin glanced at Hern, then back at Thorne.

"All right," Lewin said. "I think we're done for now."

Cal had been sitting alone in River Ridge police headquarters at Price's desk, waiting in agony.

He knew they had put Faith in another room.

A TV screen was tuned to an all-news network. Nothing had emerged about Gage. If it had, no one had told him. No word on whether Wixom had survived his suicide attempt to talk to investigators.

Cal glanced at the time. It was late and no one knew if Malko and Marsh were due to return late tonight or in the morning. Cal had overheard talk of sending him home. The uncertainty was tormenting him.

Activity and discussion spilled from the hall where the interview rooms were and into the squad room. Lewin and Hern, the FBI agents who'd been taking apart Cal's old stories, were thanking a woman, who turned toward Cal.

In a heartbeat, their eyes met. Cal recognized her instantly. It was the first time he'd seen her in years but he knew her voice—knew it all too well from their phone conversations in the past few days.

Lewin shook her hand. "Thanks again for your help, Detective Thorne."

Cal's stomach roiled. *Using her real name now, is she? Not Beth Gibson?*

Why was she here? What did she tell them? Did she tell them everything?

72

Billings, Montana

Time was ticking down on Gage Hudson.

Upon landing from Denver, FBI agents Tracy Chiu and Al Decker went directly to the FBI's office in downtown Billings.

It was well into the evening and Billings agent Scott Nesbitt, who'd kept the office open, helped them heft their equipment in hard aluminum cases to the second floor of the five-story white stone building. "This way." Nesbitt led them to a meeting room where he'd placed Abel Wixom's recovered laptop on the conference table.

Aware that the key to Gage Hudson's location could be hidden in the device, Chiu and Decker wasted no time setting up their computers. Concentrating on speed and vigilance, they ran a few tests on Wixom's laptop. Screens beeped, flashed with graphics and coding as Decker typed on his keyboard. After several moments, Chiu bit her bottom lip.

"It's just as we feared," she said.

"How bad is it?" Nesbitt asked.

"It's locked with a six-digit password. We could submit passcodes to attempt entry but the system is designed to autoerase the entire contents after ten failed password attempts."

"So that's it?" Nesbitt said. "We're locked out?"

"No, not yet," Decker said as he shifted to one of the laptops they'd brought with them. "We've got a few options."

"We're going to try loading a software image file through a protocol," Chiu said. "It'll run from the random access memory. If it works, we'll then be able to run a password recovery analysis without risk of activating the autoerase function."

"It could be a while before we know," Decker said.

Nesbitt nodded.

"Okay, I've got to reach the case agent and update him."

Nesbitt left the meeting room and called Malko. Afterward, he returned and watched Chiu and Decker, who were immersed but nodding.

"It worked," Chiu said. "We've bypassed the autoerase. We're running a passcode recovery analysis. With a little luck we should be able to unlock it and gain entry. No telling how long this could take."

Nesbitt stepped away and made fresh coffee.

When he returned with steaming cups for everyone he saw Decker hunched over the laptop working to the staccato clicking of his keyboard.

By nightfall the tense mood in the room became upbeat.

"Bingo!" Decker pumped a fist into the air. "We're in!"

The Fifth Day

73

"The Hudsons have not been ruled out as potential suspects in their son's disappearance..."

The next morning in Chicago, Gloria Sayer picked up her phone. She wanted to tell the FBI what she knew but abandoned her call.

She'd come in early to catch up on work but had been engrossed in the all-news channel she'd cued up on her computer monitor. It had been reporting the same facts in the Hudson case all morning.

Gripped with indecision she looked out her window at Parker Hayes and Robinson in the Willis Tower, which everyone still called the Sears Tower. She searched the skyscrapers and Lake Michigan for an answer.

What really happened to Gage?

Yesterday, Gloria had returned from a vacation in Southeast Asia. She'd first learned about the disappearance of her coworker Faith Hudson's son while watching CNN between flights in the airport in Honolulu. Gloria had arrived back in Chicago to find the office devastated by the news. It was all people talked about. Some of Gloria's colleagues had taken to wearing little ribbons; some were volunteering to help search efforts in River Ridge; others took up a collection, to add to the firm's contribution to the reward for information on Gage.

And everyone, as Gloria had discovered, had spoken to the FBI.

"They want to talk to you, too," Eve Moore in records had told Gloria yesterday. "They want any information that can help, like who might've taken Gage, or if we think Cal or Faith could be involved."

"Cal or Faith? Really?"

"Can you believe it? Yes, as absurd as that sounds, they asked if we thought Faith or Cal had acted strange, had said or done anything unusual or out of character in the time before it happened."

"Anything?"

"Anything that might help. You're supposed to call the lead agent. He left a card on your desk."

Now, after watching the news coverage out of Montana, Gloria grappled with a decision. She knew things all right, things no one else knew about Faith—things that clouded her mind with a vengeful bitterness.

Everyone in the office thought Faith was so wonderful, so pretty. With her handsome husband and beautiful son: the perfect family. They don't know who she really is—that she cheated when she beat Gloria in the competition for the job she has.

That was Gloria's job. Gloria was more qualified than Faith. But Faith was the pretty one. That's why someone on the hiring committee had slipped Faith the questions before her interview segment so she could prepare her answers ahead of time. Rosalita, Gloria's pal in office admin, had confided that little tidbit to her.

She picked up the agent's card.

Yes, Gloria knew things the FBI should know about that bitch Faith. Like how in recent months she'd talked to senior management about a position at one of the firm's subsidiaries in New Zealand. Rosalita, who hears everything, told Gloria how Faith was very interested in the job abroad, almost like she needed to leave the country.

She'd also sought a cash advance and had asked for it to be documented as some sort of performance bonus. She wanted it kept off the books.

Gloria tapped the card in her hand.

Yes, it's terrible her son's missing but if the FBI is still considering her a suspect, well, maybe for the sake of that little angel, someone should step up and tell the truth. Rosalita wouldn't do it—she feared police because her brother had had some trouble with the law.

Someone should enlighten the FBI on what Faith was up to long before her son disappeared. Maybe she was involved.

Gloria looked at the card again, gritted her teeth and made the call.

74

River Ridge, Illinois

Malko was back at River Ridge headquarters that morning and on the phone.

In the short time since he and Marsh had returned from Montana they'd been engulfed with developments.

Searchers in Lone Pine still hadn't located Gage. They'd brought in cadaver dogs in case Wixom had buried him in a shallow grave. They'd found nothing so far. Meanwhile, in Billings, the cyber team was working on opening Wixom's laptop.

They needed to nail down Wixom's claim that a partner beyond McCain and Griner was involved, Malko thought, making calls when Lewin leaned into his office and flagged his attention.

"Remember Ezekiel Lyman Ezili? He murdered six-year-old Teddie Turco. He claimed police and press framed him for the murder and called on his followers for a 'day of reckoning.' We interviewed

Thorne, the lead Chicago homicide detective. She doesn't think there's a threat or a connection."

"What's your assessment?"

"We don't agree. Thorne says Ezili had the boy's DNA, which sealed the case. An internal investigation into Chicago homicide's Ezili case fizzled. But Ezili claimed he was framed, and he was stabbed to death in prison ten months ago. What's your take on this, Tibor?"

Malko thought for a moment.

"Until we can analyze the contents of Abel Wixom's laptop we can't rule out a possible connection. It's something we need to put to Cal and we should talk to whoever led the internal investigation."

Malko resumed dealing with his calls when Price appeared at his desk.

"We've got the Hudsons waiting in separate rooms," she said. "We've had them here for a long time and they're demanding answers and updates. Not sure how much longer we can hold them."

"We need to talk to them. For one, we need to resolve the question that each of them moved several thousand dollars in cash, enough to cover the amount Wixom paid McCain and Griner for their help. And we'll need to talk to McCain and Griner again, too. We've got to determine who paid who, and who Wixom's partner is."

Malko's phone rang and he took the call.

"Tibor, this is Bill Caffrey, ERT. Got some preliminary analysis on the T-shirt found near the Hudson home."

"Go ahead, Bill."

"The boy's DNA is present and consistent. The blood matches his."

"Any other DNA or trace on the shirt?"

"Yes, we found canine DNA."

"Dog? From our units?"

"Not ours. We've run it through our Canine CODIS system, but no hits. That database usually collects DNA from animals in illegal dogfighting. But there's a strong indication that stray dogs may have dragged the T-shirt from the Dumpster where the shoe was found, possibly following a scent to the boy's home."

"So how does one shoe end up in Wixom's camper and other items in River Ridge, Bill?"

"Well, given the proximity to the fairgrounds, it would be consistent with a frantic effort to change the boy's appearance, altering it from what the reported description would be. Get him into different clothes, toss what he was wearing. Blood would be consistent with the boy struggling at the time. He may have got scratched or scraped in the struggle."

"That fits." Malko saw Marsh waving to him. "Thanks, Bill. Gotta go." He ended the call. "What do you have, Sue?"

"Got a woman on the line, Gloria Sayer. She works with Faith. Says it's urgent. She was away when we interviewed people at Parker Hayes and Robinson."

Malko took the call, listening as Sayer calmly and quickly told him her concerns about Faith's behavior in the time leading up to her son's disappearance and her inquiries about working in New Zealand.

"Oh, and one last thing, Agent Malko," Sayer said. "One day, when one of our assistants was off sick, I saw Faith at the assistant's desk using her computer. She said hers wasn't working. I walked over to the supply cabinet for staples. She didn't notice me and I was taken aback when I looked at her screen. She was searching sites on how to change her name."

After the call ended Malko removed his glasses and massaged the bridge of his nose, thinking that they should seize Cal's and Faith's passports while cautioning himself once again not to get tunnel vision.

He looked up to find Marsh holding her phone out to him.

"Tibor, it's Nesbitt in Billings. They just hacked into Wixom's computer. They're sending everything they found to us now."

75

"Dear Lord."

Marsh took in the dizzying array of file folders on the large wall monitor in the darkened River Ridge conference room.

Agent Joanne Jepson, a cyber expert from the FBI's Chicago office, was sifting through the files from Wixom's laptop, which they'd connected to remotely.

As she worked, nearly a dozen investigators sat at the table, poised to act on any information that would point them to Gage. LAPD detective Norm Howell and his team in Los Angeles were on the teleconference line and simultaneously viewing the data through a secure link.

"Where do we begin to search?" Malko asked.

"We'll start searching files that Wixom would've accessed most recently and work back from there." Jepson's cursor moved quickly from folder to folder, stopping on the most recent, which was labeled The Operation.

"Open it," Malko said, then raised his voice for

the speakerphone. "Are you guys in California seeing this, Norm?"

"We're seeing it fine." Howell's voice was tinny through the speaker.

Jepson clicked and the folder displayed a file list. Her cursor moved over the dates coming to a document entitled "Vengeance Is Mine."

"It's the most recent file," Jepson said, clicking on it.

The document was headed with "Day of Reckoning."

"To all the guardians of Illicitum Passio, this is my final dispatch…"

Howell interrupted. "Hold up. Can we stop, please? I just want to emphasize that Wixom was writing exclusively to an ultrasecret group within Illicitum Passio, a group that supports the abduction, torture and even ritualized murder of its young victims. Illicitum Passio members are pathologically loyal to each other. It's common for them to exchange details of their activities. They get off on it. As well, Wixom would believe all of his communications were impenetrable, totally secure."

"So noted, thanks, Norm." Malko nodded for Jepson to resume.

"To all the guardians of Illicitum Passio, this is my final dispatch. As we all know, Ezekiel Lyman Ezili was murdered for a crime he never committed. His death was a result of his imprisonment following his persecution by police and the media. Chief among his tormentors: Detective E. Thorne and Calvin Hudson of the *Chicago Star-News*.

"They know what they did.

"To ensure ELE's death was not in vain, the guardians of Illicitum Passio have enacted a plan of retribution. We'll get to Thorne but our first target is Hudson."

Murmuring rippled around the table as Jepson continued scrolling through the note.

"I worked with the Decanus..."

"Stop. What's the Decanus?" Price asked.

"The Decanus," Howell said, "is an ancient Roman military rank, like a sergeant."

"This could be the partner," Malko said. "We'll work on the ID. Keep going through the document, Joanne."

"...the Decanus, who had stalked our target for months. We knew where he lived, how he lived."

Clear photos of Gage Hudson appeared in the document. Here he was in the schoolyard; here he was walking on the street with friends, at the mall with Faith, at the ballpark.

"We had considered taking possession at a point of vulnerability. It would've been easy.

But the Decanus presented another, more fitting strategy, mined from our ability to infiltrate the earLoadzone. There, posing as young enthusiasts of midway thrills, we learned of our target's desire to experience the Chambers of Dread. He was consumed by it for it was all he talked about. How deliciously fortuitous, given our situation, given our knowledge, given our access! We engaged our target in conversation on earLoadzone and nurtured his desire to the point of success. When we discovered he would be visiting the attraction, preparations were made and we set our operation in motion. Once he entered, he was but a fly caught in the web…"

A few soft curses went around the group at the table.

"Events unfolded flawlessly. Once our target was captured in the Chambers, he was secured in a hockey bag and transported through the empty lot behind the apparatus to a van driven by the Decanus. The target's appearance was hastily and dramatically changed…the Decanus left the area cleanly."

The document continued with the next steps of the operation.

"I cooperated with police in the ensuing investigation, then citing a family emergency

I left Chicago for Vancouver to await our arrangement to secure counterfeit passports and documentation for the prize to be delivered to Bangkok. Until then the Decanus was safely hiding with our cargo in our so-called Fortress of Solitude, a location so befitting as a tribute to ELE. You must see it!"

A color photo surfaced showing an old log cabin nearly swallowed by dense woods, a rusted metal wagon wheel leaning on a post near the hand pump water well on the sagging porch.

"However, I regret to report that I've been overtaken by circumstance and have failed in my duty. In my exhaustion while driving to my destination, I crashed in this godforsaken and forgotten corner of Montana and severely injured my head. I am in great pain. My plan to obtain a rental and continue was futile. I saw my name and face televised nationally. Police here have moved with terrifying speed. And now, as I talk to you, I hear them calling for me.

"My hands tremble as I write for my journey in this life has ended. But all the guardians of Illicitum Passio must never forget: ELE committed no crime. He knew what Thorne and Hudson did, but no one—not even his lawyer—would listen to him. In their minds he'd already been convicted. Thorne and Hudson are the guilty ones. A

toll must be exacted. We started with Hudson.
I hope the fortress will one day be a secret
shrine that will be a destination for guardians of Illicitum Passio to make a pilgrimage.

"Because Hudson helped cause the death
of an innocent man, I call on the Decanus, to
take the blood of his son."

The face of every investigator in the room hardened.

A still photograph flashed on the screen showing Gage, his hair shorn, his eyes wide with fear,
as he lay in his underwear, gagged and bound to a
bed as the message ended.

"To the Decanus, I cry: Save yourself and
kill him now!"

76

They had brought Cal back to headquarters that morning and had hurried him into the conference room, seating him at the end of the table closest to the wall monitor.

The screen was blank.

He saw an agent, at her laptop, ready. He took in the others, looking at him, assessing his unshaven face, his mussed hair, his red-rimmed eyes. Their expressions were taut, sober. Something horribly monumental was coming and a moment of silence passed before Malko started.

"Cal, new evidence has surfaced and we need your help with it."

"Did you find Gage?"

"No."

"Is he alive?"

"We don't know."

"You don't know? What the hell happened in Montana with Wixom?"

"We need to show you something and it'll be extremely hard to face."

Bracing himself, Cal cursed under his breath.

"Remember that after you see this we need your help." Malko nodded and someone cut the lights.

The agent at the laptop began typing on her keyboard. The wall monitor came to life as she moved her cursor along the same path to the folders and files the investigators had seen. For the next several minutes as she clicked and scrolled, the only sounds in the room were the hum of the ventilation fan and Cal's breathing as he read the message calling for revenge against him and viewed the photographs.

When they came to the last one, Cal was confused and thought, *Is that a mannequin? A horror-house zombie doll? Some sort of twisted joke?* Then in a sickening heartbeat he realized it was Gage on the bed, stripped to his underwear, bound and gagged, head shaven, eyes bulging with fear.

My son.

The screen went blank with Wixom's last words thundering in his brain. *"Save yourself and kill him now!"*

Cal felt his soul ripped from him, his mind flailing as he plunged from reality into an abyss. He slouched in his chair, cupped his hands over his nose and mouth. His eyes burned; his breath locked in his lungs. His throat ached with rage at himself, rage at Thorne—all wrapped with guilt at being so selfishly stupid, so unforgivably stupid, as he fought to cry out for his son.

Malko put his hand on his shoulder.

"Cal, I'm so sorry to put you through this. But

it's crucial that you hear me. We believe Wixom sent his message out to his underground group. We're working against time doing everything we can to locate the cabin and find Gage. We're going through every database we can for records on Wixom, Ezili and anyone possibly linked to them. We've got our cyber and photography people studying the image. We've reached out to national security to use satellite and GPS mapping protocols to identify the images. We've called in Elka Thorne to help us determine who Wixom's partner, the Decanus, is. This is where we need you."

Struggling to think, Cal nodded and Malko rolled his chair so that he was sitting directly in front of him and staring hard into his eyes.

"What is Wixom's allegation against you about Ezili?"

Cal stared back, slack-jawed, without speaking.

"Cal, what does he mean when he claims Ezekiel Ezili committed no crime? That you and Thorne are guilty, that you know what you did?"

Cal was silent—dumbstruck.

"In his letter from prison published in the *Sun-Times*, Ezili claimed he was innocent, that he was set up for the murder of six-year-old Teddie Turco, that your reports about him were police-fed fiction, and called on his supporters for a day of reckoning. Cal, is it true?"

Cal began shaking his head; tears streamed down his face.

"What did you do, Cal?"

Cal swallowed.

"Listen to me!" Malko cried. "This information could be the key. This is no time to hold back. What in the world could be more important than your son's life?"

"I can't—I can't..."

"You can't what?"

"I can't carry this anymore— Oh God, I never thought it would—"

"Cal, we're running out of time."

"I'll tell you. I'll tell you what we did."

77

Cal dried his eyes and nose with tissues.

"I never believed this was connected. Ezili was dead—the case was buried. I swear to God that if I knew it was connected, that it would help us find Gage, I would've come to you—but I just couldn't believe it was possibly linked. I was such a fool."

Malko was stone-faced, waiting for answers.

"You've talked to Thorne," Cal started, "you've studied the case, so you have most of the background on Ezili and Teddie Turco. How, nearly every weekend, Teddie's mother took him to the General Union Mall on the West Side. Ezili was a part-time security guard there and became obsessed with Teddie.

"He learned their routine. Ezili knew that Teddie's mother let him go to a pet store alone while she shopped at the clothing boutique across from it. She could see him but not all the time. There were gaps. Ezili knew this as he stalked them, just as he knew when the security cameras worked or didn't work, just as he knew nonpublic entrances and exits. Ezili was good at luring and, one day on his day off, he lured Teddie away from that pet store and took him to his apartment where he raped and tortured him for several days before dumping his body in a ravine on the south side.

"I led on coverage for the *Star-News*, that's how I know Elka Thorne. She came to like me, trust me, leak details to me. In covering the case I talked to Teddie's family." Tears slid down Cal's cheeks. "I'll never forget how his mother held his framed photograph in her arms the whole time she talked to me. I thought of Gage and it ripped my heart out."

Cal paused for a minute, trying to compose himself.

"I interviewed store staff," he then continued, "mall security, including Ezili. I found him intelligent, a charmer, and I struck up a rapport with him. He seemed the most interested in the status of the case and would meet me on his own time, even invited me to his apartment to trade ideas and information.

"At the time, I never knew he was the prime suspect.

"After a couple of weeks the story faded and I moved on to others. But I kept chipping away on the Turco case. I'd go to Ezili, and other security guards, to see if they'd heard anything new. Of course I'd check with Thorne on the status of the investigation.

"One day Thorne reached out to me. She wanted to talk off the record and made me swear that I'd never repeat a word. I agreed and when we met she opened up about Ezili. I've never told anyone what I'm telling you. Thorne said they knew without a doubt that Ezili killed Teddie. She told me how Ezili was also suspected of killing a seven-year-old boy in Pittsburgh the same way a few years earlier but that detectives there never had enough evidence to charge him.

"In Teddie's case, Thorne said Ezili's alibi didn't hold up but absolutely everything pointed to him. But all they had was circumstantial evidence. She feared that he was going to get away with it, move away and kill again, leaving a trail of child corpses in his wake, and there was no way to stop him without irrefutable evidence.

"I grew angry and said that they needed to nail Ezili. That's when she said there was a way and only I could help because Ezili trusted me. Thorne suggested I visit Ezili, then secretly leave something in his apartment."

"Leave something?" Malko said.

"Yes, but I was reluctant. I told her that it was wrong but then she showed me crime scene photos of Teddie and the Pittsburgh boy and said, 'What if this was your son? What if he does it again? Will you be able to live with yourself knowing you could have saved the life of the next boy?' Those pictures were…" Cal released a shaky breath. "I thought of Gage, thought of Teddie's mother hugging that photograph of her murdered child. All the while Thorne kept telling me that we had to stop this monster."

"So you agreed?" Malko asked.

He bit his bottom lip and nodded slowly. "Yes. She gave me a small vial of Teddie's blood she'd gotten from the crime scene. I contacted Ezili with some BS tip that they had a suspect, another guy. He was eager to talk and invited me to his apartment. At one point I used his bathroom and dabbed the tiniest dot of blood on the side of the counter, a towel and cleaning brush under his sink, as Thorne directed. The next day, she got a search warrant and Ezili was charged and ultimately convicted."

"So you planted evidence?"

"Yes."

"You and Thorne committed a crime?"

"Yes."

"And none of this came up in court?"

"No. We'd heard that Ezili, through his lawyer, tried to dispute the evidence but the court dismissed it because it was overwhelming. Teddie's blood pulled all the other evidence together."

Malko kept shaking his head.

"Ezili had to be stopped," Cal said.

"This is why his disciples in Illicitum Passio carried out the vendetta and targeted Gage," Malko said. "We found secret dispatches where he'd claimed to them that you and Thorne had set him up. Cal, why didn't you tell us at the outset?"

"Because Ezili was dead. For me that ruled out any chance he'd be involved. How could he? When I dug into his life, I never turned up any solid connection to this underground network. Ezili was smart but he was largely a loner and didn't come across as being skilled at using the dark web, even though I should've realized that's where monsters like him like to dwell. He struck me as a pitiful loner. And with his murder in prison, how the hell could he ever be connected to Gage? First, I suspected a carny or a stranger took Gage. Then because of Faith's affair, I thought maybe she and Tate really were behind it as some sort of pre-emptive custody move. Or maybe I just built a wall around the idea that what I did to Ezili could be connected to Gage. It was a secret I'd kept for years, one that would end my career and take away my freedom if anybody ever found out. I just never, ever thought it would turn into a war against me. What have I done?"

His hands were shaking when he covered his face with them.

"Cal, planting evidence is a felony. You could face prison time."

He nodded. "I know. I expect that. Are you going to arrest me, charge me, now?"

"We're not charging you at this time. You're free to move about for now, but we'd advise you to get an attorney. Maybe you could plea and seek felony probation, but we're getting ahead of things because we first need to talk to the state's attorney, so charges are pending."

"Does that mean I'm no longer a suspect in Gage's case?"

Malko took a long breath and let it out slowly. "Let's just say recent events have allowed us to focus the investigation. Right now, we need to identify Wixom's partner and locate the cabin. Do you have any information that can help? Anything from your dealings with Ezili?"

Cal concentrated. "I can't think… I—" He lifted his head and studied the wall monitor that was now blank. He searched it as if he could decipher or extract the key to finding Gage from the horror displayed there minutes ago.

It was futile.

"I'm sorry, there's nothing."

An agent entered the room and spoke softly into Malko's ear. He nodded, stood, reached for his phone, then said to Cal, "We just got two possible leads on the cabin."

"Where?"

Malko weighed the risks of telling him.

"Tell me, Malko. I deserve to know."

"Minnesota and Wisconsin. We've got people moving on both."

"Which one is stronger? I'll go there."

"No, Cal. Go home."

"You just said I'm free to go wherever I wish."

"Yes, but we think you should go home. We've already sent Faith home. We'll have someone drive you. Go, be with her. We'll keep you updated."

A few minutes later, a River Ridge cop was driving Cal back to his house.

The officer didn't say much and kept his radio low. Neighborhoods rolled by but Cal didn't see them. He sobbed in silence as the image of his son, his only child—bound, gagged and condemned to death—burned in his mind.

Oh, Gage, I'm so sorry.

78

Cal stepped from the patrol car and shouldered through the news crews clustered in front of his house as questions were hurled at him.

"Did they find Gage alive?"

"Did Wixom confess?"

Cal made it to his door, fumbled for his keys and rang the bell, with the officer waving reporters back to the street—*You're trespassing now, people, step off!* But the questions kept coming.

"What happened in Montana?"

"Cal, give us a statement, come on!"

The door was opened by Rory Clark.

Family friends were in the living room, huddled around Faith. Detectives Price and Lang observed from the side.

Faith looked at Cal and stood.

As if a switch were thrown, the air tightened. Some of the women tried to hold her back before she walked up to Cal and slapped him full across the face.

The whip-crack of her palm against his cheek

was followed by embarrassed silence. Startled by the blow, ears ringing, Cal ached to explain. Tears were streaming down Faith's face, which was twisted with rage and disdain.

"I hate you," she shrieked as if trying to inject her words into him. "Because of you they're going to find my baby dead!"

"Faith, please, you have to understand—"

"Oh, I understand. Price and Lang spoke to Malko and told me everything, told me what you did to Ezili. You set this all in motion! You knew about this all along and said nothing! *Nothing!*"

"Faith, please, it was complicated. I—"

"No! It all comes down to your selfish, insane pursuit of a glorious story. Well, you've got one *and you killed my child*! Are you happy now? Get out of my sight, get out of my life—*get out!*"

Shaking, gasping with choking sobs, Faith closed her hands into fists and punched at Cal's face and chest. He struggled to hold her before she surrendered and went limp, collapsing at his feet, broken in her grief.

Like comforting angels, Samantha Clark, Michelle Thompson, Pam Huppkey and their husbands swooped in and took Faith up to her bedroom to recover while most everyone threw piercing, accusatory looks at Cal.

Overcome with shame, guilt and fear, Cal retreated to the kitchen where he stood alone in his anguish, staring into the backyard. Their yard, where Gage had played as a toddler in the wading pool, where he'd learned to throw and catch a baseball, ride his bicycle, where he'd lived the everyday life of a kid.

Lived.

Was he dead?

The image of Gage nearly naked, eyes bulging, hair shorn, gagged and bound to a bed in some isolated cabin, burned through his mind like acid.

Why did they have to take him? This was my war, take me. *Kill* me.

Cal gripped the counter.

Stop feeling sorry for yourself. Do something!

The cabin.

Where was it? Malko wouldn't reveal the location, but Cal had caused this so he needed to fix it. He needed to be there to fight for Gage—or to hold him one last time.

I can't wait here, helpless, letting it all happen.

Where was that cabin? *Think!*

Something pinged in Cal deep beneath the surface of his consciousness, a blurred idea, or memory of somewhere remote, secluded, solitary.

Fortress of Solitude.

Now, in his moment of absolute desperation, he prayed as he summoned all of his concentration to remember. Maybe it was triggered by the horrible image of Gage at the cabin, maybe it was psychological sting of Faith's slap, or the savage guilt gnawing at his heart, but with a Herculean effort Cal drew upon every fiber within him, straining and clawing like a madman to smash through the door where the answer lay.

Something twigged.

Maybe it was an answered prayer.

Recognition hit like a sledgehammer to his head.

Fortress of Solitude, like Superman's remote base.

He knew where the cabin was.

Fear and hope whirled in Cal's mind when he heard someone reaching into his thoughts, saying something now. "Cal?" *Why was someone saying his name?*

Rory Clark stood next to him, compassion in his eyes.

"Cal, I don't know what to say. We're all praying for Gage. Tell me if there's anything we can do, anything at all."

Cal's thoughts shot through him like the chaos of the spinning room of the Chambers of Dread, echoing with the last instructions by the recorded demonic voice: *Choose your exit now, or perish!*

Cal seized on one thought. "Rory, I've got to get out of here."

"Where? Why?"

"I think I know where Gage is, where the FBI's going."

"What?"

"I've got to go now. I've got to be there when they find him."

The concern on Rory's face deepened. "You haven't slept or eaten. You're going through hell. I think you should just sit with us, let the FBI do their job and wait for news. Have something to eat, a shot of whiskey, something."

"No, no, I'm useless here. I've got to get out. I

can't take my car. I need to leave through the side so the mob out front doesn't see."

"But what about—" Rory gestured to Price and Lang.

"I'm free to go. I'm not under arrest. Not yet. I've got to do this. Rory, help me."

His friend blinked several times, considering his plea.

"This is my fault," Cal said. "I have to fix it! I have to be there, no matter what. Even if Gage is... even if he's...dead. Please help me!"

Rory found something in Cal's eyes that sealed a decision and he reached into his jeans. His keys jingled as he put them in Cal's hand.

"Take my Subaru. It'll need gas."

"Thank you. One more thing, and keep this confidential." Cal was writing on the pad Faith used for their grocery list. "Ask Jack to use his real estate skills and search all property records for this name ASAP and call me with the result."

"Ezili," Rory read the name. "But wouldn't the FBI do this already?"

"Yes, but they won't tell me anything. I need to confirm where they really are so I can be there."

"Okay, okay."

"Thank you and don't tell a soul. I've got my phone—call me with any news."

"You do the same." Rory glanced at the detectives, then back at Cal to wish him luck but he was already headed to the side door of his house.

It was shielded by a tall wooden fence and

shrubs, which would provide enough cover for Cal to make his way through the neighboring yards to Rory's Subaru.

shrubs, which would provide enough cover for Cal
to make his way through the neighboring yard—to
Rory's Subaru.

79

Somewhere in Illinois

Westbound on I-88 beyond Chicago somewhere between Aurora and De Kalb, Cal looked out at the rolling green countryside as he pushed the Subaru past the speed limit.

The car's GPS put the driving time from Chicago to his destination at over two hours. Nothing had broken on radio news broadcasts. Other than press interview requests, which he ignored, he'd received no messages on his phone. He adjusted his grip on the wheel and forced himself to breathe evenly and think clearly.

God, please let me be right about this!

Fields floated by, pulling him back to when he'd visited Ezekiel Ezili's apartment. Back to its peculiar smell, a mix of drugstore cologne and baby powder. The place was neat, spotless, nothing out of order.

Ezili had few pieces of furniture, giving his home an air of stark, desperate stillness. Cal thought it strange how he'd kept a bowl of candy at the door, evocative of Halloween, as if he'd expected children to visit.

Then there was Ezili himself, his shirt always tucked in, belt buckled tight. Cal remembered his pale face and weird, jagged bangs of thick black hair. "I cut it myself," he'd said, "to save money."

During their conversations there were long, odd silences and Cal broke one by inquiring about a framed photo on the wall.

"That? Oh, that cabin's been in my family for ages. One of my ancestors built it in the early 1800s near Savanna, in the hilly forests overlooking the Mississippi, in the northwest corner of the state. A good place to get away from it all, to think, or to hide. I call it my Fortress of Solitude."

Fortress of Solitude.

That's exactly how Wixom's message had described where the Decanus was keeping the "cargo," in a location that honored Ezili.

Cal realized that the photo of the cabin in Ezili's apartment had the same features as the photo pulled from Wixom's computer: nearly covered by dense forest, the water pump on the ramshackle porch, wagon wheel leaning on a post.

It had to be where they were keeping Gage.

Cal was nearing Dixon when he left the interstate and the phone rang.

"Cal, it's Rory. Jack says he had his people search all property records and nothing comes up for the name Ezili. Could it be under another family name or a company name?"

"I don't know. I'll find where the FBI is somehow."

Cal could've had his newspaper check if they had a lead on where the FBI was, but he didn't want to risk anyone knowing what he was doing.

Now, well over halfway to his goal, he accelerated along Route 52, a lonely two-lane ribbon threading past farms, churches and rural cemeteries. The power poles zoomed by and he soon came upon Savanna, a sleepy town of a few thousand people.

Time hammered against him as he eased along the quiet tree-lined main street, searching the two- and three-story nineteenth-century buildings. He saw the opera house, the food store, the VFW hall, before he locked on to what he needed.

Cardinal, Violet and Carroll Real Estate.

After parking, he entered the agency. It had a waist-high counter and three desks in an open-office area. Maps and pictures of properties covered one wall, while pleasant photos of the region, awards and framed certificates covered another. The only person he saw in the office, a silver-haired man, was at his desk talking on the phone. He interrupted his conversation to acknowledge Cal.

"Be right with you, sir."

Cal then noticed a large enclosed office at the far end of the floor. The door was open to a woman working at her desk, looking like a person of some authority.

"Yes, sir, what can I do for you?" The man came to the counter smiling.

"I'm interested in a specific property, a cabin, and I was hoping you could help me locate it."

"Certainly, is it listed with us?"

"I don't know."

"Do you have an address or a name?"

"I don't have much. It was built in the 1800s. It overlooks the Mississippi and may belong to the Ezili family."

"Ezili? Can you spell that name for me?"

Cal spelled the name and the man returned to his desk and typed at his computer keyboard. "Hmm, nothing comes up in our listings." The man scratched his chin and turned to a large wall map.

"I'm sorry I don't have more," Cal said.

"Well—" the man studied the map "—I know of cabins from that period near Palisades, with gorgeous views of the river from the bluffs. Got some up near Galena and near Chestnut Mountain. What was that name again?"

"Ezili."

"Ezili. The name doesn't ring any bells with me. Course, I've only been here since last fall, moved from Kansas to be with my daughter."

"Are you talking about the Ezili who murdered that boy in Chicago a while back?"

Cal and the man turned to the woman who'd just spoken, having overheard them and stepped from her office. She was in her sixties, hair swept back in a sharp, streaked wave.

"Yes."

The woman shook her head. "No, I don't think

there's any property out here connected to that business."

"Are you sure? The cabin may have been called the Fortress of Solitude?"

"Like in *Superman*?" The silver-haired man smiled.

"That's right," Cal said.

"The Fortress of Solitude?" The woman's eyes narrowed with curious intelligence. "You look familiar. Who are you?"

Cal had to think fast, had to be careful.

"I'm a writer from Chicago."

"And why're you interested in the property?"

"A friend suggested that it might be coming up for sale at a good price. That it offers a lot of privacy and solitude. I thought I'd drive by and take a look, but I don't know where it is."

"You could go to the town hall and ask the clerk, Muriel, to look through property records."

"Guess that's my next stop, thanks." He smiled and turned to leave.

"Hold on." The woman had walked to the map, tracing her finger on it. "I don't know anything about an Ezili property. But this Fortress of Solitude thing has me thinking. Now, if memory serves me..."

The silver-haired man whispered to Cal, "Lynn grew up here. She knows everybody and every inch of the county, even served as mayor for a few terms."

Her finger tapped on the map.

"Here." She turned to Cal. "Got a pen and paper?"

"I do." Cal reached into his pocket.

"It's on Timberline. Drive right down Main Street, turn left at the high school." Cal took notes. "Turn left at Lucky's gas station, that'll put you on Pioneer, then take the second right. That's Timberline. You go about four or five miles, maybe longer, on Timberline. You won't miss it—there's a big square white stone at the entrance to the lane, and it's got the word *Fortress* painted on it. Heard a local say once that whoever lived there called it the Fortress of Solitude."

Cal finished his notes. "Thank you."

"You should know that no one goes out that way. People tend to stay clear of that property."

"Why's that?"

"Nobody living there. It's all but abandoned."

"I understand." Cal put his notes in his pocket. "Well, I'll be on my way. Thank you for your help."

Lynn watched Cal through the window as he drove off.

"That man looks so familiar," she said. "I've seen him but I can't recall where. Does he look familiar to you, Tom?"

"No, first time I've ever seen that fellow," he said, lifting the counter so he could pass through. "Excuse me, I've got to step out and pick up my prescription. Be right back."

Tom had walked about half a block when he stopped and patted the pockets of his jacket. He'd forgotten his wallet on his desk. When he returned to the office, he heard Lynn at her desk, talking to someone on the phone.

"He said he was a writer from Chicago. He asked a lot of questions, and I'm telling you, something about him didn't sit right... He's up to something... Yes, he's headed out there now..."

80

Minutes after leaving the real estate office, Cal cursed under his breath.

He suddenly realized he was low on fuel and pulled into Lucky's gas station, anxious about the time he would lose.

Tires and motor oil were stacked neatly in front of the station. A sign over the door said Open and one above the pumps where he stopped said Self-Serv. Cal filled the tank, then went inside to pay. A radio was playing the end of a country song—"Beer for My Horses."

"Just the gas today?" the large, tired-looking, woman with a rose tattooed on her upper arm asked from behind the counter as the radio news began.

Cal hesitated, keeping an ear cocked to the broadcast. The top story was a political scandal out of Washington, then something from Iraq.

"Sir?"

"Sorry?"

"If it's just the gas, that'll be thirty-six dollars."

Cal nodded, reached for his wallet and froze at the next story.

"Citing unnamed sources, the Associated Press is reporting that moments ago the FBI launched an operation in an undisclosed location in the case of Gage Hudson, the nine-year-old boy who recently disappeared from a Chicago-area midway ride. No other details were reported. Switching to sports..."

"Is everything all right, sir?"

"Uh, right, yes." Cal slapped two twenties on the counter and rushed to the Subaru with the clerk calling after him about his change.

Please, God, let them find Gage alive.

Cal's knuckles whitened on the wheel as he consulted the directions, accelerating on Pioneer, watching for the turn for Timberline. It came up faster than he expected: a paved, worn ribbon of twisting road that cut into forest so dense treetops blotted the sunlight. Cal blinked as his eyes adjusted. He had to be less than five miles away now.

I've got to get there before it's too late. I've got to see him.

The car shook as the paved road abruptly transformed into a dirt road. No signs of life, other than an occasional No Trespass sign, or a gate. Any buildings were concealed, the forest underscoring the isolation in this corner of the state. That's when worry that had been gnawing at Cal flared.

Why hadn't he seen a single police vehicle?

He knew how these operations unfolded with command posts, perimeters, road closures and SWAT teams.

He wished he had an emergency scanner, or had made some calls to sources, something more to help.

Dust clouds rose and churned in his rearview mirror, gravel popcorned against the undercarriage, and he searched the shoulders for a square white stone. He shot a glance to the odometer; he'd gone just over six miles and was beginning to panic when his phone rang and he seized it.

"Cal, it's Rory, have you heard?"

"Heard what?"

"CNN's broken the story on Gage that the FBI just moved on a property outside of Milwaukee."

"Milwaukee?" Cal slammed on the brakes and pulled to the side.

"Isn't that where you are?"

"No, I'm nowhere near Milwaukee!" Cal switched off the ignition and the Subaru was swallowed by its own dust cloud. "Did they find Gage?"

"Nothing's being reported on the outcome. I'm sorry, I thought that's where you were."

"What's being reported? Tell me everything."

"Right now they've got live aerial shots of a rural property, a heavily wooded area with SWAT types and other officers moving around. The anchor is somber—said the property is linked to a known violent sex offender. No mention of what they've discovered, or if arrests have been made."

A deepening fear coiled up Cal's spine.

"Cal, can you get there? I haven't told anyone where you went. Huppkey asked and the cops here are eyeballing me. They want to know where you are. I told them I wasn't sure. Can you get to Milwaukee soon?"

Cal didn't answer. He stepped from the car and leaned against it.

"Cal, can you get there?"

"I don't know what to do. I've got to go."

Rory's voice grew distant as Cal lowered the phone and ended the call.

Milwaukee?

He'd been wrong about this place. Dead wrong.

As if winded by a gut punch he stared through the dusty haze at the forest, tortured by his last clear memory of his son, just before they'd stepped into the Chambers of Dread. Gage was bursting with happiness at the thrill of the attraction. But the pure joy in his eyes had been lit by the fact his parents were together with him.

And it was a lie.

They'd pretended to be happy while carrying on with deceitful, hurtful acts, like the horrible people they were.

I've lost my son because of what I did. I sacrificed him to vainglory. And the last thing I did was lie to him.

Gage, I'm so sorry.

His son gone, his marriage shredded, his career over, felony charges and prison looming, Cal fell to his knees, tormented by the image of Gage— captive, bound and gagged—knowing it would be seared into his soul forever.

Cal sobbed great heaving sobs.

So loud he barely heard his phone ring.

He stared at it with dread for he knew what that call would be.

They were going to tell him his son was dead.

81

Staring at the ringing phone Cal wiped his face and braced for the news.

Fingers trembling, he answered.

"Cal, it's Rory. It's all happening fast. NBC says *USA TODAY* and the *Chicago Tribune* are reporting that law enforcement sources have found nothing at the Milwaukee site. It's a false lead."

"A false lead?"

"The wrong place! Is there police activity where you are?"

Cal's mind was spinning. If Milwaukee's the wrong location does that mean that he was at the right one? He clenched his eyes to digest the possibility.

When Cal opened his eyes the dust cloud had settled and in the distance he saw a square white rock with the word *Fortress* painted on it.

"Cal? Where are you?"

"I'm near Savanna on Timberline Road and I'm going to check something out. I'll get back to you."

"What? You're breaking up—I can't—"

Cal moved the Subaru as far off to the side of

the road as possible then he walked to the stone. Looking in all directions he saw nothing but thick forest, heard nothing but birdsong.

Some ten yards deep into the woods from the stone he saw a rusted steel gate nearly hidden by undergrowth. A sign affixed to it with wire said Keep Out Private.

Cal caught his breath. The locked chain wrapped around the latch and gatepost was new. Past the gate he saw a dirt road disappearing into heavy woods, but one thing stood out.

Fresh tire tracks in the dried mud.

The place was supposed to be abandoned.

Cal's pulse quickened as he climbed over the gate.

His stomach tightened and he headed down the dirt road penetrating the property as breezes fingered through the treetops. He estimated the road twisted for a hundred yards before he came to a hill and spotted a structure.

A cabin.

Cal crouched down, stepped into the forest to study the building without being seen. There it was, in the small valley below: a log cabin. It had a satellite dish on a roof corner, a water pump on the sagging porch and the wagon wheel leaning against a porch post.

It matched Wixom's photo.

This was it.

No vehicles, no signs of life. A quiet stillness enveloped the property.

He should call somebody—Rory, police, somebody.

Before Cal did anything, a sudden, muffled noise broke the silence. Like a cry—soft, deadened as if far away. It was there, then gone.

He couldn't wait another moment.

Using the forest as cover, he rushed to the cabin, his back to the side wall, feeling the hewn logs through his shirt. Fighting to slow his breathing he listened for more sounds, hearing nothing but his own heart.

Peering around a corner behind the cabin, he caught a glint of chrome from a vehicle nearly covered by a large tarp. Cal moved closer to it, seeing the plate. California. He copied it down, reached for his phone.

Thud!

Cal stopped. That noise—whatever it was— had come from inside the cabin. He positioned his phone to call Malko for help but cursed with disbelief. The signal was weak; the battery was low. The call refused to go through.

Damn, damn, damn!

He shoved the phone in his pocket and went to the cabin, looking in windows. One revealed a bedroom. Cal recognized the bed by the landscape painting above it.

That's where Gage was being held in the photo.

But the room was empty.

He pressed his ear to the glass and heard voices inside.

Moving to another window he saw a TV tuned to an all-news channel.

Moving to other windows and looking inside, Cal saw no one.

He'd come to the front door and a decision.

He knocked—hard, repeatedly—wishing he had something for a weapon.

Nothing happened.

He placed his ear to the door and heard the TV. He turned the doorknob.

Locked.

He went to the back door and tried the knob. It clicked and turned all the way but the door wouldn't budge more than a quarter inch, stuck.

"Hello!" Cal called.

Nothing happened.

Every instinct began screaming at him to get inside.

But he needed something, anything, to serve as a weapon. Casting about he found an ax handle, looking something like a baseball bat. It would do. He turned his shoulder and slammed against the door, causing it to swing inward, and he was hit with a wave of body odor and rotting food.

The kitchen.

A portrait of chaos, counters plastered with dirty dishes, dishrags, empty tins of canned beans, spaghetti, potato chip bags, beer cans, take-out wrappers.

"Hello?"

Cal moved to the bedroom, certain it was the same bedroom in Wixom's photo.

Empty.

He looked under the bed and in the closet. Nothing. He moved to the bathroom—it had a toilet, sink, shower stall, which was dry. The medicine cabinet held nothing.

The sound of the TV drew him to the living room. It was spacious with hardwood floors, a stone fireplace and a sofa. An area rug covered the space between the sofa and the large flat-screen TV, which was on a stand and flickering with CNN news about the Middle East.

Cal saw no one in the room before his attention went to the coffee table in front of the sofa. Splayed copies of the *Chicago Star-News* and *Chicago Tribune* covered it. Each edition was open to stories reporting Gage's disappearance.

Cal's stomach twisted. He was on the verge of screaming out for Gage when he heard the creak of a plank in the floor. Sensing a presence he cast about the room, looking everywhere—the crossbeams of the ceiling, the living room—and found nothing.

Then he saw it.

Almost imperceptible.

As if beckoning him.

A ripple in the area rug exposed a darker seam between the floorboards. Cal lifted the rug. The seam outlined a rectangle, about the size of a fridge door, in the floor. A recessed latch at one end.

A cellar door.

Cal yanked on the latch and lifted the heavy door.

It opened to stairs that descended into blackness. He hesitated, tightening his grip on the handle.

Should I go in? What if this is a trap?

Cal was motionless.

It's too quiet.

"Hello? Anyone home?" He called down only to be answered with silence.

Then something stirred in the dark below.

Cal froze at the sound of the voice he suddenly heard.

"Gage, always remember Mommy loves you. You have to be strong and remember that no matter what happens I love you, sweetheart."

His wife was speaking—to their son.

82

What the hell's happening?

Cal's heart hammered in his chest.

"Faith? Gage?"

He was answered with silence and called again.

"Faith! Gage!"

Darkness had swallowed all but the top few steps. He searched the frame of the door for a light switch but found nothing. He fumbled for his phone but its light was too weak. Then he remembered the miniflashlight on Rory's key ring.

It provided enough light.

"I'm coming down!"

The stairs squeaked as if awakened; the black, dank air smelled earthen—like a grave. The narrow light beam hinted at a confined subterranean space, revealing water seeping down the uneven stone walls, glistening like those of a dungeon.

"Faith, Gage?"

Baby-soft breathing, bordering on frantic panting.

Cal pivoted, his light piercing the dark, capturing the edge of a stained mattress on the floor, a bare foot, little legs, a small chest, bound hands, a taped mouth and small eyes enlarged with fear, tears streaming.

"Gage!"

Half sobbing, Cal flew to his son. Gage, his head shaved, looking so small, so fragile, trembling.

"Oh God, son, I'm here. Dad's here!"

Cal dropped his handle and felt the chilled skin of Gage's cheeks as he worked to remove the duct tape from his mouth. In that instant snot erupted from Gage's nostrils, his cheeks puffed and his teary eyes ballooned as he groaned a warning. Cal heard a quick, rustling movement behind him, the light diffused, then a sudden force to his head turned the world black.

83

Semiconscious, Cal's eyes fluttered.

He couldn't move.

Squeak-creak. Squeak-creak. Squeak-creak.

The base of his skull throbbed with pain. Pressure was on his mouth, face, arms and chest. His nose prickled with familiar pungent, clammy air.

Where am I? What's that sound? What happened? Think... Go back... Cabin... Cellar... Faith's voice... Gage...

Cal's eyes flickered open to a filmy, underwater vision.

Disoriented, he stared woozily. A metal chain was creaking. The room swayed in black and white as an interrogation-style naked bulb swung from the ceiling. The cellar was oscillating between light and dark...light and dark...

And in the rhythm, in the light, Cal saw Gage.

So small, so terrified, and trembling on the mattress.

In that instant their eyes met—Gage's overwhelmed with fear; Cal's filled with love, guilt, shame and anger.

Cal moved to be with him, to save him, to comfort him, but was paralyzed, stripped to his underwear, his upper body restrained to an old wooden chair, wrists pulled behind him and taped to the backrest.

A spent roll of tape was on the floor.

He cursed into the tape sealing his mouth.

The chain squeak-creaked, throwing the light across the cellar onto the large figure standing before him. He was muscular, about six feet tall, wearing combat pants and boots, a sleeveless T-shirt exposing his powerful tattooed arms.

And in that instant of light Cal's blood turned to ice upon seeing the man's head enshrouded in a black leather hood with sliding zippers open for his eyes and mouth.

The Decanus.

Questions burned through Cal's mind: Where was Faith? He'd heard her voice…

The hooded man stared at Cal.

As the light swung, Cal saw in the fringes of the confined cellar a workbench, a laptop sitting on it. It was frozen on a frame of a TV news story and it dawned on him. That was Faith at their first news conference at the fairgrounds, where she encouraged Gage to be strong. Cal had heard her voice as she spoke to the cameras, addressing their son.

The hooded man turned away from Cal to the workbench.

As the light swung, the man moved a tripod with a video camera closer, training it on Cal and Gage.

The man then turned to the bench and pulled

on a rubber apron, then shoved the light so it continued its rhythmic swinging.

A metallic rattle sounded as the hooded man rolled a cart bearing tools and surgeon's instruments, positioning it before Cal and Gage.

84

Behind the wheel of her parked patrol car, Deputy Alexa Sloan finished her burger and fries.

I shoulda had the salad but what the heck.

She removed the straw and tipped her take-out cup to her mouth for the last of her chocolate shake but it got away from her and dripped onto her shirt.

"Darn." Sloan dabbed the stain with napkins she'd soaked with her bottled water as her radio crackled.

"Hey, Alexa, got a report of a possible suspicious person at a property on Timberline. Sending you details now, copy?"

Sloan reached for her microphone. "I'm close by. Ten-four."

The mobile computer in her car beeped and, while tidying up, she read the information: a report of a man asking questions concerning an uninhabited property on Timberline. Sloan looked at the address. She knew the place, the Fortress. Caller said the man had a "suspicious demeanor," and indicated he was going to check out the property.

He was driving a blue Subaru. Caller was Lynn Violet, the former mayor.

All right, let's check it out.

Sloan started her car and headed for Timberline.

Veteran cops might regard the call as small potatoes but being twenty-two and four months out of the academy at Springfield, Sloan drove with a twinge of excitement.

Tilting her visor mirror to inspect the stain, she wished she'd had a spare shirt in her car. *Can't do much about it now*, she thought as stones popped under the wheels and the dust churned behind her. Within fifteen minutes she eased off the accelerator as she came up to the property and scanned the area.

Bingo.

A vehicle was far off on the side of the road half-hidden in the bush. Sloan stopped, radioed her position, then prepared to step out to inspect it. She still found it awkward exiting her car with her heavy utility belt. She positioned her cap but it kept slipping, reminding her that she needed to adjust the band.

The car was a blue Subaru, all right. She called in the plate, observing that it sure as heck was suspect, parked the way it was. As she surveyed the area for any sign of people, her dispatcher responded.

"Vehicle's registered to Rory Clark, River Ridge, Illinois. No wants, no warrants. No report of it being stolen, copy?"

"Ten-four."

Seeing nothing in the area, Sloan got back into her car and moved it up to the square white stone and gated entrance.

She typed on the keyboard of her car's computer, submitting her position and status. Then she got her portable radio, clipped on her shoulder microphone, tested it and climbed out. She debated on whether to bring her shotgun, deciding that her sidearm would do.

Sloan hefted herself over the gate and headed down the twisting forest road. Walking in the tranquil shade the loudest thing she heard was the leathery squeak of her utility belt. It would take time for its newness to soften, she thought.

Her shift had been quiet so far with a medical call for someone who'd broken their wrist in an off-road vehicle crash. She also tried to serve papers in a child custody case, but the person was not home. Her last call was to help a man who'd flagged her down on the highway—his truck quit and he needed a tow.

Who knew what this call could yield. In this neck of the woods she'd learned that some of the locals were a little odd but there was never any trouble. Maybe she'd find a drug operation like a meth lab. Or maybe it would be a simple trespass issue.

Or maybe it would be nothing at all.

As the old-school cops told her, the job was ninety percent boredom and ten percent sheer terror, which suited Sloan, a farmer's daughter, just fine.

Reaching the cabin, she knocked on the front door. No response.

She cupped her hands to her eyes and pressed her face to the window. The TV in the living room was on and the rug in front of it was raised.

She tried the door. Locked. Moving around the cabin she saw a car covered with a canvas, noted the California plate and requested her dispatcher run it through NCIC.

"Stand by, Alexa."

While waiting, Sloan took stock of the property. Light winds hissed through the surrounding trees, giving her a sense of dread. Something wasn't right here. She could sense it in the air.

Her radio sounded with a burst of static.

"Alexa, that California tag is flagged by the LAPD and the FBI."

"What for?"

"Stand by."

As Sloan waited, her eyes were drawn to the cabin's back door.

It was open.

Something's definitely not right.

"Alexa, you're being advised to stay put, and await further instructions. Vehicle is connected to the abduction of a nine-year-old boy from Chicago. Hang in there. Stay put. We're reaching out to the FBI. You copy?"

Abduction? Nine-year-old boy from Chicago? The story in the news?

Sloan's heart was beating faster as she concentrated on the back door.

Why was it open? Why was the Subaru on Timberline nearly hidden?

Pulling pieces together Sloan moved to the back door. She hesitated, considered the situation, then stepped inside to the upheaval of the kitchen and the rank air.

At that moment she heard a noise.

Instantly Sloan unlocked her holster, drew her weapon and proceeded to the living room.

85

I'm not going to die without fighting back!

Shooting a glance to Gage, then at their captor, Cal began shaking with rage. Adrenaline jetted through his body. His nostrils flared with hard breathing as he summoned every molecule of strength and battled his bindings. The tape bit into his wrists, but his legs were unbound, and the chair creaked and wobbled.

The chair was old and the legs were loose. The thing was weakening, and if Cal used all his strength, he could stand.

With blind fury he rose to his feet, turned and—using the chair's legs as a weapon—drove himself backward into the hooded man. Cal's surprising violent explosion knocked the man to the ground and sent the instrument cart crashing. Standing over him Cal lined up, then stabbed the chair's splintered spear-like legs over and over into his groin, his torso, his head, before jumping up and heaving his full weight on the chair into the man's chest.

As the man lay groaning Cal got to his feet and smashed the chair full bore into the stone wall.

Pain webbed through his back and arms as the chair broke apart, partially freeing his arms. Bleeding with broken jagged pieces taped to him, Cal found a knife from the tray on the floor. Hands shaking, cutting swiftly and cutting himself in the process, he removed tape from his arms and mouth.

Then he cut away the tape from Gage's hands and face, got him moving up the stairs.

"Hurry, son, run! I'm right behind you."

As Cal climbed the stairs behind Gage, a hand seized his ankle, stopping him cold and dragging him down.

86

Gage scrambled up the stairs, squinting into the light of the living room, and froze.

He was staring into the barrel of a gun aimed at him.

"Jee-zuss!" Deputy Alexa Sloan blinked at her target.

A sobbing, frail little boy—trembling in his underwear, skin streaked with blood, strips of tape affixed to his body, hair shorn from his head, eyes bulging—raised his small palms.

"He's fighting my dad down there. He's going to kill him!"

Sounds of mayhem spilled from the cellar as Sloan immediately grasped the situation, seizing her radio.

"This is Sloan. I need back up and EMT now!" Then to Gage, lowering her gun and pointing to the kitchen: "Sweetie, get out of the house through the back. Follow the road to my car and wait there for more police."

Gage inched toward the kitchen, crying, "Help my dad. Please!"

"I will. Go! Go! Go!"

Adjusting her grip on her gun, Sloan started down the stairs, the lamplight bursting like lightning flashes amid the thrashing of two people on the floor locked in a savage life-and-death struggle.

"Police! Freeze!"

Sloan's command was ignored. She saw the gleam of a blade. One man, wearing only underwear, his skin laced with blood, the other clad in black and hooded. Grunting and panting in their struggle, one of them shouted, "Help me! Help me!"

Sloan's fingers were sweating as she aimed her gun at them.

Who is the victim? Who is the attacker?

Unsure, she holstered her weapon, grabbed her expandable baton and, drawing on her training, delivered quick blows to the backs of hands, fingers, thighs, then bones and joints. Relentless, Sloan knew her strikes were disabling, impossible to withstand, and soon the two separated to deal with the excruciating pain she'd inflicted.

Sloan then shot streams of pepper spray into their eyes and as they screamed at the burning sensation, she put both men in plastic handcuffs, pulling them tight.

"You two sit there. If you move I sure as hell will shoot you."

The blood rush thumping in her ears, coughing

from the pepper spray, Sloan sat on the steps and reached for her radio but hesitated. She went to the masked man and peeled away his hood.

She did not recognize him.

Sloan drenched a towel in water for their eyes, then called again for help and more paramedics, advising her dispatcher to alert responding units to watch for Gage at her car. Then Sloan lifted her face to the ceiling, her breath coming in heaving gasps.

Whatever happened here was now over.

87

Gage sat on the grassy side of the road by Sloan's car, knees drawn to his chest, shivering and crying to the sound of approaching sirens.

More deputies and ambulances arrived and everything moved like a slow-motion dream with someone draping a big jacket over him while conversations mixed with radio dispatches.

"He's in shock."

"We've got to open that gate for EMT."

"We've got to seal the property and protect the scene."

Two paramedics tended to Gage.

"It's okay, buddy," one of them said, checking his signs. "We'll take you to the hospital to make sure everything's good, okay?"

"Where's my dad? Let me see my dad."

Paramedics and deputies talked; there was more radio chatter and soon an ambulance emerged from the cabin road, stopping at the gate. The rear doors were opened.

"Dad!"

Gage climbed in, threw his arms around Cal, who was bloodied and scraped.

Cal embraced him so tightly he could barely get a breath in. "It's okay, son. We're going to be okay."

Deputies insisted that the paramedics transport Cal and Gage to the hospital in separate ambulances because the FBI would need separate statements from them and didn't want them talking to each other just yet.

The suspect, whose ID had yet to be determined, had been treated at the scene, then transported to a hospital in Galena. Later, he'd be taken to a jail cell in Savanna to face several charges.

In the aftermath, more deputies arrived, then state police and the FBI. A helicopter circled as the investigation mounted with local TV crews arriving, then media from Chicago, Milwaukee, St. Louis, Kansas City, Indianapolis and eventually the national press as the story reverberated across the country.

Detectives Price and Lang drove Faith from Chicago to the medical center in Sterling where they'd taken Gage and Cal. FBI Agent Malko was talking to a doctor in the hall outside Gage's room when they got there.

"I want to see my son!" Faith said.

"We gave him a sedative. He's awake but resting," the doctor said.

"Is he hurt?"

"He's dehydrated, suffering shock. We want a psychiatrist to talk to him. We're going to do a few more tests. Otherwise, he's in good condition."

"Let me see him."

The doctor looked to Malko.

"For a moment," Malko said. "I'll go in with you. We don't have his statement yet."

Balloons and a stuffed dinosaur—gifts from the deputies and hospital staff—were next to Gage's bed and the IV pole. He sat up when he saw his mom and, in a rush of tears, Faith took him into her arms.

"Oh, honey, I love you so much."

"I love you, too, Mom." Gage sounded groggy.

"Are you hurt?"

"My arms are sore and my jaw."

Faith brushed his hair, smiling and crying at the same time.

"Dad saved me from the scary creep. I thought it was all part of the Chambers of Dread, but it wasn't."

"Sweetie, did he hurt you?"

Gage blinked several times but didn't answer her.

"I was so scared. He cut off all my hair and made me wear a wig to look like a girl. He said we'd be going on a long trip but I thought I was going to die. He kept playing your voice from the news to keep me calm but I only cried more for you."

Malko indicated that it was time to go.

"You're safe now," Faith told Gage. "There are a lot of big police guys just outside your door and all over the place. They're here to protect you."

Gage nodded.

"I can't stay but I'll be right here, okay?"

"Okay."

"Get some rest."

Faith kissed Gage and was at the door when he called to her.

"Mom?"

She stopped and turned.

"Am I in trouble?"

She rushed back to him, hugging him again.

"Absolutely not. Don't you ever think that, okay?"

"Okay."

Leaving Gage's room with Malko, Faith saw Cal at the end of the hall, alone, his face bearing bandages; he was leaning on a cane, staring out the window.

He cut a lonely figure and she was torn between her anger at him and her joy over Gage's rescue.

The significance was not lost on Malko and he signaled to the other investigators to allow the Hudsons a private moment. Malko turned away to take a call as Faith went to her husband, giving him a gentle hug and kissing his cheek.

"Price told me in the car what you did. Thank you."

"Don't thank me. This was my fault. You're right to hate me."

"I was angry, out of my mind with fear."

He stared out the window, shouldering his guilt.

"Cal, we've both made painful mistakes."

He nodded and she continued.

"We've been horrible people to each other, horrible parents to Gage."

"Yup." Tears rolled down his face.

Faith found his free hand, entwined her fingers in his, and they stood together looking out the window for a minute until Cal cleared his throat.

"There's a request for you and me to participate in a press conference later today. We can decline, but just think about it and remember all the people that helped us from the get-go."

Faith nodded. "All right."

Malko's reflection appeared on the window and they turned.

"Excuse me, this just came in." He turned his phone to them. "This is the suspect's arrest photo. He's not cooperating and we're still working on confirming his ID. We know from reading Ezili's files on his computer that he shared access to his family's cabin with a small number of people in his network. This man is obviously one of them. Do you recognize him?"

Cal studied his face. The man was white, in his late thirties. His eyes were defiant, accentuating his sneer.

Faith put her hand to her mouth. "This is the man who had Gage?"

"Yes."

"I don't recognize him," Cal said.

"Faith?"

She shook her head.

Malko looked at both of them for a long moment.

"Do you believe us?" Cal's anger was rising.

"After all this, do you believe what we're telling you?"

Malko blinked and looked through the window as if the right words were somewhere out there.

"Tibor," Faith said. "Detective Price told me in the car about the case that haunts you."

Malko kept looking out the window.

"Every night before I fall asleep, I see her face," he said. "Every case is extremely complex. Everyone lies, everyone has something to hide. It's never black and white. Never." Malko looked at Cal and Faith, looked at them sincerely, his Adam's apple rising and falling. "I was fighting for Gage."

"We didn't make it easy," Cal said. "It looked bad because it was bad. We still have a lot to deal with."

Without speaking all three of them accepted the truth.

Epilogue

Satellite trucks dominated the seventy-three news vehicles that overwhelmed the hospital's parking lot for the press conference.

No room inside was large enough to accommodate the number of media people so it was decided to set up on a side lawn in an area where some staff had lunch on sunny days. Now it was webbed with cables running to large news vans.

Cal and Faith sat at a folding table, flanked by officials from the hospital, local and state police and FBI Agent Malko. A small mountain of microphones rose before them; cameras clicked and flashed as they began.

Malko spoke for the investigation by reading a bare-bones statement. Within a couple of minutes, he was wrapping it up. "The suspect has been identified as Augustin Rudulf Yutellim, aged thirty-nine, of Riverside, California. We'll provide his photo. Yutellim faces several felony charges. Charges are also pending against other individuals for their role in the kidnapping. Our investigation continues and we'll provide more information when it becomes available. Now I'll pass things to Cal and Faith Hudson."

Questions for them came in a sudden wave with one from the reporter for *USA TODAY* emerging as the first.

"Cal, Faith, how is Gage doing?"

They both turned to the man at the table wearing a white coat.

"Dr. Jacob Hennesy," the man said, spelling his name for reporters. "Gage is in good condition. He suffered some trauma, some weight loss. He'll be provided counseling. But under the circumstances he's doing well. He's a resilient boy. He requested pizza and a milk shake."

Laughter rippled across the group.

"Doctor," a woman from a Chicago TV station, shouted. "Given what is surfacing about Yutellim, Abel Wixom and their activities with this network known as Illicitum Passio, is there any indication Gage was abused?"

Hennesy looked to the Hudsons, who nodded for him to continue. "We're still endeavoring to ascertain the full extent of his experience during his confinement. As I said, he will be provided counseling."

"This is for Cal," a reporter for the Associated Press said. "Your connection to Ezekiel Ezili was just reported by the *Washington Post*. We understand you played a role in your son's rescue. How did you know to go to that particular cabin?"

Cal outlined his reporting on Ezekiel Ezili—

how he'd visited his apartment where he saw a picture of the cabin, how it all came to him after Wixom's capture and reports connecting Wixom to Illicitum Passio, the group to which Ezili belonged.

For the next ten minutes they continued their back-and-forth with journalists on general questions before things took a turn.

"Cal, coming back to Ezili and Illicitum Passio," a man from the *Chicago Sun-Times* said. "The *LA Times* is reporting on its site that your son's abduction was a vendetta against you for your reporting on Ezekiel Ezili. Is that true?"

"That's my understanding, yes."

"On that aspect of the vendetta," a reporter from the online arm of NewsLead, a wire service, started, "our sources inform us that you and a detective may have planted evidence that led to Ezili's conviction in the Turco case and that you're both facing charges. What's your response?"

Cal was silent, then another reporter, whom he recognized from the *Star-News*, continued to press him.

"Cal, what's your reaction to rumors surfacing now on social media that Ezili had always proclaimed his innocence and that you had planted evidence that led to his conviction?"

Cal's face whitened, and as he struggled to answer, Malko interjected.

"It has come to our attention that evidence may have been planted in the Ezili case. Any charges are pending. The matter is under investigation. That's all we can say at this time. One more question and we'll wrap this up."

The last one came from a woman from the *New York Times*.

"Faith and Cal, throughout much of your ordeal the FBI regarded you as suspects. Can you tell us why, and what that was like for you?"

Faith leaned to the microphones.

"We know that investigators have a job to do, and that until they have all the facts, everyone is considered a suspect. Cal and I are not perfect people." Faith paused, never having uttered those words before. "We want to thank the FBI, the River Ridge police, all the investigators, all the volunteers, our friends, everyone who helped look for Gage and who prayed for him. We want to thank God for returning our son to us."

In the days and weeks that followed, Gage received counseling in Chicago from Barbara Minovich, a leading psychiatrist who specialized in helping children who've suffered traumatic experiences.

As part of Gage's therapy, Minovich also met with Cal and Faith, and for the sake of their son, they agreed to reveal to her their innermost private information about their broken marriage. Nodding behind her glasses, Minovich took notes before addressing their questions and providing her observations.

"Your son has experienced a life-altering tragedy. I cannot say if he was sexually abused. He tells me he wasn't, but children often don't tell because of the confusion, fear and shame. At this time I cannot say with certainty that Gage was not abused sexually, but he is still processing many other aspects of his kidnapping, namely his psychological trauma arising from it."

Cal and Faith listened intently as she continued. "Now, taking into account your marital disintegration and your plan to separate, I must make this observation. To break up Gage's family at this time would be devastating for his healing. Bear in mind, his sense of security and well-being are shattered and he clings to his parents as the only constant he can trust in his world. His father is his hero, his mother his emotional sanctuary, making his family his only safe refuge. Setting aside that criminal charges are looming against Cal. I'm not encouraging you to live a lie, or a make-believe marriage, but I urge you both to think hard about the potential impact on Gage's recovery if his family were to be torn apart at this time."

After considering Dr. Minovich's concerns, Cal and Faith decided that, for Gage, they would live together and maintain the semblance of a marriage, taking things one day at a time as they braced for what was to come.

In the days after Augustin Yutellim's arrest, midway workers Alma McCain and Sid Griner were formally charged with several felonies for their part in Gage's abduction.

The FBI's further investigation and questioning of Yutellim yielded more details. Shortly after the abduction, Yutellim shaved off all of Gage's hair, cutting him slightly in the process. He then changed Gage's clothes, discarding them in the Dumpster at Emerson Plaza, because it was a few miles from the fairgrounds and because he was confident it would be emptied before any discovery of Gage's clothing could be made. This was all part of his plan to disguise Gage with a wig and dress him as a girl.

Yutellim and Wixom had drawn on their connections and support through Illicitum Passio to arrange for a fake passport and documents for Gage, identifying him, or her, as it were, as a refugee whose entire family was killed in the Middle East. Wixom and Yutellim had records identifying them as international aid workers. They had planned to smuggle Gage into western Canada at a weak border point, travel to Vancouver, British Columbia, then fly to Thailand, delivering Gage to an orphanage operated by people affiliated with Illicitum Passio. Gage would then be sold into a global pedophile ring and lost forever.

The FBI's investigation confirmed that Gage's abduction and planned enslavement was an act of vengeance to honor Ezili and to demonstrate Illicitum Passio's reach and power. The group never accepted Ezili's conviction, for it maintained that he had never murdered anyone, that he was framed. Moreover, the group would never be convinced that Ezili, or any of its members for that matter, could possibly abuse children "because he dated them with their consent." The last aspect was a pillar of Illicitum Passio's belief system, that there should be freedom to have unfettered sexual relationships between people regardless of age. The secret group's fringes supported zealous forces around the world who were lobbying lawmakers to radically reduce, or strike, the legal age of consent between an adult and young person for a sexual relationship.

The FBI's investigation of the underground group continued.

Nearly two months after Gage was found, Cal was charged with obstruction of justice for planting evidence in Ezili's apartment. Detective Thorne was also charged, fired, convicted and sent to prison. Thorne's case gave rise to a cloud over all investigations she'd been involved with and became a major controversy.

As expected, the *Chicago Star-News*, facing severe financial pressure, cut forty-five percent of its editorial staff. Cal would have been among those on the list of dismissals if he hadn't been fired for evidence planting already. After he lost his job, Cal and Faith took out a second mortgage on their house in River Ridge to pay Cal's legal costs. At the same time, a prominent Chicago law firm agreed to represent the Hudsons on a contingency basis in civil action against Ultra-Fun Amusement Corp and the River Ridge fairgrounds for failure to protect Gage's safety.

Meanwhile, across America, Ultra-Fun continued operating the Chambers of Dread. The notoriety the attraction had gained fueled a legendary status, resulting in increasingly longer lines as the attraction continued breaking attendance and revenue records.

Before Cal's trial, which was nearly a year away,

Kay Donahue, Cal's criminal defense lawyer, was pushing hard with the Cook County state's attorney to work out a plea bargain. A case for felony probation, so that Cal would avoid prison, was rejected. Donahue worked hard to ensure Cal's conviction, which was inevitable, would result in as little prison time as possible.

During that period, the FBI had succeeded in gaining access to Yutellim's computer where they'd discovered encrypted files, which they eventually managed to unlock. Hidden deep among them was a video made by Ezili in which he boasted about "abducting, dating, then sending to heaven" the missing little boys in the Chicago and Pittsburgh cases. The video revealed details that only the killer would know, eliminating any doubt as to Ezili's guilt.

The video was eventually obtained by several news organizations and, with graphic parts redacted, was made public. The revelation ignited a social media furor. No one knew what, if any, impact the video would have on Cal's case, or Thorne's prison sentence, but Cal's lawyer was hopeful it would be a factor.

In the months after his abduction, Gage had nightmares and several breakdowns for he feared elements of Illicitum Passio were coming for him, stalking him at school, hiding in cars, in bushes and dark places like his closet or under his bed. Cal, Faith and Dr. Minovich did all they could to reassure him, knowing that he might never be fully assured.

Almost a year later, Cal's case was heard by the court.

He entered a guilty plea. The judge called Cal's willful planting of evidence against Ezili a highly serious offense. After hearing all of the agreed upon facts and evidence, and after considering Cal's spotless criminal record, the judge sentenced him to ten months in a minimum-security prison.

That his dad was going to jail meant little to Gage because to him Cal would forever be his hero. Faith took Gage to the prison regularly to visit his father. Apart from the family visits, it was during the phone calls that Cal was allowed that he and Faith struggled to work out what their future should be. They discussed all options with Gage being the priority, but there were many wounds that needed time to heal.

They settled on not making any decisions until closer to Cal's release.

Each night as Cal tried to sleep in his cell, he thought of his family, while miles away Faith looked in on Gage before going to her bedroom and getting into her side of the bed she'd once shared with her husband. In those moments, Gage, Faith and Cal were helpless against the anguish that assailed them in the desperate night. They each grappled with the truth on their own: their lives would never again be the same, the degree of happiness they had once known now only as certain as a falling star.

* * * * *

Acknowledgments & Author's Note

In bringing *Last Seen* to you I benefitted from the hard work, generosity and support of a lot of people.

I want to thank David Heinzmann, a reporter with the *Chicago Tribune*, Shane Gericke, formerly with the *Chicago Sun-Times*, and Laura Caldwell, former civil trial attorney, now a professor at Loyola University Chicago School of Law. David, Shane and Laura are superb authors in their own right and you'd do well to seek out their work.

If any part of *Last Seen* rings true for you, it's because of their kind help. If this story fell short for you then blame me; the mistakes are mine for I have taken creative license with police procedure, jurisdiction, the justice system and Chicago's geography.

My thanks to Amy Moore-Benson and Meridian Artists; thanks to Emily Ohanjanians and the incredible editorial, marketing, sales and PR teams at Harlequin, MIRA Books and HarperCollins.

As always, my thanks to Wendy Dudley for improving the tale.

Very special thanks to Barbara, Laura and Michael.

For readers who follow my work, my apologies for the long gap between stories. Other commitments vied for my time but I worked faithfully on *Last Seen*, taking it with me when I traveled, as I do with all of my works in progress. Parts of this book were written in hotels, in airports, on jetliners, in train stations and on trains in Toronto, New Orleans, Montreal, New York City and Quebec City.

This brings me to what I hold to be the most critical part of the entire enterprise: you, the reader. This aspect has become something of a credo for me, one that bears repeating with each book.

Thank you for your time, for without you, a book remains an untold tale. Thank you for setting your life on pause and taking the journey. I deeply appreciate my audience around the world and those who've been with me since the beginning who keep in touch. Thank you all for your kind words. I hope you enjoyed the ride and will check out my earlier books while watching for my next one. Feel free to send me a note. I love hearing from you!

Rick Mofina
www.RickMofina.com
Facebook.com/RickMofina
Twitter.com/RickMofina